Dark Passion

Dark Passion

a novel

Sarala Barnabas

PRESTIGE

Published by
Prestige Books
3/28, East Patel Nagar
New Delhi 110 008

All characters are imaginary. Any resemblance with persons living or dead is purely coincidental

ISBN: 81-7551-013-X

1997

Photo Typesetting by
Pivot Computers
Delhi 110 006

Printed at
Mehra Offset Press
New Delhi 110 002

Foreword

I have often wondered about the accuracy in reporting past events. Embellishments are added, each teller adding a frill or two to make the narrative more exciting. Interpretation also plays an important part. Years after an event, new factors are discovered which put a whole new perspective on the entire picture. *Dark Passion* presents one such story. In a sense, it also continues a theme from the earlier novel *Nayantara* about the sins of the fathers being visited upon the children, with the past casting a long shadow over the present.

Dark Passion is a companion piece to *Sakshi, Nayantara, Anjolie* (Calcutta, 1993, Writers Workshop), and *Incident at Waverley* (1995, Writers Workshop), in all of which the central character is a woman. Almost always, much of the background is India. In most of the novels, the narrative is in the first person.

I wish to express my very grateful thanks to my husband, the Reverend Professor Joseph Barnabas for suggesting the central theme of this story. His encouragement and enthusiasm make the process of writing even more pleasurable. Warmest thanks to my daughter, Nandita, and Dorothy Blake of Philadelphia for prompt and timely help; to Meher Baba Lovers for useful information; and to my colleagues in the Department of English, Ahmednagar College, for many suggestions and discussions: Professsors Dnyate, Barnabas, Rathi, Swarna Kant, Bhat and Tiwari.

SARALA BARNABAS

DEDICATED

to

My husband Jay

in grateful appreciation of

the wonderful years of

partnership and sharing

PART ONE

The evil men do lives after them,
The good is oft interred with their bones

Julius Caesar, III. ii.79

1

We mortals are not gifted with foresight, all palmists and astrologers notwithstanding. If we were, and if I had had an inkling of what lay ahead for me, what secrets so deeply hidden for decades would be uncovered, I wonder if I would have changed my plans for the future? And had I done so, would it really have made a difference? Or ultimately, would everything have ended in the same way? The ancient Greeks believed in Destiny, in Fate. Witness Oedipus. In their mythology were the Three Fates, or Moerae who controlled the lives of men: Clotho who spun the web of life, Lachesis who measured its length, and Atropos who cut it off. Spine-chilling, isn't it? Then too, the Greeks believed in Nemesis. And further East, in *The Rubaiyat* which I read so avidly in my teens, Omar Khayyam in his own inimitable way, claimed about life: "'Tis all a Chequer-board of Nights and Days/ Where Destiny with Man for Pieces plays:/Hither and thither moves, and mates, and slays,/ And one by one in the Closet lays." Yet the thought comes to me—suppose I had known, and therefore altered my plans, would I then not ever have met my beloved, or the beautiful unforgettable one who had suffered so cruelly at the hands of one of my own family, or come to know a kinsman whose existence none of us had even guessed at? My answer to myself is that though pain and heartache, separation and anguish were my lot, I feel certain I would have changed nothing at all.

Instead of talking in riddles, I suppose I should first identify myself. From the several names bestowed upon me at birth, as was deemed only befitting, the shortest, and least pompous one of only three syllables came into use, and I have been called Piyali ever since. I belong to the former ruling family of the erstwhile princely state of Divyasthala in Northern India. I use those two words advisedly, for the princely states were abolished by a newly independent India, stripping the maharajas, the rajahs and the nawabs of their titles and power, merging their kingdoms into the various states of the Republic of India. I shall not enlarge here on the after-effects suffered by the princely families at the collapse of a centuries-old system. There are parallels enough of similar fates suffered by European royalty I will say, however, that in a land as ancient as India, traditions live on. Deep respect and homage are still accorded to certain men who in other times would have occupied the *gaddi*, the throne. Who doesn't love an occasional display of pomp and grandeur, a reminder of the good old days that were? Indeed, in some states, the public treasures these observations of royal birthdays, or processions at religious festivals complete with gaily caparisoned elephants, the present ex-king enthroned on a glittering *howdah* as his forefathers had been, the populace cheering as lustily as they have done for hundreds of years. So also does Divyasthala have a present ex-maharaja, Uday Singh, cousin to my father. Now Uday Singh's own father was the renowned Maharaja Digvijay Singh, remembered with gratitude for his unceasing devoted efforts to better the lot of his subjects. Our family name, Chandravats, goes so far back that its origins are lost in the mists of time. A proud name, found in history books, Chandravats connotes a favourite child, in the spiritual sense, of the Moon.

My father. Daddy. Tej Pratap Singh. He was what is called 'a fine figure of a man' with the aristocratic lineaments of the Chandravats. In his late forties now, he had taken a decision about himself while he was still at college. Envisioning the future for himself as a member of a former ruling family, he took off on graduation with his bride for the United States to Cornell University's School of Agriculture. I was born in Ithaca, New York, destined to be an only child, for Mummy was unable to have more children.

Daddy always said later how much the Cornell experience had taught him, and not just for the horticultural training he received. There he was not a prince, but just 'Tej' to his wide circle of friends and fellow students. Minus the retinue of salaaming servants they had been used to since birth, Mummy and he kept house, shopped for groceries, carrying their bags themselves, cooked, and after I arrived, cared for my needs. The intellectual stimulation he experienced at this elite Ivy League school was unlike anything he had known before. Daddy had chosen Cornell because it had one of the finest programmes in the United States, eminently suited to his plans for the future, for he intended to devote it to apple-growing. I was three when we returned to India.

In the Kotgarh area of the Simla Hills in the vicinity of the Himalayas, an apple-growing estate came on the market when the owner died. Having no issue, the widow was anxious to find the right buyer out of sentimental reasons, and was therefore choosy. She was immensely impressed not just by Daddy's title and qualifications, but by the man himself. And who could blame her? Daddy had that innate courtesy and gentleness with women which some men are born with. Tearful but satisfied, the lady accepted his substantial offer.

Within five years, Daddy had effected an amazing transformation. Although he had an excellent estate manager, he supervised every step of pruning, spraying and thinning himself. His experiments in grafting and budding were extremely successful. These untiring efforts were rewarded by the finest quality fruit one could find anywhere, and widely exported.

I was definitely Daddy's girl. He was my hero. As a very small child, I remember sitting perched up in front of him on his big horse, Shah Rukh. The workers always paused to smile and greet me fondly. For my part, I sat very straight, and responded gravely to their greetings. Later, I went astride Lady Fair, my own lovely dainty mare. Mummy wasn't always well, and spent quite some time resting. I think it pleased her that Daddy and I were so close, and that since she couldn't join in actively participating in his work, I did.

Inevitably, the vexing question of my schooling came up. I could hardly attend the local school for village children. One possibility was an exclusive school located at some small hill station in India where affluent parents sent their children. In fact, such schools existed right in Simla and Mussoorie. Mummy would have none of it. For her only child, it had to be a school fit for a princess, and where but in Switzerland would one be found? Looking back now, I'm sure Daddy felt the deepest sorrow in letting me go so far away. I did not realize it then, but Mummy's health was causing him worry, and dissent between them on this issue was the last thing he wanted. If that was what Krutika had set her heart on, he was not going to deny her, no matter how much he hated sending his little Piyali away. As for me, I was all choked up at the thought of leaving my adored father, my dear mother, and everything I loved and knew so well.

I will not linger over those school years though I would love to narrate several tales about them. Inevitably, I was miserably homesick at first. Then I reached the point of acceptance. From then on, it was smooth sailing. Needless to say, pupils here represented the most elite classes. Drawn mainly from the Continent, there were also some Americans, a couple of Australians and Taiwanese. Two Arab princesses who were sisters, Piyali, and girls from the English and French nobility, added further snob appeal to the liberal sprinkling of daughters of millionaires, industrialists and cattle kings. I learnt a great deal in the classroom, for the instruction was of the finest, and much outside it. A sound grounding in languages and mathematics went hand-in-hand with art, music, Cordon Bleu cookery, to say nothing of riding and skiing. On the other side of the coin came lessons in deportment, how to walk and sit gracefully, and the gracious art of hostessing. Enduring friendships were forged in those years. On vacations that were too short for me to go to India, I was invited to the homes of friends in England or France. There it was then, a fine very expensive schooling just as Mummy had wanted for her child. Poor Mummy who did not live to see me complete it.

The moment of decision came now. In my mind, there were no doubts about the career I wanted. As far back as I could remember, gems and jewellery had been part of my life. Indeed, how could it be otherwise? Apart from the truly magnificent pieces passed down from generation to generation, each with its own special history, worn by both men and women on state occasions, there were ones of lesser historical value for everyday use. Unconsciously, I must have absorbed their colour and glitter, their beauty and fashioning. At school, whenever we were taken for trips to say, Paris, and visited the Louvre, Piyali always managed to linger in the sections displaying jewellery excavated by archaeological expeditions, and brought to light after centuries out of the earth. In London for any length of time, I often went back to the Tower of London to see the Crown Jewels, the British Museum and Tate Gallery and the like.

When I went home that summer after graduating from school, and told Daddy I wished to train in jewellery design, he was silent for some time. Yet when I asked him if he disliked the idea, he shook his head. "No, little one. It isn't that I disapprove at all. In fact, now that I think over it, I'm proud of you for wanting to. It's a great idea. You'll excel at it, I'm sure. The truth is I'd hoped my little girl would stay with me for some time. Selfish of me, I know," with a half-smile.

I went over to him, and he held me close. Pangs of guilt assailed me. In the careless way of youth, it had not occurred to me my father must be a very lonely man ever since we lost Mummy almost ten years ago. He always seemed so self-sufficient, very busy with the task of running a vast estate. And here I was, his only child, come straight home after years in Switzerland, and already thinking of taking wing again.

I kissed his cheek, and said impulsively, "Daddy, what made you send me so far away all these years? Couldn't I have gone to school in India?"

"You could have, of course. But to give you the kind of education we wanted for you, it had to be Switzerland. Your mother was adamant about it, in any case. And suppose we had sent you to South India, for example, it would have taken you as long to make the train journey to Simla, as the flight took you from Lausanne. Besides, this way, I could be sure this was what Mummy wanted for her child—an education fit for a princess, she called it."

"Truly, Daddy? " I said wonderingly.

"Yes. And then, we could afford it. What is money worth if it can't be used for a most beloved child?" I hugged him. "Even though," he teased, "she's almost my height now."

My height again, I groaned to myself. True, the Chandravats men were very tall, but why did I as a girl have to inherit that trait? I suppose the good Swiss food also played a part in adding inches. In Europe, I was not an oddity, but in India, at five feet ten inches, I either dwarfed, or at least was on a level with most men.

I chose Parsons School of Design in New York, and loved every moment of being there. Jewellery design was my main focus, but other forms of art were absorbing as well. I found myself revelling in painting again which I had studied at school, and photography, ceramics and sculpture. Then too, I fell in love with New York. I've heard people say it's too this or too that. Not for me. I became a part of it effortlessly. I had my own circle of friends, and as course work permitted, an exciting social calendar. Yes, I did have dates, and enjoyed the outings with my companions. However, I drew the line at having any one serious relationship. Several of my women friends had live-in arrangements. I attended parties they threw at their apartments, but recognized this was not for me. I hadn't yet come across that one person with whom I would like to share the rest of my life. I was waiting for him. Casual relationships did not figure in my life's plan. And, of course, he was the one I would marry.

Another realization on my part had come some five years ago when I came home for the summer vacation. Daddy and I had attended the wedding of his niece, my cousin Mallika. It promised to be one of those gala affairs, and I quite enjoyed the ceremonial pomp—until I found Mallika all by herself in a hidden corner of the garden weeping her eyes out. Until then, I'd had no inkling of her feelings about this—yes, arranged marriage. My first guess was that these were pre-nuptial nerves, brought on by the thought of leaving home and loved ones. But when she saw me, she fell on my neck, and would not be consoled. Gradually, I made sense of the incoherent words, and came to know she hated this marriage, the whole idea of it, and the man who was not of her choice. Of course, no one had even considered her wishes. It had been arranged entirely by her elders and the groom's. And most of all, she hated her husband-to-be. Allowed to meet him once long enough to speak to him, she had found his looks, manner, attitudes, repellent. It had become very clear to her that she was to be confined to the women's quarters, for that was the way of it in his family. Also clear was his expectation that her role in his life was to be merely that of a brood mare, providing him with sons for the continuation of the line. As an individual with aspirations, ideas, desires and feelings, she did not exist for him.

I had managed to soothe my poor little cousin, and taken her back to her rooms, slipping in quietly. Then I had gone straight to Daddy. He had listened to my outpourings, and then said, "If you are thinking, dear girl, that I—or anyone—can call the whole thing off, you haven't understood the familial structure at all. First, there's a pecking order where rank, status and age, all come in. I'm far too much younger than Mallika's father to approach him on this matter. Second, in the short span of one encounter, has she really summed up the man and his set-up accurately? She is so young. Probably seen little of the world. She may find all her fears are quite unjustified, and be extremely happy. I haven't met the groom yet, so I can't venture to make any judgments." He had laid a hand on my shoulder. "It bothers you terribly, doesn't it, Piyali? I can make you a promise. When the time comes, you are free to make your own choice. I have to tell you I have received several feelers—and some actual offers for you. I rejected all of them. You are very surprised, I see, but why should you be? That's the way things are done here. I want to give my firm assurance that I shall never impose my choice on you," he had said quietly. Much comforted, what could I do but hug him warmly?

In the next few years, Mallika duly presented her lord master with two sons and a daughter, a baby every year. Whenever I returned to India, there was news of another birth. I hadn't met my cousin since her marriage, for she seldom came home, and certainly had never done so when I was around. I could only hope she was happy.

To come back to New York. The one man I did go out with most was David Asscher. He was at Parsons with me, also specializing in jewellery design, and for a very pertinent reason. His family owned a famous chain of jewellery stores across the United States. His fascination for the art form, as much as mine, had begun in childhood. "The administrative side of the business seemed an utter drag to me," he said. "I had this obsession with design. At first, Papa was astonished that, so to speak, I wanted to be at the other end of the business. Mama was great though. She's an artist herself, and I am sure I inherited my talent, if that's what we can call it, from her. She backed me to the hilt." He grinned engagingly. "My brothers teased me unmercifully. Said I was just trying to get out of the more arduous part of the business. Take the easy way out."

Other men might escort me to exclusive restaurants, to the theatre or a symphony. David's idea of giving me a good time was to take me on weekends to such places as the Metropolitan Museum of Art. While other sightseers admired great landscapes or still lives, we avidly studied the jewellery adorning the portraits of royalty and nobility. Our sketchbooks overflowed with drawings we made. We were most systematic, and went through one section at a time. So here was David, youngest member of one of the wealthiest families in the country, dressed in baggy pants, T-shirt, and sneakers, earnestly going over the finer points with me of Lady X's brooch or King ABC's necklace. I must confess, I enjoyed myself enormously. Later, those ideas were to inspire me time and time again. I especially recall Queen Elizabeth I's jewellery which was always so spectacular.

In the three years I was in New York, I couldn't get one conversation with Daddy out of my mind. He had sent me to Switzerland for the best schooling, thus honouring my mother's wish. When I mooted the idea of Parsons, he had given his consent generously. At the same time, I was ever conscious that if I continued to stay abroad I was being utterly selfish, uncaring about my parent's welfare. Which was why I had every intention of returning to India once my training was done. I promised myself I would visit Europe and America frequently. I had friends scattered everywhere who would welcome a visit from me any time. Among them were David's family. I wonder sometimes if his very sophisticated mother and his distinguished-looking father had worried about their son's friendship with me. David took me home often, but there was never anything remotely romantic about our relationship. I think once this became very clear, the Asschers accepted me with great warmth and affection. And by going back, I could keep in touch with the latest trends in jewellery design.

I had written to my cousin in Bombay to make enquiries. Born a Chandravats, Suvarnalata, known to all as Lata, was married to the Yuvraj of Sonal Mohur, Devendra Singh Dhanraj. Lata had always been one of my favourite people. I should have addressed her respectfully as Lata Didi, for she was truly a big sister to me. Typically, she would allow nothing of the sort. But I did call her husband Bhaiyya. As a small girl, I had thought he was one of the handsomest men I had ever seen, tall and broad shouldered, with the brown hair and green eyes bequeathed by his maternal grandmother, Elizabeth Shelbourne, who had been his grandfather's third wife. It was as romantic a story as anyone could find, for he had fallen in love with the English governess to the children of the Yuvraj of the kingdom. Bhaiyya held degrees from Stanford and Harvard, and settled in Bombay where he carved out for himself a brilliantly successful business career. Lata herself was an extremely talented dress designer.

In her reply, Lata wrote that there would be no dearth of opportunities for one with my qualifications. Given the fact that Indian women used jewellery in profuse quantity, to say nothing of weddings et al, the jewellery business in Bombay, and in India at large, was not only alive but kicking, and extremely frisky. Any number of big houses would be glad to employ me. Alternately, there were more producers of costume jewellery than one could count. For one, Bombay's film world, perhaps the largest anywhere, needed an endless supply. Then those women and girls who could not afford the genuine stuff relied most on costume jewellery for their adornment. All of which greatly cheered me.

Lata also wrote: "Why not just come and stay with us in Bombay? You can survey the scene yourself, and then decide. In the meantime, I have a big surprise for you. You are invited to a wedding, not an ordinary one, but a big big splash, unlike any you or I have seen because of who the bride and groom are. I don't think you've met my sister-in-law, Nayantara. She completed a doctorate in Biophysics—at least I can spell the word! In the best romantic tradition, Tara is marrying the man she loves. And he isn't royalty! It's a long story, and I can hardly begin to tell it all in a letter. But he is so famous, he quite puts the Dhanrajs in the shade. I don't have to ask if you have heard of the young composer, Lekh Sebastian. You may not know his compositions—the *ghazals* and so forth—but surely you know he and Julian Chatwick brought out an album recently which hit the top of the charts. The two are now collaborating with American balladeer, Hamilton Brubaker. Lekh is a very very special person. So why not come—Uncle Tej is invited too, of course— and just relax and enjoy the wedding? Did I say relax? I take back the word. I could use your help in a million ways. We are woefully short of women in the family."

Lata's advice and invitation sounded very good to me. Yes, a wedding would be great fun. And how intriguing that one from among us should choose—well, a commoner. Even if this man Bhaiyya's sister was marrying wasn't everything my cousin claimed him to be, as far as I was concerned, her daring in flouting all royal tradition held fascination for me. How had she managed to convince Dev Bhaiyya, and those very formidable grandparents of theirs whom I had seen once when I was a little girl? Frankly, the ex-Maharaja of Sonal Mohur had been quite terrifying with that autocratic bearing he had. One steered clear of the Maharani too, for in her own way, she aroused similar feelings. I couldn't imagine this Nayantara being cuddled on that lady's lap.

Daddy responded in a gratifying way. Of course, he was delighted to attend. He looked forward to being with me most, but this marriage which had created a tremendous stir in princely circles everywhere was one he would not miss for anything.

And so I begin to finalize plans. I was very sad to leave New York, and my wonderful circle of friends, but this wasn't the end of the world. I would be back, I promised them—and myself. I didn't know then the circumstances under which I would keep my word.

2

I arrived in Bombay with a mountain of luggage, the accumulation of my years in New York. Whether it was my American passport which helped me to whisk through Customs, I do not know. Lata and Dev Bhaiyya were at the airport to receive me. Bhaiyya threw up his hands in mock horror, and asked if I'd occupied all the luggage space in the plane by myself. Bombay's humid air struck me in the face but once we arrived at the lovely old Dhanraj mansion at Breach Candy, and I had showered off travel stains, I felt quite human again.

Lata examined me with interest, for we had not met for years. "Hmmm, you've inherited the family height, Piyali, but none of the family looks. Very different from the rest of us. From another planet, I'd say."

I grinned. "Just another E.T."

Bhaiyya amended, "Let's say from the other side of this planet. I can see we're going to have young men haunting the place, Lata."

"I wonder though," she said thoughtfully, "which of our ancestors is responsible for those dazzling looks. And the colour of your eyes. Mmmm, I'd call them grey, but I see they're quite blue in some lights. Remarkable. Now Dev's colouring is easily explained, but yours—I don't know about those Chandravats of long ago."

"You mean another Shatvijay?" I asked slyly, and that made her laugh. Shatvijay, a kinsman, was a cheerful womanizer whose sexual escapades brought stern disapproval from the elders of the clan. It was said he had sired so many children by various women, that he had lost count. Among the young Chandravats, it was a joke that the erring charmer's name which meant 'he who has a hundred victories' had a special significance.

I looked at my hosts. Lata, slender and very pretty with the charming manner and sweet smile which won everyone who came within her orbit, now a most successful designer for The Honey Bee Boutiques under the label, Suvarnalata Creations, catering to the most elite circle. Bhaiyya as handsome as I remembered him, the perfect example of what a man of royal blood could achieve in changed circumstances. A graduate of Stanford and Harvard Business School, he now belonged to the top echelons of industry. They made a perfect couple, completely in tune with each other. Here was one arranged marriage that had been outstandingly successful. Only the lack of a child marred their happiness. I had overheard talk about this in family circles when I came on holiday. I thought it a pity, not because I agreed with the whispered comments, but because a child born to these two wonderful people would have been very special indeed.

The topic of the day was naturally The Wedding. I was brought up-to-date on the state of preparedness. The Honey Bee was going all out on the bridal outfit and trousseau. The owner, Madhur Monal, had designed the first, and contributed to the second. Lata's designs played a large part. For the rest, everything was being catered. The wedding reception was to be held on the spacious lawns of the exclusive club of which Bhaiyya was a member. Hotel accommodation had been booked for out-of-town guests. Lata told me privately that Dev had not invited anyone from Sonal Mohur. Tara had not wanted anyone of the family either. But, Lata groaned, though some members had gone into a huff, not so others who all agog with curiosity, on the pretext of fulfilling family duties, had been unable to resist attending this most exciting event, the like of which had never taken place in Dhanraj royal circles. Dev had been informed they were arriving.

"And horror of horrors," Lata went on, "Dev's grandmother is coming. No one informed any of them about wedding dates. There must be a spy somewhere who kept them informed! The Maharani is the last person anyone of us wants. H.H. isn't very mobile after a stroke, or we'd have had him too. I might as well tell you, Dev and his grandparents are far from being on cordial terms—following a lot of unpleasantness. I won't go into details now. He wouldn't have her under his roof in any circumstances. It's a hotel suite for her."

To say the least, the situation was rather intriguing. I did not probe. If Lata wanted me to know more, she would tell me.

"Piyali," Lata continued, "Brace yourself. Your special charges at the wedding are going to be a pair of foreigners. You have to pilot them around, explain things, be their guide. It's their first time in India, you see. And be warned. Wherever they go, they'll be mobbed by admirers."

"For heaven's sake, Lata, who are these paragons?"

"Great pals of the Lekhs. Being the groom, however, he will hardly be free to entertain them." Watching my face and with relish, she intoned, "Julian Chatwick. Hamilton Brubaker."

A full minute must have passed before I realized my jaw had dropped. I took hold of myself, and sank into the nearest seat. Lata was gratified. "Oh, my goodness," I said weakly.

"Lekh says they're great fun," Lata said consolingly. "I hope the cultural shock isn't too great for them." She moved to another subject. "Tara will be back tomorrow. She's in Sinhadurg visiting her in-laws."

"Where's that?" blankly.

"An hour's drive along the coast from Bombay. A lovely peaceful place. And such nice people. It's a mutual admiration kind of thing."

"Lucky Tara. And the groom?"

Lata leaned over to pick up a framed photograph from the table to give me. When I looked at it, I exclaimed accusingly, "You said he was a composer! This man looks like a movie star!"

"I'll say he does. And has immense charm. Very suave. Polished. One of the most wonderful people to know. When you meet him, you'll understand why Tara threw every convention to the winds, and decided to marry Lekh. They have faced some horrid problems before things settled down at last."

"And Tara?"

"I'll let you form your own opinion. I will say she's more than a sister to me. And I 'm so thrilled for her. You know she was in boarding school in England after her parents died so tragically young. In a sense, she's never really had a home of own."

"So have I been in boarding school since I was very young! And lost my mother too! " I told her indignantly.

"Yes, I know. But, Piyali, you have an adoring father, and therefore a loving home. Tara has had Dev, and they couldn't be closer. And all she had besides him were those two cold fish in Sonal Mohur."

I had not expected Tara to be so beautiful. She being a Ph.D. in Biophysics, University gold medallist, and who knew what else, I had built up this vague image in my mind of a very scholarly-looking female, drably dressed, a little stooped, wearing glasses, pretty enough to have caught the eye of this composer. The reality could not have been more different. I wondered at myself for not guessing that Dev Bhaiyya would have a sister who matched him in looks as well as intelligence. She was strikingly like him, with the same colouring, and those identical green eyes. Only, where he was big and tall, she had a slim lovely figure. Had she not taken up research, she could have been a very successful model. It was her warm informality that endeared her to me at once. She danced into the house, kissed Lata with great affection, hugged her brother exuberantly, and turned to me. "You're Piyali! And I'm so happy to meet you. I quite envy you your height! Now you look the part—straight out of the Divyasthala Palace. Though I'm not so sure about the jeans," she added laughing, glancing down at her own trim pants and blouse. Had I closed my eyes, I would have guessed it was an Englishwoman talking. The boarding school in Kent had left an indelible imprint on her speech. But then hadn't my Swiss schooling done the same for me? Overlaid with an American touch, I really couldn't say what my speech was like. Yes, Tara was a lovely person to know, and I was relieved to find that so.

3

Breathes there the man (or woman) with soul so dead who never to himself hath said, oh, how I do love a wedding! I'm sorry about the mutilation of Sir Walter Scott's immortal words, but I have yet to encounter such an individual. When I look back, I cannot decide which one of us enjoyed Tara's wedding most. At numerous family weddings, the pomp had been appropriate to such royal affairs. In our senior year at school, our class had been privileged to attend the wedding of our pretty Music teacher, Mademoiselle Renaud, and the Assistant Headmaster of the Boys' School run by the same establishment. The other girls had been green with envy, but they could not possibly have squeezed into the beautiful little School Chapel with all the Staff of both schools, and guests. That wedding had been very Swiss, quietly elegant, and in complete contrast to the kind we had in Divyasthala. Tara's wedding surpassed them all.

I had met Lekh Sebastian at last. Who could help being impressed by this man who carried off his good looks and success so effortlessly? Certainly, I was bowled over. Within moments of meeting him, we were chatting away and laughing like old friends, Tara with us. I have to confess that the three of us at various awkward moments in these days of celebration, resorted to communicating in French. Yes, I could understand now why as Lata said, Tara had consigned all convention to the winds, and chosen to marry this extraordinary man. Lata and he were great pals. Bhaiyya and he seemed a little less close, but then, not many people had Lata's sweet winning personality. It pleased my romantic heart to see the bridal pair together. Anyone could tell they truly belonged to one another, and that not just because of their frequently linked hands, or close proximity when seated. It was more a fleeting look, a gesture, which sufficed to prove how deeply in love they were. Was it my imagination that made me feel they also wore a look of peace and contentment, as if after great stress, all was right with their world now?

A week before the wedding, Lata hosted a dinner for the groom's family. I met Tara's future in-laws for the first time. The resemblance between Cressida Sudarshan and her son was very marked. A tall handsome woman, she looked as if she possessed some inner strength that would carry her through every crisis. Lata had told me she was a brilliant pianist in her own right, and surely had passed on her talent and love of music to her illustrious son. I liked Mr Nand Sudarshan on sight. Slight, grey-haired, with a gentle face, and the eyes of a poet—which I discovered he actually was—he was the easiest person to talk to. Zelda Carvalho, very smart and well-groomed, well known in advertising circles in Bombay, was Lekh's aunt. Conversation with her was interesting and enlightening. The one Sudarshan who won my heart was Lekh's nephew, Vivek Nicholas, whom the privileged—I was graciously allowed to join that group—called Skeet. Closest to me in age, college-going, he seemed to be everyone's favourite.

I was wrong, of course, but I felt I had seen him somewhere before. Since this was absurd, I dismissed the thought. I must have met someone who bore a strong resemblance. I guessed that the girls at college fell for him left and right like the proverbial nine pins. Besides being tall with a breadth to match, he was very personable, and kept the assembly laughing. For all that, I noted he was very well brought-up, full of courtesy to his elders and the ladies present.

What was really most pleasing was the way in which the two families meshed. There was none of that awkwardness that accompanied such affairs where two familial groups still new to each other are cautious, over-polite, wary about committing any faux pas that might mar the relationship. Rather they seemed to know each other well, totally relaxed, and chatting away like old friends. I supposed they had reached this stage after frequent visiting back and forth. Lata's domestic staff—two were from Sonal Mohur—were perfectly well-trained and much practised, for perforce, she was always throwing dinner parties for Bhaiyya's business associates, as well as for those from the elite social circle in which they moved. Tonight, however, was different. Skeet brought the delicious canapes around several times. At the buffet table, Madame Sudarshan personally served the men. It was astonishingly cosy. More, Lata's servants seemed to enjoy it all. Particularly, they beamed at Skeet. Oh, well, who could blame them? Here in this beautiful mansion, the one thing lacking was the presence of children, for sadly, Lata had not been able to carry any of several pregnancies to full term. It was the one great sorrow in an idyllic marriage.

Back in the drawing room which bore the stamp of Lata's wonderful taste, Skeet brought me a cup of coffee, and sat down beside me.

"I've been trying to decide all evening which of the three princesses in the room is the most beautiful." He looked at Tara who was putting a spoonful of sugar into Lekh's cup, smiling up into his face as he spoke. Tonight, she looked truly bridal, the green eyes glowing softly in her lovely face. Skeet's eyes moved to Lata. As if she sensed his regard, she looked our way. Her face lit up, the smile she gave him was so special I was taken aback. As if she could not stay away, she crossed the room swiftly. Skeet was on his feet.

"No," she said in dismay, "I didn't mean to disturb you."

"You aren't at all. Here's a place just waiting for you," and Skeet seated her on his other side.

"Skeet is trying to make up his mind." I told her what we were discussing.

"Oh," she exclaimed, "you and Tara are both lovely, but so different that one isn't really able to compare. And I'm not beautiful at all!"

Skeet said quietly, "To me you are." Lata quickly searched his face. A small indeterminate sound came from her lips, and the soft brown eyes filled with sudden tears. She put out her hand to touch his cheek, and he held it there for a moment. The byplay lasted a fleeting minute, and I was the only observer. It troubled me because it was so inexplicable. Why was there this special bond between Lata and this young man, and what would Bhaiyya think of it?

The thought nagged me until I joined in the singing at which the musical Sudarshans excelled, and which Bhaiyya had requested. Tara claimed she couldn't croak a note, but would help by clapping to the rhythm. Skeet mourned the lack of a guitar, but it hardly mattered. They all sang so beautifully, their glorious voices blending so harmoniously that it was obvious they had sung together for years. It was obvious too that the domestic staff had never enjoyed any guests so much. They had grouped together behind the curtains to listen, but at Bhaiyya's signal came in and settled on the carpet. It was Lekh's solo pieces which enthralled all of them and us most. Seldom had I heard such a mellifluous voice. I liked Tara's fiance even more when he asked for requests from the staff, and sang for them alone. A memorable start to the wedding festivities.

If I were using sub-titles here, I would head this section with one word: ARRIVALS. No one counted the number of journeys to and from the airports which were made by various chauffeured cars to receive the guests, and ferry them to their hotels. It is mandatory according to the dictates of social custom in India for someone from the family to personally welcome out-of-town guests and relatives. I need not spell out who was the fortunate one this task fell upon mostly. After the seventh such trip, my jaws ached with the polite smiling I had subjected them to. The answers to surprised questions about my presence here, and current activities I reeled off by rote. I think the hotel staff regarded me as an old friend after the third set of guests was unloaded, and turned over to their tender care. Lata said guiltily, "Piyali, I'm so sorry I didn't anticipate it would be so taxing for you. Are they being a nuisance?"

"Not at all," I said brightly. "I'm enjoying myself." After all, I was only fulfilling family obligations. One reason why I had come early was to help Lata.

And then Daddy flew in, accompanied by my cousin, Anahita, who was Lata's eldest sister. He took me into his arms, and kissed me tenderly. "Let me look at you." He nodded proudly. "Anu, do you see how lovely my daughter has become?"

"Lovely? I'd say gorgeous, even if she makes me feel like a midget. My dear," kissing me warmly, "I'm delighted you're here. Lata told me on the phone last night that without you, she would just collapse. Between the three of us, we ought to be able to relieve Lata of more of her worries."

"I'd like to do whatever I can," Daddy said. I was seeing his dear face after a whole year.

True to her word, Anu rendered invaluable help, never so much as when she joined Lata in receiving Bhaiyya's grandmother. This once, I was spared. Bhaiyya had refused to go with them. I had overheard Lata pleading with him, and Tara saying, "Of course, she'll expect him, but I don't think she'll be surprised if he's not there, Lata. No one actually issued an invitation. It's her own decision to come. Do you want me to go with you? Hmmm? I don't care a bit what convention dictates, and I'm the bride! Well, if you are sure. Yes, Anahita will do the honours very well. No, Grandmere will just have to accept certain things. I think you'll find she's changed, Lata."

"If such a thing is possible," Lata said gloomily.

4

The venue of the wedding had been transformed into a veritable fairyland with lights of every hue, banks of flowers, a delicate scent in the night air all around from perfume sprayed at intervals. Lekh's troupe, ensconced on a dais of their own, played the most beautiful numbers, many of them Lekh's compositions.

Bhaiyya stood at the glittering entrance arch, Daddy beside him, to welcome the guests in the best traditional manner. Though in impeccable suits and ties, they both looked as princely as could be desired. Significantly, Bhaiyya had requested Daddy to stand with him when the honour should have been bestowed on the seniormost of the Dhanraj princes who had come all the way from Sonal Mohur for the wedding. I could not fathom why Bhaiyya had deliberately slighted them thus. They now sat at a large table reserved for them, Maharani Chitralekha in the centre. One had to admit, in their regalia, they all truly looked the part, representing the bride's family. Only last night, Lata and Anahita had ceremoniously presented to Tara the jewellery and gifts the Maharani had brought for her granddaughter, and a full trousseau such as a princess was equipped with at the time of her wedding. Patently, the lady had been determined to follow every tradition possible under the circumstances when neither the bride nor her brother had presented themselves to her, to say nothing of the said brother who was, after all, the Yuvraj, asking her to stay under his roof. Tara had been touched by the gesture, and looked over everything. Lata asked anxiously if Tara would prefer to dress in the bridal outfit that had been included rather than the one Madhur Monal had designed. Before Tara could speak, Bhaiyya had said sharply—unusual for him—that such a thought was not to be considered for a second. Anahita was requested to lock away everything upstairs.

I spent almost the entire evening with Julian and Ham who were my special charges. When I had gone in the limousine to collect these two, I had been astonished by the huge crowds waiting outside the exclusive club where the reception was taking place, being controlled by policemen. I realized then that these were fans of Lekh, of the film crowd that was surely coming, and, yes indeed, of Julian and Ham. At the sight of the car, they had surged forward. For me, it was a new experience to have excited faces peer in, shouting words, camera lights going off in my face, and autograph books being waved. Somehow, we were safely in. We made a stir when we entered. Apart from the fact of who my companions were, I suppose we made an interesting trio. Our English companion in the perfection of his Savile Row tailored clothes, correct to the last fold, lean, upright, sandy-haired, couldn't have offered a better foil to the American balladeer in his fringed suede outfit (no one had warned him about Bombay weather obviously), long blond hair sweeping his shoulders, the diamond in his lone earring winking. As for me, I had refused Lata's suggestion about wearing a glittering *salwar-kameez* set she had chosen for me. Instead, I chose to wear a dress I had particularly enjoyed wearing in New York. It was full-length, dark red, the skirt graceful and swirling around my legs, the bodice draped across my breast, low-necked, leaving one shoulder bare. Matching shoes and a set of rubies and diamonds which had belonged to my mother's family completed my attire.

We three were certainly having a whale of a good time. Julian had a wicked dry wit, while Ham's use of the more pungent Americanisms kept fuelling us into more laughter. People came over to greet both men, and tell them in fulsome words how they enjoyed their singing.

Skeet looking very handsome in suit, ruffled shirt and cummerbund, and his youthful companions, were busy directing waiters as more and more guests arrived. Often as he passed our table, he paused to point out who various people were. For instance, one group comprised scientists from Tara's Research Centre. Cerebral they might be, but they were having a rollicking good time away from the test tubes. Another very merry group was made up of Zelda Carvalho's advertising crowd. Easily recognizable, though Skeet added footnotes, were Bhaiyya's friends from the business world, some industrialists. With their elegant-looking wives by their sides, they all had that aura which power, authority and untold wealth brings. One especially striking couple was identified by Skeet as young industrialist, Jai Samartha, and his beautiful auburn-haired green-eyed wife, Sakshi. An older man dressed in a heavy silk tunic with a necklace of amber beads also stood out in the crowd. Skeet whispered this was none other than famed painter, Prithvi Gaurav. And my word, the filmi folk! Glamour, glitter, glitz, these words spring to mind, as stars both female and male, lesser rank-holders in the stellar firmament, producers, directors, composers, and screen writers, went up to the bridal pair to offer their congratulations, and pose prettily for the ever-whirring, ever-clicking cameras.

What can I say that will do justice to Tara and Lekh? They made a spectacularly beautiful couple, he as splendid as a movie star himself, perfectly at ease with every guest, laughing in that charming way of his. Madhur had out-done herself, keeping the bride's beauty of face and form in mind. Nor had she forgotten that she was designing for a princess. Madhur's first query had been to ask what kind of jewellery Tara would be wearing, and having seen the priceless antique emerald-gold set which had belonged to the English grandmother of the bride, Elizabeth Shelbourne, gifted to her by her adoring husband whose third wife she had been, and now passed on to Tara by Bhaiyya, Madhur had sat down to create an extraordinary bridal outfit. And so here was Princess Nayantara, absolutely resplendent in gold shot with green, as radiantly beautiful as any groom could wish. She seemed to take all guests in her stride, greeting them with perfect aplomb. Julian and Ham had been all admiration for their friend's choice.

The Sebastian orchestra began playing a piece softly, its music catching me unawares by the throat. Ham spoke for me when he said, "That's the most haunting melody. Wonder what it is."

"It's The Princess Sonata. Lekh wrote it for Tara. I first heard it in London, and reacted exactly as you did," Julian told us.

I saw Tara put out a hand, and Lekh take it. They exchanged a long wordless look. I thought with a pang, will there ever be someone for me with whom I shall share a tender love like that? I shook myself out of my reverie. This was a wedding, a festival, not the time for gloomy thoughts.

The three of us had arrived just a little too late to witness Maharani Chitralekha's first meeting with the bridal couple, but I heard Lata and Anahita discussing it later. This was before most guests had appeared. Flanked by the Dhanrajs who had come with her, she had advanced towards them determinedly. Bhaiyya's gaze had locked with hers for a long moment, then without a word, he had turned away. Tara had done far better. She had embraced her grandmother briefly, thanked her for the gifts, and then said, "This is Lekh, Grandmere." For the second time, the Maharani's gaze locked with another's, this time a very cool one. In that moment of tension, Lekh had bowed without smiling. Perforce, Her Highness had done the same. With the other Dhanrajs, however, as Tara introduced uncles, aunts and cousins, the tension visibly diminished. The groom was most cordial and welcoming. It was a gracious gesture on his part. The interesting fact was, Lata concluded, they were completely bowled over to the point of being awed by his fame or personality she did not know which. Lekh had then drawn his parents forward. Lata said she had never thought to see Dev's grandmother at a loss for words before. Mr Sudarshan had said, "Welcome, Highness," to which Madame had added, "We are so happy so many from Tara's family could grace the occasion." That was all. The bridal couple went to the throne-like chairs waiting on the dais with its backdrop of roses and lilies, for the orchestra had launched into a special rendition of Lekh's famous *Bhavishya ghazal*, very spirited and lively.

My attention was arrested by the sight of Bhaiyya talking to an important-looking man. Other than a few stragglers, most guests had already arrived, and were sitting at tables eating the sumptuous fare so Bhaiyya could leave the entrance where he had been standing. Skeet had approached the twosome. He waited patiently for Bhaiyya to notice him. Which he did a moment later. Patently, he was murmuring an excuse to the guest. Bhaiyya turned aside, putting his head close to Skeet's. The latter gestured as he spoke. Bhaiyya put a hand on Skeet's shoulder while they conversed. As I watched, realization hit me so shockingly that I had to choke back a sound. The resemblance between the man and the lad was so plain I could not understand how I had missed it. So many facts tumbled into place. No wonder Lata had warned me to say that Skeet was Lekh's cousin and not his nephew. No wonder Skeet was so completely at home in Bhaiyya's house. No need to ask about the special bond between Lata and the boy, the one which had disturbed me so much earlier, or why he and Tara were so close. Probably, I would never know the whole truth, but the proof of their relationship was there right in front of my eyes. Skeet must have said something comic, for Bhaiyya laughed. One hand folded into a fist, and gave Skeet's chin a gentle affectionate push. Skeet grinned, and went off. Bhaiyya resumed his conversation. That was all. I glanced around. Everyone else was eating and chatting away. I sighed with relief that I was the only one who had noted that little byplay. I was wrong.

A waiter came by shortly to ask if the Rajkumari would please accompany him. The Maharani wished to see me. For a moment or two, I did not move, then I braced myself. As I moved away, I murmured to my companions, "If I'm not back in ten minutes, come and rescue me."

"We shall come galloping on our trusty steeds," Julian assured me.

I greeted the Sonal Mohur contingent with folded hands and a bow. I was welcomed cordially. Maharani Chitralekha fixed her eyes on me unwinkingly.

"Child, who is that boy, do you know?"

"Which boy, Ma'am?" innocently.

"The one who was talking to Devendra just now," with controlled impatience.

I said vaguely, "Was there a boy with Bhaiyya?" She snapped, "Yes. Tall, big. Wearing what is that called—around the waist like a flamenco dancer." Her head swung around. "There in the corner by the orchestra."

I glanced across. "Oh, that one. He's a cousin of the groom's. I met him just once. Working hard isn't he, with all his friends? Nice chap."

"What is his name?"

I shook my head. "Sorry I've only been here ten days, and met so many people, I'm utterly confused with names. Perhaps you can ask Bhaiyya, Ma'am," I suggested glibly, knowing full well that she would not dare approach her grandson in his present mood.

She was cross with me, and came back with a terse, "We shall see. Now," fixing her eagle regard on me, "who are those two foreigners, and why are you spending all your time with them? The one in those ridiculous clothes—with that over-grown hair—looks especially dangerous. Not the kind of person a young girl should associate with, and certainly not one of royal blood."

I said politely, "Those foreigners, as you call them, Ma'am, are world famous entertainers. They are very special guests of the groom but of Bhaiyya too, and have come all the way just for the wedding. I have been given special charge of them. I've never met such perfect gentlemen. In fact, I must get back. Was there anything else, Ma'am?" politely, standing up.

She said in exasperation, "This generation has lost all sense of proportion. I truly fear for the future. As for you girls who were in schools abroad, the less said the better."

"That is so," I agreed courteously. "May I take your leave, Ma'am?"

She opened her mouth to say something more which, no doubt, would shrivel me on the spot. I bowed, to her first, and then to all the others before moving off.

I wasn't upset. A faint feeling of pity stirred my heart. Poor lady, I thought, so out of tune with the times, alienated from her nearest and dearest, still unable to learn tolerance, or come off her pedestal. And I was glad I had managed to deflect her enquiries about Skeet. Knowing her, however, I was sure she would not leave it at that. Thankfully, I joined my two friends again.

One of the pleasantest surprises awaited us. The two most famous playback singers took centre-stage now to sing Lekh's songs to the delight of the guests who listened with rapt attention. It was astonishing how well these Hindi film song hits were known to all. From the look on Lekh's face, he had not been expecting this. But he laughed in that way he had, applauding after each song.

All good things must come to an end. To round off the evening, there was a magnificent display of fireworks. At some point, when all faces turned skywards to see each splendid burst of colour, the bride and groom slipped away. I could truthfully agree with Ham when he said, "Some wedding this! I wouldn't have missed it for the world! Sure was great!"

5

It always happens. After great excitement, the aftermath is always a letdown. And so it was with us all once the wedding was over. The bridal couple were winging their way to Paris first, then on to New York where Lekh would be working on a new album with Julian and Ham. Most wedding guests left promptly, Daddy among them, but there were some who stayed on to see the sights of Bombay. Bhaiyya had little time to spare for them now, having spent more time than he could afford from his work. Lata flopped wearily for a day, sleeping late the next morning. She had earned the extra hours of sleep. Anu and I, however, were up bright and early from force of habit, though she said very firmly that she had promised herself a post-lunch nap. Between us, we cleared up everything possible by the time Lata surfaced around 11 a.m.

"You're so good, both of you," she said gratefully.

"Nonsense," her sister said, "it was the least we could do. Except for one thing which only you can take care of." She handed Lata a cup of strong coffee to fortify her. "Drink this. You'll need it." Alarm showed in Lata's eyes. "Yes, I'm afraid so. Dev's Grandmere called. She's leaving by the night train, but wants to see you and Dev before that. I told her Dev left early, and was not reachable, but had to admit you were around. She said if you were that weary, she would come here to see you. I sense she's eaten up with curiosity about many things. Intends to get to the bottom of many matters—one especially. Lata, don't look like that! I fobbed her off. Didn't succeed all the way. She's much too shrewd. I did say you and I would come to see her off, but she would have none of it. So we are to have lunch at her hotel. She didn't mean to invite me at all, but I said we'd be delighted to come."

"Oh, my God!" Lata said weakly. "I think I'll go back to bed. Call her and say I'm ill—something highly infectious!"

"I'll do nothing of the kind! We'll go and beard the lioness in her den. Buck up," bracingly, "I'm there. She can't say much in my presence."

"Thank God for that!" Lata clutched my arm. "Piyali, you come too. I need all the reinforcements I can muster."

"I wish I could," I told her, truly regretful, "but our singing duo insisted I have lunch with them . They're at the Taj, as you know."

Anu said severely, "Piyali, watch out! Chatwick looks staid enough. Quite the propah Englishman. It's that long-haired blond one I'm not sure you can trust!"

"Ham's old enough to be my father!" I protested laughing.

"Hah! As if that was ever a deterrent to that sort! Any man who wears a earring—And I ask you, why one earring?"

"I wouldn't know. Ham's very nice. And they're both great fun to be with. In any case, they're flying out tonight."

"A lot can happen between lunch and flying time," she said darkly. "Are they married?"

"Julian is soon to be. Ham," I added reluctantly, "is just divorced."

"I knew it! You just be careful, Piyali!"

"I shall," I said, and fled upstairs to get ready.

Now that things had settled down, it was time to think of other pressing matters. Lata took me to the main Honey Bee Boutique where she worked. It was much larger than anything I had visualized, the decor elegant, bustling with clients and saleswomen attending to them. Later, I was to visit the workrooms where the expert tailoring was done.These were The Honey Bee headquarters, with other branches all over the metropolis. But first. I had to meet the owner, Madame Madhur Monal.

No one could have looked the part better as the creator of this enormously successful fashion enterprise than this svelte, perfectly groomed woman with her very English accent. Her manner was warm and welcoming.

"I'm so glad to meet Lata's cousin at last. I did see you at the wedding." We looked at each other with equal interest. "I can't be the first one to tell you you're most people's idea of what a princess looks like." I smiled. "You've done some modelling, of course, besides designing?" And was genuinely surprised at my answer. "Now tell me about yourself. I know you trained at Parsons and I'm impressed!"

I gave her a brief resume of my schooling , and the courses I had offered at Parsons. As a businesswoman, she would need to know my credentials. I produced my portfolio of designs which she examined with great care. Then she sat back, and gave me a straight look. "These are excellent. And I have a proposition to put to you."

The gist of what Mme. Monal said was that I could, of course, approach some of the big jewellery houses for which the city was famed. They would be more than interested in my work. But as a beginner just launching on my career, it might be better to take each step one at a time. Once I was established, and my name known, the sky was the limit. At this point, experience was important. She was offering me a position here at The Honey Bee, designing jewellery for the class of very affluent customers for whom Lata's designs were exclusively created. In any case, although still classifiable as costume jewellery, it would be quality stuff, using semi-precious stones, corals, or whatever. After Lata had first consulted her about me, Mme. Monal had thought up this idea. Doing a bit of preliminary scouting, she had located craftsmen in Hyderabad, Jaipur and elsewhere who would do the actual work.Yes, it entailed frequent trips to those places, but that presented no problems with daily flights there and back available. Now what did I think of the entire plan?

I hardly needed to think it over. As she spoke, I had realized here was an invaluable opportunity for me to gain experience. As one new to Bombay, and certainly to the Indian market, what better place than this to learn, especially with Lata around, and this lady now awaiting my reaction to her plan there to pilot me?

"You'll want to mull over this. Discuss it with Lata and Dev, I'm sure. Does the basic idea appeal to you though?"

"Yes, very much so. I'll talk it over with the family."

She spoke next of a basic salary, commissions, and more, which she said Dev in particular as a businessman would ask about. Could I get back to her within two days with my answer? I didn't tell her I had already made up my mind, but promised to see her again the day after next. I wouldn't take any more of her time now, and took my leave.

Bhaiyya gave his full approval. "Whatever one might say about Madhur, she's as straight as they come. Has a very shrewd mind, I'll grant, and why not? She's made it to the top because of it. In this business jungle, one has to be."

Lata was delighted. "We'll be working together a good deal, Piyali. I can't wait to get started!"

I sensed a quiet elation when I went to see Mme. Monal again. She said she was very glad. And thus was my immediate future taken care of.

One of the pressing problems I faced concerned a place to stay. I had enjoyed every moment of staying with Lata and Bhaiyya but I had no intention of becoming a permanent guest. Then too, I prized my independence. I needed a place where I could work. I had been offered office space on The Honey Bee premises, but in the midst of such bustle, I doubted if I could accomplish much. When I sounded Madhur out—she had told me firmly she didn't care to be called Madame—she had thought briefly, and come up with a possible solution. It seemed that one of her young models owned an apartment of her own. She was married now. Madhur did not know if the place was rented, or used by Ruhi whenever she came to Bombay from Sinhadurg, but she would find out. No sooner said than done. She called right away, and received a favourable answer. In fact, the young lady would be in Bombay that day. Madhur made a lunch appointment for us.

Within moments of meeting the Nevilles, Ruhi and Robin, I knew they were my kind of people. It did not surprise me in the least that this lovely person was one of India's most successful models. She had the fresh youthful looks that made one think of springtime. Even if Madhur had not briefed me about this magnificent-looking man, towering above everyone else in the restaurant, I would have guessed he was someone important. Indeed, as photographer extraordinaire, one who produced prize-winning documentaries as part of his wide-ranging interests, his was a name highly respected in knowledgeable circles. In no time, we were engaged in animated conversation. It appeared Madhur had told them about me, and they regarded me with friendly interest.

After lunch, Robin glanced at his watch to exclaim it was nearly three, and he had to get to his studio. He would leave it to his wife to give me a guided tour of the apartment. Putting us in a taxi, he went off in his car.

Part of a new complex, the apartment was charming. It was fully furnished, and in excellent taste, reflecting the owner's personality.

"I've become so fond of it. It became my refuge at a rather painful time in my life," Ruhi said. "That's why I haven't sold it though I have offers all the time. But I'm very glad to let you have the use of it. Will you require a maid-cum-cook? There's a very nice one who used to work for me. In fact, still comes in a couple of hours twice a week and cleans the place for me. She doesn't like the new lady she works for. I'm sure she'll jump at the chance to work for you."

My spirits brightened by the second. The rent Ruhi quoted seemed absurdly low to my Americanized ears. She mentioned it diffidently as if it were exorbitant. I was new to housekeeping in India, and realized that having domestic help would leave all my time for my own pursuits. Thanks to Ruhi, the place was equipped down to the last spoon, and I could move in immediately. When we parted that afternoon, we were already firm friends. I promised to visit her and Robin at their beautiful home, Waverley. But before any of this, I had to tell Lata and Bhaiyya.

Lata was mad at me. What had possessed me to think up this crazy idea! And I hadn't even discussed it with her before going ahead with investigations! Patiently, I explained. "Oh, Piyali," she scolded, you're family, not a guest. This is such a big house for just the two of us. I've loved having you around. I—haven't had time to tell you," biting her lip, "but Skeet is moving in with us." I hid my astonishment. "We—Dev and I— thought he commutes every day from Sinhadurg—we have plenty of room—and Lekh and Tara are married now so—" Her voice trailed off as her eyes met mine.

I said gently, "That'll be great. Skeet is so full of beans. He'll fill the house with fun and laughter."

She blinked back the sudden rush of tears. "Yes, he will," she managed to say. "I'd thought both of you would be here."

"I'll spend a day with you on weekends," I promised. "This will always be home to me, you know. Where can I find a small car, Lata? Even a second-hand one?"

"Dev," she said at once. "Or Skeet might know. In the meantime, feel free to use mine. I don't enjoy driving in Bombay during the rush hour, and Dev drops me off, or I take a taxi." She touched my hand. "I'm sorry I was cross. I know the Nevilles very well. Ruhi often models my designs, and in between assignments, Robin has done photography for us. They're really charming people." She gave me a watery smile. "At least you'll be in the same city, and we'll meet at The Honey Bee. Madhur was so impressed by you."

Bhaiyya was more understanding. "We'll miss your beautiful presence, Piyali," he said gravely, "but I understand that creative people need peace and quiet. And you will come often, won't you? Lata misses having a woman around. Tara and she always have a rollicking time. I'm afraid I—and now Skeet—won't quite fill the gap your going will leave. Call upon me for the smallest problem, okay? I'm going with you when you move in. I want to check out the security system in the place."

A month later, I was very well settled. The apartment was just right for my needs.. The maid, awed by my so-called title which Ruhi had mentioned, kept the place spotless. I preferred to manage breakfast and lunch on my own, the former comprising only toast and fruit juice, the latter a large salad. But whenever I was going to be at home, she made tasty little dinners for me.

Work was tremendously exciting. Mostly, Lata and I worked as a team. I confess I had to adjust to a whole new side of my cousin. I had not guessed she was so talented a designer. The clothes which bore the label of Suvarnalata Creations were exquisite, extremely expensive, but snapped up by The Honey Bee's wealthier clientele. It was upto me to create jewellery to match. I put my all into the task, loving the challenge of it.

Madhur and I flew to Jaipur first, and then to Hyderabad to supervise the making of the first pieces. Here too we selected the semi-precious stones, pearls and other materials needed. The craftsmen were masters at their work. To gauge the response of the customers, it had been decided to make no announcement or to advertise, but to display the jewellery in the Boutique's showrooms. Laid against the rich backdrop of Lata's outfits, sometimes by themselves against satin or velvet, and on mannequins, the whole brilliantly lit, they looked spectacular. That first day, I was nervous. I need not have worried. Lata's clientele took one look, demanded to know if the pieces were on sale, and promptly bought them. News spread, and by the end of the second day, the entire first consignment was sold out. It would have been hard to know which one of us was the most elated. Indeed, the whole Boutique buzzed with excitement. Madhur promptly ordered tea and cakes for everyone to celebrate. I had never been so relieved or satisfied in my life. The runaway success signified that I had indeed launched on my career at last.

It was Lata who added one more new dimension to my life. There I was all unsuspecting, deeply interested in the Fashion Show that The Honey Bee was putting up in collaboration with Coquette, makers of fine soaps and cosmetics. I exclaimed over each new outfit distinctly bearing the stamp of its individual designer. One, a scarlet and black affair, rich with gold embroidery, was especially enchanting. I lifted it against me. Mmmm, not too bad, I thought about my reflection in the full-length mirror.

"Try it on," Lata urged.

"Oh, I couldn't! I'm too tall for conventional sizes anyway." Actually, I was dying to see how it would look on me. Lata insisted, and I found it not only a perfect fit, but if I do say so myself, it seemed just made for me. "Not bad," I said modestly, privately thinking it looked rather good. A thought struck me. "How come it's in my size? Do you have a tall client who ordered it?"

My cousin glanced at Madhur who was a silent spectator. "Well, not exactly. It was—well, made to your measurements."

I was confused. "But why? Why would you do that?"

The words came out in a rush. "Because, Piyali, I've been hoping so much you'll model some of my designs at the Fashion Show." I stared at her speechlessly. "With that height and carriage, you'd be perfect. And you have that air about you. Haughty. Regal. You know what I mean. Think what a splash it will make—a real live princess modelling Princess Suvarnalata Creations!" Her speech was still hurried. Now she clasped her hands together. "Just try it this once, Piyali." She glanced at Madhur. "How does she look, Madhur?"

That lady said succinctly, "Perfect. Stunning."

"See? And this is the expert talking!" Lata managed to look anxious and pleading simultaneously.

I spoke for the first time. "No way! I refuse to go mincing down the catwalk wiggling my hips, and being ogled by all male spectators! I'm not a model. I'm a designer. I've never modelled in my life!"

Later, Bhaiyya chuckled. "Piyali, you don't know your cousin very well, do you? But I do. The things she makes me do against my will—" More seriously, "But this time, I concur with her wholly. Little as I know about fashion, I'm convinced you'll make a great model. We're going to be proud of you all over again."

That was the beginning. I was in the Show, and many more to follow. On occasion, I agreed to pose for photographic sequences in fashion magazines. That was as far as I would go. I turned down all offers from advertising agencies. One plus point was that I met many people which was both enlightening and interesting. They were quite different from my circles in Europe and New York. Did I mention that Lata presented me with the scarlet and black outfit because, as she said, I had been a good girl?

6

The journey went smoothly enough until I reached the outskirts of Sinhadurg. The car seemed to falter, and slow down. At first, I thought I was imagining it, but no, it was real. A case of so near and yet so far, I told myself grimly. I nursed, the car along, cruising till the first signs of habitation appeared. A bus stop, shops, people, and thank heavens, the strong smell of diesel, stacks of used tyres, and other paraphernalia that pointed to a petrol pump-cum-garage. Thankful indeed, I pulled in carefully, the car giving several jerks which rocked me. Patently, luck was with me, for it seemed like a respectable place where I could trust the mechanics not to ruin Lata's car permanently. PETER'S GARAGE the sign said. All was bustle as cars, trucks and two-wheelers filled up their tanks at the pumps. In another section, an expensive-looking car was being lowered on the ramp, almost certainly after being serviced. I waited for someone to notice me, then honked impatiently. A man in greasy overalls, wiping his hand on some waste cotton, came to me. He spoke fluent English, so I surmised this was Peter himself.

I came out, of course, glad as I thrust my legs through the door that I had dressed sensibly—narrow beige pants and a blouson-style top, moccasins, my hair swept up for coolness in a topknot. I suppose a woman driver, and one dressed as I was wasn't a common sight here, for I was attracting a great deal of attention. Drivers stared out of their windows, attendants manning the hose pipes at the pumps likewise. It must be my height, I thought, and held my head high. So what if I was taller than many of them?

Peter or whoever he was, had the bonnet open, and his head bent over the engine. Moments later, he emerged. The fan belt had broken, he told me, and needed replacement, and there was some leakage in the petrol tank. I stared at him. How long would it take, I demanded, and was horrified at the answer. If it had to wait till tomorrow, what would I do now? It was late evening already. I should have reached Waverley half an hour ago. How did I get there? I put the question to Mr Peter who looked at me with renewed interest. A taxi? A rickshaw? He shook his head regretfully.

The expensive car was being given a final rubdown. The rays of the setting sun picked up the gleaming maroon paintwork, and the sparkle of plateglass. As if the sight gave him an idea, Mr Peter snapped his fingers, and called out to someone in the Office. In a moment, a man sauntered out. He was so disreputable-looking that I fervently hoped the summons had nothing to do with my problem. The man surveyed the scene briefly, then slouched to the nearest wall, and propped himself lazily against it. I couldn't make out his features very well in their unshaven state. In any case, he wore a cloth cap, something like golfers wear, and the visor obscured his eyes. For the rest, he wore shabby faded pants, and a shapeless shirt that looked none too clean, plus dusty sneakers with the laces missing.

In Hindi, he growled, "*Mujhe kisne bulaya?* Who called me?" Peter admitted he had. "*Kyon?* Why?" the fellow barked. He reached over to one of the mechanics, pulled out a matchbox from his shirt pocket, extracted a match, bit off the head and spat it out, then stuck the rest in a corner of his mouth and began to chew. I wasn't the only one taking this in. It seemed to me everyone had suspended work, and was watching. Fleetingly, I gave thought to why an inflammable object like a matchbox should be permitted on the premises. Peter seemed to choke a little before explaining that this lady's car had broken down, and no repairs were possible at this late hour. Would the man be willing to drop her off at Waverley? I was stunned. Go with this creature? What was Peter thinking of? Why, he wasn't the kind of person one would wish to encounter on a dark night in any case, but more, no one sensible would want to face him even in broad daylight!

"*Ismen mera kya fayada hai?*" he asked cunningly turning around the matchstick, and spat out a sliver of wood. "What's in it for me?"

Another paroxysm of coughing attacked Peter. He dived under the open bonnet of Lata's car, and did not emerge for a couple of minutes. When he did, his colour was high. How much would the Memsaab give him, the man was asking. I looked at him haughtily. To Peter I said, "Is there no one else who can take me?" He shook his head. "All right," I said impatiently, "how much does he expect?" Peter glanced at the oaf who said affably, "*Kum se Kum sau rupaye.* Nothing less than a hundred rupees." Really, this was daylight robbery! I glared at him, and was subjected to a leer. And why was everyone around grinning so broadly? Coughing badly, Peter managed to say feebly, "Twenty five should do it," which was still exorbitant for a journey of some six miles. Still, beggars couldn't be choosers. I nodded. "How do we go? The man straightened, and approached the now gleaming car. Surely, the owner of it, didn't employ this scruffy creature as a chauffeur? Peter was asking if I had luggage. I unlocked the boot to take out my bags. With the amount I was paying him, one would think the fellow would have the decency to pick them up, but no, the man simply watched me. I thought angrily if this had been Europe or America, it could never have happened. I lugged the bags over myself to the other car. At this point, Peter came to the rescue, and lifted into the other boot. I took the opportunity to speak to him alone. Ostensibly, I was talking about repairs, but what I wanted to know was if it were safe to go with this individual. Very safe, Peter assured me. I wished I had his confidence. I didn't care that the man had heard.

When Peter opened the front passenger door, I asked to sit in the back. The other man sliding into the driver's seat said sarcastically, "*Memsaab naukaron ke sath nahin bethin janab. Ye bade log sab ek jaise hote hai.* She doesn't sit with servants, my friend. These big people are all the same." Then impatiently, "*Accha mujhe der ho rahi hai. Jahan chahe wahan beth jaiye.* Sit where you like. I'm getting late." I slid in quietly next to him. The ordeal would be over in a very short time.

This was the hour of twilight. A few last birds winged homewards. On the road, all vehicles had their lights on, but there was enough light to see trees flashing past. The breeze that poured in through my window held a tang of the sea. It tugged playfully at my hair, so that tendrils came loose which I brushed away from my face. The thought of the Nevilles, and a pleasant weekend ahead lightened my mood. The man beside me had spoken no word. Evidently he was sick of me, and couldn't wait to dump me off. I noted how confidently his long hands held the wheel, the nails well-trimmed and very clean. They seemed too finely shaped for a servant—but then who could say how they should be? When we slowed to let a car pass, I took a quick look at the face below the visor. The eyes were still obscured, but the profile astonished. The nose straight, high-bridged, the lean jaw and firm chin spoke of his character. I moved my gaze back to the road hastily. Such a scrutiny was unbecoming on my part.

Lights had begun to appear, a great many to our left where obviously lay a dwelling, then the headlights picked out two pillars, and the name WAVERLEY in Gothic lettering, and a quick glimpse of a pair of stone lions. We were climbing a slope, coming closer to bright lights. I was gripped by a wave of anticipation. Quite suddenly, still a hundred feet away, the car came to a halt. I turned my head in surprise, but the man was out of the door, going to the back, opening the boot. Quite bewildered, I was out myself. He dumped out my luggage on the side. Neville Saab's servants would collect the stuff, he said briefly. I was to go on up to the house. Before I could utter a word, he was back in the car, slammed the door, reversed, and I was looking at his tail-lights vanishing in the darkness. Crazy man, I thought. And he hadn't taken his money! And then voices were coming closer, Ruhi's calling my name. Robin loomed up.

7

I loved Waverley at once. If ever a house had personality, this one had a most distinctive one. Grand though they had been, I had not experienced this in any of the palaces associated with my childhood. I learnt it was more than a century old, and had belonged to a retired British colonel who had lived in it until his death. It had then become the property of the Navalkishor family, generations of whom had lived under its roof. Ruhi said Robin was related to that family, and had bought the house when it came on the market. He had commissioned extensive renovations, as well as a completely new interior design. The work had been undertaken by a husband and wife team though they hadn't been married then. Ruhi assumed I knew the names of Anjolie and Geet Adityaraj. It wasn't the first time since I arrived in India that I had felt like an ignoramus.I had to agree they had both done a superb job. The interiors were perfectly in keeping with the gracious architecture of Waverley. Ruhi went on to explain that the young architect had designed the house-cum-studio of their nearest neighbour and one of Robin's best friends, Neel Gregory. I hoped my face did not look as blank as I was about the name. A neighbour who could afford the services of a leading architect—a studio—and spoken of with genuine affection by Ruhi, I would have to do some homework in order to come abreast of the current scene—prepare a kind of private Who's Who in my mind. And here was a tidbit. This Geet was the stepson of Madhur Monal! Gracious me, I told myself, and what was this Gregory fellow anyway? An artist—a fellow photographer like Robin?

I was having a marvellous time. If sometimes I was challenged to do things I hadn't done in years, I responded with total abandonment. The morning after my rather unorthodox arrival, I was awakened early by birdsong. I leaped out of bed, and ran to the window. My room faced the back where thick trees stood, and beyond were undulating plains, and low hills in the far distance. I breathed deeply of the clean bracing salty air. I had laughed when Ruhi asked if I would like bed tea. It made me sound like something straight out of P.G. Wodehouse, I teased, and unless she could produce a Jeeves, I wouldn't emulate Bertie Wooster. Since Robin was the first one up, and always made a potful, I would come down for my first cup of tea. Recalling that, I showered happily, dying to go down and explore in the daylight.

I had barely finished dressing when Ruhi knocked. She laughed when she saw me. "Piyali, I came to rout you out of bed, and there you are, all ready!" Like me, she was in a T-shirt and pants, her hair in a single braid. She looked so young and lovely, her skin quite without make-up, dewy fresh like a little child's. No wonder she was the most sought-after of models. When I told her that, she looked at me. "Oh, Piyali, you say that to me when you're so gorgeous yourself—the perfect Princess!"

That Ruhi was still very youthful in impulses as well as looks was proved when at the top of the stairs, she looked at me out of the corner of her eye, and then without warning, slid down the banisters. I stared down. She had landed gracefully, and was urging me to do the same. It was all very well for Ruhi, so neatly proportioned. Given my height and long legs, could I do it? Impossible to resist. We were alone, and no eye was watching. I sat down gingerly, told myself it was no different from tobogganing which I had done hundreds of times, and let myself go. I whizzed down, and landed at Ruhi's feet in a flail of legs and arms. I sat up to recover my breath—and my dignity. Ruhi clapped her hands in delight. I stood up. No, it was definitely not like tobogganing. For one, no soft snow cushioned one's tumbles, and the polished tiled floor was very hard on one's posterior. I said indignantly, "I'm not going to let this defeat me, Ruhi!" She choked with laughter, giving me instructions, and making encouraging little sounds. And I did it! True, not at once. But by the third attempt, I had taken note of the pitfalls. I summoned all the expertise I used on ski runs, and voilá, I slid slowly and gracefully down the curving wood, and stepped off still upright quite nonchalantly. This time Ruhi's laughter mingled with that of a man. Robin said, "So my little wife is leading you astray! Watch out for her, Piyali. She'll make you do all kinds of crazy things." He swung her off her feet and twirled her around till she begged for mercy.

The banister episode set the mood for the day. I was taken all round the estate, then for some last-minute shopping for the party my hosts were throwing in my honour. I had protested at that. Ruhi told me she and Robin loved to entertain, but in recent months had been out of the country so much that this was the first opportunity they had to return hospitality to many people—and this was a perfect excuse. It was to be a small group. And, she added mischievously, they would enjoy meeting a real live princess.

I discovered Ruhi was a marvellous cook. And why wouldn't she be when her mother, Mona Jagmohan, was the author of several cookbooks? She had trained her daughter very well. Robin said ruefully that with a wife who made such delectable things, he had to watch out for his figure. I looked at his grand physique with not a superfluous ounce on it. He always took measured quantities, and no second helpings. For a party, Ruhi and Hannah divided up the cooking, and it worked very well. Hannah and her husband Benny had been with Robin's family since his childhood, and were a dear couple. When hesitantly, I offered my services, they all stared at me. Did I know how to cook? Princesses didn't have to learn how, did they? I told her dryly I couldn't speak for others, but this princess had been given little choice. It was all part of the curriculum at school. I had kept in practice at the Dhanrajs, I added. The final outcome was that I was put in charge of the canapes.

By five o'clock, all was in readiness. Waverley waited with open arms to welcome her guests. Here was gracious living, I thought, looking at the beautiful drawing and dining rooms, adorned with fresh flowers.

I was ready early, wearing Lata's scarlet and black gift. I went straight to the kitchen to put the finishing touches to the canapes. Hannah lifting her hands when she saw me in my party finery, enveloped me promptly in an apron to protect my dress. The sound of cars arriving, voices and laughter impinged on my consciousness. The platters of tiny morsels looked most tempting. I could vouch they would melt in the mouth. After all, reluctant pupil though I had been, a Cordon Bleu master had taught me. I washed my hands, smiled at Hannah as she whipped away my apron, and went into the drawing room.

The place seemed full of people. Robin was the easiest to locate. He seemed to be having the most enjoyable exchange with a male guest, laughing uproariously, punching the person on the shoulder. Who must be the comedian type, I concluded. I had come across plenty of those. They thought they were the soul of the party. Ruhi spotted me, and came over at once. "Piyali, I thought you weren't down yet! Everyone's dying to meet you!" A hush seemed to fall over the gathering, as Ruhi took me by the hand, and we moved from person to person. They seemed to be very fine people, and I knew I would enjoy getting to know them better.

When we reached Robin's corner, his eyes were still full of laughter, but with perfect gravity, he said, "Piyali, meet our very dear friend, Neel Gregory. Neel also happens to be our neighbour." My first impression was that of a powerful physique, and extraordinary eyes, midway between brown and gold, the only man in the room besides Robin whom I did not have to look down at. He had bowed gravely, murmured the conventional words of greeting. Could that insufferably rude creature be his employee was my next thought. I must ask him before the evening was over.

"What do you do, Mr Gregory?"

After a pause, "I—er—play with clay."

I stared. What did that mean? Robin said hastily, "Neel is one of our most brilliant young sculptors. Can hardly handle the offers of commissions that pour in. The most recent exhibition of his work was much acclaimed."

I said quickly, "My apologies, Mr Gregory. I haven't been in India long enough to become knowledgeable about a lot of people." I was intrigued. At Parsons, I had enjoyed the sculpture course. At that moment, Ruhi swept me off to meet some new arrivals.

At the dinner table, consuming the delicious fare with great enjoyment like everyone else, I was having a very good time. As the conversation flowed and eddied, I discovered that everyone at that table was a person of consequence. And our hosts made each one feel very special. Those around me as I sat on Robin's left had many questions to ask about my work, and background. To my regret, Mr Gregory sat across the table, too far to carry on a conversation. Still, I noted the finely tailored suit which sat well on the big shoulders. The features were strong and very masculine, but laugh lines around mouth and eyes confirmed my earlier impression that he had an irrepressible sense of humour. From those around him came fresh bursts of laughter, and affectionate looks. Whenever that happened, Robin smiled to himself. This Gregory man seemed to be very well liked. And, ye gods, what was I seeing? Two deep indentations appeared in his cheeks frequently. My gracious, the man actually had—what would one call them but dimples?

Then it happened. Ruhi was explaining how my interest in jewellery design came naturally, it being part of my heritage. Inevitably, someone asked which princely state I belonged to. As I uttered the name Divyasthala, I could have sworn Neel Gregory stiffened. I did not imagine that he stared at me incredulously. Then he turned away. It was a puzzling reaction. Had he not known who I was? And what was so shocking about the revelation? Titles had little significance now. No one else had reacting so, and indeed, many asked interesting questions. But the one exception bewildered me.

Nor did I imagine that after dinner when everyone told Ruhi they had eaten too much, and flopped down on the most comfortable seats to aid digestion, they said, Mr Gregory was definitely avoiding me. He sat far away with two couples, but talking seriously. It was too much for me. I had to put the matter to test. Benny was serving coffee as Ruhi poured. I seized a bowl of salted nuts in one hand, and a dish of chocolates in the other, and went around. Naturally, I exchanged a word or two with each one. My ploy failed utterly. By the time I reached the far corner, my quarry had escaped to join Ruhi, and accept a coffee cup from her hands. He stood there talking to her. So I was left in no doubt whatsoever. It was shocking how hurt I felt. There was more to this than met the eye. It was the name Divyasthala that had signified something to him. Did it link me to Lata and therefore to Bhaiyya? Could there be bad blood between the two men over something connected with business? As a newcomer, I couldn't possibly know.

After the guests left, we three relaxed, too wide awake to go up just yet. I said casually, "Robin, I wonder if your sculptor friend would mind letting me see his studio? I've done a course in sculpture, you know."

"We'll have to ask him, Piyali. I imagine when he's at work, he doesn't welcome visitors. But, after all, he may not turn down a beautiful lady."

"He seems to have quite a sense of humour."

Robin began to laugh. "You've guessed!" Our faces must have shown our puzzlement. The same roars of laughter came from him which I'd heard earlier. He managed to say, "I met Peter today when I stopped to fill up, and he told me they were still savouring the whole incident. Neel is a great favourite with them all, you see. Sometimes, when he needs a change of scenery, he goes there to spend a couple of hours."

The words barely registered. The whole scene unraveled in front of my eyes in explicit detail. How could I have guessed that the surly disreputable creature was the polished urbane gentleman, centre of attention because of his wit and charm? A slow burning anger began to build within me. How dare he make a laughing stock of me! Why, even Robin thought it prodigiously funny. It was the kind of story Neel Gregory could regale guests with at dinner parties. And they would laugh heartily over his having completely duped this girl, so naive and unsuspecting.

"And it was Neel?" Ruhi was saying, "and that's why he wouldn't stay and be recognized?" Her silvery laughter tinkled.

I sat in stony silence. In any case, I had no words to say. When the phone rang, I was glad of the respite. Obviously, from the way Robin spoke, the caller was someone special. Ruhi joined him, and spoke eagerly. I spied a glass we had overlooked, and took it into the kitchen. Here all was sparkling, the counters and sinks spotless, the food put away. A sudden gush of water proved the dish washer was doing its share of cleaning up. I drank some water, and tried to take a grip on myself. I mustn't spoil my little holiday, or be ungracious to the Nevilles who were being so kind to me. Nor must they guess at the anger in my heart.

Ruhi said joyfully the call had been from her cousin. They were as close as sisters, and indeed, had grown up here at Waverley. That was why it was a double delight for Renu to come. I murmured a reply.

That night, I lay awake, making my plans. The impending visit opened up new vistas for me. I felt infinitely better by the time sleep claimed me. I was taking the matter in hand—into both my hands.

I liked Ruhi's cousin on sight. Her intelligent face with its fine features somehow missed matching my friend's loveliness, but she was a most interesting person to talk to. I enjoyed meeting her husband and daughter. At mid-morning, I declared firmly I was going out to explore. After all, I was sure they needed time together. I ran upstairs to change into shorts, sleeveless shirt, and rubber-soled sandals. Besides dark glasses, I carried a wide-brimmed hat to shade my face. Robin was very sweet about coming outdoors with me. The beach lay that way a quarter of a mile away, he explained, and also pointed out other places that were close enough for me to go to. "We'll expect you for lunch. Enjoy yourself." He smiled and waved. I waved back, and set off blithely. When I glanced back as I went down the driveway which led to Waverley, Robin had gone in.

Dear Robin, how could he know his guest was going no further than the outskirts of his estate? I halted briefly by the stone pillars I had just glimpsed on the night of my arrival. The stone lions were very handsome. I must ask Ruhi about those noble-looking sentinels. When I looked to the right, there appeared before my fascinated eyes an edifice which even at this distance beckoned for a closer scrutiny. Through the tall mesh fence that bounded the property, it stood proudly, double-storeyed, gleaming a dazzling white in the mid-morning sunshine. My sandals carried me to the big gates on which the beautiful lettering resembling medieval script spelled out the word ROMOLA. I repeated the name softly. It sounded beautiful like something out of a book from long ago with expensive leather binding and gold-embossed lettering. I could almost see the silk ribbon marker, and a pressed rose in between the pages. The name brought me up short. Did Neel Gregory have a wife? If so, no one had mentioned her. Where had she been last night? If this Romola was inside, my plans would have to undergo some rapid last-minute changes. I squared my shoulders, ready for anything. Why should I feel a pang at the thought of a wife being around when my sole purpose in coming was to take my pound of flesh from a man for whom I felt only dislike and contempt?

If I had hoped to walk straight in, I was greatly mistaken. A low growl warned me, then the deep barking of a large dog. A man appeared, a golden retriever loping by his side. Dog lover I might be, but I knew better than to attempt to go further. The man spoke to me in Hindi. I managed a few words, judiciously mixed with English. Without a twinge, I strung together some truths and a few white lies. I was from Waverley. Neville Saab had sent me. Was Gregory Saab at home, and if so, could I see him? At the mere mention of Robin's name, the man's face cleared. *Hah ji,* Saab was in, but, doubtfully, he was working, and one did not disturb him at such times. Oh, I said airily, Saab was expecting me. At that, he moved to unlock the gates. Earlier, at his bidding, the dog had quietened, but still sat there, very intent on me. Would he bite, I asked. A small chuckle escaped the man. Never bite, he assured me. He said a few words to the beast whose ears flickered. I was instructed to put out a hand. It was sniffed, then a paw was held out to me. I shook it gravely, and dared to say, "Good boy." In English, the man told me, "She lady dog. Name Sheena."

I was actually in! More, through a very beautiful carved door, I was being escorted in. No time to look around. We traversed a long corridor at the end of which the man halted before another door, indicating I was to go in. He pushed it open, and shut it behind me. The first thing to catch my attention was the sound of music, rich, pouring out its golden notes—not at all what I had expected. I recognized at once the passage from *La Traviata.*

I was in a very large studio where light poured in from several skylights. My third impression was of the all-too familiar distinctive odours of clay, paint and turpentine. These were external impressions upon the senses, but what riveted me was the sight of the lone occupant.

From where I stood, I could not see what he was working on, nor his face. His feet were bare on the tiled floor. Minus a smock, he wore only a pair of faded jeans, cut off at the knee. The muscles of back and arms rippled as the hands moved with perfect sureness. He was so totally wrapped in his work that he had no inkling of another presence.

Slowly, I studied the rest of the studio. And as I did, the artist in me felt a wave of envy. Three factors made the place ideal for anyone involved in such artistic creativity—space, light, and complete peace and quiet if desired. All were there in superabundance. This artist's creative flow evidently required the inspiring background of music. Strange, but it was exactly how I worked. Before I sat down with my designs, I first switched on whatever music suited my mood. That fact disturbed me. I hadn't marched in here to establish a fellow feeling with Neel Gregory. Equally disturbing, one part of my mind was actually admiring the way he moved. It was almost like a ballet, this concerted motion of both arms, the bend and sway of torso, the movement of the long powerful legs. In each of my three encounters with this man, I mused, I had seen the most different facets of the same person—the down-at-heel one in the garage; the beautifully groomed gentleman of last night; and now the artist who was shaping with his hands a creation that was part of himself.

Deliberately, I turned my eyes away, for the thoughts and sight were distracting me from my purpose. On the next level of the studio was a built-up section running along three fourths of wall space. A glimpse of rows of bookshelves made me realize it must be a kind of library. Had I dared to ascend the carpeted steps, I would have loved to explore. Instinctively, I guessed those books would be just the kind that would interest me.

Willy nilly, my eyes came back to the splendid young physique. How long had I been standing here I did not know. I was strangely content to do so. Had I not been so preoccupied, I would have been prepared. As it was, I should have realized what would happen. With a final flourish, the music came to an end. I stood as frozen in motion as one of Gregory's own statues. He ceased his work to go and eject the cassette, but perforce, could not insert a fresh one with clay-covered hands. In the act of turning away, his eye fell on me.

Now two of us were absolutely motionless in the deafening silence, eyes locked. Incredulity written on his face, he moved first. Then as light dawned, words burst out: "How the hell did you get in here?"

Unlike him, I was well prepared, very calm. "In the usual way—through the gates, admitted by your man. Who, I must say, is much better mannered than his employer."

"Impossible! Sheena wouldn't have let you get past!"

"*Au contraire,* Mr Gregory, she shook hands—paws—very cordially," I said composedly.

His fury was palpable. It was hard to remember he was known for his sense of humour. "Why the hell are you here?"

"Such language," I said reprovingly. "Why—the hell—am I here?" I tilted my head as if pondering. "First, this is a courtesy call. Being neighbourly, you know. Such a good friend of my hosts must be well worth knowing. Second, I'm very interested in sculpture. Took a course in it, you see. I wondered if you'd let me see some of your work—see you at work."

"No!" The word seemed to strangle in his throat. "Out of the question! What did you think—that I gave demonstration lessons?"

"Third," I went on as if he had not spoken, "for the same reason, I wondered if you'd kindly let me do a bit of sculpting. It's been a long time since I worked with clay, and I'm dying to get the feel of it again. Who knows, with a brilliant sculptor like you to give me pointers, I might turn out something good. Then I can tell people I worked under the guidance of no less a personage than Neel Gregory."

At some point, he became conscious of his attire, or rather the lack of it, and snatched up a shirt flung over a tall screen. He thrust his arms into it, and pulled it together to cover his chest without buttoning it. Clearly, he meant to wear it for a very few minutes until he threw me out, and went back to work. He strode purposefully to where I was still standing.

"You know, Mr Gregory, it's almost eleven. You are going to offer me some coffee, aren't you?"

Very slowly, and with great emphasis on each word as if to a retarded person, "I'm asking you politely to leave."

"Oh, I'm not in a hurry. Ruhi's cousin and her family have come, and I thought it best to give them time to themselves." I tilted my head up to look at his face. Earnestly, "Do you take commissions, Mr Gregory? If I commissioned a sculpture, would you accept?" His eyes were taking in every detail of my appearance from head to toe. "And another thing, Mr Gregory. Do you use live models? Can you use me, for example, Mr Gregory?"

"If you call me 'Mr Gregory' once more, I'll—" he said in a strangled voice. So I was getting under his skin, I thought gleefully.

I opened my eyes very wide. "But you haven't said I could use your first name. Do you want me to? How nice and friendly!" I tried it out. "Neel. Mmmm, nice!"

"Why are you really here?" more quietly.

His eyes were steady on mine. The earlier fury seemed to have subsided. A scant foot between us, my glance locked with his. For the life of me, I couldn't think of another word to say. Some kind of current seemed to pass between us. I could not have analysed it. He felt it too, for I saw it in his eyes. With a shock, I recognized it for what it was—and that it was no more welcome to him than to me—a powerful sexual magnetism such as I had never felt before.

I said quietly, "You really hate my being here, don't you? Why am I so unwelcome? Have I offended you in some way?"

He bit his lip, which deepened the indentations in his cheeks.Then he took himself in hand. "You guessed right. You aren't welcome here—ever."

The words pierced me though I should have expected them. "Very well," when I could speak, "I have something of yours. I came to give it to you." I reached over to tuck something in his shirt pocket. "You need not be afraid that I'll trespass again. Goodbye, Mr Gregory."

Head held high, I walked very quickly across the width of the floor before he could pull out the twenty-five rupees, opened the door, and fled down the corridor. Sheena was lying in the front, and she loped over to me. Perhaps she sensed I was a dog lover, for I was graciously permitted to scratch under her ears. But most of all, I wanted to get away. The man servant appeared. At the sight of the dog blissfully enjoying being fondled, he shook his head, grinning. "Looking big. *Dil* very soft." Cheerfully, he unlocked the gates. With a word of thanks, I was out, walking away swiftly.

8

It is not to be supposed that I spent all my time posing in gorgeous clothes for the cameras, or doing the hectic party round. The truth was very different. I literally slaved over my designs, spending hours at my desk. After all, I was in the process of establishing myself in a big way. Tremendously valuable for my career was the exposure I was able to get through The Honey Bee. My explorations with David Asscher of museums had resulted in several sketch-books filled with designs from every period, and many lands. These became invaluable for me. It was amazing how Lata's designs and mine complemented each other. No one was more pleased than Madhur Monal. I knew that with her, it was not the zooming of the sales charts alone that was so satisfying, but that her Boutiques were now offering clients this additional facility of being able to buy jewellery that went with their exclusive outfits.

And then, one day, Madhur sounded me out about other jewellery. Her Boutiques also offered a full range of clothes affordable to middle income customers. Four designers worked on those designs. The range was immensely popular. The same care and meticulous tailoring went into them as into Suvarnalata Creations. Could I extend my creativity to this range also? Perhaps Madhur doubted I would be interested, or even capable of it. For me, it was a challenge where I would be testing myself.

I put every ounce of my being into the task. It wrung me out at first. I had been told that the market was flooded with gimcrack stuff of the shoddiest quality, notwithstanding its external glitter. My stuff had to be extremely eye-catching, and durable. And it worked! The clients loved the designs—and the price range. There were cases where they bought just the jewellery, and not the clothing items—which was surely not Madhur's intention! Needless to say, this was why I was so hectically busy.

There was an unexpected development here. I was approached by three different prestigious jewellery firms in the city. It started when a few young ladies of the family that owned the largest one came in to select some dresses. Evidently, it was not beneath them to pick up the accessories that went with their beautiful clothes. I suppose the jewellery caught the attention of those involved in running the firm. Having unraveled the mystery of who had done the designing, the next step was to sound me out—in a subtle way, of course. I was a guest at a dinner hosted by one of Bhaiyya's good friends and his wife. Among the invitees was the scion of the famous firm, and his glamorous wife. I was inveigled into a corner, and the subject carefully approached.

There was not the slightest question of my accepting, though the offer came with a fabulous salary. I would never do anything disloyal to Lata or Madhur who had launched me, a total unknown. I was under no illusions about these would-be employers. They would squeeze me to the utmost, extract the maximum they could. Then again, I wished to stay free of commitments and contracts that would tie me down for years. I wanted to be free to fly away if the occasion rose. No, I hadn't forgotten Daddy. Just now, I spent a few days with him as often as I could, averaging perhaps once every two months. And Daddy came to Bombay whenever he could. Still, I wanted to keep my options open. One never knew what might come up. So I refused very politely—only to have the offer upped accordingly. I could not make out if my services were sought for my abilities as a designer, or the snob appeal of my so-called title.

A last-ditch attempt was made now by approaching Bhaiyya. Lata and I had some unfinished work left, and she carried me home for tea. Bhaiyya joined us, watching me quizzically over his cup. "Piyali, I must tell you I've been asked to use my good offices to convince you to take up a certain offer." Lata sat up. " What offer?" she demanded.

"Haven't you heard your little cousin is the envy of every reputed jeweller in the metropolis, to say nothing of other boutiques and the like? And one or two are already dangling very tempting bait in front of her. In fact, Ritesh asked me to use my 'influence.'"

Lata said slowly, "And are you going to use it, Dev?"

"You know me better than that, Lata. It's Piyali's life—her decision. For what it's worth, Ritesh thinks she's wasting her great talent on costume jewellery, and should really be involved with the real stuff."

Lata looked at me. I shrugged. "He's entitled to his opinion. I'm simply not interested. I hope he and the others will accept once and for all that I mean what I say."

"Others?" she said in shocked tones. "How long has this been going on? You never told me."

"Didn't see the need to. I'm very happy where I am, thank you."

Bhaiyya said, "I'm proud of you. You could have succumbed so easily. Some day, you will go beyond costume jewellery, but for now, you're getting valuable experience which will stand you in good stead."

Lata hugged me. "And I'm proud of you! Though I won't deny it's a great relief. Madhur will have ten fits when I tell her!"

Tara and Lekh returned from the States with only the family in the know. It was a time of excitement. Both were glad to be back, though they'd had a wonderful time, Tara told us. Wonderful, her husband echoed, when he had been hard at work most of the time? Lekh's teasing notwithstanding, they still looked like newlyweds, very happy and madly in love.

If Lekh had wished for a respite, it was a vain wish. In that mysterious inexplicable way, news of his return spread rapidly, and as Tara said wryly, the phone never stopped ringing after that. They had settled into Lekh's beautiful new home, designed by the same Geet Adityaraj who had designed ROMOLA, a house I may have noticed when I was at Waverley. No one observed I winced inwardly at the name. One piece of information came my way inadvertently that a certain sculptor was a great friend of Lekhs as he was of Robins.

With film producers beating a path to his door, and his P.A. staggering under the onslaught, Lekh was plunged into work. I marvelled that Tara, a scientist and a Ph.D. at that, had slipped so easily into this new milieu. "I'm savouring the difference in life styles," she told Lata and me. "When I look back, I think I was just existing before I met Lekh. Now I feel I'm living for the first time—a wonderful feeling. Someday I may want to do other things, but for now, I'm content." The green eyes glowed. "Now tell me how my darling Skeet is doing! Of course, he fills the house! You and Bhaiyya look like different beings! Lekh is very happy over it all." Lata's eyes filled with quick tears.

Depending on Lekh's schedule, Tara began giving a round of parties, averaging one every fortnight. She kept the numbers down to twenty or so, and took care the invitees were congenial. So it was that I found myself attending a dinner with other young people. I looked forward to an enjoyable evening.

It began that way. Some of the guests were known to me, and with the others, I quickly established a rapport. Almost all the women present had careers as I did, and it was interesting to exchange experiences. I turned to place a few empty glasses on a tray—and that was when I saw them—the pretty petite figure in pink looking up adoringly at the man who towered over her, head bent protectively. I hadn't seen Neel Gregory since that last encounter in his studio when I stormed ROMOLA, and I confess, the sight of the pair riveted me. Was this a girl friend, or perhaps a fiancee? They were talking to Tara and Lekh, and laughing with the ease of old friends. I tore my eyes away. In a moment, they would turn. I turned my back, and began to talk animatedly to a small group of people.

It was too much to expect I would remain unseen. Somehow, I knew the exact moment when Neel caught sight of me. As people joined my group, I had been forced to change my stance, so that I was now facing the other way. Across a sea of heads, our glances collided. His expression was unfathomable, registering neither surprise nor disgust. I cut off eye contact at once. I thought grimly, you won't be able to throw me out of this place, Mr Gregory! I vowed to myself that I would leave early on some pretext. Tara would be very understanding, but first, I had to get through the evening. I managed to have a good time after all. Dinner was superbly prepared and served deftly. My appetite not too keen, I consumed with pleasure the little I served myself with. Rather pleased with myself for the way I had managed to stay far away from a certain couple, I went to set my plate down from where a waiter instantly whisked it away. A voice said, "Hello?" It was the girl in pink. "You're Princess Piyali. Tara said you wouldn't mind if I came over. I'm Jyoti Swarup." She touched her throat and ears. "You recognize these, of course?" smiling. "Yes, of course," I replied. I saw she was rather pretty with a kind of gamine charm, hair cut in pixie style which suited her pert looks. "My friends and I are crazy about your designs!" she was saying. They would be pea green when they heard she'd actually met me in person. Was she in college? "Not any more. I graduated last year. Now I'm at home learning domestic arts—waiting to get married. Mummy is putting me through the paces in the kitchen. I hate cooking." I tried to visualize this girl conjuring up delicacies for her sculptor husband at ROMOLA, and failed. Would he allow her at least to enter the studio when he was working? Who knew, perhaps she might model for him.

". . . just my idea of what one should look like." I blinked. I had lost the first words. "The way you look. You're beautiful, so tall and regal as a Princess should be. I asked Neel—my escort—and when he told me, I thought you must be very proud. You have the look. He thought you probably were. But you aren't at all. And I'm so glad I could come and talk to you."

"I am too." Over her head, I saw a male figure moving towards us rapidly. "I think your fiance is about to rescue you from my dubious company. Tara is beckoning. It was very nice to meet you, Jyoti." And I left her.

I joined a merry group, and was warmly welcomed. In a little while, I would slip away, bid farewell to Tara and Lekh. I couldn't endure being in the room with Neel Gregory much longer. I had congratulated myself on handling one situation very well. They were premature congratulations. A now familiar deep voice said in my ear, "I believe this is yours, Princess?" bending low to offer me a slim gold envelope which I hadn't missed yet. After a moment, I took it. "Thank you," I said stiffly.

Someone in our group hailed him joyfully. "Neel, sit down, man! Something I want to ask you." He sat down promptly next to me on the arm of the sofa, and leaned forward expectantly. How dared he, I thought furiously. He could have sat on the arm of any other chair, not mine. True, there were no spare seats. And I was hemmed in, unable to move. It was all part of his intention to rile me.

"Know this fellow, Faberge, Neel?"

"Peter Carl, you mean? That one? Yes, I've heard of him," smiling.

"Made those fabulous jewelled eggs for the Russian royal family—the—the—"

"Romanovs."

"That's it! What I want to know, Neel, is why someone else can't come up with stuff like that? Can you, for example?"

A sleeve brushed my bare shoulder. The long strong hands so strangely familiar were held out. "I'm very flattered, Somesh, but I'm only a humble sculptor." An outraged cry from all present. "No, wait a moment. You're talking of an item that falls within the purview of jewellery, not sculpture. Faberge was one of the world's geniuses. It would take another genius to create such objects. But in any case, why not ask the expert in our midst?" One good strong push, I was thinking, would send him sprawling to the floor. A jab in the ribs with my elbow, very sharp and unexpected, was another possibility. In the old days, a very small but effective dagger could have been slipped under my sleeve—except that my black chiffon dress had no sleeves. I realized everyone was waiting for my response.

"I suppose it isn't impossible. But as we've just been reminded, we'll have to wait for another Faberge to be born."

"But, Piyali, you design fabulous jewellery. Suppose you give it a try?"

"That would be presumptuous of me."

The hateful voice closest to me said, "Oh, I don't agree with that! The Princess is being over-modest. From what one sees of her work, let's say she has all the potential of becoming a Faberge some day." Loud cheers and applause greeted the words. For the first time, I lifted my lashes to glare at my tormentor. If looks could kill, he would have been stretched out on the floor by now. The face which I could have touched just by raising a hand was so close, I saw the laugh lines around eyes and mouth.

"What do you say, Piyali?"

"When India's young Michelangelo says so, Somesh, who can argue? I'm truly honoured. All of you are witnesses. He gets the first Piyali Faberge egg—if one is ever created."

Cries greeted that. In the noisy confusion, a glass of water was upset over a guest who jumped up. And everyone else moved to help. I left the group quietly.

Tara was very understanding about my early departure. She knew I had an out-of-town shooting appointment. Lekh asked how I was going home. By taxi, I told him. "I don't think you have to do that, Piyali. Neel Gregory is catching a morning flight himself, and is leaving early. He can drop you off." I said quickly, "I wouldn't dream of bothering him," but my words made no impact. Tara said, "But we'll be happier if he drops you off. It's rather late for you to go alone." Lekh was speaking to someone behind me about the matter. Did I imagine a slight hesitation? The answer came smoothly enough. "An honour for Jyoti and me." Short of having a tantrum right there, or pretending to faint—neither of which I had ever done, I had no alternative but to go quietly.

Farewells achieved, we were out in the street where an all-too-familiar car was parked. Jyoti said happily, "What fun to have you with us, Princess!" I murmured a reply. Neel asked where I lived, and when I told him, he said, "Then Jyoti better sit near the door so that I can drop you off first." I opened my mouth to protest that I could still take a taxi, but the door was held open, and both were waiting. I slid into the centre of the big roomy seat followed by Jyoti, and we were off.

I can't remember much of the conversation, but Jyoti chatted on brightly. I think she asked about my background and school, but that is mere guesswork. There was admiration in her voice, and small gasps of wonder. From the other side, there was only silence. At some point, the car slowed and halted off the road. Jyoti said, "It was wonderful to meet you, Princess!" I said something suitable in reply. The two figures walked to a lighted house the door of which opened. A man was silhouetted against the light. Apparently, Neel was explaining why he couldn't come in. To me, he hadn't uttered a word, or said he'd be right back. All his worst manners were reserved for me. To everyone else, he was the soul of courtesy. Oh, well, just a little longer, and the ordeal would be over for both of us. He was shaking the man's hand, bestowing a kiss on Jyoti's hair. Had I not been there, he could have gone in to be with his future family. Well, the situation was not of my making.

If Neel noticed I was now sitting practically against the door, he gave no sign except to lean over and test the lock. A whiff of masculine cologne reached me. I blanked my mind to everything. We had barely braked outside my apartment complex when, after a muttered thank you, I was out of the car. I was free at last. Only I wasn't. Neel must have moved like lightning to roll up his window, and lock the car, for he was by my side.

"I'll see you to your door." I exclaimed it wasn't necessary. Without missing a step, he added, "I want to be able to report to the Sebastians that I left their ewe lamb safely in her apartment." Ewe lamb indeed! What a ridiculous phrase for someone of my size and looks. Done deliberately, of course. The security guard saluted me smartly, and looked with interest at my companion. To my astonishment, he saluted him too. We went up in the elevator, and along the tiled corridor to my door. "Thank you again, Mr Gregory." He merely took the keys from my hand, and opened the door, entering before me. I was too outraged to speak. Unerringly, he found the light switches so that the room filled with a golden glow. Then he moved on. Lights came on briefly in other rooms. Now I understood. He was checking for intruders! He reappeared to say all was well.

"There was no need for such dramatics," I told him coldly. "We have a very efficient security system."

"Perhaps so. But I prefer to be sure."

I waited stiffly for him to go. Why did this man always make me feel so helpless? He brought my keys over, but when I put out my hand, he did not let go. "Oh," I said passionately, "why do you persist in such torture? I thank you again for the lift. Will you leave me alone now at least?"

"You haven't paid me yet."

I stared at him. "How—much do you—want?"

"*Kum se Kum sau rupiyah*," he quoted. "No, I'm not a cabbie. I don't want that kind of payment."

"No," I said bitterly, "just your pound of flesh, Shylock."

His mouth quirked so that a deep indentation marked one cheek. "Not tonight, Princess."

I said steadily, "You told me I wasn't welcome in your home ever, Mr Gregory. I must tell you how distasteful it is for me to have you in here. Tara said you have a plane to catch. So do I have an important appointment. So will you please go now?"

After a moment, he held out the keys which I snatched away. He began, "Some day . . ." but stopped. "Au revoir, Princess."

When he had passed out of the door, I said, "Adieu, Mr Gregory." Then after I had locked it, I leaned limply against its solid frame. I was totally drained by the events of the evening.

9

We arrived early, the van right behind us. At the hotel we had been booked into, we were taken straight up to a reserved suite. Lata had planned well. Two hours later, we four models were ready. Bobbie, Neena, Karen and I looked as perfect as the hair dressers and makeup artists could make us. Lata herded us out, muttering something about the sun, and hurried the whole caboodle down. It is no exaggeration to say that as we swished and clinked our way across the crowded lobby, everything came to a complete standstill, and we were the recipients of spontaneous admiration. Once in the cars, the van following, we were on our way.

The year before, driving with Bhaiyya, Lata had seen this picturesque spot in the beautiful hilly tract called Khandala located between Bombay and Pune. With its verdant valleys, and waterfalls cascading down slopes, it is an artist's dream. Our photographer was young Kamlesh, until recently under training in the art of photography with Robin himself. Kamlesh was the son of a family friend, and had insisted on specializing in photography. His affluent father, quite exasperated, had begged Robin to take the boy under his wing, and try him out. The condition was that Robin's assessment would be the decisive one. Robin had discovered the young chap's genius with a camera. Which was why now after the initiation period was over, Kamlesh did much work for Lata and Madhur.

Three hours of unrelenting work, and we were all ready to call it a day. As usual, I had to pose alone, and it had been gruelling. All I wanted now was to get back to the hotel, have the finery and makeup taken off, a long hot shower, and lunch. Kamlesh and van with the beauty assistants tootled off ahead of us. The three girls piled into one car, Lata and I into the other.

I sank into the seat, put my head back wearily. From the open windows, the cool breeze played havoc with our hair. Lata said, "You know, Piyali, that dress was designed with you in mind. Only someone tall can carry it off." She grinned at me. "Are you still grumbling to yourself because I asked you to model today?"

I said feelingly, "Did you say 'asked'? I was practically blackmailed into it!" She patted my hand. "Wait till the pictures come out! You know, if you tire of designing jewellery, you could slip into full-time modelling with ease." I shook my head. Then I sat up. "Am I imagining it, or are we wobbling a bit?" I wasn't the only one who had felt it. The chauffeur pulled off the road. In a moment, he had the bonnet up. Then when steam billowed out, he leaped back. We both groaned simultaneously. It had to happen just when I was so anxious to reach the hotel.

The chauffeur's head appeared at the window. He explained apologetically that he would have to find a mechanic. He would be back right away, he assured us. If the Rajkumaris wouldn't mind waiting—as if we had a choice. Lata waved him away. I thought longingly of the little icebox that had gone with the van, full of cold drinks. A tall glass clinking with ice, I dreamed, like a man lost in a desert conjuring up the mirage of an oasis.

Never one to sit still, Lata was out, looking around. I thought crossly, It's all right for her in her comfy pants and shirt, whereas I'm still in full war paint, wearing a most expensive gown. Lata said suddenly, "Piyali, there's a house there. Several houses. Nice ones. Looks like a colony. I'll go over—find a phone—call the hotel and explain. Want to come?"

The words were barely out of her mouth when we saw the figure coming towards us, moving fast from the direction of the houses. It was a man, patently a domestic, and young. He saluted. His *malkin* had seen us, and wanted to know if we were in trouble. "*Malkin* said I was to bring you home if you wished to come."

Lata murmured, "Reprieve at last. We'd better take the offer." The man had waited respectfully. He was well-trained, for he leaped to open the door for me. He helped to roll up windows, and lock the car before leading the way.

Affluent people lived here. The houses were most pleasing to the eye, surrounded by blooming flowerbeds, and an abundance of trees. Our destination was a large pretty bungalow set somewhat further back with a larger garden area. It was painted a soft green, the doors and window frames a darker shade. A fine roomy veranda furnished with comfortable cane furniture led into a big cool sitting room. I had a fleeting impression of a glass cabinet covering an entire wall, handsome pieces of furniture, deeply upholstered sofas and chairs. Then I concentrated on the only occupant of the room.

She was seated in a rocker, perhaps in her late seventies, soft white hair drawn into a knot on her neck, wearing a blue and white silk sari. She spoke in beautiful English, her voice soft. "You are most welcome. I was on the veranda when I saw your car stop, and what happened afterwards. Please do sit down."

Lata said smiling, "Madame, I can't tell you how much we appreciate this. I was just about to come in search of a phone when your kind message arrived. The others in our group went back to the hotel ahead of us, and they will worry when we fail to appear."

"Oh, then do call them at once. If you do not mind stepping into the next room, the telephone is there."

Lata flashed her charming smile, and vanished. I had not uttered a word so far. My appearance was being studied with interest. I felt obliged to say, "We came up from Bombay for a shooting assignment."

The lady's eyes lighted with interest. "But how exciting! For a movie?" I explained, adding Lata was a designer. "Did she design what you are wearing? It's beautiful—and elegant. As you are."

"Thank you," I said awkwardly.

"I think you have great poise and grace of movement. This sophisticated dress demands it. It could have been made for you."

Returning, Lata said gaily, "Indeed, it was. I told Piyali that just a few minutes ago."

"Piyali." The name was repeated as if to get the feel of it. "Not a name I've heard, but it's charming. Did you make your call?"

"I did. And they were so relieved to hear my voice. I told them to have lunch and a siesta. All thanks to you, Madame."

"Oh please don't thank me! Such an interesting encounter for me. I seldom have visitors like you. But I'm neglecting my duties as a hostess.

What can I offer you? Of course. You must be parched. And till the drinks arrive, would you like to wash up?"

I said fervently, "It would be heaven to wash off this wretched makeup."

A smiling young maid took us to a bedroom. "You first, Piyali," Lata said, and stretched out on the big bed.

What bliss to slip out of my dress, and in the bathroom, to scrub my face and neck. I pulled pins from my hair, and combed it out. Drying myself with a fresh towel, I looked around. It was a lovely little bathroom, well-appointed. It must belong to a man, for on a glass shelf was a row of men's toiletries scenting the atmosphere. I stood still for a moment. Where had I come across this scent, and that too very recently? I could not recall it. Back in the bedroom when Lata had vanished into the bathroom, I took in further evidence of male occupancy—the unusually large bed, the books packing the lower shelf of the little bedside table, a pair of slippers, and on the dressing table, a little container in the shape of a sea shell holding a tie pin. Oh well, it was hardly my business. We were chance visitors, and it was not for us to probe into the complexities of this household. Lata came out very much refreshed.

"Piyali, do you realize we don't even know our hostess' name, and haven't mentioned ours? Very discourteous, isn't it?" She powdered her face. "Did you notice the lady's looks? In her youth, she must have been very beautiful." I made a sound of agreement. I was a little ashamed that hot and uncomfortable as I had been, I hadn't really paid enough attention.

Downstairs again, we were given a warm smile of welcome. Gratefully, we accepted our drinks. The sweet chilled liquid was like nectar. If surreptitiously, I now studied our hostess. Lata was right. Even at this age, she had great beauty of the kind 'age cannot wither' which very few women are blessed with. It came, of course, from a very fine bone structure, large eyes of an unusual golden-brown colour, and the most delicate features. Again, age notwithstanding, she was very fair-skinned, hinting perhaps at mixed ancestry. I could not see her feet in small embroidered slippers, but the hands were very pretty, slender with oval nails.

"Yes, a very nice neighbourhood. The climate is wonderful. Many owners are retired people, but others commute to Bombay every day. It's a very congenial atmosphere, and we all care for each other's welfare. Oh, I have a lady companion. Kusum takes very good care of me. She's a widow. Used to be a nurse before she married. Is out shopping now. I expect her back any minute. She'll be sorry she missed all the excitement." The long golden eyes twinkled. "Very strict about my regimen." We smiled back. "And someone from the family calls almost every day. They all visit often. Yes, I have a daughter and a son. And grandchildren—two grandsons and a granddaughter. And can't wait to become a great grandma. One of my grandsons is grown-up, you see," gaily. She was so charming when she said that, both of us joined in her laughter. We liked her more by the minute.

Something nagged me a little. To my certain knowledge, we had never met before. Why then did I have this sense of familiarity? It was the colour of the eyes, I discovered, after some thought. Yet when I searched my memory, I could not recall anyone who resembled this lovely lady. On the table by my side were framed photographs, almost certainly family ones, but I did not attempt to examine them.

"Dhanraj," Lata was saying. "My husband works for a corporation. Yes, I love dress designing. Except when we have mishaps like the one today! Your car? That will be splendid! And your man will keep an eye open for our chauffeur? Wonderful! No, how can we mind waiting for a few minutes? Oh, no, lunch is waiting for us at the hotel. We're expected. But you're so kind to suggest it."

"You've made my day, you know. My son teases me about this thirst for knowledge. He calls it inquisitiveness. But I like to learn. It gladdens my heart that young women are able to have careers if they wish. In my day, the question simply did not exist. We were given an education—in a girls' school—then married off, and expected to run our husbands' households, and have babies. When I think of your designing, and see this beautiful dress of your creation, I wonder how many women in my generation blessed with great talent fell by the wayside. But I think even today in India not every woman is permitted to develop any special interests."

"How true, Madame, and it is a great pity. I think I gave you the wrong impression about my cousin here. You'll be interested to know she isn't really a model at all and is here under protest—as a great favour to me. Piyali is a jewellery designer."

The information brought astonishment, then a delighted smile. "Oh, do tell me all about it!" Which I did as briefly as I could. The lady gave a deep sigh of satisfaction. "My feminine curiosity has been fully aroused. How I wish I could see some of your work! Both of you live in Bombay? I believe Dhanraj is not a Maharashtrian name, is it? And Marathi not your language?"

"I speak it a little—very ungrammatically! But I speak Hindi very well. And Piyali knows a few words of the latter, none of the former—though she can orate in French and German."

Later in our dismay when Lata and I went carefully over this dialogue for a possible clue, we both came to the same conclusion that it was the next innocent question, so logical in its sequence, and its reply which made all the difference.

"Then you both come from another state?"

"My cousin and I belong to the former princely state of Divyasthala." What was in that simple statement that turned the lady suddenly to stone, her hands gripping the arms of the rocker, a curious stillness on that expressive face? Lata and I exchanged puzzled glances. "You've heard of Divyasthala, Madame?" The answer was slow in coming. "Yes," very low, "I've heard of it."

If the sound of a car arriving had not interrupted, I don't know what might have happened. Doors slammed, and voices spoke. A middle-aged woman swept in, hands full of parcels. All unaware of our presence, she called out, "Romolaji, I had such luck! I—" the words trailed away. "I'm so sorry! I didn't know we had visitors." She looked at us with frank interest.

Madame came slowly to her feet. "Kusum, these ladies had a problem with their car. Tell Sunder to drive them back to their hotel, please."

Lata took both Madame's hands. "How can we find words to thank you?"

"No, it was my pleasure." But the words seemed forced.

"I hope we haven't tired you out, Madame?" I asked, shaking hands. She shook her head, and murmured a reply.

The lady companion led us out. Lata left our car keys with her. She looked jolly, cheerful and capable of handling any situation. Lata said, "This is a bit awkward—but we don't know the lady's name. I'd like to send a thank you note."

"It's Mrs R Nalin." She added the address and phone number which Lata jotted down. She was still studying us with great interest.

We could not say anything in the car, but after lunch when we both stretched out on the same bed before leaving for Bombay, we concluded that mention of the name Divyasthala had been the turning point. Why had this been so, we pondered, not a little disturbed. We were anxious about the well-being of the lady who had been kindness itself to us. When Lata dozed off, I lay thinking. This was the second person who had reacted so visibly to the name. It had made Neel Gregory shun my company, and throw me out of his house. And the other name. The companion had clearly addressed Madame as 'Romolaji'. It was a second link, and surely could not possibly be a coincidence? The name wasn't common at all. But what connection was there between a young sculptor who lived in Sinhadurg, and an elderly lady residing in the

Khandala Ghats? So many unanswered questions, but they were hardly my business. I would not encounter either of these people again.

10

After Bombay's sultry humidity, the upland air was delicious. Apart from the reunion with my father which was as wonderful as ever, I felt much more uplifted in spirits than I had been when I arrived five days ago, and especially after the disturbing interludes of recent days. I went for long tramps and rides on my own when Daddy was busy, but at night after dinner, we sat in front of a crackling blaze, for the nights were cool, and discussed every topic we could think up. At least, Daddy sat in his favourite old deep chair. I stretched out on the rug, and lazed there. This kind of contentment I could find only in this one place.

"Asleep, darling child?"

I rolled over and sat up. "No, but given the slightest encouragement, I will be." I hugged my knees. "Daddy, does the name Nalin mean anything to you?" I had not anticipated his reaction. The question had shaken him. He removed his pipe from his mouth slowly, eyes on my face. "Now what makes you ask that, Piyali?"

Astonished that this most forthcoming parent of mine should prevaricate over a simple question, I said casually, "No special reason. We met someone of that name—Lata and I—and when she heard where we were from, she said she knew the place. I just wondered if you'd heard the name." Also casually, he replied, "I believe there was a family in Divyasthala long ago. I doubt if any one of them lives there now. In fact, till you reminded me, I'd forgotten." Still casually, "Where did you meet this lady?" I shrugged. "Oh, somewhere near a place where we were shooting. I remembered because in the Bombay area, one doesn't often meet people who know the name Divyasthala. Lata was a little nervous," I went on, knowing he would tell me nothing more, "because we had a young photographer, but the pictures came out very well."

Daddy seemed relieved I did not press him for details. He couldn't know that his reaction had simply whetted my appetite to find out more.

". . . great pride in all of you. Each a career woman and doing us proud. You put your young male peers to shame—Lata, Tara and you."

I gathered my wits together. "But you've forgotten Dev Bhaiyya who's the perfect businessman-prince. And we're not to forget a certain very successful apple grower," which made him laugh.

"Darling child, there's something I've been wanting to bring up—but haven't known where or how to begin." I turned a shocked face to him. "Not a marriage proposal for me!" He shook his head. "No, not at all." I sat up again. He seemed to be having difficulty finding words.

"I'm doing this very badly. Piyali," in a rush, "what do you think of the idea of my marrying again?"

I think the word 'flummoxed' aptly describes my state. I saw he was waiting tensely for me to speak. My heart melted. My adored father who had lived alone for ten years deserved a companionship and love no daughter could give. I was up, and across the dividing space, kneeling down in front of him. "Is this a hypothetical question," I asked solemnly, "or does it have a more solid basis?" The uncertainty in his eyes was too much for me. I flung my arms around his neck and hugged him, felt his arms enfold me in a great bear hug. "All right, Daddy, it's time you came clean. I think it's the greatest idea! Now tell all."

I saw he was very moved. For that matter, so was I. "I—don't know where to begin," he said helplessly. I thought gleefully, this is truly role reversal. Helpfully, "There is someone special then?"

"Hmmm. The thing is—I haven't—well, approached her. I haven't known how to go about it. And hadn't consulted you anyway. That's why I was so anxious to have you come up."

"And I thought you missed your charming daughter's company!" Relenting, "Do I know her, Daddy?"

"It's Kanan Hanspal."

I sat back on my heels. Of course. She and her husband owned the estate that ran parallel to Daddy's on the far west. We had known them for years. Vijesh had died tragically in a tractor accident some five years ago. He couldn't have been more than forty two. And as I recalled they had children. Kanan. A rather good-looking woman. No wonder she had caught Daddy's eye.

"I like her," I told him, and saw relief in his eyes.

It seemed Kanan had retained the orchards. Daddy had found her a good manager, and kept a vigilant eye on everything. The children were aged fourteen and ten, were at boarding school, and came home for vacations. They were extremely fond of him. How was Kanan with him? As a friend, or big brother, he said ruefully.

"I wish I'd known days ago, Daddy. I'm here just for tomorrow. Suppose I do some discreet investigating of my own, will that help? I won't give a thing away. Trust me with that. At least we'll know how the land lies."

"I'm nervous." Something tugged at my heart-strings. I squeezed his hand. "It will be all right, Daddy."

I slowed to a canter when I came within sight of the sprawling bungalow set amidst thick trees. It seemed very quiet as if no one were at home. I dismounted anyway, groaning to myself, for this was my last day. I had just looped Sugar Plum's reins over a fence post when to my great relief the screen door to the front porch opened, and a slim sari-clad figure came out. It was Kanan. "Piyali!" she exclaimed. "But what a pleasant surprise!" I stooped to hug her. "I was afraid you might not be at home." A wry laugh from her. "And which hectic social round am I involved in? But let me look at you. So Tej wasn't exaggerating! I thought as a fond father, he might be. Yes, you look the perfect princess." I waved the word away. "No, it's true. You're really beautiful in a stunning kind of way. I've seen you in magazine fashion features wearing those luscious dresses. You're not wearing a bit of makeup now, and still look great." She took my hand. "Would you like to sit on the porch here, or go inside?" I said firmly, "Here. I'm trying to absorb as much mountain air as I can before I go back to Bombay."

Settled in comfortable bamboo chairs, I looked at her. She was much the same as I remembered her, a little older, but not much more, figure slender, face oval with large dark eyes, and a fine clear complexion. Like most widows in India, she was wearing little in the way of adornment, hair coiled in a knot on her head, wearing a white sari, tiny earrings of plain design, and a wrist watch. Did I detect a slight droop to the mouth as if she were weary and dejected? On request, I told her all about my work and Bombay, alert for the right opening. She told me how without Daddy's help, she could never have coped. She couldn't repay Tej for standing by her throughout those first dreadful days, she insisted.

"He'll miss you terribly when you go, Piyali."

I seized the moment. "I know, and I feel very bad about it. I came back to India especially to be within visiting distance. I sometimes feel it isn't right for him to be alone. He loves company—people and talk and laughter. Paradoxically, he loves it here. He's put the best years of his life into this place. When he comes to Bombay, he enjoys every moment—but I know he loves to come home. It saddens me to see him rattling around all alone in that big house. We call each other once a week, but it hardly fills the void. I wonder why he didn't remarry years ago."

"Perhaps he's still mourning for your mother."

I lifted my eyes to watch a humming bird fly to its tiny nest. "He is—and he isn't. I think he came to terms with her loss years ago. And cliche or not, Time is a great Healer. I ask myself what I can do under the circumstances, and come up with no answers."

"You can't do more than you're doing, Piyali. Children have to grow, and follow where their star beckons. I miss my children, but they have to go away to school. I retain the estate for their sake. Where else can I find support for their education and maintenance? Vijesh's mother was very clear about it. She blamed me for his death, you see." I stared at her. "Oh, yes, that's the way of it in India. Never mind that I was miles away from where it happened. I should have prevented it. It was due to my carelessness."

"But that's utterly absurd! Kanan, do you mind my asking you if you're still mourning for your husband?"

It took her a moment to answer. "As you said about Tej—I am—and I'm not. I've accepted the fact Vijesh will not come back. I've never told anyone, but he wasn't the easiest man to live with. Moody—lost his temper all the time. And I took the full brunt of his rages. He was a good man—and he loved us—but how difficult it sometimes was to love him. His mother knew none of this. Probably would have blamed me for it anyway."

"Have you never thought of remarriage? "

She gave an unamused laugh. "You don't know Indian men if you think they'll want to marry a widow—with children. Yes, I know I'm still young enough to have children. A lot of good it will do me!" She said, speaking carefully, "You spoke about wishing Tej would remarry. Someone in the family could find him a royal wife."

"Neither Daddy nor I care a fig about royalty! And he would never accept some strange woman, no matter how blue-blooded. No, for my beloved parent, I would want him to do his own choosing. I can't say how. He's very shy about such matters." I changed the subject. I had said all I wanted to, and much more. In the process, I had learnt a great deal. At this stage, it would be wrong to belabour the point.

In time, I rose to go. "Don't tell me you're going! I've been enjoying your visit so much!"

I said promptly, "Come for dinner tonight. Your mother is most welcome."

"Dinner! I don't know when I last dined out! How exciting!" Her eyes sparkled. "Wild horses won't drag my mother away from the idiot box, and our elderly live-in servant woman is equally crazy. I thank you, Piyali. You've made my day!"

I pulled the elastic band of my hat under my chin. "We'll love having you. Pick you up in the Rover at six thirty ."

As I rode away leaving a bright-faced woman behind, I reflected I hadn't done too badly this morning. Now to tell Daddy.

I teased him about his formal dress which he never wore in my honour. And he looked very handsome, beard newly trimmed, hair neatly brushed. When I had told him Kanan was coming for dinner, he had been astounded. His eyes had not moved from my face when I recounted the entire exchange we two had had. But once the telling was done, he had hugged me tightly, and kissed the top of my head. "Piyali—my baby—thank you. I can't say more." I was close to tears. What had I done which merited such gratitude? I managed, "Daddy, suppose she doesn't like beards?" He grinned. "I'll shave it off! And my head too if that's what she wants," he said jubilantly.

Needless to say, dinner was a runaway success. We were all in a buoyant mood, and matched each other wit for wit. Kanan very pretty in a cream sari with a narrow gold border, her hair loose on her shoulders for the first time I could recall, veritably sparkled. And dear Tej Pratap Singh had trouble keeping his eyes away from her. After coffee, I asked to be excused to complete my packing—which actually was all done. When close to midnight, she stirred at last reluctantly, I begged off from accompanying her, and Daddy drove her home. When she left, we hugged each other with genuine affection. Well, I thought, as the Rover drove off, it's up to Daddy to take it on from here. Still, I felt the same anxiety a mother must feel for her child on the first day of school.

11

When Lata told me, I was appalled. With enormous effort I spoke normally. "Sounds great—but I can't make it, Lata. Hmmm, a prior engagement which I can't break."

"Oh, Piyali, you can't refuse! They'll be very hurt. They like you so much, and Cressida mentioned you more than once. What is this date you have? Maybe I can think up a way for you to wriggle out of it. This is going to be a very select group, not a big noisy crowd. Lekh rearranged his trip and Tara's just so that they could be here. They fly out the next night." I asked that most important question about who else would be there. Zelda Carvalho, Lata and Dev, the Sarans, and, of course, the immediate family. The Nevilles were unfortunately going to be away, and their young sculptor neighbour also. This last piece of information cheered me. Actually, I liked Tara's in-laws very much, and Mr Sudarshan and I, almost as much as Tara, had a very close bond between us. Tara had told me he had lost his only daughter tragically when young. Could I let him down? It was his sixty-second birthday that was being celebrated. I guessed that Neel had invented an excuse for the same reason that I was reluctant to go.

I set about making my own discreet enquiries. I put a call through to Waverley. Ruhi was delighted to hear my voice. I gathered that Robin and his partner, Fali Chhapkhanawala, had been commissioned to make a documentary on Kerala. They had already completed much of the footage, but were now to finish the film. Ruhi was going with him. She was extremely excited. Doubtless, much of that feeling came from just being able to be with Robin. They were driving, she told me, and had to allow for possible breakdowns, so couldn't delay by a single day. They hated to miss the party, and being with all of us. I mentioned how awkward I was feeling. After all, I wasn't really family as Lata and Bhaiyya were.

Ruhi exclaimed, "But I have an idea! Why not come straight to Waverley? Come early and rest, then shower and dress up. Hannah and Benny will love having you. They get lonely when we go. And they liked Princess Piyali so much. Stay on that night."

A deep male voice took over. "Piyali, I've been eavesdropping. Why don't you just stay on for a few days—as long as you like. Call it a working holiday. What do you say?"

Half-laughing, I said, "Robin, you and Ruhi take my breath away with your generosity. It sounds heavenly! About staying on, I'll have to check and get back to you tonight. And, Robin, thank you!"

But after I had hung up, I asked myself what I was doing, actually agreeing to stay on at Waverley, practically on the doorstep of that obnoxious creature. Yet, the opportunity to work there on my designs was most tempting. In the end, I called the Nevilles and said I would accept their gracious invitation.

When I told Lata about the Waverley plan, she looked surprised, but did not comment. I set out for Sinhadurg the afternoon of the party. Passing by Peter's Garage, I kept my eyes on the road. Ruhi had been right. Hannah and Benny gave me a warm welcome. I acknowledged it was splendid to be back. I took the dogs for a stroll before going up to shower and dress for the beach party.

It was a most enjoyable party after all. Lekh and Skeet had built an enormous camp fire, and around it, we ate and laughed, talked and sang. Mr Sudarshan's birthday celebration was one I would not forget.

Ruhi had told me once that she could write the children's stories for which she was justly making a name for herself, only at Waverley. Away from it, inspiration simply died. Some of Waverley's magic seemed to touch me, for I worked almost non-stop till my eyes, hands and back rebelled. Hannah would scold me for doing too much, and drag me off for lunch. By four in the afternoon, reaching the end of my physical endurance, if not of my creativity, I put away everything. Hannah would have given me a bounteous tea, but I would accept only a cup of tea, just as at lunchtime, I had only soup and salad. It displeased her, for she was all set to fatten me up. I insisted on her leaving my dinner for me to heat in the microwave when I was hungry. I had no wish to be waited upon hand and foot. They were not to wait up for me. Hannah agreed reluctantly. So it was that every afternoon, I went up to change into shorts and a shirt which knotted at the midriff, donned rubber-soled sandals and my sun glasses, picked up a paperback to put in my handbag, and drove off to the beach.

On the fourth day after my arrival, I parked the car as usual off the road, and made my way down to the sands. I had found a little cove where I could sit. The westering sun cast long shadows on this stretch of beach. Far out, a boat skimmed the surface of the ocean. Occasionally, a bicycle or rickshaw came along the road and passed on. I settled down to enjoy the peace, my book lying neglected beside me. My mind wandered from the state of Daddy's courtship—he hadn't mentioned it at all in our weekly calls—and the frequent calls from the Nevilles which were made from Kerala. Subconsciously, I registered the presence of a small boy perched on a rock at quite some distance from me. He was fishing, or trying to. Fleetingly, I wondered if a parent was around.

Of the owner of ROMOLA, there had been no sign—which was all to the good. Had he been in residence, he would certainly have come to check on the well-being of all at Waverley. This much I knew, for Hannah told me so, speaking as fondly of 'Neel Baba' as she did of 'Robin Baba.' It was a dimunitive old retainers in a family used for the children they had served so faithfully. 'Baba' made one think of a small boy, I smiled to myself, and here was Robin so big and tall. For that matter, it didn't suit the ruggedly masculine persona of the other man either.

When the sun went down a little more, I would go for a long walk. The peace here was so precious. . . . A long-drawn yell of terror shattered the calm. I was on my feet, staring in its direction. In front of my eyes, the small fisherman teetered on the very edge of the rocks, lost his footing, and fell in. I didn't wait to see if he could swim or not. At such times, instinct takes over. Sandals and glasses flung off, I raced into the water, and began to swim as fast as I could. The child came up once at some distance from the rocks. Clearly, the waves were towing him away. Some sort of commotion erupted on shore, and I heard yells, but my whole attention was on one spot. And then when a head surfaced, I was there to grab first the hair, followed by an arm holding the child securely. He struggled, but my voice seemed to calm him, and he went limp. I set my sights not on the rocks where he had been, but on the shore.

Progress was slow, painful, but I kept on doggedly. A shout came over the waves, and two heads came steadily closer. A wet furry head reached us first, and strong jaws seized the child's shirt. A man's arm clamped itself around my burden, and I was free of it. "I've got him. Keep going," a voice said. The final laps were an ordeal. Then blessedly, I was in shallow water, my feet touched the sandy bottom, and I was out of the sea.

My companions had preceded me. The child was lying on the sand motionless. Sheena sat by him, tongue lolling, sides heaving, streams of water running from her hide. Neel had already begun mouth-to-mouth resuscitation. I ran to kneel by his side. "Let me try now," I told him. He moved to make room, his own chest still rising and falling rapidly.

I cannot say if seconds passed or minutes before the small chest suddenly heaved, and the boy began to retch. Neel turned his head to one side as he began to throw up the water he had swallowed. He stared at us, wailed loudly, and began to cry loudly. "Reaction," Neel said briefly. A spatter of applause made me blink. We were surrounded by people—perhaps ten or eleven. Some bicycles and rickshaws parked by my car identified them as passersby. They must have spotted the rescue attempt and come running. Neel helped the boy to sit up. "I think he's okay now." The child was shivering with cold, not crying now, but an occasional sob still escaping him. I drew him close. The nearness seemed to comfort him.

Neel was asking the group if they knew who the boy was. No one actually did, but one man pointed to a distant spot where a hutment colony stood. When asked, the boy nodded. Neel's eyes were on both of us. We were very chilled. It was late now, and a brisk breeze had sprung up. Sheena kept shaking herself.

"Your car, I think," and when I nodded, "You'll catch cold. Time to move on." From his wet pants, he extracted a purse. "Take the child home," he instructed a rickshaw driver, offeing him a note. The man put his hands behind his back, and protested he could not take money at such a time, but would certainly do his bidding. More, he would scold the parents soundly. Yes, Saab? Tea with lots of sugar? And take him to a doctor? That he would do himself. He did accept a fifty-rupee note for the doctor. "Let's go," Neel said, as the boy was carried away. One of the men darted off to bring my things. We had an escort all the way to the car. Neel took the keys from me. "I'll drive," he said briefly. Sheena leaped to the back seat on command. I slid into the passenger seat, and

Neel under the wheel. Clearly, everyone was loath to have the excitement end. One man asked if Neel was Neville Saab's neighbour, for he had seen him before. "Saab, you—and your wife—saved the life of a poor man's child today. You will get *punya* for it."

Neel shot back, "Not a matter of *punya,* my friend. A fellow human was in need. And you haven't forgotten my dog's help, have you?" Guffaws greeted that, and the car went into motion.

We must have taken a route I did not know. I wasn't paying much attention , for I was huddled in my wet clothes, my teeth beginning to chatter. It was just as well Neel was driving. In a very short time, we were slowing. I saw we had halted by the the gates of ROMOLA. Neel is hopping off first, I thought. He had opened the door for Sheena who leaped out. About to slide over to the driver's side, I stopped when Neel opened my door next. He bent his wet head. "Come in and dry off."

I said stiffly, "Thank you, but no. I'll be home in a few minutes."

"You're here now. And you'll worry Hannah when she sees you like this."

"Not if I explain." I accepted the invitation for what it was—meaningless polite talk. He didn't mean it, and wild horses wouldn't make me do it. Neel said, "It isn't wise to delay. You're shivering. At this rate, you'll get pneumonia. Come, Princess."

I stared straight ahead. "You're the one who's holding me up."

He made an exasperated sound. "Please, I'm asking you to."

"You're very kind. I appreciate it. The keys, please?"

He growled, "If you're not out of there in ten seconds, I'm going to drag you out, and carry you in over my shoulder in front of Manohar." The man servant I had met on my only visit had arrived, looking shocked at his master's state.

"Such he-man tactics, Mr Gregory! You don't really mean I should come in. Last time, you told me in no uncertain terms to get out—and that I wasn't welcome ever." Gooseflesh had broken out over my skin, and I rubbed my arms. I was miserable now. Probably, another girl might have burst into tears.

Standing on hind legs, head inside my window, Sheena peered in. She gave a short bark as if enquiring what was holding up the show when she was wet and uncomfortable. Neel's mouth quirked. The man was being given a brief explanation. Eyes wide, he exclaimed, "The Rajkumari mustn't sit around in wet clothes!" A gleam in his eyes, Neel stepped aside. "This way, Rajkumari, this way. My wife will make you a nice cup of hot tea." He was bowing, bending almost to the ground in cordial invitation. If looks could kill, Neel would have fallen flat on the ground by now. What could I do but step out?

We must have made a ludicrous sight, man, woman and dog, all bedraggled, following our eager leader through the front door. I was taken straight up as instructed to the east guest room, and shown the bathroom. In fact, Neel was at our heels as we went up the graceful staircase, and along the corridor. He said, "There's a dryer in the top drawer of the bureau, and a robe behind the bathroom door—my mother's. Come down when you're through."

With chilled hands, I struggled to take off my wet clothes. They fell in a heap, and then I was standing blissfully under the streams of warm water, letting it wash away the sticky salt. With a cake of delicately scented soap, I made a wonderful lather, rubbing it into my scalp. Feeling human again, not just a bit of flotsam washed up by the tide, I stepped out. After drying off, I found the robe, and went into the bedroom.

It was the prettiest of rooms, gay flowered curtains matching the bedspread, the other furnishings well-chosen. At the triple-mirrored dressing table, I located the dryer. My scalp felt good, clean and warm, the hair restored to its silky state. A pocket comb from my bag took care of the tangles. The heavy curtain hung over and below my shoulders. Minus makeup, I looked young—and defenceless? What did it matter? As soon as I could, I would be out of here. A knock, and a woman came in. She was the wife of Manohar, it seemed, and had come for my wet clothes which she put in a plastic basket. Much curiosity in her eyes, she bowed and told me I was asked to go down. Tea was ready.

Feeling a bit foolish in my kimono-style flowered robe, I went down. It reached only a little below my knees, but was so ample that I had crossed the edges over each other, and tied the sash as tightly as I could. The woman had taken me into a living room, bowed and gone away. I stood there looking around at its beautiful proportions.

It was the kind of room that is so interestingly done up that one needs time to take it all in. A long curving settee covered in nubby oatmeal fabric, a perfect foil to the brilliant heaps of cushions; deep chairs and sofas; a coffee table so unusual and eye-catching that I was instatntly covetous; an enormous seascape which covered half a wall, and which I could have studied for hours. Long windows overlooked the garden. Something peculiar was happening to me. I did not realize it at first, then when I crossed over to a sofa and sat facing the painting, it came to me. From my first visit, I had loved every moment of being at Waverley. But here was something curious, the more so because it was totally unexpected. A feeling of homecoming engulfed me. It was as if I had been wandering for a long time, and had at last reached the destination I had been seeking. How ridiculous to feel that way about a place I had been ejected from once, where I was now under protest, and which I would not enter again. But it was there. It combined welcome and warmth, a sensation of complete relaxation. I curled my legs under me, put my head down, my cheek against a cushion, utterly soothed.

It could have been minutes or hours, but when I became aware of my surroundings, a single lamp cast a golden circle of glowing light on the table beside me. It illuminated the features of the man sitting very close by my side, eyes on my face. Shocked at the proximity, confused, I struggled to sit up, only to be pushed back gently. "It's all right. You fell asleep," Neel said quietly. "Tea is ready whenever you want it. How do you feel? Not cold now?"

Could this be the same man whose studio I had invaded, who had nearly throttled me, speaking so gently in concern? I could only shake my head. I discovered that in my sleep, I had stretched out my legs, and someone had thrown a light cover over me.

"If my clothes are dry, I must go now."

"I don't know if they are. Why must you go?"

"*You* ask me that? You know you hate me, but felt duty-bound to make me come in. I thank you for your hospitality."

"You are very mistaken. I don't hate you. What I feel—is very different." His voice was very low. "You know, when I first saw you—at Lekh's wedding—no one could tell me who you were."

"You were there? Yes, of course, you are Lekh's great friend. I'm not surprised. I'd just arrived from New York ten days before the wedding."

"You were with that British singer who brought out an album with Lekh. And that other fellow with the long blond hair—the American. I wondered if you were a foreigner. You were so unlike any other girl there that I even thought you might be the wife or fiancee of one of those chaps. I couldn't very well march to Lekh and ask him. And Ruhi and Robin didn't know either."

"Why did you want to know?"

"Because I'd never come across anyone like this girl in the beautiful red dress with those long legs, that carriage, and that unforgettable face."

We were so close to each other, speaking almost in whispers that anyone else in the room would have found our words inaudible. I was oblivious of the darkness that had fallen, for we were both wrapped in each other.

"Then you recognized me at the Garage?"

"Instantly. I saw you through the glass wall of the office, so imperious—watched you speak to Peter—the whole thing. When he called me, it was too much to resist. The situation was ready-made. And you rose splendidly to the bait. It was delicious the way you looked me up and down in horror." Ruefully, "I've never been able to resist practical jokes—and when a beautiful girl is involved—well, it's exactly the way Robert Frost said of himself, 'Spring is the mischief in me'. I still didn't know your name, but if you were bound for Waverley, then I would find out soon enough."

"You were very wicked." His mouth quirked. Unwillingly, I smiled back. "But I didn't recognize you at the party at all. If Robin hadn't laughed over the incident—he thought it terribly funny—I still wouldn't have known. And Ruhi thought it was the cutest thing."

"You were angry. That's why you came to see me."

"Nowhere as angry as you when I came here." I searched his face. "When you learned who I was, you withdrew completely, isn't it? I sensed it happening. And when I came into the studio, you considered it an abominable intrusion because this creature had dared to enter the sanctum."

He was silent, neither admitting nor denying it, eyes on my face. He said huskily then, "No one ever taught me how to talk to a princess."

"Oh, what do such titles matter? I'm as ordinary as anyone."

"If you're ordinary . . . do I dare. . .?" His hand came up to cup my face, his head down to mine. Nothing had prepared me for the warm tide of feeling that swamped me now. It was as if he had intended a light caress, perhaps because of the episode of the little boy, or perhaps as a small gesture towards a new beginning in our relationship, making up for its disastrous start. But at some point, the powerful physical pull that had always existed between us engulfed him, and drawing me completely into his arms, he kissed me with driven hunger. And I, I was lost, blind, deaf to everything else except the closeness of this one man, the warmth of his body, and his mouth that was evoking sensations I had never felt before. My hands had moved to the dense curly mass of his hair. And then Neel lifted his head to murmur, "Piyal—Piyal, I shouldn't be doing this—not with you—not with you." His clasp tightened, a deep groan leaving him, "But, oh God, how can I help it? How can I?"

I lay still, my face against the warm strength of his throat, the strange words ringing in my ears. It felt so right to be here, then why was Neel saying such words? I had clarified that point about my status, and indeed, wasn't that why he had relaxed his guard, and taken me into his arms? All the while, mouth still throbbing, my cheek on the soft cotton of his shirt, I felt I never wanted to move. My body was still, but my mind pondered over the words. Neel seemed as loath to let me go, yet he loosened his hold at last. "Piyal, I —don't know if I can trust myself when I hold you like this. As it is, I—"

"Because you're engaged to Jyoti?"

"To Jyoti? Of course not! Nor to anyone else! Her father and mine are old friends. She's a little sister to me. I escort her if I'm around. That's all."

"I misunderstood her. She said she was preparing for marriage."

"Of course, she is. But not to me."

He stood up. "I haven't even given you a cup of tea yet. What do you take in your tea?" removing the tea cosy, and pouring the steaming amber liquid. The mundane question brought me down to terra firma with a thud. "Just milk." I threw aside the cover, and swung my legs down, sitting up straight to take my cup.

Neel walked to the window, his in hand, to stare out into the dark garden. An awful feeling gripped me. Do we go back to the old footing now, hostile strangers again, and if not quite that, then polite acquaintances perhaps? I went to place my cup on the tray. "More tea?" I shook my head. "You're staying at Waverley?" I explained briefly. "I didn't know. I came back last night. Usually the grapevine carries such tidbits back and forth. I was going up to see Hannah and Ben tonight. And you've been able to get work done? That's very good. How long will you be here?" "We were exchanging this polite small talk as if minutes ago we hadn't been locked in a passionate embrace.

"I really must go now."

"Stay and have dinner with me."

"Thank you, but not this time."

"Will you come to see the studio tomorrow?" I couldn't believe I was hearing the words. "I'll keep the time free if you tell me when you can come." Relief rendered me speechless. "Piyal, you will come, won't you?"

Suddenly, I was light-headed with happiness. "I'd love to. But I won't disturb your morning hours or mine. Will afternoon suit you? Around four?"

He let out his breath, and smiled. "I'll look forward to showing you around."

Neel drove me home, parking the car in the garage. The Neville's watchman had run up to open the garage door, the dogs all over us. When it was locked, he asked if Neel Saab and the Rajkumari were all right. "That rickshawalla—he is my brother's wife's brother-in-law saw the whole thing. Gave the boy's parents a lecture they won't forget. The boy is fine."

With an avid spectator watching, we exchanged polite goodnights.

Neel walked away into the night.

12

I was up with the birds next morning. Filled with anticipation, I showered and dressed, slipping out of the side door after letting the cat out. It promised to be a glorious morning, and I laughed aloud, twirling around, my arms stretched out. Rocky and Reba came leaping to join me. At breakfast which I insisted on having in the kitchen, Hannah spoke about yesterday's incident which she had just heard of via the milkman. I grinned to myself. She and Benny had to be told all, and they exclaimed in horror, concerned about me and Neel Baba. The Rajkumari should have woken them up. What Robin Baba saying to them? I assured them I had been fine, and there had been no need at all to call them. They smiled fondly at the mention of Sheena's part. Yes, she and Neel Baba swimming in the sea every day in summer.

She was impressed when I said I had been invited to the studio. Neel Baba not letting many into studio. Yes, I told her, but I did sculpture sometimes too, and that convinced him. I must take advantage of his offer before he changed his mind. Hannah shook with laughter at that, and Benny chuckled. They both nodded when I added that we both had to work in the mornings, and I would be going only in the afternoon.

Sheena gave me her warmest welcome. "Look at that disgusting hound!" Neel exclaimed. "Slobbering all over you! She's the sort who'll invite a burglar in for a cup of tea."

I stroked the golden fur. "She knows I'm not a burglar, don't you, Sheena?"

At the door of the studio when she was firmly banished, she trotted off with a hurt reproachful look at us. Neel's eyes met mine. He shook his head. "If I'd let her, she'd stay in the whole time. That's why I have to give her so many outings in compensation."

The studio was just as I remembered it, only now I was entering without rancour in my heart, secure in my welcome. The familiar odours were all around, and the afternoon brightness poured in through the skylights. Fresh air came through well-placed ventilators. A dais with a tall stool indicated that live models were sometimes used. Shrouded objects were undoubtedly sculptures, perhaps yet to be finished. Neel did not uncover any of these, and knowing how important privacy is to an artist, I did not ask to see them. He stood aside to let me through a door he had unlocked. In front of my dazzled eyes were a number of sculptures, each tremendously powerful, and therefore riveting.

A hammer thrower caught in the act, face contorted in utter concentration, every muscle of the big body in coordination, so realistic that one could feel them straining. Flanking him were two wrestlers locked in combat, feet placed just so to withstand the mighty strength of the opponent, skin slippery with sweat, grim determination on each countenance.

Behind me, Neel said. "These have been commissioned for the central hall of a new sports complex. The others are in the studio, ready for casting."

"They are absolutely—what can I call them but fantastic? I could study them for hours."

He said huskily, "If you feel that, Piyal, then I'm happy." There was the name he had used before—and I loved it. No one else called me that. We were so close, I could have leaned against him for support. He seized my hand. "Piyal, this way."

He had led me to the figures of a man and woman, backs to each other, and as the body language made crystal clear, totally unyielding, neither willing to give way an inch. Stubbornness dominated their facial expressions, but there were subtle differences. The man's held a mixture of indignation and outrage; in her eyes was a sly gleam of—triumph? Without doubt, all communication between them was at a standstill, each wallowing in self-righteousness, convinced the other was in the wrong.

I stammered, "Neel, it's superb." Unconsciously, I put a hand on his shirt front. "I feel I know them. That—I've met them. Yet they could be any couple anywhere. There's something—universal about them."

He picked up the bronze head of a small child. "My god-daughter. No question of her modelling for me, but even making sketches was a problem. She wouldn't sit still. The number of lollipops I had to bribe her with! Her father and I were boyhood friends, and the friendship has endured. This head is an anniversary present for the parents." He moved to a larger bronze. "My mother. Quite a character, my Mama. No, she doesn't like it all. Says it makes her look years older." He laughed. "I'm going to do another one, and lop twenty years off."

That was when I saw it. Instantly recognizable, all that delicate beauty captured in white marble. I stood very still, waiting for Neel to speak. When he said nothing, I did. "This is truly a work of art, Neel." He laid a hand caressingly on the lovely sculpture. "My grandmother," he said briefly. I murmured, "She's very beautiful, isn't she?" He was silent, then he said, "That she is. More's the pity." Before I could react to that cryptic statement, he was urging me out of the room. "Come. I've lots more to show you!" I protested that I hadn't even begun to really study his works. He was locking the door. "You can do that any time, Piyal."

We climbed one of those short intriguing carpeted flights of steps that had caught my attention the first time. At the top, I paused in delight. Going around three walls of the studio was a gallery. Railings ran along its length. In deep recesses, glassed-in bookshelves lined the walls. A large table with comfortable chairs was placed in each recess. The largest section was a study, complete with a handsome enormous desk, deep armchairs, and a long sofa where one could recline in luxury, or relax and read. The lighting was superb.

"One could spend a lifetime up here on research," I said. "It's quite the most novel study-cum-library I've seen in a long time. Your idea, Neel?"

He shook his head. "The credit goes to my architect friend, Geet Adityaraj. I told him my requirements, and he came up with this studio-study under one roof. It's tremendously convenient. This door leads directly into the house."

"Quite brilliant!" I had been looking at the book titles. "I could spend days here just reading. Exactly the kind of books I love."

"You're always welcome to do that—or anything else." His next words were even more incredible. "Piyal, why don't you bring your work tomorrow morning, and do it here? In the studio, I mean?" When I did not speak, he added, "Unless you think it will be distracting?"

When I could, I said, "More to the point, will it distract you?"

"No, not at all. I'd like you to come. Will you, Piyal?" I searched his face. It was very serious. Finally, I nodded. "I am glad," he told me, relief in his voice.

"So am I. I think my own company was getting to be a little too much. I need fresh inspiration. If this place doesn't provide it, nothing will. To say nothing of the presence of a most distinguished sculptor."

I grinned back, feeling my spirits rising. There were too many unanswered questions, but for now, I would not let them mar our all-too new relationship. Neel's impulsive offer was at war with what he had said after he kissed me. Just now though, I was too happy to think of that.

I was deeply touched to see Neel had made preparations on my behalf. A table large enough for me to spread out my stuff, a very comfortable chair with extra cushions, and even a footstool. They were placed in the work area, I was happy to see. As if he had been unsure if I would show up, Neel greeted me with warmth. He asked what else I needed. I said there wasn't a single thing he had overlooked. Briskly, I set out everything. The last thing I wanted was to disturb his work.

"Piyal, you once said you'd like to work with clay again." I had said that during my first disastrous visit here. "Feel free to do that, won't you?"

His generosity startled me. Recovering, "Why, thank you. I will sometime."

"Good. Will it bother you if I put on some music? I don't have to if it will spoil your concentration."

"I'd love it. I always have music when I work."

"Any preferences? No? Well, then. . . ."

A few minutes later, the studio filled with the wonderful rhythms of Zakir Hussain's *tabla.* It was the signal for both of us to start working. Neel began to unwrap the wet cloths on the piece he was working on. I bent over my design. To tell the truth, I was so far ahead of my timetable that now I was doing such designs as pleased me. A half-finished bracelet lay in front of me. All around us the *tabla* rose to an exciting fast-paced climax. To tell another truth, I had never felt less inclined to jewellery design than at this moment. A quick look showed Neel was already absorbed—with his shirt on. His back was towards me, and I could not see his face, or what he was doing. But an idea came to me. I took a fresh sheet, and began to sketch quickly. Under my pencil emerged the fine curly head and strong neck, and from the glimpses of profile, the broad brow, straight high-bridged nose, curve of mouth and chin, the clean-cut jaw. It all added up to a very striking personality. From memory, I added one dimple, and the laugh lines around the mouth that were so much a part of Neel's personality. As my pencil moved, I was thinking that for the last two days, Neel had been rather serious.

A second *tabla* crashed out a response—to which the master came back with great eloquence and beauty, the beat unbearably stirring. The subject of my drawing had gone into his own rhythm. Like the one time I had watched him, I was struck again by the movements of the powerful body, ballet-like in form, as if a choreographer had planned every move.

I had completed several sketches when the music fell silent. As if conscious for the first time of his surroundings, Neel paused, clay-covered hands held up, then turned around completely to face me. As if in relief, he said, "Piyal. How is it coming? Good. Will you change the cassette please?" I went to look through his impressive collection. I chose the same piece from Verdi which had been playing when I first came. Neel nodded at my choice. An unusual follow-up to the *tabla*, but a favourite of both.

I said, "You don't always work with a shirt on, do you? I thought not. And you're uncomfortable. Is it for my sake—because I must remind you I grew up in the West, and a shirtless man is no shocking sight to me there or in India. So, please do what you always do."

His mouth quirked. "I didn't want to hurt the sensibilities of a princess."

I snorted in un-princesslike fashion. "Believe me, this princess isn't hurt by such things!"

He stripped off his shirt without more ado, and now the broad beautiful structure of neck, shoulders and back faced me. I seized my pencil and set to work. How much time elapsed I could not know, but adding finer details to the almost completed sketch, I looked up to see Neel standing by the table. There was no time to snatch up the scattered sheets.

"So your work's been coming along well, Piyal. Mine has too. I usually break for coffee at this time. May I see? I'd like to see how jewellery looks in the designing stages." What choice did I have? I passed him a sketch. He drew his breath in sharply. "This is what you've been doing? But it's tremendously good! I had no idea you. . . ." I met his gaze. "Piyal, I never expected to be the subject of a drawing. Role reversal, isn't it? Is this how I look?"

"Yes, but I wish I could do one of your face."

He grinned and struck a pose. "I'm all yours, Princess."

It was too good to miss. I worked rapidly on that wonderfully expressive face. Patently, he was amused, for the laugh lines and the deep indentations in his cheeks were in evidence, mischief in the eyes. When it was done, I turned it to show him. He bent over it for a long moment. "Will you sign it for me, Piyal? May I keep it as a memento?" And to my question, "It's better than good. And I'm honoured you did it at all. Do you paint too?"

"Not as much as I'd like to."

"Let me get cleaned up, then we'll have coffee. Why don't you go ahead? I'll join you."

In the living room, I stood in front of the seascape to study every detail. There was just enough light in the sky to reveal the immense span of the ocean, the thundering waves in their ceaseless round, and at the shoreline, creaming at the edges. A distant lighthouse sent out its steady beacon, for this was just before the hour of twilight. But the centre of interest was the approach of two large fishing vessels laden with the day's catch. Several figures were visible, and one man, no doubt the leader, had an arm raised in victorious greeting. A timelessness characterized the whole painting, for had the sea not pursued its eternal cycle since the beginning of Creation, and from time immemorial, had not man brought home the catch at close of day? And for how long had lighthouses renewed hope in the hearts of desperate ships, guiding them through the shoals to safe landings?

So lost in the picture, I jumped when Neel said behind me, "It's yours, Piyal."

I said in shocked tones, "Oh, I can't take it away from you! it must be worth a fortune!"

"I don't know about that."

"But didn't you pay an enormous sum for it?"

"In cash, no. In time, some hours, yes."

Light dawned. My eye went back disbelievingly. In my absorption, I had completely overlooked the initials NKG. I stammered, "I'm terribly sorry. I never dreamed. . . ."

"I paint sometimes in between assignments. This is what I saw on my first visit to Sinhadurg when Robin was still trying to sell me the idea of settling here. This is a little fishing village just beyond the town. Robin's taken quite a few pictures, and I wanted to record it on canvas. It will give me the greatest pleasure if you accept it, Piyal."

"I don't have anything of this value to give in return, Neel."

"Not to think in those terms. You've given me forgiveness, friendship, companionship—all priceless, more than the value of this painting."

"Neel—what can I say—but thank you?"

Our eyes met. He made an involuntary movement towards me, then controlled himself at once. His voice was unsteady. "Coffee coming up."

We had five glorious days together. Work came first, and we were very firm with ourselves over that. An astonishing amount was achieved which made us feel we deserved a change of pace in the afternoons. Though Neel pressed me to stay, I always went home for lunch because I felt he needed some time to himself. With Sheena, we went swimming in a little bay Neel had found, drove to picturesque spots, or simply sat either in the living room or study, talking for hours. Hannah and Benny were pleased at our friendship. And that summed up our relationship. We were very good pals. Two things were noticeable about our exchanges. One that Neel spoke freely about himself and his work, but was most reticent about his family. Two, he kept our relationship on a strictly platonic level. Not by word or touch did he go beyond the bounds of friendship.

Robin had called twice. Like Hannah and Benny, I had a brief exchange. All was well, he reported. The filming was coming along well. Ruhi was having a ball. They were leaving for Kanya Kumari shortly. He was happy my stay at Waverley was proving fruitful. I was to stay as long as I wished. He would call again.

The disturbing call which shattered everything came on the morning of the sixth day just before breakfast. It was from Lata, and she was very disturbed indeed. Bhaiyya's Grandmere was making a most unwelcome and unexpected visit to Bombay. It was so unusual for her to do so that her motives were suspect. I was not to know, Lata went on, how both grandparents had made her life—and Dev's—miserable, urging him to take a second wife who would give him children. Had Tara and Lekh not been away, it would have been a different matter. Tara handled her grandmother superbly, and Lekh had done very well, giving no quarter the only time they had met at the wedding. I could hear desperation in Lata's voice, see her practically wringing her hands as she begged me to get back to Bombay. I must move in with them, for the Maharani was to be there under their roof, and deflect whatever was coming. My heart sank. Oh no, I thought miserably to myself, not now. Not when Neel and I are just getting to know each other. Lata's anxious voice brought me back to the present. "I'll come," I said briefly. "Today? I see. I'll need time to pack. I should be there by lunchtime. No, don't start to thank me. I don't know how well I'll cope, but I can give it a try."

But after I hung up, waves of misery washed over me. To leave Neel now—how cruel it seemed. We would never be together in exactly this way again. If I came back to Waverley, I could hardly spend my days with their neighbour, and no time with my hosts. No, it was over for all time—our wonderful idyll. Meeting the Maharani did not alarm me. Formidable she might be, but I wasn't a Dhanraj or her kinswoman. Lata really wasn't asking much. And I owed her so much, the question of refusal simply didn't exist.

Hannah's voice recalled me to the present. I told her who was coming, and that I had to go, knowing she would enjoy that tidbit. Her eyes grew round in wonder. She trotted after me to help with the packing. Benny helped me to put my bags in the car. To please Hannah I choked down a piece of toast. A word of explanation to Hannah, and I was racing down the path to ROMOLA.

Neel was at his desk in the study. I went up silently, and stood watching him. Hair unbrushed after his shower, curling all over his head, grew low on his neck. It made me long to sink both my hands in its thickness, and smooth back one errant curl on his brow. Sensing my presence, he lifted his eyes. They reflected shock at seeing me, then concern, for my own face must have revealed my feelings. He spoke my name, and rose swiftly, coming around the desk.

"Piyal, what is it? Tell me."

Stumblingly, I explained. "Today? Now? But if no one's ill, or even in trouble, why do you have to go? She isn't even related to you, is she? Lekh would come to the rescue!" My words must have been garbled, since I was finding speech increasingly difficult. He became silent.

"Will you come back after the lady leaves?"

I shook my head. Tracing the pattern on the floor tiles with the toe of my sandal, I explained I was going to see my father. Something was wrong with my eyesight, for the pattern wavered and disappeared. I turned away to the desk, my hand covering a crystal paperweight, my back to Neel. With effort, I managed to say, "Neel . . . I must tell you . . . it's been a tremendous pleasure . . . to be with you. You've been so kind. Thank. . . . "I could not go on in any case because a hand had covered my mouth." I stood very still, my whole being conscious only of the man behind me, the tang of aftershave and talcum I remembered from another room far away mingling with the fresh scent of soap. The hand came away, and I was turned by the shoulders to face him.

I pressed my lips together to keep them from trembling. The same stark misery I felt was reflected in his eyes. For a long moment, we stared at each other. Then Neel held out his arms to me, and I went into them like a homing pigeon, burying my face in his shoulder.

"Piyal, Piyal, how can I let you go?" As if the tight control he had imposed upon us both for all these days had snapped, he kissed me feverishly all over my face. When the warm mouth touched mine, I responded with all the feeling I could command. We were both shaking when Neel lifted his head at last, still holding me tightly. He put his cheek on my hair. "Piyal, I—shouldn't be doing this. Not with you. Never with you. But, oh God, how long can I keep away? I tried—God knows I tried. But how hard it's been! Your stunning beauty and sweetness—your companionship—your sense of humour which is exactly like mine—I love every smallest thing about you. But I shouldn't, Piyal, I shouldn't." He groaned the last words, and put his face in the curve of my neck.

If he had poured a bucket of icy water over my head, I could not have been more stunned. Both hands on his chest, I leaned back to stare at him. "Neel, what are you saying? And not for the first time. You've said something like this before. What does it mean? You have to tell me. Why have you kept your distance—and why shouldn't we be doing this?"

His arms dropped. He said tonelessly. "There can be nothing but friendship between us, Piyal. Anything more is impossible."

I tried to quell my rising panic. "Because of who I am? My stupid title?"

"There's that too," he said tiredly.

"I've never heard of such rubbish! My father will never raise objections! And Tara has blazed a trail there." I paused. "Unless there's something else?"

"Yes, there is," after a pause. "I can't spell it out, Piyal. All I can say is—well, that someone very dear to me—would be immeasurably hurt—and I can't do that to—this person."

"Then you can't have any real feelings for me, Neel." He made a sound of protest. "What about my being immeasurably hurt? You can do it to me, but not to someone else. What I can't understand is why you didn't let me go in peace the time we rescued the little boy. Then none of this would have come to pass—or reached this stage."

"If I'm hurting you—and I can't tell you how sorry I am about that—I'm hurting myself too, Piyal. If I didn't let you go—it was because I couldn't. Don't you think I tried?" He lifted his hands and dropped them. "What can I say to make amends, Piyal?"

I had come here practically running, and now in my deep hurt and confusion, all I wanted was to get away. I said steadily, "Thank you for all you've done, Neel. For your time and hospitality—for letting me share the facilities of your studio. And for the great experience of working with such a brilliant artist. It's been a wonderful working holiday." He said nothing, but his eyes were on my face. "Goodbye, Neel."

Why was it, I asked myself as I raced out of ROMOLA, that I was fated to leave the place in this fashion? Back at Waverley, I managed farewells to Hannah and Benny. Experience had taught me they would never accept tips, so I had given Hannah a pretty frilly apron with capacious pockets to house her glasses, and other little objects she liked to have around her, while Benny acquired a fine hat to keep off the sun when he went shopping. The simple gifts brought great pleasure.

I drove away towards ROMOLA. A tall figure stood behind the gates. Neel made no attempt to stop me. Once past him, I let the hot tears fall.

13

Lata was pathetically grateful to see me, as well as profoundly apologetic. "I interrupted your holiday, and am so sorry about it, Piyali."

"Don't be. It was time I came back anyway. And my work is way ahead of schedules. So now, what's the battle plan?" I had never felt less like smiling, but was determined no one would guess at the state of my battered heart. It wasn't that easy at all. I hadn't succeeded in pushing away all memories of Neel, the wonderful ones, and others I would have given a great deal to forget.

Skeet had moved for now to Lekh's house. That he lived here was not to be mentioned. In fact, he was not to be mentioned at all. Lata gave me a quick glance, and said someday she would explain all. I nodded. Goodness knew I had my own secrets to conceal. Then the Maharani knew nothing of Lata's career, which would inevitably be revealed to her. Dev said it was none of her business, and he would not tolerate any criticism from her about that or anything else. And that was another factor. Dev's relationship with his grandparents had become very bitter. Since the last confrontation, he had not stepped into Sonal Mohur, not even when the Maharaja had a stroke. Tara had gone alone. I realized the seriousness of the situation, for after all, Bhaiyya was the Yuvraj, heir to the throne, whatever that meant in this day and age, the last male of his particular line. If the Maharani brought up the matter of the succession again, Lata did not know what would happen. My task was to deflect any impending trouble. As one fairly new on the scene, I could do things Lata could not. Taking the guest out was another. "Oh," Lata concluded vehemently, "if only she weren't coming at all, we wouldn't be in this state of unrest!"

Lata would have considered it treachery on her cousin's part, but the royal visitor proved a welcome distraction for me personally. Yes, she was formidable, but I enjoyed her acerbic remarks whenever we went shopping, or sightseeing. I did not pass on to Lata and Bhaiyya the many probing questions I was asked about the young lad at Tara's wedding. As it was, Bhaiyya hardly came home for the duration of the visit, hardly exchanged a word with his grandmother. Lata was out all day at work. Surprisingly, that fact did not bring forth any adverse reaction, though many interested questions were directed at Lata—and at me—about our designing. I was given a cordial invitation to come and see the Dhanraj family jewels which might give me some ideas. I sensed the Maharani in her own dry way, had become rather fond of me. If she had thought of extracting information about Skeet, she was doomed to disappointment. I acted puzzled at her interest, said the young fellow was Lekh's cousin, that I had understood he was in college. The indication was that I had had nothing to do with him since the wedding. But, I added helpfully, Tara would be able to supply more details. I received a sidelong glance at that, and no more questions came my way. In an odd sort of way, I missed the lady when she left. Lata breathed a heartfelt sigh of relief, and kissed me. My presence had made all the difference, she insisted, and Bhaiyya concurred. But my misery came back to haunt me all over again. It must have shown because Madhur asked me if I were coming down with a cold. Lata said escorting the Maharani had exhausted me, which didn't surprise her in the least, she claimed. Why not go back to Waverley to recoup? I parried the suggestion.

I began deliberately to accept all kinds of invitations including several from personable young men-about-town. I told myself my attempts to forget were working out very well. And then the Nevilles returned from their trip. Ruhi phoned, sounding happy and excited. Why didn't I come up to Waverley for the weekend? She had so much to tell and show me. I managed to make some plausible excuse, instead inviting them both to dinner at any restaurant of Ruhi's choice the next time they were in Bombay.

Even in a place frequented by the rich and famous, we three attracted much discreet attention. It was a merry evening, and we laughed and talked away.

Out of the blue, Ruhi said, "Oh Piyali, tell me about the rescue of the little boy!"

I was startled. Here I had put those memories on hold, and now they were being recalled. A pause, then I shrugged. "It wasn't my rescue really. Neel and Sheena took over."

"That wasn't the way I heard it, Piyali," Robin said. "You're the one who saw the child fall and dived in. It was the most amazing coincidence that Neel and Sheena happened to be walking on the beach, and could help. If it hadn't been for your prompt action, even if they'd found the lad, it would have been too late. Neel said he had no idea someone had fallen in. It was when he saw you fling off your footwear, and race in that the truth dawned on him. The child came up once then, and the two of them started swimming to you."

"Perhaps so," I said stiffly, "but the fact remains it was a joint effort."

Ruhi exclaimed warmly, "I think both of you are tremendously brave! How could you have such presence of mind, Piyali? I'm sure my mind would have stopped functioning."

"No, it wouldn't have. Tell me about my dear Hannah and Benny," changing the subject.

Ruhi said, grinning at her husband, that they were very excited at having Robin Baba back. They had told her how I had worked and worked. Ruhi was happy about that.

"As you said, Waverley provides just the perfect setting. Ideas just crowded into my head, and I achieved a tremendous amount of work. And for that I have you two to thank."

From Robin, "Come back at any time you can, Piyali, whether we're there or not. I'm happy you and Neel were able to share some time together, both spectacularly talented. He's truly one of the finest people I know." Teasingly, "I think you've forgiven him for his little act at Peter's Garage?"

"Don't remind me!" I retorted, trying to push away memories of the one person I was trying to forget.

It wasn't that easy. Robin had left us briefly to go across to greet some friends when Ruhi gave me a jolt. "Piyali, do you see the group just coming in, and that girl in the fuschia dress, sort of off the shoulder? She happens to be Neel's ex-girl friend." I stared in startled interest. The girl in question was both attractive and glamorous. "Enormously rich. That's her father—the stout one. Looks like a family party. I've met her at parties. Probably owns enough clothes to stock a boutique."

"Why is she an ex?" I managed.

"Neel broke it off. He never said a word to me, but maybe told Robin. I guess he found she was too much of a pampered darling—and didn't care for the crowd she moved about with. You know the kind—rather on the wild side—discotheques all night. Many of them definitely into drugs. The few times I spoke to her, the conversation revolved around trivia so that I was glad to escape. Boastful too. I can't imagine how he liked her in the first place."

"Perhaps he's in love with her."

"I don't know about that. He was rather quiet for weeks after. Kept to himself. Long outings with Sheena. As a matter of fact, he's doing that right now. More actually. A lot of pressure with commissions piling up. Couldn't be Natasha after all these months. It'll do him good to have his parents visit him soon. You know his father is that renowned archaeologist, Denzil Gregory? Oh, you don't? His mother accompanies him everywhere. Called Jana—abbreviation of Sanjana." Ruhi poured more coffee into my cup. "Oh, I've met them many times. And really enjoyed it. The father is quite a character. Very big-made, a little stooped now, wears hornrims. Has a habit of blinking behind them. Very thick iron-grey hair, sort of rumpled. I guess one reason the mother goes with him is because he's so very absent-minded. Robin says he has the sharpest brains, and the forgetfulness is deceptive. Has written any number of books and research publications. The wife does the editing, and prepares manuscripts."

I was a fascinated listener. "What is the mother like?"

"It's strange, but one would never know either was Neel's parent. His mother is so different in looks. not one of your pretty dainty ladies. Handsome features though. No frilly clothes for her—wears practical no-nonsense stuff, mostly pants. Maybe a long skirt for parties. Hair short and simple."

"I suppose their life style demands it."

"Yes, it does. But they're both very kind. And so devoted to each other."

"And where does the son fit into all this?"

"I think he was raised by a grandmother. His house is named for her, you know. And he enjoys his parents. When he was old enough to travel, they had him fly out to wherever they were on a dig during his vacations. Neel has seen the most interesting places. I've seen him tease his father about his forgetfulness, and make his mother laugh and laugh. I sense it's a warm uncomplicated kind of relationship."

"When they're not on digs, do they stay with him?"

"No, just for short visits. They have their own establishment somewhere—part of the Gregory estate. Robin says the family has inherited wealth. Did I tell you Denzil Gregory is an opera buff? Has a fine voice too. And Neel's picked it up from him. Is a wonderful baritone. I think their love of music drew him and Lekh together from the first time they met. They often sung duets for us. I love it when they sing."

Robin slid into his chair. "So you two have been gossiping."

"Mmmm. Telling Piyali all about your girl friends."

"Not about all surely! You'll shock her!"

"Piyali is quite unshockable," I said dryly.

The talk with Ruhi had thrown so much light on Neel—and left so many questions unanswered.

14

Rukmini and Jagdish Saran were dear friends of the Dhanrajs. They had known Bhaiyya's parents, Yuvraj Vikramjit Singh and the beautiful Sukanya who had lost their lives so tragically when Tara was still a small girl. A former career diplomat, as Mr Sudarshan had been—they were good friends—the Sarans had taken up residence in Bombay. Like the delightful couple they were, they enhanced the social life of the metropolis considerably. Rukmini was a patron of the arts—which meant she took special interest in all creative artists, especially young aspiring ones. Often she invited artists who had already made their mark to meet groups of interested girls and boys. These get-togethers were informal, relaxed, no lectures being involved, more in the nature of a question-answer session. This is what Rukmini told me when she invited me for one such meeting. I was a shining example, she coaxed, and an inspiration to would-be young artists. What could I do but accept?

About fifteen college-age young people, all bright and eager, greeted me with enthusiasm. Our hostess served a high tea first which was demolished with gusto. I was glad I had come. I was enjoying the informal chatter, and I could see Rukmini was pleased. So occupied, I missed what was happening until behind me, Rukmini said, "Prin—Piyali, may I introduce Neel Gregory whose sculpture is admired so much everywhere?"

The shock I felt was reflected in Neel's eyes. We hadn't laid eyes on each other since I left Waverley. Patently, I was the last person he expected to encounter there. For a moment, neither spoke or moved. I don't know what imp of mischief prompted my next actions. Wasn't Neel known for his love of practical jokes, ever ready for a laugh? I'd had my turn at his hands. Today the joke was to be on him for a change.

Clasping both hands together, I gushed dramatically, " No! Not Neel Gregory, the famed sculptor? Why, I *adore* your work! It's a *supreme* honour to meet you, Mr Gregory! Had I known, I'd have brought my autograph book!" The indentations in Neel's cheeks deepened, but not in a smile. I could not make out if he was angry. I called out, "Folks, look who's here! None less than India's Michelangelo!"

The group didn't disappoint me. They crowded around Neel, so that only the top of his head was visible. Rukmini seemed pleased, but a little mystified by my enthusiastic welcome. My spirits had risen so much that I felt light-headed as if I'd been imbibing champagne instead of Darjeeling tea. Neel was actually here, in the same room, and would be for some time. I could look at him, listen to his voice after a break of months. My mind told me severely to stop being a moonstruck idiot. This was a dead end. I know, my heart replied, but let me have this much at least.

Eventually, Neel had to be rescued. Rukmini put him in a chair and gave him a soothing cup of tea. I kept my distance warily. Neel was perfectly capable of repaying me by doing something outrageous. In fact, his behaviour was exemplary. He fielded all questions very well, made the group laugh, but gave them plenty to think about. I wasn't really listening to the actual words as much as to the deep voice. The boys were clearly much impressed, the girls compeletely under the spell of those sheer male good looks. I was the last to blame them. When my turn came, I had to gather my wits. I guess I acquitted myself well enough. All the while, I sensed Neel's eyes upon me.

We came in for profuse thanks. Neel excused himself when the others left. He had another engagement, he told Rukmini. I came in for a half-bow, then he was gone. My heart had sunk to the soles of my sandals. It was truly all over for Neel. There was no place in his life for me. Somehow I managed my farewells to a grateful Rukmini. Then I drove straight home.

It was dark when I arrived, and parked my car. I did not turn on the lights, but went to sit on the balcony. A breeze off the sea cooled my face, tugging at my hair. I pulled off the scarf that held it back, and shook it loose. The lights of the city twinkled unconcernedly. Several storeys below, traffic flowed on in unending stream. So, I told myself, Life goes on—as mine must. I thought hotly it wasn't fair of Rukmini not to have mentioned her other guest. I would have backed out somehow. It struck me Neel would have done the same had he known. We've become antagonists, I told myself, circling each other warily, avoiding a confrontation. Neel had not exchanged even a conventional greeting with me.

When the doorbell pealed, I jumped. Probably a neighbour. Sometimes an item of mail was wrongly delivered. I peered through the peephole. Then I leaned against the doorframe, taking deep breaths. Was it really Neel? The bell rang again. My hand went out to pull back the bolts.

Neel said gravely, "May I come in, Piyal?"

Silently, I unfastened the safety chain, and let him in. We were both tongue-tied, and stayed on our feet. I hadn't the presence of mind to offer him a seat, though I had switched on a lamp. Neel was examining the leaves of a potted plant in a ceramic jar as if it were some rare object that needed careful study. He was half-turned from me. The glossy hair curled on the back of his neck over the collar of his striped shirt. The big powerful frame dwarfed Ruhi's dainty furniture. Why was he here?

As if he knew what I was thinking, he said without looking up, "You're wondering why I've come, Piyal." He moved to where he could look out over the balcony. "All these months—I've kept away." I waited wordlessly. "Even my trips to Bombay have been curtailed."

"To avoid me."

"To avoid hurting you all over again. When I saw you at Rukmini's, all my resolves went up in smoke."

"You didn't say one word, or look at me."

"Oh, I was looking at you all right. I could describe each detail of what you wore and said." Neel turned around to face me. "And, idiot that I am, I kept thinking, 'Why don't they all go away, and leave me alone with Piyal?' I'm here because I couldn't stay away."

"We're alone now. What—did you want?"

He said steadily, "I want to kiss that luscious mouth again—see those eyes darken from grey to blue—to just hold you in my arms. It's all I could think of since I laid eyes on you this afternoon."

A giant hand squeezed my heart. Neel was putting into words the kind of feelings I had had myself. Where were all the brave words uttered, the firm determination to stay away from each other? I whispered, "What—are we going to do about it?"

A deep groan as out of anguish broke from him. I can't say which one of us moved first. All I know is that we were locked in each other's arms, and we were exchanging feverish kisses. Words, some incoherent, spilled out in broken whispers. I don't know how much later Neel lifted his mouth from mine, his hand tangled in my hair moved to my waist. He gathered me up, and carried me to the sofa where he sat down holding me on his lap. He said huskily, "Your eyes have turned blue, Piyal." I looked my fill at the beloved features. I reached up to press my lips to each deep indentation. Neel smiled tenderly at me. "Tell me what's been happening in your life, Piyal."

"No," I said firmly, burrowing my head into his shoulder. "I want to hear all about you."

"I've been wanting so much to share my news with you. I have two exhibitions coming up abroad." I made a sound of pleasure, but didn't move.

The strange aspect of it, Neel said, was that it had all come about without any effort on his part. The Dutch owner of a gallery in Amsterdam had a two-day stopover in Bombay on the way from Tokyo. Not being the type who enjoyed tourist spots, he had checked in the newspapers for exhibitions being held in the metropolis—just when Neel's work was being shown. Neel hadn't known him, of course, but they'd met at the gallery, and talked at length. Finding him knowledgeable, Neel had had dinner with him. That was it. A chance meeting with an interesting visitor. Then two months ago, the Dutch fellow had contacted him again. And voilá, Neel Gregory's work was to be shown in Amsterdam. The one in Stockholm had come about in another strange way. Apparently, there was a kind of brotherhood between some gallery owners in Europe. When this Swedish friend had discovered his pal was exhibiting this Indian sculptor's work, saw the brochure and photographs, and instantly thought up the idea of a show in Stockholm since the sculptures were to be in Europe anyway. Frantic calls were made to Neel. "As if I'd refuse!" he said.

I'd been listening quietly, watching his lips move, the animated expression on his face, the dimples come and go. I was very proud of him. For an artist of his age, it was truly an acknowledgement of his genius. Yet I could not suppress a kind of foreboding. Neel continued. He had been working round the clock to complete some smaller pieces for the exhibit. Nearly through now. He hadn't wanted to accept Rukmini's invitation, but she was his mother's schoolmate, and also a dear person. Yes, there was so much to do before his stuff was shipped out. He himself was leaving in six weeks. The way things were scheduled, he wouldn't be away more than two or three months. In between exhibitions he meant to do a great deal of sightseeing and research, things he had missed before. Then his uncle in the States was urging him to hop over from Europe for a visit. His voice changed suddenly, and he pulled me into a fierce embrace. "Piyal—I kept thinking—if only you were coming with me, it would be heaven. We could go to all your childhood haunts, see your favourite places." The words were muffled against my throat.

"Why can't I?"

"Oh, Piyal, what can I say? That's why I told myself not to come here tonight. For both of us, it's too wretched to meet and then tear ourselves apart, Piyal." He saw the look on my face. "Don't! Don't look like that!" He laid me back against the length of the sofa, and began to kiss me with desperate intensity. I closed my eyes willing myself not to think.

We were to have one more encounter before Neel left for Europe, this time at a fashion show. Robin was the official photographer for it, commissioned by Coquette, and I was a reluctant model. Needless to say, Ruhi was modelling too. I came in at the end in the show's piece-de-resistance because my height and carriage would show off the exotic number best, Lata had claimed. The compere took care to emphasize my so-called title, that of the designer of the dress, and the fact that the jewellery I wore was my own creation. It was after I had walked the length of the ramp, and duly twirled before walking back to stand in the centre of all assembled models that I saw Robin. He was the tallest there, of course, armed with his camera. My eye moved on, and stopped. My gaze locked with Neel's. I was jerked out of my detached state. I told myself bitterly that just being in the same room with him, surrounded by a host of people, was enough to crack my composure. I tore my gaze away.

Later, when the other models were being helped to change and remove their makeup, I walked away to be by myself where it was completely deserted, a long corridor with what must be rows of offices, now locked. What had brought Neel here? Fierce resentment burned in me. It wasn't fair for him to keep showing up. I still hadn't recovered from our last parting. Neel must be about to leave for Amsterdam now. At the end of the corridor, a figure instantly recognizable, loaded with stuff, halted outside a locked door. I was too close to beat a retreat. Neel unlocked the door, and began to carry in the bulky objects. He glanced up, and saw me standing there. How could I wait there like a dummy? I strolled forward very casually.

"Piyal." His eyes were running over me swiftly.

"What brings you to a Fashion Show of all places, Neel?"

"Francis was ill, and Robin needed an assistant urgently. I volunteered." He spoke jerkily. "You were—are incredibly beautiful."

"When—do you leave?"

"In two days."

A scant foot separated us. In his eyes I read the same agony of the approaching separation—the unchanging situation that always lay like a sword between us. Neel held out his arms, and I went into them. As I buried my face in his shoulder, lost in the warmth of the powerful frame, the familiar scent of him, I felt him shake with strong emotion. "Piyal," cupping my head with his big hand, "I—can't bear the thought of leaving the country—where you are. But what good is that? We mustn't have anything to do with each other in any case." His face twisted. "And there's nothing I can do to change it. But, oh God, how I miss you! You're with me all the time—when I'm awake—and in my dreams."

"I know—because it's the same for me."

We clung together in longing and grief.

That was the night I made up my mind. In those long hours when I lay awake, I remembered how Neel had wrenched himself away from me at last. This state of affairs had to end. As long as we lived in such proximity, it was inevitable that we would keep running into each other. The only solution was to remove the possibility of such meetings. In short, one of us had to go. Neel belonged here. It was his home. I was the newcomer, the interloper. I had to take myself away. There never would be a time like the present. Neel must not know. When he came back, he would find me gone. I was making the hardest most painful decision of my life, but I had no choice. Whatever the circumstances that kept us apart, they were unchangeable. And Neel would never disclose the truth. Perhaps, in time, my removal from the scene would bring us both peace. Our hearts would heal, and a new future begin. The ramifications were grave and wide. Drastic changes were indicated. Already a small possible opening had presented itself though I had not given it a second thought before. Now there was no time to lose. Tomorrow I would start enquiries.

15

Among the many friends I had kept in touch with, David Asscher was the most faithful about writing. He complained jokingly that his bride couldn't care less about jewellery or its design. A fine spouse for an Asscher, he wrote with wry humour. Katia was the daughter of the department store tycoon, Saul Aaronson. That fact notwithstanding, she was a most capable freelance journalist. If jewellery did not interest her, Katia's passion was painting and sculpture. Her father was an avid collector of both. David recounted many interesting amusing tales, but reading between the lines, it was obvious he was quite besotted with his wife. David and I often exchanged sketches of designs, and threw new ideas back and forth. It was an exercise I enjoyed. One time, I sent him clippings from a magazine which had covered a recent Fashion Show I had participated in. The close-ups detailed my work very well. Ruhi and I were the two models featured. David had been all admiration, discussing the ones he had specially liked. "Quite by chance, your letter and pictures were lying on my desk," he wrote, "when my pal, Quentin Wirth, happened to drop in. He took one look, and whistled. Was most interested in hearing all about you. You'll be tickled at what he said. 'Tell this princess she can come work for Danae any time!' Quent doesn't throw compliments around. You can take that as a genuine accolade." That was the item that had sprung to my mind now. I faxed David. Within a couple of hours, I had an answer. I was to send my CV, and a portfolio of my designs to be placed before the top brass at the New York headquarters of Danae. David had suggested that I despatch, if possible, actual samples of my design, and photographs of myself wearing some of them. That should work wonders, he claimed. I was to get on with it right away.

I did get on with it, and without delay. I mailed everything by Speed Post, except the box of jewellery samples. I had remembered Bhaiyya's friend mentioning he and his wife were to be in New York the following week. When requested to deliver my box to the Head Office, they had readily agreed. That done, I waited.

The next weeks were tense ones for me. I had asked no one's advice, told no one. This was purely my idea, born out of desperation. I had decided that if it failed, I would leave anyway. Once I arrived in New York, I could scout around on my own. If I succeeded, it would mean a giant step in my career.

Many thoughts gnawed at me. First, there was Daddy. I hadn't given him an inkling when we had our usual loving telephonic exchanges. By leaving, no, running away, I was going against my own resolution to be in India, within distance of my father. Then I couldn't imagine how I would tell Lata. To me, her kindnesses—and Bhaiyya's—had been legion. And Madhur. How was I to face her? Ruhi and Robin, my dear dear friends. A score of others who had become part of my life. I'd lie awake for hours thinking. I wasn't happy, though I didn't let it affect my work. If anything, my output doubled, but my state of mind must have shown because at least three people asked if I was on a diet. One, more discerning than the rest, guessed something was up.

So it was that one afternoon when I brought in a set of fresh designs, Madhur looked straight at me, and said, "Something's up, isn't it, Piyali? And it's bothering you very much. I think it's something you can't share with Lata. Will you remember if you want to unburden your heart that I'm here—and that I shan't pass it on to anyone else?"

I realize now how great was my need to confide in someone, to share my problem with a fellow human being. I knew Madhur well enough to be aware that behind that remarkable business acumen and great talent, lay a warm sensitive person. It all poured out as and when I could speak. There were details I omitted, of course, and Neel's name was not mentioned, nor his profession. When the telling was done, I sat back drained and limp with exhaustion. Madhur rang for coffee. She said nothing till it came, and I had gratefully drunk two cups of the hot beverage.

Then she said, "I guessed it was an *affaire du coeur*, Piyali, so I'm not surprised. I can't say what you're doing is the right answer to the problem. I've been through some hellish days myself. I would have stayed and fought this out. You say the man concerned is helpless to change anything. Since I don't know all of it, I shan't comment on that. Isn't there some way you can get to the bottom of this mystery? He need never know. At least you'll be able to go, knowing the true facts."

I was silent. Her words made excellent sense, but how could I take her advice? "I'll think about it, Madhur, though I haven't a clue about how to go about it," I looked at the finely featured face. "I feel so badly about letting you down. You've been so good to me. Set me on the right path. Boosted my career. Whatever I've achieved so far is due to The Honey Bee—which means you,"

"I won't deny this is going to be a tremendous loss, Piyali. It's good of you to say those nice words. I wish I could take full credit for your success which has been stupendous. The true fact is that The Honey Bee may have been your launching pad, but it was the brilliance of your work that did it." She smiled wryly. "To tell you the truth, Piyali, when your first designs sold out overnight, I was elated, of course, but in my heart, I wondered how long we would be able to keep you. I felt that one day, some international concern would snap you up. Yes, you told me about the Bombay jewellers who kept after you to join them.You didn't fall for their offers. Which company are you considering now?" When I told her, she was stunned. "Well, well!" And when I told her I hadn't received any confirmation yet, "Oh, you will! I'm sure you will!" She poured herself more black coffee. "As I was saying, I've kept my eyes open for possible substitutes for you, should the event arise." This was Madhur, the businesswoman talking. "I've tracked down two—one a man. Neither has your flair. They've been working freelance, and I think they'll snap up the chance to work here. Piyali, what if you don't get the expected offer?"

"I'll go anyway, Madhur. I can't stay on. I'm in a perpetual state of misery, and Ne—he is too. It's too much to bear, Madhur."

She reached across the table, and patted my hand. "It will be all right, Piyali. You'll make a new life for yourself." There was a lump in my throat. "Does Lata know?" I shook my head. "I see. Tell her. Yes, she'll hate the thought of losing you, but you'll be surprised how level-headed she can be. And maybe, she'll find the answers to some of those questions."

"I'll think about it," I rose to go. "I promise to complete a lot of designs before I actually leave. And, Madhur, thank you for being so understanding. I won't forget that."

"Good luck, Piyali—though I hate to see you go."

I did not tell Lata after all. I couldn't. Every time I made up my mind to do it, the words simply wouldn't come. I confess the delay in receiving word from David troubled me. Without the firm assurance of the job, I felt insecure. I wasn't worried about having to starve. That was one thing about being in America—one could work in any capacity, and no one would turn a hair. For instance, I could be a salesperson in a store there. Here in India, that would be impossible. But I wasn't breaking off in the middle of such a promising career in order to be reduced to something like that. So I waited each day in growing anxiety.

One other matter loomed very large. How and when should I tell Daddy? It didn't seem right to do it on the phone. Nor could I dare take time off now to go and see him. I must stay right here in Bombay in case David wanted to contact me urgently. Actually, a break would have been wonderful because I desperately needed some respite from the emotional stress I was undergoing. And then Daddy himself pulled a welcome surprise. It came without warning through a call from him. At first, he was jubilant enough to be incoherent, then it all came out. He had proposed at last, and Kanan had accepted! Tears came to my eyes. If anyone ever deserved happiness, it was my father. I let him finish, and then told him warmly how happy I was.

"You set the bali rolling, dearest child. Kanan says it was your conversation with her that opened her eyes to so many things." He laughed happily. "Will you believe it, Piyali, she's been in love with me for years, but thought it a hopeless attraction? And here I was, seeing her prcatically every day, and never daring to open my mouth till you paved the way!"

"It was bound to happen, Daddy. So what plans have you made?"

"None—till we consulted you. We both want it to be as quiet as possible, with as few people as we can get away with inviting. And, of course, we don't want to delay the wedding at all. Do you have any ideas?"

I thought rapidly. I had to consult Lata, for she would be very hurt if I didn't share the news with her. Besides, she was one who never lacked ideas. Daddy agreed readily to my plan, as long as I called him back soon.

Her initial surprise and pleasure notwithstanding, as might be expected, Lata came up with a plan right away. Why not have the wedding in Bombay? It would take care of their request for a small private wedding. Between the two of us, we could set it up with ease. I liked the idea very much. When I told Daddy, relief was uppermost in his voice. He said Kanan had been worried about Vijesh's family, and possible repercussions. This way they would come to know only after the marriage was a *fait accompli.* Kanan's children started vacation shortly, and would be able to attend. Daddy's gratefulness to Lata and me was immense. With Bhaiyya's full concurrence, preparations began in earnest.

Putting away my troubles for the moment, I was a happy witness to the nuptials along with the immediate family, Kanan's sister and brother, and her children. The latter's excitement knew no bounds. Uncle Tej was their adored friend, and the impending relationship thrilled them. Their first visit to Bombay was a marvellous experience.They were to stay with me while the newlyweds were away for a week, and I had planned all kinds of outings for them. At Daddy's request, and unknown to Kanan, Lata and I had a trousseau waiting. an exercise we enjoyed. No more widow's garb for her, I thought to myself more than once as we bought lavishly the most beautiful saris, and *salwar-kameez* sets, the choicest The Honey Bee had to offer.

When she met Kanan, Lata accorded Daddy's choice full marks. They were perfect for each other, she applauded. Yes, Uncle Tej had done well. It was true. Daddy looked years younger, and Kanan had blossomed into quiet beauty. For all of us gathered there, it was the most heart-warming satisfying experience to see these two united in holy matrimony.

Daddy had tears in his eyes when he held me after the wedding. I did too. There are times when no words are needed, and this was one of them. Embracing me, Kanan said with a catch in her voice, "If it hadn't been for you, we wouldn't be here today, Piyali." I laughed at that. "I'd love to take the credit, but I knew my dearest parent wouldn't be able to keep silent much longer!"

I held a hand each of the children as the bridal couple drove away laughing, and I thought to myself, it was rather strange, but these two were my family now. Looking down into the young faces turned up to me so trustingly, I found I rather liked it!

The week was so filled with seeing the sights that before we knew it the last day before Kanan and Daddy returned was upon us. We staggered home after visiting the zoo. Worn out with excitement, the children fell asleep the moment their heads touched the pillows. I flopped into a chair. I thought to myself it had been worth getting footsore, for my small companions had had a glorious time. I confess I had indulged them in many small ways from buying them trendy clothes to sampling all kinds of culinary delights Bombay offers. Such an opportunity would not come my way again. Besides, was I not a veteran of boarding school myself?

When the phone rang, I groaned. I wasn't in a mood for small talk. I put out a lazy hand to pick it up—and was galvanized by the pips that announce an international call. It was David.

Daddy was silent after I told him. I hated to spoil his joyous mood, yet it was too good an opportunity to miss. I had barely six weeks before I was due to report to Danae for an interview. He said heavily, "I've been afraid of this. I haven't been so preoccupied with my own affairs that I've missed noticing you didn't seem your usual self. I'm so proud of you, my sweet child. This Danae offer is a giant stride for you." He took my hand, and said quietly, "Are you in love, darling? Is it an unhappy love affair that is behind this urgent desire to get away? Is it?"

I looked at his dear face through a veil of tears. An exclamation broke from him. "My dear, what is it?" I went into his comforting embrace. "I'm ashamed my daughter has been in pain, and I haven't been able to help." Into his shoulder, I mumbled shakily, "You couldn't know, Daddy."

He held me away. "Piyali, I want to know. Tell me."

It wasn't that easy. This wasn't Madhur who accepted as much as I told her. My father asked searching questions. Wary as I was over the answers, he managed to squirrel out more facts than I intended to give him so that Neel's name, occupation and status came out. I told him about Neel's parents, and stopped there. To my relief, he did not probe further. Plainly, he was pleased that the man in my life was not a ne'er-do-well. That was one thing. I didn't need to be apologetic about Neel. Daddy could not fault his achievements, or object to his parents. In fact, he said so in actual words. What he found hard to take was the point about family objectons to marriage with me.

"A beauty like you, so talented, already a name at your age! And I can't see a darned thing wrong with marrying a princess! Sebastian did it!" indignantly, very much a Chandravats now.

"Probably, they'll want a bride for their only son from their own circle, Daddy. I'm just too different,"

"What kind of wishy-washy fellow is this anyway who can't put his foot down, and lets them lead him by the nose!" he demanded incensed, very much his daughter's defender. "Can I help, Piyali? Shall I go and see them or him?" I said hastily that none of them was in the country right now—which happened to be the truth fortunately. "So I lose my only child because of such foolishness!" he said wrathfully.

He calmed down eventually, but his feelings towards all Gregorys had not improved. I thought thankfully that by the time any of them returned, Daddy would be back amidst his apple trees. Seldom had I known him to be so upset. When they all left, he kissed me with tender warmth. "Be happy, darling. Look ahead. Things will come right again."

I could only nod as I blinked back my tears.

And I was left with Lata to face.

16

"Piyali?" I turned around, wishing people would leave me alone. Tara's green eyes searched my face. She said abruptly, "You're miserably unhappy, aren't you?" I was unable to answer. "I recognize the signs, you see. I've been through it all myself." My eyes questioned. Tara put a hand on my arm. "If you need a shoulder to weep on, you have one right here. No need to spell out the details, Piyali, but if I can help in any way—You're in love, I think, and things are going badly, I take it?"
"They couldn't be worse. And it's all over,"

"That's what I assumed about Lekh and myself. We faced crisis after crisis. Strangely, there was no quarrel between us. It all related to people close to us. I wouldn't wish that situation on anyone. It's too harrowing. Piyali, do you have serious clashes with this person?"

"No clashes or dissensions between us. I was so struck when you mentioned other people close to you being the reason for your separation. That's exactly how it is with us. Tara," I had to ask, "How did you learn the reasons which caused all the trouble between you?"

"Lekh told me. I was very direct. Said I'd been in England for years, and knew nothing about the Dhanraj involvement in anything. It took a lot of convincing, but I did it. That was when he told me—a bare outline, true, leaving many very vital clues out. But at least I had the basics."

"Oh, Tara," I said in despair, "at least he told you that much. N—won't say a word about it. All I know has been gathered from bits and pieces here and there. And I can't be sure if I'm making two and two add up to five. Lata will confirm some of it."

Tara leaned forward. "Does Lata know? About this whole affair, I mean?" I shook my head. "I'd share the problem with her, Piyali. She's absolutely trustworthy. Won't even tell Bhaiyya. She and I—well, we've kept secrets to avoid hurting him. I can tell you now Lata has been worried about you. Told me you seemed so unhappy," Tara touched my hand. "I know she's a wonderful sister—and I can always turn to her for anything. She has more than her share of practical wisdom. Tell her, Piyali."

With one more person urging me in that, what else could I do? I badly needed to talk to someone, and who better than these two caring persons? I would not be able to conceal names and identities, but what did that matter? Neel was lost to me. All I wanted now was the truth behind the whole story, no matter how dark the secret, and how heinous the part played in it by any of my family.

Tara was sitting quietly, waiting, giving me time to decide, not trying to influence me in any way. I met her eyes. "Do you know where Lata is?"

Tara was right. After the initial shock, Lata recovered quickly. "I understand so much now. I did suspect you might be in love—but never saw you with any one special individual though you've never lacked for escorts. I'm so terribly sorry, Piyali. And now you're leaving us." She dashed away a tear. "Madhur? Not a word to me. We'll miss you much. I've loved having my tall little sister around!" She listened to the rest in wonder, then became thoughtful, "We're not going to leave it dangling this way! We have to get to the bottom of this story—if we can. How? Leave that to me," firmly. Tara smiled at me.

I did not join in the converstion in the car, too keyed up about what might happen. Would we be told the truth at last? The greatest worry was the possible effect of our visit, any shock that might have an adverse effect on health and well-being. Neel would never forgive me. And here were Tara and Lata who had jointly come up with the plan seemingly quite calm. It was Lata who had phoned ahead, and asked to speak to Madame Nalin. And when that lady came on the line, Lata had asked in her most charming way if it was all right for her to drop in whenever Madame found it convenient. The initial response was hardly encouraging. Hesitation first, then a question about the reason for the proposed visit. Once again, Lata's persuasive charm came to the fore, and reluctant consent was obtained. Which was why we were now speeding toward our destination.

It was the companion, Kusum, who greeted us, and led us into the familiar sitting room. The rocking chair was unoccupied. We were asked about refreshments which we refused politely. Patently, Kusum was dying of curiosity, but went away to inform Madame of our arrival. I was all keyed up. The sound of slow footsteps alerted us so that by the time Madame entered, we were standing up. It was a moment fraught with tension. She looked at each one of us, clearly recognizing Lata and me, bowing courteously.

Lata said warmly, "Madame, this is very good of you. We appreciate it more than we can say. You've met my cousin, Piyali. This is my sister-in-law, Tara Sebastian."

Madame spoke for the first time. "Sebastian? Then you are Lekh's wife. Cressida sent me an invitation for your wedding. I read a magazine article about it. A princess from Sonal Mohur. You are as beautiful as your pictures. But I can't have three princesses standing in my honour! Please, please sit down." She seated herself in the rocker. "Has Kusum offered you refreshment? I see. Perhaps later then." I could see Tara taking in the fragile beauty of our hostess. Today she was in white, printed with tiny blue and pink flowers. She said to Lata, "The stole you sent me was very lovely—but I did not feel I deserved such a gift."

"Of course you did, Madame. Without your timely and gracious help, we would have been in serious trouble."

Madame's eyes moved from face to face. She said, "I confess to being rather alarmed. I welcome visitors. They bring me a glimpse of the outside world. I ask myself now though why three princesses would want to see a simple person like me. I get the feeling that this is Judgment Day—as if the Hour of Reckoning is at hand." The last was spoken whimsically, but she did not smile.

Tara replied quickly, "Madame, please believe the last thing we want is to disturb your peace of mind. We ask you to bear with us. Had it not been for the fact that someone is in great distress, we would not have dreamed of troubling you."

"I am very intrigued. How can an old woman who does not go anywhere be of assistance to this person?"

Lata spoke quickly. "Madame, we seek some information. If you can give it to us, it will clear up so many doubts. Our only fear is that it may disturb you to tell us." A flicker crossed the beautiful face. "Last time we were here, Madame, when you were so kind, we told you we were from Divyasthala, and you were very shocked. Your reaction bothered us very much." A delicate hand came up involuntarily to cover Madame's throat. "At that time, my cousin and I wondered why that should have been so. We guessed the name of the former princely state had some very unpleasant connotations for you. Our conclusion was that something—some event—took place there, and it was connected to our family—the then ruling family—and yours, Madame. It must have happened a long time ago, because we have never heard a word about it." Lata leaned forward. "Madame, we ask not out of idle curiosity at all, but because the lives—the future—of two young people are involved. And I promise you that whatever you tell us will remain in strictest confidence."

The snowy head went back to rest on the padded backrest, and the slim hand to cover the eyes. We exchanged worried glances. Other than a conventional greeting I had not spoken yet. Unable to sit still, deeply anxious, I crossed the room, and bent over the rocker. I said gently, "Madame, please do not distress yourself. May I fetch you some water? Are you all right?"

A long moment passed before she moved her hand and let it drop to her lap. She looked up at my face, and said shakily, "A Chandravats princess being so kind to me. No, I'm all right. Though very shaken." Her gaze moved to Lata. "Of what use will any information be?"

"You are thinking we may misuse the information? We shall not in any way. Our only purpose is to clear up doubts—and know the truth."

She murmured almost inaudibly, "Ye shall know the truth—but will it set me free?"

"To beg forgiveness if it is acceptable to you at this late juncture," I added.

A strange expression crossed her face. "I never thought to hear such words from a Chandravats. And for events that occurred before any of you were born." She rang a little bell by her side. "I think I will have some water after all." Iced water was brought for all of us. Madame drank deeply, then set her glass down. She said slowly, "You may not know this, but you are asking me to rake up my most painful memories which I have buried in the farthest corner of my mind for more than fifty years. No one has heard of them from my lips other than the most immediate family. But somehow—somehow I feel I can trust you." Then passionately, "But, oh, how painful it is going to be! You cannot imagine the anguish I feel over it!"

We were silent. Indeed, what could we say? Hardly breathing, we listened.

I suppose I should begin with my background. My brother and I were the children of the Principal of a famous English public school in Divyasthala. You must remember that this was still the British Raj when quite a few Indians went to England for higher studies. Papa held a B.A. from Oxford, and a Teacher's Diploma from London. T.D., they called it then, considered to be very prestigious. Papa was insistent about my receiving a good education. He sent me to an exclusive girls' school. With our sweet Mama, our very comfortable life style, we grew up in a happy home atmosphere. Nothing prepared me for what was to come.

When I was eighteen, an outstanding marriage proposal came for me. Offers had started coming in for two or three years, but the law in Divyasthala prohibiting girls from marrying before eighteen was strictly followed. It caused a lot of grumbling amongst families who wished to dispose of their daughters early, and especially when there were too many of them. Papa had waved away earlier offers. For his Romola, he wanted the best. I was his favourite, named after George Eliot's heroine. The offer that made him sit up and take notice came from no one less than Silvanus Nalin—and what an honour that was! Retired now, Mr Nalin had held the post in Divyasthala of what today would be Director of Education. The one on whose behalf the offer was being made was a worthy son of his father. Kushal Nalin belonged to that elite order, the Indian Civil Service—now the Indian Administrative Service. He was a brilliant young man with a most promising future. Papa did not hesitate. In the time-honoured way, the senior Nalins came to our home. I was very nervous, of course, but Mama had coached me well. The Nalins had seen me with my family at a Carol Service in church, and made enquiries about my identity. The next round brought Kushal Nalin himself. He came alone—and I was truly petrified. I need not have been. He was so gentle with me—so courteous to my parents. We listened with absorbed interest to his stories. He had been educated in England, and travelled widely in Europe. While he spoke, I took the opportunity to look at him, and I wondered why such a handsome young man, already Assistant Collector, who could have chosen any girl in the community, should have come to see me. At that moment he glanced up—and smiled at me—and won my foolish heart forever.

Madame stopped her narrative abruptly. We did not speak, caught up as we were in the drama unreeling before our eyes. Then with great effort, she went on.

I cannot tell you how happy we were in those first years of marriage. We loved each other to the depths of our beings. Kushal's parents had their own beautiful home where we often spent a few days. They were kind to me as if I were their own daughter. Which was fortunate because Kushal in his capacity as an ICS officer and later Collector for the British Raj (he was promoted soon after we were married), was often away on tour of the district under his jurisdiction. When he was absent, I missed him deeply, and waited for his return. Our daughter's birth was a joyous event. She was a bonnie baby, no trouble at all. Both sets of grandparents adored her. Sadly, I lost my parents within a short time of each other. Not long after, Kushal's father passed away. We comforted each other in our bereavement. Paul—my brother—had left Divyasthala—and had a flourishing medical practice. I used to visit him with the baby, and when he could get away, Paul came to us. Kushal's mother went to stay with two sisters who were also widowed.

As Collector, Kushal had his own spacious official house at the District Headquarters. He was also responsible for the collection of revenues from the princely state of Divyasthala. As the son of Silvanus Nalin, he knew most important people, but in his administrative capacity, he was in touch with officials of high rank connected to the running of the State, and therefore to the Palace itself. As representative of the British Raj, he attended formal occasions where Maharaja Digvijay Singh presided.

My time was divided between the two places. When Kushal was on tour, I went to Divyasthala, a journey of two hours by train, to see if all was well with the Nalin house. We had a couple of servants to keep it clean, and the garden tended. It made a change for the little one, and for me, because when Kushal was away, I missed him immensely. It was good to visit old friends, mine and those of my parents. In those days, domestic help was cheap and plentiful, so I always brought along my cook and the baby's ayah. I could leave her for short spells to go shopping or visiting.

One day, I went to see a former classmate who had just had a baby. I hired a *tonga* for the purpose. The *tongas* were not like the closed victorias one found in Bombay. These were two-seaters, rather small, quite open, except for an awning-like canvas cover for protection against sun and rain. Passengers sat with their backs to the driver so they faced the other way. I was homeward-bound when something very embarrassing happened—something no woman should be subjected to. Floating free, the *pallav* end of my sari was caught in a wheel of the *tonga*. I was all unaware until a sound of tearing fabric drew my horrified attention. The cloth was so firmly enmeshed in the big wheel that as we moved along, more and more of my sari ripped off my body. It was worse than anything that had happened to me before. If I called to the driver to stop, he would see me in this state. Stopping might bring a crowd of onlookers. In any case, the sari was irretrievable. No, the only line of action open to me was to keep going without any fuss, and hope fervently that none of the passersby would notice this woman clad in just a blouse and petticoat from which shreds of sari dangled. I kept my face down, praying we would reach home quickly.

And then I realized we were slowing down, and going off the road, coming to a standstill. I called out sharply to the driver to ask why we were stopping. He was clambering off his perch, leading the horse off the road. In an awed scared voice, he told me, "*Maharaj padhar rahe hain*, Mem Saheb. The Maharaja is about to pass by." That was when I noticed all traffic had indeed come to a halt, and vehicles lined up on either side of the road. And then I did the most foolish thing. I should have sat very still. No one would have spared me a glance. Acting on impulse in my state of confusion and shame, as the first car went by, I grabbed for the bundle of green grass placed by the driver's seat, and held it in front of me like a shield to cover my half-dressed state. The movement, when all else was so still, did not go unnoticed. How often have I blamed myself for that thoughtless act of mine. Faces from the

Rolls Royce that was passing at that moment turned to me. I wanted to sink down and die on the spot, for surely, this was the car where the Maharaja sat.

Looking back, I know I over-reacted. I was perfectly well-covered. Women wore longer blouses then that tucked into their petticoats, trimmed with lace or frills, the sleeves elbow-length or upto their wrists, nothing like the modern brief *cholis* which have plunging necklines, and large areas of back and midriff exposed. But most Indian women are innately modest, and one is supposed to keep one's breast covered. Social rules decreed such matters in our youth.

The cavalcade went on, and spectators let out their collective breaths, the driver hopped on, and our journey was resumed. I was shaking inside, for had I not been utterly disrespectful to the ruler of the state? And I the wife of Collector Nalin? Would there be repercussions? Oh, this was not like the old times when the Maharajas were all-powerful. The British had seen to that. Nevertheless, even if I were not to be cast in a dungeon, there were more subtle ways of punishment. My great fear was not for myself, a nonentity, but for my husband.

Somehow the journey ended. I dashed in, sending the fare out with the ayah. Respectably dressed again, I could not get the incident out of my mind. And the burning question was if I should tell Kushal. I could not do it ultimately. To my overwhelming relief, there were no repercussions. Not then. In fact—and this astonished me—I was invited by the Senior Maharani to join the Palace ladies in their own private quarters to celebrate the ruler's fifty-fourth birthday. Kushal, of course, always attended these festivities with other VIPs, but it was the first time, I had been invited. I was all in a flutter. What did one wear for such occasions? How did one behave? I had plenty to guide—and misguide me.

It was quite an experience. I did not know a soul. The Senior and Junior Maharanis were gracious to me. In the privacy of their women's quarters, the ladies, noblewomen, no doubt, had their heads covered, but not their faces. They wore the most beautiful clothes, very ornate and in brilliant hues, gold embroidered, the jewellery worth a king's ransom. I felt like a sparrow among peacocks. What I wore—and it was my best—was very modest beside their splendour. There was singing and dancing. For the latter, some of the ladies would rise and join in, the others clapping to the beat. We sat on thick mattresses covered with spotless snowy covers, bolsters to lean on. I overcame the feeling of strangeness, and took it all in with interest.

The only men present were a couple of elderly musicians who accompanied the songs and dances. I wondered how Kushal was doing. For him, of course, it was nothing new. And then there was a stir. Every lady rose swiftly to her feet when the announcement came. The Maharanis went forward to bow before the ruler and the young Yuvraj. They were in splendid garb with gleaming silk turbans, and glittering jewels. I learnt later they were the only males who ever entered in here.

Escorted to honoured seats, the best items were presented. We ladies had resumed our seats. I took care to sit so that I was half-hidden. The Yuvraj was very young, not more than fifteen. He chattered boyishly with the Junior Maharani who was his mother. The ladies watched him fondly. The Maharaja's gaze swept the assembly keenly. When it fell on me, I felt like a butterfly on the end of a pin. I had lowered my gaze at once, my heart beating very fast. Doubtless, H.H. was amazed that a commoner should be in this noble assembly. I told myself he could not possibly have recognized that distraught creature in the *tonga.* To my great relief, in a short while, the men rose to leave. I remember little of the rest of that celebration.

Madame Nalin paused. No narrator had a more captive audience than she. It appeared that this part of the story had made for fairly easy telling, but whatever was about to come was causing difficulties. From the restless movements of her delicate hands, we saw the memories were extremely painful. Yet how could we leave the story unfinished even though it smote us to see her plight? I knew my companions were as tense as I was, not knowing what was about to be revealed. With effort, Madame resumed.

For two or three years now, Divyasthala had been subjected to great harassment by a gang of dacoits. Their leader, Bhairav Singh, was an evil ruthless man, totally without a conscience. The gang had started on a small scale, raiding remote villages, killing anyone who resisted, looting, and then on departure, setting fire to the flimsy huts. These, however, were small pickings. Becoming greedier, the gang began making forays into small towns, also attacking travellers on the highways under cover of darkness. It was a very serious situation, and the public demand was for drastic action. Certainly, there had been encounters with the police, with many killed on both sides.

One day, Kushal announced he was leaving for Divyasthala. The Maharaja had summoned him and other leaders to discuss the dacoit menace. I told him that the baby and I might as well go with him. When Kushal came back from the meeting, he was very thoughtful. He told me little, but did mention that one avenue they had decided to explore was the possibility of holding talks with Bhairav Singh. No doubt, he would make exorbitant demands in exchange for peace, but it was well worth investigating.

The first conference was followed by a lull, and then another one was called. As Collector, posted out of Divyasthala, the matter did not fall within Kushal's purview. Yet, he was a long-time resident of the kingdom, and the Nalins had lived there for three generations. It seemed that the dacoit leader had agreed to meet the Maharaja's representatives. He had chosen the meeting place in rugged hilly terrain. One condition was that they come without armed escort. The last created a furore. The man was not to be trusted, most people said vehemently. Oh, but he would not dare to harm the ruler's chosen emissaries, others claimed. Still, the majority agreed on the wisdom of posting a guard in the vicinity. Of the four men selected for the confrontation, three were senior highly respected leaders. The fourth was Kushal.

I wept and clung to my husband, begging him not to go. He laughed at me, made light of my fears, and said he would march back like a conquering hero. Besides, H.H. had personally requested him to go. Thus was Maharaja Digvijay showing his esteem for the young Collector.

Madame fell silent. We did not utter a word, or move. Then with supreme effort, she went on.

Bhairav Singh—had planned his answer to the Maharaja. The four didn't have a chance. They were ambushed—shot to death. That was how—my Kushal—was brought home to me. . . .

I could not sit still any more. I went and knelt by her, took her cold hands in my warm ones. "Madame, please don't distress yourself," I begged, chafing them. She looked at me with tears in her eyes, and I folded her in my arms, saying nothing, just holding the frail form shaking with a grief she had carried with her for five decades and more. It seemed to comfort her, for she stayed there, one hand clasping my shoulder. Behind me, I sensed movement, and knew Lata and Tara had risen to their feet. When Madame moved at last, I loosened my hold. She laid a hand against my cheek, and said in a trembling voice, "You are so good and kind to me." I said, "No, I'm not. Are you all right, Madame?" She nodded. Lata said, "Tea is on its way. I took the liberty of asking for it, Madame."

She said in wonder, "I never thought princesses could be so—informal—kind—like anyone else."

Tara told her dryly, "It's this generation, Madame. My grandmother abhors my so-called flouting of all norms. But she's resigned to it now,"

Kusum came in bearing a tray. It was a welcome interruption.

Madame certainly needed a cup of tea, and so did we. She seemed much better, I was glad to see. Kusum appeared delighted to be in our company, and to look at us from close quarters. When it was time to clear the cups away, and depart, she did so with patent reluctance. We were relieved to see Madame looking more her usual self, but the strained look in her eyes still remained. Clearly, the ordeal of going on with her story weighed heavily upon her. Valiantly, she went on.

The grief, the sense of utter loss I felt over my beloved husband's death was accompanied by a feeling of outrage, of bitterness against the man responsible for it. Kushal had been only thirty-three with a brilliant career ahead of him. I could not get over the waste of such a precious young life. And the three other very worthy men of achievement and stature had died with him. And, after all, they had not come even near completing their mission. The public in Divyasthala was outraged. Wrapped in my grief, I did not care what was being said, or what new ideas were being tossed around for further action against the dacoits.

Paul was wonderful, a source of great strength to me. He took me back, and I stayed with him and his wife for several months away from Divyasthala. Kushal's mother lived in the same city, and I visited her frequently. The shock of her only son's death caused her to lose her memory. She could recall nothing of the past, and was aware only of the present—which I suppose was a blessing in disguise. My baby—she was three now—was my one solace.

Life goes on. Six months months later, I forced myself to return to Divyasthala. There were so many matters to attend to, and a decision to be made about the Nalin house.

It was painful in the extreme to enter the home where we had been so happy. Every room echoed with Kushal's voice, his laughter, his footsteps. I told myself sternly to behave as Kushal would have wanted me to. The house was still cleaned regularly, and I was able to set to work, going through stacks of papers that had belonged to my father-in-law, the contents of cupboards, a thousand little tasks and big ones. This time, I had left the baby behind with Paul and Vera. I knew I would have little time for her. They loved her dearly, and she was very attached to both. I had slipped into Divyasthala so quietly that none of our friends knew I was back. I was able to devote all my energy to the cleaning up process. Until one morning. . . .

A servant came running to announce a visitor. He looked rather scared. I went into the sitting room. This most unexpected guest was someone I had not seen before. He was very polite, and said he had come on behalf of His Highness. The mention made me shudder, but I listened. A fully staffed house had been arranged for me. I was to move in at once. Bewildered, I said I had no need of a house when I had this one. In any case, I had no plans to stay on in Divyasthala, and was here just for a few days. For the first time, a gleam appeared in his eyes. He indicated with well-chosen but subtle words that H.H. would not accept a refusal. And at last, his meaning penetrated my dull mind. I felt the walls caving in on me. This could not be happening to Romola Nalin—this—this unspeakable disgrace.

Beside me, I felt the quiver that ran through Lata's frame, and Tara's hands clenched into fists. In my heart, a slow burning anger began to build. A long pause before Madame went on.

I—shan't dwell too long on what followed. I wanted to die. Indeed, I thought of it often. Only the thought of my child stayed me. Paul was helpless. He could not even meet me. Very rarely, I managed to get someone to post a letter to him, though no reply would ever reach me. What shall I add? So many things became clear to me now. The most hideous doubt in my mind related to Kushal's death. Had he been chosen deliberately to act as an emissary with the almost certain possibility that Bhairav Singh would kill him and his companions? I could not ever dare to ask.

I lacked for nothing. Every luxury was heaped upon me. All of it sickened me. I was a prisoner in a gilded cage. At first, I wept continuously. At some point, the human mind begins to accept even the worst with resignation. I endured the beautification rites the maids put me through under instructions from an older woman, my knee-length hair always left loose, perhaps entwined with pearls or jewels. In rich attire, *kohl* for my eyes and attar of roses which I had never used before, I felt exactly what I was—a courtesan, a kept woman, a pampered perfumed toy for the pleasure of a king. I felt besmirched, wanting to scrub myself with a wire brush till the blood ran. I could not even pray for succour though I tried several times. How fully I understood why in the Psalm the Israelites taken in captivity to Babylon cried, "How can we sing the Lord's Song in a strange land?" I was still in Divyasthala where I had lived all my life, but it was an alien land to me now.

In all truth, H.H. treated me with every consideration. More, he was gentle, even tender. He talked with me for hours, saying I was the first woman he had met who could carry on an intelligent conversation with him. He brought me gifts chosen with care—a jewelled gold watch, French perfumes, small objets d'art. Because I loved books, a regular supply of the latest was delivered. He took delight in choosing jewellery especially suited to me. He told me much later, I was the one woman he had ever loved though he was old enough to be my father, that he had seen me in the *tonga*, and been unable to believe anyone could be so beautiful. That was why he had asked the Collector and his wife to be invited to his birthday celebrations. Then he could see for himself whether his eyes had deceived him or not.

In my bitterness and shame, grieving for my husband, longing for my child, I told myself, if there was a God, He had forsaken me. I was twenty-three, and already more suffering had fallen to my lot than most people endured in a lifetime. And then, Divine intervention brought me deliverance.

Late one afternoon, at the time when most people were having a siesta, a great commotion erupted on the streets. Shouts, cries of disbelief, loud weeping caused every occupant of the house to rush outside past the armed guards. I did not go out, of course, but from a front window, words reached me clearly. Maharaja Digvijay Singh was dead. A massive heart attack while playing golf had felled him. So far out on the golf course, by the time medical aid reached him, it was too late. Suddenly, the stunning reality flashed upon me. I could not know if my life was in danger, but my position had become impossible. I had to get away immediately. In the end, it was surprisingly easy. Expecting to be caught, my heart in my mouth all the time, I slipped out when no one was looking, wearing the most unobtrusive clothes I could locate, no easy task I found. I had a little money of my own, and I took nothing—not the closetfuls of gorgeous clothes, the jewels, the beautiful gifts lavished on me. The servants and guards were still on the street, standing with people who discussed the changes imminent in the kingdom, speaking in low voices. No one noticed the woman who slipped out of a side gate. By avoiding the main roads, and keeping to lanes and alleys, my sari pulled low over my head and face, I managed to reach the railway station. A train was just leaving. I didn't care where it was going. My one thought was to get beyond the boundaries of Divyasthala. And I did.

Complete silence reigned after the low voice ceased. Madame lay back in the rocker. Strangely, instead of looking exhausted, she looked as if relieved of a burden carried too long. I was glad to see it. Anxiety for her well-being had been an ever-present companion for me.

Lata said at last, "Madame, we are more grateful than we can say. What more can we add except to ask forgiveness for your immense loss, and the terrible experiences you had to undergo at the hands of our kinsman?"

"You mustn't say that. These things happened before you were born, and you played no part in any of it. And, do you know, though the telling was as painful as I had expected, now I feel—at peace. If only my Kushal had not been taken away—that's the one bitterness that remains. I've had a richly satisfying life since then, and am very content. I don't ask for more." Unexpectedly, her eyes twinkled. "Except perhaps to see my great grandchild."

"You've been splendid about not letting the past blight your family's life!" Tara exclaimed.

"Hardly splendid," was the wry response. Then soberly, "But I'm afraid it did have an impact on my daughter. Jana avoided marriage till she was almost thirty. If Denzil Gregory hadn't swept her off her feet, things would have been very different. And then, I wouldn't have had my adored grandson." It was fortunate that Madame was not looking at me. My expression would have given me away at once. "He is so much like Kushal in looks, though much larger in physique like his own father. He has Kushal's facial features, and devastating smile—with dimples, no less," she said smiling herself. "But his eyes are like mine. Jana insisted on his second name being Kushal. Nothing could have thrilled me more."

"He's married, of course?" glibly from Tara.

Madame shook her head. "Not yet. His career has been all-important, you see. But I wish he would take it seriously, or I won't be here to see his children. By all accounts, there are plenty of girls in hot pursuit of him. I rather suspect he's waiting for someone truly special. I do wish he'd find her though before too long." She smiled reminiscently. "When his parents were away so much, he lived with me, so we are very close. Such a darling boy, all curly-haired mischief, but also loving and thoughtful towards me. Busy as he is, he always makes time to come and see me. As for his talent, I was the one who realized it first, and encouraged him. And today, I'm so proud of him—as Kushal would have been."

"You have every reason to be proud, Madame." Lata rose to her feet. "We've taken so much of your time—and hope we haven't tired you out. You will rest now, won't you?"

"Oh, must you go?" in some dismay. "Another cup of tea perhaps? I see. You were such patient listeners. I still can't get over my three royal visitors. You didn't mind what I said about—H.H.?"

"Not only didn't mind, but had far more pungent thoughts about him than we can say,"

Madame stood up. "Let me walk with you to your car.

Outside, she shook hands with Tara and Lata, but both kissed her warmly. She was visibly moved at that. When it was my turn, she lifted her face to gaze at mine. "For the first time, I feel I missed a great deal by not also having a granddaughter to raise."

I bent to hug her. "Madame," I managed to say, half choking, "I shan't be seeing you again. I—I'm leaving the country—for the States. It's been wonderful to meet—and know you. I shan't ever forget you." Dismay on her face, she reached up to place a hand on my head. "I'm truly sorry to know that. My dear dear child, I shan't forget you either," She drew my head down, and kissed me tenderly, holding me close. "Bless you, sweet one. *Vaya con Dios.*" Tears blinded me when I stepped away. Somehow I made my way down the steps, and took my seat by the driver. A last wave to the white-clad figure, and we were on our way.

17

After hearing Madame Nalin's story, the name Divyasthala made me shudder. Lata confessed to feeling the same. In time, this subsided. The association notwithstanding, commonsense told us that, after all, it was foolish to blame the place when it was a person who had been wholly responsible for those demonic actions. Now a strange compulsion drove me to visit Divyasthala once again before I left. With Daddy's advice, I made my plans. He had called Uday Singh to ask if I could come, and received a reprimand. Was that a question to ask, demanded the man who was the present ex-Maharaja. Piyali just had to walk in any time, and be assured of being welcomed home.

Mixed as my feelings were, I was left in no doubt of my welcome. The question of how to greet Uday Singh, who, after all, apart from his lofty status, was also the oldest member of the clan, was taken care of by that personage himself. He embraced me as Daddy would have done, with unaffected warmth, and then held me away to take a good look at me.

"You do credit to the House of Chandravats, my dear. Hmmm. I see a fleeting resemblance to my aunt, Uttara Devi. She didn't have your height, of course," eyes twinkling, "nor your poise. If this is what a Swiss schooling does, then I regret not having sent that imp of a granddaughter of mine to some Alpine boarding school!" He turned to his wife who had been standing by. "Urvashi, here's little Piyali, Tej's daughter."

She kissed me on both cheeks. "Except that she's not little any more! My dear, I can't tell you what a pleasure this is! Yes, even in

Divyasthala, it's very well known that two Chandravats princesses have made their mark in a place no less than Bombay. And I've seen your pictures modelling Suvarnalata's outfits. Beautiful!"

Later over the tea cups, and with my newly acquired knowledge, I tried to visualize Uday Singh, this distinguished cultured man with the strong features as a young lad in his early teens attending a celebration in honour of his father's birthday at the exclusive chambers of the Maharanis. Had he noted, or had he completely overlooked in his innocence, the beautiful young woman who was an invited guest whose name was Romola Nalin? And in the events that followed after Kushal Nalin was killed, was the youthful Yuvraj sheltered from the knowledge of his sire's actions? Probably, I would never know the answer, I thought, as tea was served in Spode cups by a bowing turbaned man servant in Palace livery. And as Urvashi Devi brought me up-to-date on family affairs, I wondered if she, so gracious and exquisitely-mannered, her simple pastel chiffon sari, and single strand of pearls not concealing the fact of who she was, had ever heard of her royal father-in-law's behaviour? I had not spent enough time in family circles to know how such a situation might be regarded then—or now. Did the clan generally take such liaisons in their stride, assuming that a monarch must have his indulgences, as kings have had since the beginning of civilization? Yet there had been circumstances which surrounded this particular liaison, heinous, shocking, which should have stunned every member of the clan.

I came back to the present, forcing myself to listen to my hostess. Mayurika was here, she was saying, referring to her granddaughter who was a couple of years my junior. She attended college now. From the way she spoke, Rika was a favourite, high-spirited, and a chatterbox. In my turn, I mentioned how eager I was to see some antique heirloom jewellery which might perhaps inspire my own designs. Urvashi Devi's eyes lighted up with interest. Of course, I could see whatever there was in the Palace at present. This was very exciting, she exclaimed. She had many questions about my work, and Suvarnalata's, but they would keep till I was rested.

Later, in the chamber allotted to me, I stood before the long narrow window overlooking the gardens below. I breathed deeply of the warm air. So here I was under my ancestral roof. Not a sentimental journey, for I had come with a purpose. In the three days I had spared, I had to uncover secrets hidden for decades. They were to be shared with no one except Lata and Tara, but for my own peace of mind, and to fit in the last missing pieces of the story, I had to know. In this, though I did not know it then, I was to have a willing, if unsuspecting helper.

Someone rapped on the open door. I turned to see a girl in jodhpurs, shirt and riding boots, hair in a pony tail. Before I could open my mouth, she said breathlessly, "I'm so terribly sorry to be late! I just got a terrible wigging over it! I forgot my watch, and the time simply flew! It's terribly ill-mannered of me, I know. You will *forgive* me, won't you?" By now, I had identified her. Since she hadn't waited for me to get in a word, I simply waited for her to run out of breath. She seemed to be many years younger than I was, I thought wryly. A cute face, large eyes, and a tilted nose added to the effect. ". . . and I'm not to call you by your name because you're an aunt, sort of, Gran said. But I don't feel you're an aunt at all! Even though I'll have to look up *at* you, it's not like looking up *to* you—if you know what I mean! I'm terribly impressed now that I've met you—you're terribly beautiful—and clever—and talented. I couldn't wait to see if you looked like your photographs. And you do—but even better!" Her lungs no doubt protesting, she came to a full stop. Then as if just remembering a lapse, said lamely, "I'm Rika."

What else could I do except laugh aloud? This pert little person—I had the advantage of some eight inches over her—had taken me out of my introspective mood. I told her to call me Piyali, and when she worried about what her grandmother would say to such disrespect, I made her grin when I said, "Tell her I'm too Americanized, and won't have it any other way."

From then on, Rika was my constant companion. It was she who took me on a conducted tour of the Palace and grounds. From her running commentary, I culled much information about family history. Whenever she mentioned Digvijay Singh, I pricked up my ears. Very gradually, a composite picture of him emerged, the details of which added up to an individual nothing like the one my imagination had conjured up. This man had been a benevolent ruler, and social reformer. In a time not noted for justice to women, he had decreed that every girl in the kingdom be given at least primary education; raised the age of marriage for girls to eighteen; built hospitals, schools and orphanages; established a system whereby clean drinking water was available for everyone. The network of good roads that had been laid in his time still existed today. A university founded after his death was named in his honour to commemorate his splendid contribution to the cause of education. Under the non-stop flow of words, I detected immense pride on the part of this granddaughter.

"Rika, is there a portrait of him I can see? And of other Chandravats? I'm woefully ignorant, having been away most of my life."

Twenty minutes later, having studied several portraits with interest, and having noted certain definite points of resemblance to various members of the family, including Lata's father, I was standing in front of the painted likeness of Digvijay Singh. I felt a tremor go over me. It must have been painted while he was still in his twenties, but even then, strength of character showed in the square chin, the direct gaze, and the firm mouth. He was standing, one hand holding an open book, the other a book mark. The resemblance to Daddy was marked, and he must have had a commanding height like so many Chandravats men. And at least one woman—myself. It gave me the strangest feeling that we should share this one physical trait. For this formal portrait, Digvijay Singh was in thigh-length brocaded coat, *churidars*, silk turban, and a heavy gold chain from which hung a pendant of unusual design which caught my trained eye.

". . . a better one in Grandpapa's study," Rika was saying. "This one's okay, but I like the other. It was done while he was the Maharaja."

I murmured I would surely see it sometime. I needed time to absorb all that I had seen and heard. The truth was that I was weary. Travel fatigue was catching up with me. I excused myself, and went upstairs to my chamber. On the huge bed with its drifts of silk curtains, looped back for the daylight hours, I lay down. The relaxed posture of my body, and my closed eyes were deceptive. My mind was weighing everything Rika told me. Was it accurate, or had it been inspired by awe and admiration for her hero? The only way to confirm her story was to talk to Uday Singh himself, and perhaps to Urvashi Devi on the subject.

"I'm not the man my father was," Uday Singh said ruefully, "or any of my forefathers for that matter. Yes, I'm aware times had changed by the time I became Maharaja, and I no longer had the authority he had had. He was one of those rare people—a man of vision. I've often wondered what other great plans he had for his people had he lived the full span of his years. I was just sixteen when he died—a shocking event—and an irreparable loss to Divyasthala—and I'm sorry to say, I hadn't really appreciated him fully. One doesn't, you know, till it's too late."

We were in the big comfortable book-lined room which was his office-cum-library. My hosts had carried me off here after dinner, for, as they said, if Rika was around, no one could get in a word edgewise. Quite unabashed, that individual had grinned impishly, said there was a terribly exciting serial on TV which she never missed, and went off jauntily with a wave all around.

"Did you know him, Auntyji?" I asked.

Urvashi Devi shook her head. "No, I regret to say. We weren't married for two years after he died. But Uday's mother who was the Junior

Maharani—and the Senior Maharani—both spoke of him for years, so I have always felt I knew him."

My eye went to the big portrait of Digvijay Singh. It had caught my eye the minute we entered the room. I had gone straight upto it. With a sense of shock, I realized it was this older man whom Romola Nalin had known. A little heavier than when he had posed for the other painting, there was much more character on his face here. He was seated on a throne-like chair, hands loosely clasped, with a half-smile on his lips. One of the heavy rings he wore now adorned his son's hand. His head was bare, the hair just lightly touched with frost at the sides.

"There are statues and busts of my father everywhere in Divyasthala. I think the best one is an equestrian one on the grounds of Maharaja Digvijay Singh University here in the Capital. And a fine portrait in their Convocation Hall," Uday Singh said behind me. The opening I needed had thus presented itself, and the talk went along the lines I had hoped it would take. It continued as we drank our after-dinner coffee which the man servant had served us with great ceremony. "Dev Bhaiyya tells me you are brilliant in financial affairs, Uncleji, and a stockmarket whiz."

"Devendra says that? Then it must be true." His eyes twinkled. "Coming from him, I take it as the opinion of one who stands out as a shining example to all princely scions."

"And how is dear Dev?" Urvashi Devi was asking. "We haven't met since last year. What were his reactions to his sister's marriage? I've been waiting to hear all about it, and about the wedding."

I regaled them with a spirited account of it which had them laughing.

Uday Singh asked, "And does Piyali mean to follow in Tara's footsteps?"

The question pierced me. "I don't know," I said at last. "But eventually, I hope so."

"One hardly needs to ask if there's anyone special. With those spectacular looks, I'm sure you come in for a great deal of male attention in Bombay," Urvashi Devi said.

I shrugged. "I suppose so."

"Tell us about Tej's marriage. Were you happy about it? Is she a nice woman?"

I gave a glowing report which seemed to relieve both of them. They looked forward to meeting Kanan when Daddy brought her home for a visit, they said.

"I've been a little disturbed about stories that have come to my ears about Devendra being estranged from his grandparents. God knows they aren't the easiest people to get along with. I haven't liked some things reported to me by Lata's mother. Yet Dev was the adored grandson. As I've heard it, it concerns something which happened a long time ago, and which he came to know recently." Uday Singh paused as if waiting for my comment. I said nothing. "A great pity Lata couldn't have sons, of course, and that has been a bone of contention, I know. Even in these days when the princely states no longer exist, this is still important. No, Devendra should have had a son."

The image of a young boy flashed in front of my eyes so like Bhaiyya and Tara that every line of face and form declared him to be a Dhanraj.

"Lata has never mentioned any details to me except that the grandparents had wanted Bhaiyya to marry again." They both nodded as if this was not new to them. I said casually, "But then rumours true or false always float about, don't they? I believe, in the old days, courts used to be hotbeds of gossip." Uday Singh was smiling. "Why, will you believe it, we've even heard a tale about Maharaja Digvijay?" I put my cup on the tray, and raised my eyes. On Uday Singh's face, there was comprehension. Would he explode with anger at the slur upon his revered father's name? I waited a little apprehensively, for it took him a moment to answer.

"This tale—if it's the same one I think it is—isn't a false one, Piyali. And you can't know how sorry I am to admit that. Did you hear of it from Tej?"

I shook my head. "Daddy is the most loyal of Chandravats. He told me nothing."

Uday Singh said wearily, "Yes, Tej is that. But one can't deny a fact of history. If my father is remembered for his great deeds and achievements, he still did something so reprehensible—Where did you hear of it, Piyali?"

I told myself to be very careful now. "Lata and I ran into a lady somewhere. When she heard we were from Divyasthala, she seemed to recall something most unpleasant associated with it. We were dismayed—and intrigued, unable to imagine what it could be. You know how charming Lata can be. She coaxed it out of her."

"And you were completely shocked."

I nodded. "But I wonder if she was mistaken about certain factors. I would really like to know, and so would Lata." And when they asked me to specify, I did so, for after all, how could they guess what we had been told?

"It was the one act on my father's part," Uday Singh said slowly, "that I have never been able to fathom. It was so unlike him. Call him what you will, he was not a cruel man, not a womanizer, nor a lecher preying on young girls. No," in answer to my question, "I don't recall seeing the woman—but I'd met the husband more than once. To my youthful eye, he was very handsome; highly intelligent, of course, to have reached where he did at that young age. I admired his height and fair skin. His was an old Divyasthala family, had status and respect. Likewise the young woman's family. Their fathers had been distinguished educationists. If I hadn't come across my mother crying one day, I wouldn't have known anything about it. Her weeping made a deep impression on my mind. But I loved my father—worshipped him. I was truly confused."

Urvashi Devi added, "Uday's mother told me the woman had extraordinary beauty. They had seen her at some women's get-together." She glanced at her husband. "I've often thought—well, the attraction must have been so overwhelming, the Maharaja lost all sense of right and wrong—simply gave in to temptation."

Uday Singh had risen to his feet. He took a restless turn around the room, and came back. "And for that, four men died. A child was left fatherless. A marriage destroyed. A young woman left a widow. And as a final touch, her reputation trampled in the dust. I cannot condone it, Piyali. For me, it has overshadowed all his good deeds."

We were all silent. Then I asked, "Does anyone know—what happened to the woman?"

He shook his head. "No, she simply vanished. For a long time after my father's untimely death, there was so much confusion, no one gave her a thought. When at last the chamberlain in charge reported her disappearance, and wished to know what to do with the house and contents, the Staff, my uncle who acted as Regent till I achieved majority, ordered everything to be dismantled."

Urvashi Devi added, "For some years, a story floated around that she had committed suicide. There was no proof to give the rumour credence."

We sat quietly, thinking sombre thoughts.

I said into the silence, "Speaking hypothetically, Uncleji, suppose someone from that family showed up here in Divyasthala—how would you react?"

"Oh," he exclaimed, "I would welcome him or her! I cannot make amends for another's actions, but I can do my bit by being cordial."

"You're very good and noble about this, Uncleji."

"No, I'm not, Piyali. Part of it would be selfishness on my part. It would relieve me of a weight I've carried all these years."

I thought with a pang of Madame Nalin. What would she think of such words? I wish I could have told her. What use to speculate? We would not meet again.

"One last question which has been nagging me. What happened to Bhairav Singh?"

"Ah, yes. It happened a few months after I became the Maharaja. After the horrendous murder of those four men, public revulsion against him had reached such a degree that groups of vigilantes were formed. They went at it on a war footing, training themselves to shoot. These were respectable citizens, but such was the anger in their hearts that they took on their new roles with total dedication." Uday Singh paused. "Bhairav Singh was killed one night in a shootout when the gang was on one of their raids. You can imagine the jubilation that followed. The gang? It fell to pieces without its leader. There was no one who could compare in leadership qualities to Bhairav Singh. The dacoits who were wounded that night were brought to justice, of course. The rest drifted away, I would guess, for the kingdom was freed from that particular menace for all time."

I sat back to ponder over this, and could not help sighing again over the earlier events which had brought so much tragedy in their wake.

That night I went to bed a little lighter in spirit. My visit to Divyasthala would not resolve the situation between Neel and myself, but my knowledge of the man long gone who was in a convoluted sense responsible for our separation had vastly increased. Added to that was the feeling of homecoming to our ancestral place, made all the more precious by the warm welcome from my kinfolk. More than ever before, I was conscious of my Chandravats heritage. I was proud to be a member of this noble clan.

If I had achieved what I had set out to do by coming here, one more aspect of the case was revealed to me in quite an unbidden manner. I had busied myself taking photographs of the Palace and grounds, of the portraits, with special care of one particular subject, and the jewellery which Urvashi Devi so kindly displayed for me. For some of the detail on certain intricate pieces, I had made quick sketches. I was trailed by Rika everywhere who chattered on regardless, of course. I lent only half a ear to most of what she said, but after I was done with the camera work, she said something which brought back my full attention.

Hesitantly, "Piyali, would you care to see a very special collection?" She glanced over her shoulder. "Grandma won't like this. It's terribly hush-hush, you understand?" I waited indulgently. "Have you heard the story about Grandpapa's father—and his—well, mistress?" My face must have shown my shock, but after a moment, I nodded. "Oh, you have?" in relief. "Well, this stuff belonged to her. Grandpapa's mother passed it on to Mummy, and she to me. It's never been used by any of us, you see. I mean, how could it be? It's terribly awkward. But I have it upstairs in my safe."

I said, "Lead on, Macduff," hoping Rika had missed the quiver in my voice.

For once, Rika's flow of words lessened. She brought out a casket from the safe after locking the door. Against the red velvet backdrop of Rika's bedspread, a profusion of the most exquisite jewellery lay in scintillating loveliness. All of it was of most delicate design, not one as ornate as some of those I had seen in Urvashi Devi's collection. Yes, I thought, H.H. must have chosen these himself to match the beauty of the woman he loved. A slender gold chain from which hung a single sapphire caught my eye. I could picture Romola wearing it, and the tiny earrings that formed a set, blue fire catching the light. There were tiny flacons of French perfumes from which a faint fragrance still emanated, and which surely must be collectors' items. A beautiful painted Chinese fan. A pair of jewel-studded powder boxes. A set of tiny animals wonderfully crafted in blown glass.

". . . wondered why she didn't take any of this. Piyali, do you think the story that she killed herself is true?"

"No, I don't think so. And I think that the fact she didn't carry off anything speaks volumes about the nature of their relationship, and about her character."

"Oh, it does!" fervently. "They say she was always so sad. That's what the servants reported later—when it was all over. She'd sit for hours just staring out of the window. I think that's terrible, don't you, to be so unhappy?"

"Yes, it is terrible," huskily.

"Don't you want to take photographs of this jewellery?"

"No. I've run out of film." It was the last thing I would want to do, tantamount to prying into someone's deepest most secret grief. "You were kind to show it to me, Rika. I appreciate it."

"I seldom look at it, you know. It makes me feel terribly sad—and rather ashamed—though why I should be, I don't know."

"I know the feeling exactly, Rika. I have it too."

The Irkal saris and *cholis* to match which Lata and I had chosen together, one in rich turquoise silk with a wide red border, and the other a dark chocolate bordered in gold and royal blue, made an instant hit with Urvashi Devi. "I love them!" she exclaimed. "I'm going to be the envy of all female Chandravats. I have always wanted one of these typical Maharashtrian saris." Of the several sets of jewellery of my own design, I asked anxiously if my cousins would look down upon wearing what was, after all, costume jewellery. Urvashi Devi snorted. "Why on earth would they do that? You should see what junk some of them wear! And these are beautiful! I'm going to keep that set for myself. And wear it proudly because it's your creation, my dear." She kissed me warmly. As a safeguard, since we had not known who else would be there, Lata had added a couple of choice outfits from The Honey Bee collection, and these were immediately appropriated by Rika who dashed off to try them on.

"My dear, I know you wear saris only under protest. I have these for you. Have Lata design something formal with them. I thought you could wear them in New York."

She had three lengths of the most beautiful fabrics for me, all heavily embroidered, one in deep red and gold, another in shimmering gold, and the third woven with the same iridescent colours as a peacock's plumage. They made me catch my breath with their beauty. "I thought these would suit your exotic looks. I've been saving them for just the right person. They wouldn't suit anyone else in the family," thus dismissing daughters, and daughters-in-law with a wave of her hand.

"Oh, they are gorgeous! I'll enjoy every moment of wearing them! And I'll send photographs when they are made up for you to see," I promised.

She had one more gift for me, so costly I saw at a glance, I was struck speechless. They were earrings made up of waterfalls of sapphires and diamonds. I gasped, "But, Auntyji, surely these should belong to your daughters—or Rika?"

"Nonsense! All of them have more jewellery than they can ever use. No, Piyali, these are for you. I thought of them minutes after I met you, and saw your eyes. Only you have the flair to carry them off. They belonged to my mother. I've never worn them. Not quite my style. It's a shame to let them lie in a vault. So take them with my blessing, and wear and enjoy them."

I bent to put my arms around her. "You are too good to me," I said shakily. "I've come to realize how much I've missed without having a mother. No mother could have been more welcoming and loving than you've been. And Uncleji too. This visit to Divyasthala has been many things, but most of all, a homecoming, and all because of you. I shan't ever forget."

She stroked my head. "My dear child. Uday and I were saying last night we've felt as if one of our daughters has come home—and what a lovely intelligent daughter! Will you come again when you're back for a visit? We claim some of your time."

"Of course, I will," dashing away my tears.

I discovered Uday Singh in his library-cum-office.

"Piyali," he said gravely, "I've been thinking how much we've missed by not meeting you earlier. And now you are going far away from us. When you come to see Tej Pratap, don't ever go without paying us a visit." He looked at me keenly. "You've said you were very happy about Tej's marriage—which speaks well of you. So it can't be the reason why you're leaving India, especially when your career has reached such a high point. I've been wondering—is it an *affaire du coeur,* Piyali?"

I hadn't been expecting the question. It brought back all my misery and desperation in a powerful wave. I couldn't articulate a reply, but looked at him dumbly.

"Piyali." He came to sit by me, and took my hands in his. "I shouldn't have asked you. It is very painful, I can see." Then gently, "Then I guessed right. A quarrel perhaps? No? Your background then? I assume he's not of princely blood. Not that either. What does he do?"

I managed to say, "He's an artist."

"Ah. A struggling one perhaps? Is that the problem?"

"No." I groped for my handkerchief to blow my nose. "He's extremely successful. Has his own studio. Gets more commissions than he can handle. Exhibits abroad." I looked at his kind face, concern for me written all over it. "I wasn't going to tell you. I thought you might object to my following Tara's example, and falling for someone not of our background."

He shook his head. "I'm well aware of changing times, Piyali. Of course, I feel sorrow that our best girls are marrying outside—but I understand the situation. Now Nayantara has made a brilliant marriage, according to all reports. Surya Mohan was quite livid, I was told. Does Tej know? I see. And could do nothing? Can I help in any way, Piyali?"

"No one can, Uncleji. You see, it's a family thing. His people—one in particular—would be quite shattered over a match like this one." He was clearly quite astonished that anyone could object to marrying into royalty. Quite the reverse. "He's very close—to this relative who's rather aged—and will not jeopardize her well-being. So an impasse. I couldn't take it any more. Inevitably, we run into each other. It's equally harrowing for him. So the only solution is to take myself off. Fortunately, I'm going into a wonderful job situation. I love New York, and have umpteen friends. So I'll be all right, Uncleji."

"I can hardly believe that, dear child. But you have courage, I know. Still, it disturbs me that you have been so sad. Dces Lata know."

"Yes. And has been wonderfully supportive."

"I can believe that. I want you to promise me, Piyali, that if there's ever anything I can do—whatever that might be—you'll let me know." Fresh tears threatened, but I held them back. "I mustn't forget to thank you for those cassettes. I was so carried away by Sebastian's compositions that it was midnight before I went to bed. You couldn't have given me anything I would enjoy more. Tremendous genius there. It explains why he has scaled such heights. I'm a lover of classical music, as you know both Western and Indian. Which is why the selections had me spellbound. I hope some day to meet this young man. Do you think it's feasible?"

"Tell Lata," I said promptly. "She'll do the rest."

He reached out and put an arm around me, one hand on my head. "All my blessings, Piyali. I pray you will find peace of mind, and the happiness you deserve."

"Thank you," I said unsteadily. "I can't believe how I was rather alarmed at the prospect of meeting you, Uncleji."

His eyes twinkled. "You assumed I'd be an ogre."

"Not quite. But formidable like Tara's grandfather."

"God forbid! Not like him!" he exclaimed.

On that cheerful note, I was able to leave. One last farewell remained. I found Rika sobbing on her bed. At my hand on her shoulder, she sat up, revealing a wet face. She flung herself at me. "Why can't you stay, Piyali? Don't go!"

"I have to, Rika. My flight's booked, and my job is waiting. Write to me. And if you want anything from the States, I'll send it to you. Okay? I'll make sure your Honey Bee order is taken care of right away." I smiled at her woebegone face. "You were a wonderful guide and companion. Terribly patient. Terribly informative." She did not notice the use of her favourite word.

"I'll miss you terribly."

I hugged her. "I'll miss you terribly too. Take terribly good care of yourself." And that last brought a watery smile.

In less than a fortnight, I was winging my way to New York, leaving behind my nearest and dearest, turning my face resolutely to a new future.

PART TWO

Ask me no more: thy fate and mine are sealed:
I strove against the stream and all in vain:
Let the great river take me to the main;
No more, dear love, for at a touch I yield:
Ask me no more.

Tennyson, *The Princess*, Song VII

Danae. The name went back to Greek mythology where King Acrisius, concerned at the prospect of having no heir, consulted the Oracle at Delphi. The Oracle replied that he would have a daughter whose son would slay his grandfather, and rule in his stead. When the daughter Danae was born, she was of exceeding beauty. To prevent the latter part of the prophecy from being fulfilled, she was imprisoned in a subterranean chamber. But a shower of gold sent by Zeus fell upon her, and she became the mother of an infant destined to fulfil the oracle, named Perseus, perhaps because he was a son of the great god of light. The shower of gold signified a great beam of light. Perseus, of course, one of the great ancient heroes, became the slayer of the Gorgon, Medusa. It was for the multinational enterprise which took its name from this legend, and whose logo displayed a shower of gold, that I expected to work.

When I entered the imposing edifice, I went straight up to the floor where the offices were situated. Only later did I discover that the others were sales departments, and stores. But for now, my whole concentration was on the confrontation with the top bosses of this great firm.

The four men around a small conference table rose when I entered. A grey-haired man introduced himself as Harrison Roxburgh, and we shook hands. The presence of the one named Quentin Wirth made me feel infinitely better though neither showed any signs of having heard of the other. I memorized each name carefully. When we sat down, I was the object of intense scrutiny, not covert, but very open. And why not? If I were to be inducted into this organization of world renown, samples of my work having preceded my appearance notwithstanding, I had to win the final stamp of approval in person. It was the gaze of the fifth member, the woman, Charlotte Metzger, which I felt most keenly.

Rejecting anything of an ethnic nature, I had chosen a pants suit bought in Paris, superbly tailored, its simple classic lines in style even after three years. Other than tiny gold drops and a pearl ring, I wore no jewellery. I had swept my hair into a chignon, and wore heelless court shoes.

If I had felt some anxiety before, it dropped away now. No questions were asked that I could not answer. Whether I was finally selected or not, I had every reason to be confident about my ability to face any challenges in the future, and about my achievements so far. And then three quarters of an hour later, they all sat back to allow Harrison Roxburgh to smile at me, and say, "Welcome to the Danae family. With one stipulation." The others were as surprised as I was. I waited in suspense. What condition was he imposing on me? "That you tell us a simpler name to call you by. I can't possibly twist my tongue around that last name of yours!" The words lifted the last lingering shreds of doubt from my mind, and I could join in the general laughter. I said most people called me Piyali. He tried it, as did the others, emphasizing the 'li' as Americans will.

Over the coffee cups, Charlotte Metzger asked me several personal questions, particularly about my family background. On my part, I marvelled privately that a woman of her rank in the hierarchy could be so careless about enhancing her appearance. In my circle of American friends, most women were exceedingly well-groomed. Ms Metzger's greying hair looked as if had been hacked with a knife; she wore no make-up except for a dreadful shade of purplish colour on her lips; and her clothes looked as if she had thrown on a few things from someone's box for the Salvation Army. She had good features, and a fine height, I saw, even if her figure was hidden in those shapeless garments. And here she was at the top of Danae, makers of the most complete range of beauty preparations which millions of women swore by, to say nothing of high fashion jewellery, designer clothes, a wide range of perfumes, and footwear to please every feminine heart. Oh well, I thought, it wasn't my business.

I was to start in a week which was pleasing, because it gave me time to settle in. Great relief in my heart, I took my leave. Now for the next step. Which brings me to Katia and David, those two wonderful friends. They had met me at the airport, and whisked me off to their penthouse apartment. If meeting my dear David again was heartwarming, then coming to know Katia was a delight. She was lovely to behold, a blonde with very blue eyes. Now here was one woman who looked as if she could be a cover girl for any glossy magazine. Daughter of a millionaire, she was warm and unaffected, highly intelligent, and with a sense of humour, all of which made us kindred souls within minutes of our meeting. David was very satisfied over the Danae interview. He said he had never doubted for a moment that I would make it, but had only felt concern I might be in for a rough time when faced with a formidable panel of interviewers.

The Asschers had done some homework for me even before I arrived. Saul Aaronson owned several apartment blocks, and they had chosen an apartment for me in one of them. It had an excellent security system, with easy access to shopping centres. Katia said she had rejected a place in a more luxurious neighbourhood, for this one had a nice homey atmosphere, and the people were really fine. She knew many of them personally. Katia had chosen wisely. The apartment was all she claimed. The moment I stepped in, I felt I was in the right place. A large living room-cum-dining room, a spacious bedroom with a pretty bathroom and a kitchen that was more than adequate for my needs. I suspected that the rent which was absurdly low for New York had been reduced by Katia for me. She waved her hand airily when I mentioned this.

I had planned to pick up second-hand furniture cheaply, some in garage sales. Katia said solemnly all that had been taken care of. Both David's mother and Katia's mother had said firmly that they had all the stuff I could possibly need in storage, and all I had to do was to choose what I wanted. According to the rather wicked account of their children, both ladies were prone to periodic fits whereby they suddenly decided that their decor looked terrible, it was out of style, boring, and they could not stand it for another day. *Voila*, summon the interior designers, and start all over again. Katia said her father simply took off for some urgent work elsewhere, while David's moved into another wing where no designer was allowed to set foot. I had to laugh at the graphic descriptions. When Katia asked anxiously if this was appropriate . . . a princess using such stuff . . . I simply hugged her. Not only did I not mind, but I would be honoured, I told her. And it was true. The fact was anything that had once adorned the homes of these two families was choice stuff, and extremely expensive.

With the enthusiastic help of Katia and David, my apartment took on a look of combined luxury, beauty and comfort. A huge settee in striped ruby red and gold satin, enough to accommodate any possible overnight guest, occupied pride of place. My Indian temple lamps converted into table lamps acquired tall gold shades. A lovely cherrywood desk placed in an alcove of the living room, flanked by bookshelves, would be perfect for my designing. For the bedroom, David had pounced on a king-size bed. When Katia had protested at its size, he had insisted someone as tall as Piyali needed its length, if not its breadth. It was the last word in luxury, and even boasted a silk canopy. Decadent, Katia muttered, of this item from her mother-in-law's store. Unless, she said brightening, it was going to be shared by someone, hmmm, Piyali? I pulled a horrible face at her, and we both fell into laughter which astonished David.

When I hung the seascape over the mantelpiece, Katia uttered an exclamation. She came close to study it carefully. I actually knew the artist? It was fantastic, she said. Watch out for Papa, she warned. If he saw it. . . . It was the only memento I had brought with me of Neel. I couldn't bear to part with it.

The purchase of pots and pans, cutlery and inexpensive crockery for daily use was augmented by a set of lovely dishes and glassware by Katia who said she had been flooded with these for her wedding, and I would be relieving her of the trouble of storing them. And so I was all set to start my great Danae enterprise, thanks to these kind and generous people who proved the meaning of true friendship.

Nothing could have been more different than the office-workplace at Danae which I shared with Peter Weisman who designed men's accessories and the place Madhur had offered me at The Honey Bee. Where the latter was comfortable and adequate, the former was the last word in convenience with every kind of equipment I could possibly need. My immediate boss, Quentin Wirth and I had a long briefing session when I was shown the kind of Danae jewellery currently being offered. However, Quent said firmly, I was to give rein to my own ideas, and be innovative. It was a constant challenge to find new ones. He pointed out the pieces in my portfolio which came closest to what he had in mind. Other jewellery designers here also catered to conventional tastes. Some customers preferred traditional jewellery, and always chose classic designs. I was not to concern myself with those.

What could have been more challenging than that? I set to work. When I went to show my first efforts, Quent was quietly elated. He did not shower me with high praise, of course, but I sensed his satisfaction. I had grasped the essence of what was to be my special area in jewellery design. Armed with further instructions, I marched back to my office. Peter looked up questioningly, and grinned when I raised my arm in a victory salute. Thus did I find my niche at Danae.

I spoke to Daddy regularly. Patently, he was very happy. I could lull his worries about me with exciting descriptions of everything that had been happening. I wrote to Lata in similar vein, and she replied with news of Bombay. She and I both avoided mention of one particular name. Once in a while, I spoke with the Nevilles, necessarily in brief.

My social life picked up considerably. Besides my old friends, I made many new ones, and there the Asschers were largely responsible. For some reason, Barbara and Saul Aaronson had taken a great liking to me, so that they insisted I join Katia and David when they went to their home for dinner. David's parents were equally kind. No, I did not lack for friends or company. If behind the carefree facade there existed a person who lay awake at nights remembering, grieving, bereft, none of these people guessed. Stern as I was with myself, unbidden my thoughts would turn in one direction, wondering what was happening in another life, if my absence was being felt, or if I had been relegated to the past, forgotten. Then I would bury my head in my pillows, and the tears would come.

19

Summer in New York can be unpleasantly hot. I was glad my vacation was to begin from mid-July till the second week in August. The Aaronsons had a summer cottage—cottage being a complete misnomer—in Cape Cod. In early August, Katia, David and I were to spend a week there. I looked forward to cool Atlantic breezes, and swimming in the sea. These five months at Danae had seen me work harder than I had in my entire life. If the results had been gratifying, the pace had been gruelling, and I was more than ready for a break. Till our threesome took off, there was plenty I wished to see and do right here in New York.

I was in a euphoric mood on the first day of my holiday. My first priority was to give the apartment a thorough cleaning, for I had neglected it the week before under pressure of work. By eleven, I was all done, and looked about with justifiable pride at my gleaming dwelling place. I dumped a load of sheets and towels in the washing machine, and that was all. You deserve a cup of coffee, Piyali, I told myself, and made a fresh brew. The mug was half empty when the phone summoned me. It was Katia.

"Piyali," she announced, "I am suffering from writer's block. I am truly and well stuck with my article. I need to do something different. Did you see the notice in *The New York Times* this morning?"

"I? Hardly. I've been slaving away at cleaning the place."

"Well," she said honestly, "neither have I, but I know it's there. There's an exhibition—Young India—or something like that—on Indian art. You know how David adores these things, and I enjoy them too. Shall we go and see it this evening? Oh, great! And we'll have dinner somewhere afterwards. Pick you up around six."

My mood brightened still more. An evening out with two of my favourite people sounded wonderful. If we were dining out, I would have to dress up. Blissfully, I went to look through my wardrobe.

Katia's father was part owner of the gallery, I learnt on the way. Which accounted for her knowing about the exhibition. I wondered which youthful painters were being represented. The place was surprisingly full. Quite a few Indians, but a large number of people who could only be tourists. Of course, I reminded myself, this was summer, and people flocked to New York from all over the country, to say nothing of those from other lands.

One had to admit they had done a remarkable job of the displays. Soft orchestral music greeted us as we entered, the poignant notes of a *sitar* predominating. Ravi Shankar, I told my companions. On David's face was an avid look of anticipation. Katia winked at me when she saw it. She herself was greeted with bows from several men who were surely her father's employees.

At some point, we lost David. From the start, he had been drifting away from us, wrapped in contemplation of every painting. The variety of talent displayed was quite astonishing. I didn't recognize any of the artists. Katia was full of questions. Patiently, I explained the finer details of a rustic scene, all earth colours, and most realistically depicted. We were studying a group of women in the act of winnowing, rust-red skirts and veils flying in the breeze, the grain falling in a golden stream from their tilted baskets when an excited David came in search of us. We were to follow him, he said, seizing Katia's hand. He'd discovered something really worth seeing, he explained. Mystified, we went along. He led us through room after room where we glimpsed handloom fabrics, embroidery, clothes and rugs, until we reached a larger one. Katia walked on oblivious. My feet froze to the ground. The room was full of sculptures. How foolish of me to be surprised, I thought. What had made me assume that at such an exhibition where multi-faceted talents were being displayed, sculpture would not be included? And surely, in a Young India exhibition, one particular young sculptor would be represented?

David said, "Over here."

We went to stand in front of a group of five bronzes, each on its own pedestal, complete in its individual capacity. They were human figures titled Loneliness, Joy, Rage, Despair and Serenity. Every line of body and face reflected feeling and emotion. Despair was unmistakable in the slumped posture of a male figure, hopelessness written in the agonized eyes and droop of mouth. Serenity was a woman, utter tranquillity smoothing the lines in her face, such calmness in her regard as if the result of meditation, or acceptance, or some divine gift, the body still but relaxed. It was Joy that made Katia exclaim—a woman, face radiant as she held up a chubby baby laughing down at her.

"I could look at them for hours," David murmured. "They say so much, and reflect all humankind." He stooped to look through his glasses. "NKG it says here." He didn't need to tell me. The stamp of the sculptor was unmistakable. Hadn't I seen so much of his work?

Katia called out, "Oh, come and see this one! It's absolutely out of this world! I just love it!"

And why shouldn't she? It was in white marble, a head and shoulders only sculpture of a man and a girl. It hardly needed the title 'Lovers'. The two heads were very close, almost touching. Each figure had a hand on the other's face, the man's strong one curving around her cheek, while her slim arm encircled his neck, the fingers caressing the back of it. If that were not explicit enough, it was the expression in the eyes that gazed into the beloved's face. As sculpture it was a work of art, timeless in theme and rendering. It could have been Romeo and Juliet, or Tristan and Isolde, or Laila and Majnu, for there was a universality about the pair that transcended man-made demarcations of time such as centuries or historical periods. Katia fortunately failed to notice that I was unable to speak or respond as she pointed out various features. "I wonder if it's on sale," she was saying, when David called yet again. This time, I did not go with her. Other viewers crowded behind me, and I moved to give them room. I wanted to be alone for a while as feelings and emotions battered at my fragile defences. I found a comparatively quiet corner.

Beyond the heads of the viewers, a door opened, and two men talking animatedly, came out. One was short and stout, an American wearing a suit and tie. I hardly spared him a glance. My gaze was riveted on the other man. Oh God, I thought numbly, Neel is here in New York, and I didn't know. No, why would he want to see me? He's here for the Exhibition, of course. My eyes registered every detail of his appearance, drinking in the sight denied to me all these months. A thought came to me. If Neel had no wish to meet me, should I not make myself invisible till he had gone? Just one moment longer, my treacherous heart pleaded.

As if his ESP told him something, Neel turned his head away from his companion to let his glance rove over the room. It skimmed over the tourists, stopped for a moment at Katia and David—and found me. Profound shock was registered on his face, rendering him motionless. Then he said something very quickly to the other man, and began to work his way through the crowd, eyes not leaving me. I stood there waiting, my heart thudding in my breast. And then he was there.

"Hello, Neel," I said, striving to sound composed. After all, I'd had more time to get used to the situation than he.

"Piyali," Katia said behind me. Her voice trailed off, and she looked with interest at my companion.

"Katia, this is Neel Gregory whose sculpture we've just been admiring."

"My goodness, you're NKG!" She put out a hand to shake Neel's. "We haven't just been admiring! We're amazed—awe-struck! My husband, David Asscher," as David came up. "This is Mr Gregory, the sculptor we've been raving over, Davy."

David's dear face lit up. He shook hands enthusiastically. In a moment, they were deep in discussion, David asking questions, Katia adding hers, though for the most part, she was studying Neel with interest. I stood quietly, glad of the respite. The questions I had in mind bore no relation to David's. I would never have the answers to mine. Very shortly, we would be going in different directions, and it would be the end of a chance encounter.

"Are you busy this evening, Mr Gregory? The three of us are dining out. Can you join us for dinner? We'd be so happy if you could come."

A swift look at my face, and a smoothly worded acceptance of Katia's invitation followed. David beamed. Patently, he felt he had discovered a kindred soul, and was loath to end the fascinating conversation.

"Your first time in New York, Mr Gregory?"

"Neel. No, not my first time by any means, Mrs Asscher. My love affair with New York began years ago when I was at Parsons, and continued during subsequent visits."

Truly startled, I looked at him directly. Was he joking? But no, Neel was telling a delighted David which years he had spent at the School of Design, and Katia saying with a groan, "Oh no, not another one! That makes me the odd man out!" Why had I never known about Parsons? Neel had never mentioned the fact to me. I was always learning new facts about him. Secretly, I was exhilarated at the thought of spending more time in his company. At least my presence hadn't resulted in his turning down Katia's invitation. It was a cheering thought.

"Do you have a favourite haunt we can go to for dinner, Neel? Oh, we love trying out new things! No, we've never been there. Let's go!"

The suggestion proved to be an excellent one. The Caravan on 8th Avenue near the theatre district was an Afghan restaurant. The extremely personable owner welcomed us warmly. Words of Hafiz hung on the walls, while music perfectly in keeping with the place, played softly. The food was exquisite.

I added a few desultory remarks to the conversation, but for the most part, I listened—and stole quick glances. David was in his element, Katia equally fascinated. I saw her studying Neel, the devastating smile, the strong features, and thickly curling hair. Clearly, she liked what she saw. Oh yes, I thought, Neel can very well charm the birds off the trees. In response to a question, Neel spoke of his parents and a dig in Israel, Katia sat up.

"I've been there on a dig myself!"

It appeared that Saul Aaronson had made a munificent contribution towards it, and his ebullient daughter, then just out of college, had managed to become part of the expedition. She had to know where exactly the Gregorys had been, describing some of her crazier adventures. The conversation became even livelier, for Neel had visited his parents at several of these sites over the years, and spun yarns with such verve that Katia fell under his spell further.

Even so, at some point, she became aware that I was contributing to the conversation rather infrequently. She lifted an eyebrow in enquiry. I gave the slightest shake of my head. Not one to leave matters there, when the dishes were cleared and we were awaiting dessert, Katia announced we ladies were going to powder our noses.

Alone together, Katia looked at me with concern as I let cool water flow over my wrists, holding a wet paper towel to my burning eyes.

"Piyali, tell me what's wrong?" and when I didn't answer at once, "Is it our guest? Do you dislike him?"

I gave a short bitter laugh. "I wish that were so." And at her puzzled look, "Oh Katia, I fled India because of him—so that we couldn't keep meeting. Every time we met, we had to tear ourselves away from each other. Why? Because of complications I can't go into now. I'll only say, a family member—his—is involved, and any relationship with me would cause untold harm to that person."

She let that sink in, then she touched my hand. "You care for him, don't you, Piyali?"

"Too much for my own good." I tried to smile. "A fat lot coming away has done me. I was determined to forget him—and what happens? I realize this evening, I've just been fooling myself." I went on painfully, "If we hadn't gone to the Exhibition today, we wouldn't have met. Obviously, he had no intention of informing me he was in New York."

"Oh, my dear, that can't be true! Perhaps he thought you might not want to see him. After all, you say you left India because of him." She nodded at my mirror reflection. "Make no mistake, he's been very conscious of your presence. Don't look so surprised. I've been aware of it. At the gallery, the air positively crackled!"

I looked at her despairingly. "Katia, he'll walk away after dinner. We haven't exchanged two words yet."

"Leave that to me," she commanded. To the two men who had risen when we returned, she said gaily, "Well, have you solved at least half the world's problems?"

"Without two beautiful ladies to inspire us, we couldn't, Mrs Asscher."

Holding her hands up in mock horror, "Please not Mrs anything! Just Katia!"

"An unusual and charming name. I'm honoured."

"You know, I'm rather curious. Is this the first time you and Piyali are meeting, or had you run into each other before?"

Smoothly, "Oh, we belong to the same social circle in Bombay. Knew each other well."

"You did?" opening her eyes wide. "But that's a wonderful coincidence—to meet in New York!"

All unsuspecting, innocently abetting her, David exclaimed in a pleased tone, "Then you two must have plenty to catch up with! Piyali, you'd better take Neel home for coffee. Then you can bring yourself up-to-date on everything."

From Katia, "My goodness, this is quite an opportunity to find out about the latest happenings."

For the first time, Neel looked at me directly. "I rather think the lady has to invite me first."

Three pairs of eyes on me, I said, "Hmmm? Oh, of course. I must hear some first-hand news about everyone, my cousin in particular." It didn't sound very warm, but then I didn't wish to sound too eager.

"That should be exciting," Katia said approvingly.

Neel looked around. "It's as beautiful as one might expect your apartment to be."

"Thank you. Most of the furniture was given to me. But it was fun doing it up." I threw my purse on the coffee table. "Do make yourself comfortable. I'll put the coffee on."

"Mind if I join you in the kitchen?"

Startled, I said, "No, not at all."

"Nice," he approved a moment later.

"Yes, it is rather. I enjoy making meals here."

"Do you miss the maid who cleaned and cooked for you?"

"Sometimes. But I manage pretty well. Breakfasts are easy enough. I have lunch at Danae. And I'm out for supper often."

"A hectic social calendar?"

"Not really, but I have a lot of friends."

We were carrying on this casual conversation as if we had parted just yesterday, as if nothing lay between us. Yet all the while, as I ground the coffee beans, and set water to boil, I was trying to believe that Neel was actually here, his big frame dwarfing my large kitchen, that it was not a hallucination at all. Had I wished, I could have put out a hand to touch him.

Behind me, Neel asked, "Where can I find some cups?"

I turned to show him—and almost crashed into the solid frame. We were just inches apart. The moment was fraught with tension.

"Where—are you staying, Neel?" very low, keeping my head down.

"With an uncle," equally low. Neither of us seemed able to move away.

"How—long have you been in New York?"

"About a week."

"How long are you staying."

"Perhaps a week or ten days."

"If we hadn't met today, you weren't going to get in touch with me, were you?"

A pause. "I didn't know if you'd resent my doing that."

"How could you think that, Neel!"

"You left to get away from me, Piyal."

"Not the whole truth. I felt the situation had become impossible for both of us, and it was best to remove myself from the scene."

"Why didn't you tell me what you had planned? Can you imagine how I felt on my return, and found you had gone? I went nearly crazy."

"I thought it best—to slip away."

"I was responsible for driving you away. I can't forgive myself for that."

"You must not blame yourself. The decision was mine."

"But you hate me for it." I bent my head lower, and shook it. "You don't? Then why won't you look at me? Does my presence bother you? Shall I go?"

At that, my head shot up. "No!" frantically, "don't go!" clutching a fistful of silken fabric. "Neel, please don't go!"

Impossible to say which one of us moved first, but we were in each other's arms, holding on as if to a lifeline, incoherent broken words tumbling from our lips. The fire that had always smouldered beneath the surface now leaped up to engulf us, fuelled by our separation of months, for having lost and found each other again. For the first time in our whole relationship, we were entirely alone as we had never been before with no one to disturb us. And of the future, this was neither the time nor the place , even if we'd had the presence of mind for it, to think dark thoughts.

I did not know if minutes passed, or hours. Into the darkness, Neel said in a shaken voice, "Piyal. Piyal, why didn't you tell me? I never dreamed. . . ."

I said in a small voice, "Did you imagine I indulge in orgies with other men?"

"No, never that! But you've lived in the West all your life, dated men. . . ."

I burrowed my head into his shoulder. "No, I've always drawn the line because I was waiting . . . for the man I loved. . . ." I couldn't add ". . and married."

Still in a shaken voice, "You make me feel very humble—You honour me, Piyal. But even so, had I known, I'd have been—well, more gentle. You—I must have hurt you terribly, my darling." He lifted my face up, and kissed me tenderly. "But never again, I promise you."

I asked in a small voice, "Are you so experienced then, Mr Gregory?"

Laughter in his, he murmured, "You don't really want to know my darkest secrets, do you, Princess?"

"Oh, I do!" I assured him. "And you'll never tell me."

Suddenly, I was overcome with happiness. Here in the warm darkness, I lay in the arms of the one I loved. For now, I asked for nothing more. I put my hands up, and drew Neel's face down. He began to kiss me, softly at first, then with hungry passionate urgency. I lost track of time again.

If I thought I knew my beloved, it was quite an erroneous impression. The Neel I'd known at ROMOLA, or gone swimming and exploring with in Sinhadurg, or encountered in Bombay, had revealed only part of his nature to me. I had always known he was a delightful companion, fascinating conversationalist, brilliant at his work. His grandmother had mentioned what a bright lively mischievous little boy he had been. The incident at Peter's Garage had given me my first taste of those qualities which had accompanied him into adulthood. But now, I was discovering a whole new set of qualities.

Woe unto me if I walked into the bathroom when Neel was shaving. I was hauled up against him, held firmly in spite of my struggles while he gave my face a foamy white shaving cream beard and moustache, even new eyebrows. Then laughing boyishly, he lined me up in front of the mirror. What could I do but laugh with him?

On the first morning over a hilarious breakfast, he declared he had every intent of sampling the culinary delights associated with New York, which he always looked forward to every time he came to the States. Asked what they were, he listed them with relish, "Lasagne. Coq au vin. Lox. Bagels. Moussaka. Chili con carne. Arroz con pollo. Corn on the cob. . . ." I held up my hands for mercy. "And that's just the start."

"Just listening makes me feel the pounds accumulating."

"Not on me, lady. Sheena and I swim and run off any excesses. I don't see any danger of your putting on any extra pounds either."

"Because, Sir, I don't let them. Besides, at Danae, we have regular aerobic sessions for those who want them."

"Which explains why your figure is so perfect."

When the mood took him, Neel sang at any time. Over the sound of water in the shower, his rich baritone floated out, perhaps singing an operatic piece. In the kitchen or bedroom, he might burst into a love song, catch me and kiss me enthusiastically, or waltz me around to some livelier ditty. Not being blessed with a singing voice, I loved listening to his.

That first morning, not having expected a guest, and certainly not one with a healthy young appetite, we had to go grocery shopping. There was a supermarket within walking distance, but I often preferred the little Italian store around the corner.

As usual, Mr Bertinelli was singing as he swept the floor with a long-handled broom. This time it was from *The Barber of Seville,* where Figaro is indulging in self-praise—his own popularity, his ability ever to be on the spot, his bravery, what a wonder, a marvel he is, king of razor and blade. Mr B halted for a moment after singing 'Ah, bravo Figaro!/ bravo, bravissimo; a te fortuna/ non manchera' to bend down and chase an errant potato which had rolled away. He straightened slowly when another voice picked up Figaro's self-eulogizing. 'Ah, ah che bella vita!' and went on to recount how if a girl needed a husband, he went out to get her one; likewise a widow. He was a messenger of Cupid, Figaro declared. Mr Bertinelli came back smartly as the Count now, wondering who this fellow might be, finally recognizing him. What is the old braggart doing here, he asked. For heaven's sake, isn't he putting on some weight? 'Ti veggo grasso e tondo. . . .' Figaro explained it was from hunger. I laughed openly at Neel's meek mien when he sang that, and Mr B told him he was a rascal— 'Ah birbo!' Neel bowed with his hand on his breast. 'Grazie.'

Movement with the broom suspended, Mr B was enjoying himself to the hilt. Passersby, many of them his customers, paused and lingered on the sidewalk to listen with pleasure. When both singers concluded in a magnificent burst of sound, the crowd clapped with great enthusiasm. Mr B's bow, a hand on his chest, would have done Pavrotti proud. Smiling, they hurried off.

"So," he boomed, "you bring me an opera star, Principessa!" He shook hands at my introduction, surveying Neel with a keen eye. "You are a Prince from India then?"

Neel grinned disarmingly. "Alas no. I'm a very ordinary commoner."

"But you can never be anything ordinary!" Mr B told him. When he heard Neel was a sculptor, he nodded as if that was no surprise to him. At the mention of his sculptures on exhibit, his eyes became round with pleasure. He would go and see them this very evening, he declared. A moment later, he was talking excitedly about a village near Amalfi where he had grown up and where Neel had stayed with his parents once. Mr B personally helped Neel to select the firmest red tomatoes, the crunchiest celery, and the most luscious fruit. As his own personal gift to a new friend, he handed over a wrapped package of his own special bologna. As we left after prolonged farewells, I was told to bring Neel back soon. As I said, I had never been the recipient of such treatment.

On the night after we met again, Neel had called his uncle's home. His aunt had been most understanding about his meeting with an old friend with whom he was staying overnight. I had no idea what reason he gave next day for packing his bags, and moving in with his 'friend'. Neel said he would be seeing them almost every day, and did not enlarge further. At no time, did he offer to take me to their home. Obviously, he had no wish that we should meet.

Katia had made one brief phone call. Neel was in the shower then. Hurriedly, I briefed her. She was truly happy for me, and rang off. Neel spent some time at the gallery every day, and it was there that he met Saul Aaronson. Needless to say, Neel made one more friend. Saul carried him off for lunch to some exclusive restaurant where they talked about painting and sculpture for two hours.

Together, Neel and I went to our favourite haunts, some the other had not seen. A place we both loved, which I had not had time to see since my return to New York was The Cloisters. The atmosphere of this medieval Gothic monastery, partly brought over from Europe, and reconstructed, still had a sacred quality. From its location on a hill, one had a breathtaking view of the Hudson River and Manhattan. As we said after a leisurely tour of the museum where Gothic art was displayed, when we sat down to drink in the scene, one always felt renewed after coming here.

No girl could have asked for a more tender understanding considerate lover, mindful of my inexperience, sensitive to my feelings and moods. The ardent look in the golden eyes was enough to make me melt, the whispered love words stirring me to the depth of my being. It was the artist in Neel that made him hold my head in his hands, tracing my features, long clever fingers shaping the contours of my body. As a sculptor, tactile impressions, the textures of soft smooth skin and silken hair were important to him.

"I could sculpt you in so many different ways, my darling," he told me, "and never run out of ideas to depict you. Your face is wonderfully mobile and expresses every mood. And your physique—just made for a sculptor—perfectly proportioned, that graceful neck, the way your waist narrows here to the curve of the hips, and these lovely long legs. You have the most remarkable bone structure, Piyal. All the fairies must have been there at your birth to bless you with such beauty." His voice became serious. "I should have asked you to model for me at ROMOLA. Will you let me make sketches of you when I want to capture a pose?" Smiling, I acquiesced. Neel did just that, keeping a sketching block handy.

We talked for hours lying curled up together on the settee which was large enough to accommodate us both, on the rug, or in the king-size bed. It seemed we were constantly discovering new things about each other. If Neel came to know now for the first time that I was born in the US, I learnt he held a green card, which meant he visited the country once a year, if not more. His uncle's home was his base. Yet one area was absolutely taboo, and if accidentally, we veered dangerously close, Neel changed the subject at once. I let him do it. The time we had been granted together was too precious to spoil. If ever he was ready to bring it up, the initiative would be his. And so while we spoke of a myriad topics, matters of the gravest import remained untouched.

20

"Piyal," Neel said, "I'm afraid I shall be out for dinner." I looked at him questioningly. "My aunt's throwing a party in my honour. Has invited all those who've been so helpful over the Exhibition, plus a few others she and my uncle want me to meet from the art world." He brushed back a strand of hair from my cheek, and tucked it behind my ear. "You don't mind, do you? I hate to waste a whole evening away from you, but my aunt and uncle—well, they've been so good to me always. Very understanding about my not staying with them this time."

Surely, I thought to myself, if they were such understanding people, and Neel had told them about me, I would have been invited too? Patently, he had told them nothing. Presumably, he had visited them several times in the past week without mentioning my existence. It hurt—deeply. And there was not a thing I could do or say in the matter. Neel was waiting, not sure of my answer at all.

I said brightly, "Of course, I don't mind! The Asschers have been begging me to come for supper. This is as good a time as any. I'll call and announce I'm coming."

Neel's face cleared. "That's good. I'll try and slip away as soon as it's decently possible."

"You shouldn't, Neel. Not when your aunt's taken so much trouble. I may be late myself. When the three of us get to talking—"

So it was that Neel went off looking heartbreakingly handsome and groomed in formal evening wear—and I left for the Asschers' penthouse. Thank goodness for Katia and David, I thought, as I drove into their parking lot. Had I stayed at home, I would have sunk into deepest gloom. I shook off the mood that was threatening to swamp me.

As a matter of fact, the evening was delightful. David dear as any brother, and Katia who had become as dear, welcomed me with open arms. We ate and drank, talked and laughed, fully at ease with each other. As a wife, Katia had achieved a miracle of sorts. The David I had known at Parsons, always so sloppily dressed, had been transformed into a rather handsome individual, very spruced up and smart. I hadn't realized before what fine features he had. David had been—well, just David. Katia rolled up her eyes when I mentioned the change.

"You should have seen the look on Papa's face when I took David home." She chortled at the memory. "He took me aside to ask if I hadn't made some mistake. This fellow was a hobo. Couldn't possibly belong to *the* Asscher family. It took a lot of convincing to make Papa believe his identity. And then after we were married, you should have seen the battle over his clothes. His wardrobe was full of down-at-heel shoes—in rows—hideous suits, shapeless pants, and shirts that were two sizes larger. There was a sweater with holes in the elbows which was his absolute favourite!

"David had been grinning at this recital. "That sweater was the most comfortable garment I owned, Kat," he protested. "It sort of grew up with me."

"Be that as it may, I was determined I was not going to grow old along with it! I knew he'd kick up the most awful row, so what did clever Katia do? I bought him the most expensive imported sweater, as soft as I could find. Did he like it? He tried it on, and said politely it was very nice—and wanted to know where the other one was. Truth was I'd bundled up most of his stuff for Goodwill, all ready in cartons for them to pick up. Except The Sweater. I felt even Goodwill couldn't salvage that dreadful object. I laid it aside to put in the trash. And what do you think this scion of the Asscher family did? He found it!" I was doubled up with laughter at the picture. "At this point, my Mom arrived. The entire saga of the sweater came out—and she scolded me! Said all men, including my Papa, had these little idiosyncracies; listed them. Then as the crowning glory, took away that dratted garment, patched the holes with matching wool, sewed on new buttons to replace the old assorted lot—and restored the whole to an ecstatic son-in-law! Now they're buddies for life!"

I had to see the famous sweater, of course, and admire it. Fresh coffee was brewed, and another hour slipped by. It was 11 when I rose to go. I had been dreading going back to an empty apartment, but it seemed likely Neel would be in sooner or later.

"Something's not quite right with you, Piyali, I think," Katia said when we carried the cups into the kitchen. "I won't ask you now. If ever you want to share whatever it is, you know I'm here."

"I know," I said gratefully. "Does it show then?"

"Perhaps not. but I could make out."

"Oh, Katia, I—" David poked his head around the door to see where we were. I said, "David, thank you." He blinked. "For marrying Katia."

I let myself in quietly in case Neel had come back, and gone to bed. It was very still. A single temple lamp was on by the big settee. Suddenly, I was overwhelmed with gladness. Neel was home! But when I tiptoed into the bedroom, he wasn't there. The bed was untouched, its cover smooth, unwrinkled. I slipped off my shoes, and laid down my purse. The bathmat in the bathroom was wet, and so was a big towel, so he must have had a shower recently. Had he gone out again? Perhaps he'd left a note. I dashed back to the living room, eyes searching—and nearly tripped over a supine form stretched out on the rug. What's wrong, I thought in panic. I knelt down swiftly.

Neel was half-lying on his stomach, one arm over his head, face partly hidden. He had shed his coat and shirt, and was barefoot. A hand laid lightly on his bare shoulder showed it was cool after his shower, not hot at all. He isn't ill, I thought in great relief, just tired, and sleeping. Still, I couldn't help feeling deprived. We had been apart for some six hours. At best, our time together was going to be all too short, and here was Neel slumbering! I told myself to get changed, but I lingered on, reluctant to draw away. Why do I love this man to the depths of my being, I mused. I've met plenty of men here and in India. Nice, interesting, knowledgeable, attractive, cultured, from fine backgrounds. I could have fallen for one of them, and it would have been so simple. Instead I had to pick someone with whom no future is possible, and the situation so fraught with undercurrents that any moment, a wrong word might be uttered, snapping the fragile thread that binds us.

I bent to place a butterfly kiss on the rumpled curly head. A deep voice growled, "Who's touching me?" I froze. "Is it Pamela?"

"No," softly, "it's not Pamela."

"Then it's Kiran."

I chuckled inwardly. So Neel was in one of those moods.

"No, and it's not Asha or Joyce or Kimi."

"Then who is it?"

"Try—Natasha."

The arm covering his head came away. Neel rolled over onto his back, and surveyed me. "That's a low blow, lady." Strong hands seized me, and pulled me down to the broad chest, holding me prisoner. "Who told you about Natasha?"

"A friend. At a restaurant. She—Natasha was there with her parents."

"What did this friend tell you?"

"Nothing much. Only that you had a sizzling affair with her."

"Liar. It never sizzled. Barely sputtered. What else?"

"That you went around looking like Lord Byron after you broke up." The grip tightened. Lines memorized at school came to me now. I declaimed, "'When we two parted/In silence and tears,/Half broken-hearted/ To sever for years, /Pale grew thy cheek and cold,/Colder thy kiss,/Truly that hour foretold /Sorrow to this.'" The words, spoken in jest, suddenly too poignant, came out falteringly at the end. We stared at each other, sharing the awful conviction that they could very well apply to us at any time now. Neel made a sound deep in his throat, then lifted me to lie beside him. He began to kiss me as if we had been parted for years instead of hours, telling me without words that the poem had pierced him as unbearably as it had stabbed me. Where was the need for words between us? Our communication lay in the hot throbbing of blood, the harsh breathing, the way an imperative need drove us to shattering heights, and then dropped us into fathomless oblivion, still in each other's arms.

In the morning, we forced ourselves into a cheery mood. I made waffles for breakfast. Neel loved them. Watching him pour maple syrup lavishly over his, I marvelled he could consume the stack on his plate. Prudently, I had just one waffle minus butter or syrup. Neel caught my eye and winked.

"I know," I said wryly, "you jog and swim off everything you eat. You don't have to be so smug about it."

"Growing boys need their nourishment."

"Yes, indeed."

He leaned over to plant a syrupy buttery kiss on my lips, grinning as I grabbed for a napkin to wipe it off. Then suddenly serious, "Piyal, I've had a brainwave. I wondered if you and I could go on a picnic somewhere today. It's such a glorious day. And since it's Monday, there may not be too many people trying to do the same thing. How about Woodstock?"

Surprised, I said slowly, "Why, that sounds great!"

Woodstock was where the Aaronsons had their estate, well out of the city. Katia had taken me to spend a day there one Sunday. I could call her parents and ask permission to picnic in the woods on the estate.

"You didn't have to ask, honey," Saul boomed. "Your friend that nice young sculptor fella? Bring him over to the house to say hello first, will you? I kinda like the guy."

A spirit of joie de vivre bubbled up within us. We dashed down to the delicatessen to load up on salads and a roast chicken, picked oven-hot rolls from the bakery and a mouth-watering lattice-top apple pie. Back in the apartment, while fresh coffee was brewing, Neel packed everything into a hamper. I dashed off to change. I should have worn something practical like the jeans Neel was wearing, but I was in the mood to wear an off-the-shoulder embroidered cotton blouse and a long skirt splashed with bright flowers which would be cool and comfortable. I coiled my hair on top of my head, and tied a chiffon scarf around it. Light rubber-soled sandals, and I was ready. I found Neel had filled a flask with coffee, and closed the hamper.

We were in gay spirits like two small children who had been given an unexpected holiday. Nothing was going to mar this day. All dark thoughts were put away.

An hour later I swung the car onto a quieter road with little traffic. On either side grew the hardy Self-heal with its spiky blue flowers. Katia had told me it was sometimes called Healall, both names indicating the plant was once used medicinally. I drove up a tree-lined lane. The Aaronsons had chosen their retreat well. The place had a charming rustic atmosphere which made it hard to believe we were not so distant from New York.

The gates stood hospitably open for us. The house set amidst magnificent oaks and elms, was an architectural marvel, single-storeyed, large enough to house all children and grandchildren when they gathered for a festive celebration, blending perfectly with the rustic surroundings. Immaculate lawns, gardens abloom with midsummer flowers, spoke of a team of gardeners. Saul came out himself, enveloped me in a bear hug, and turned to pump Neel's hand with great cordiality. Clearly, he was delighted to meet him again. He led us, talking non-stop, into the enormous living-room where a fireplace took up half a wall.

I came to a dead standstill. Neel narrowly missed crashing into me. We both stared. The sculpture titled Joy occupied pride of place, mother and child laughing at each other. So Saul had bought it! Neel had mentioned that all his exhibits at the Young India show being for sale, had SOLD stickers on them.

"Wanted to buy the whole lot of them—but was told there were too many would-be buyers asking. Had a hard time deciding on which one. Piyali, don't tell Kat, will you—I bought 'Lovers' for her as a birthday present. She raved over it. That's when I got the idea." He winked at me. I smiled back, but felt a sharp pang. I had loved all those sculptures, and now they were scattered, in the hands of many different people. Well, at least two were within visiting distance, I comforted myself. And Katia would have the one I had loved most.

Saul was explaining how he and Barb were going on a world cruise next year, planning a week's stopover in Bombay. Neel promptly invited them to Sinhadurg. They were in the midst of discussing how and when to get there when Barbara Aaronson hurried in. She apologized for being in the conservatory when we arrived, kissed me warmly, and turned to welcome Neel cordially.

"I've been looking forward so much to meeting you, Mr Gregory. Both Saul and Katia have told me so much about you. And, of course, I visited the Young India Exhibition. Your work is tremendously exciting. I had to hold Saul back from buying the whole set of sculptures!"

She had been looking at Neel with great interest. And what did that worthy do? Gave her his most charming smile, dimples flashing, bowed over her hand, and told her how having met her beautiful daughter and famous husband, he too had looked forward to meeting her. It was instant conquest. She plied him with coffee and cookies straight from the oven. Neel had both hosts laughing, Saul's big belly shaking as he guffawed. They were having such a good time with him that an hour later, it was with reluctance I had to call Neel's attention to the time. Barbara said regretfully we should have stayed for lunch. Saul produced a bottle of his choicest wine for us to take. Armed with instructions about where to go, we managed to get away.

Noted for its artists' settlement, Woodstock retained all the beauty of the countryside. Farms, open fields and pastures dotted the landscape. Many of New York's affluent and cultured folks had weekend homes here.

I parked the car in the shade by a meadow. Thick waist-high grass and a blaze of bright wild flowers beckoned. Laughing, holding hands, we ran into the midst of yellow-centered white-rayed daisies, and small colonies of petite dainty four-petalled purple Bluets making pretty patches of colour. Neel told me they were also called Quaker Ladies and Innocence. He warned, "Watch out for the thistles!" Still, we paused to watch the bees partaking of the spiny pernicious weed's rich nectar-laden yellow and purple flowers. We chased the fluffy 'parachutes' sailing off in the warm soft breeze of the Milkweeds, all parts of which contain a milky juice, latex. Brilliantly-patterned, a butterfly alighted on a clump of crimson Wild Pinks. We stood still, admiring the iridescence of the wings, marvelling at their beauty.

Neel said softly if this were India, we would have to beware of snakes and scorpions. He remembered Robert Frost's 'The Tuft of Flowers' where a mower of grass coming on his shift, discovers the clean swathe his fellow has made earlier, then sights a hovering butterfly. Going forward to investigate, he finds the other man has left a tuft of bright flowers untouched which he could so easily have destroyed with his scythe. It is so exactly what he would have done himself that he feels a warm sense of brotherhood towards the unknown mower.

I was overcome by the beauty of this warm thyme-scented day, and most of all, by the presence of my beloved. I laughed aloud, flinging my arms in the air, twirling around in joyful abandon. I ran away through the tall grass, looking over my shoulder, my hair coming undone, the scarf falling off. I didn't wait to rescue it, for Neel was gaining on me fast, his longer legs used to running with Sheena, far more swift than mine. He caught me, of course, and still laughing, I fell to the ground, cushioned by the thick springy grass, Neel falling with me. He pinned me down, holding both my arms over my head. A wisp of colour in the pocket of his half-sleeved shirt gave away his secret.

"Neel, you have my scarf!"

The indentations in his cheeks deepened. "And what ransom will you give me in exchange for it, Princess?"

Demurely, "What do you want, Mr Gregory?"

His eyes wandered to my mouth. "Hmmm, let's see. How about a king's ransom?"

"Can't be done. What else?"

"Not even a handful of diamonds?" coaxingly. "No? Then how about a kiss from a Princess?"

Breathlessly, "That might be arranged. Just one?"

"As a starting point, yes."

Our eyes met. Neel put a hand through my hair, lifting my head, cradling it in his hands. He asked huskily, "Do you know when I first knew I loved you?" I shook my head. "It was at the beach—the day the little boy nearly drowned. We were all wet and cold, and you took the child into your arms, and held him close. I thought to myself—this girl is royalty, and she does this?"

"But, Neel, he was shivering as I was," I protested. "He was just a little child."

"A slum child who almost certainly hadn't encountered soap for weeks. I'd felt this powerful attraction to you at Lekh's wedding, and every time we met, the feeling intensified. The first time you came to the studio, I had to fight the impulse to kiss you. I put it down to the presence of the most beautiful girl I'd ever seen, a strong physical pull. But that day at the beach—that was when I knew. I couldn't bear to let you go back to Waverley—and out of my life."

"Oh, Neel," I whispered, utterly moved, putting my arms around his neck.

As his head came down, I closed my eyes. The clamour of the senses would not be denied. I shall never forget the scent of crushed grass and wild thyme, the drowsy murmur of bees, and all around us, the soft gold of that summer day.

21

The apartment was full of the delicious odours of Hawaiian Roast Chicken. With Neel so appreciative of my efforts, I made it a point to make a variety of dishes for him. Of course, we ate out often, but after yesterday's picnic, we were still basking in the memory of that precious time together, and preferred to stay at home this evening. I loved going out with Neel, for he made every outing very special. Yet I loved staying at home with him.

The chicken was doing beautifully. I had stuffed it whole with all kinds of good things such as coconut, pineapple, grated orange peel to go with the usual breadcrumbs and celery. I opened the oven door to brush it again with Golden Pineapple Glaze. It looked good enough—well, to eat. The plain white rice was almost done, the salad ready to be dressed. I set the table quickly, and went off to shower. I sang as I used bath gel on my skin, thinking happily this was one thing I had learnt from Neel. My voice was hardly a match for his, nor could I burst into an aria, but my warbling was a measure of my uplifted spirits.

I slipped on a sleeveless cotton dress which changed my eyes to sapphire, touched gloss to my mouth, but didn't bother with more makeup. It was warm this evening, and all windows stood open to catch the smallest breeze. Back in the kitchen, I removed the roasting pan from the oven, and admired the golden-brown contents. Even the rice was done. Where was Neel?

When I heard the key in the lock, my heart sang with happiness. He came in, locked the door carefully—and turned to look straight at me without advancing more than a few steps. It was so unlike him not to greet me with his warmest smile. My heart began to thump in my chest. Almost, I guessed what was coming.

Then the bald statement without embellishment: "Piyal, my flight leaves tomorrow evening."

When I could, I said, "I see. How—do you know?"

"My uncle's office. They were handling it for me."

"Had you—asked for this particular one?"

"No, of course not. But since I'd changed my booking once, this is the only one available for another six weeks."

It was a bolt from the blue. But it shouldn't have been so shocking. Sooner or later, it was going to happen. Which argument did nothing to take away the awful feeling which invaded my being. Neel's next words were a worse blow.

"I have to say this also, Piyal. It's—truly the end for us this time. We—can't meet again."

I looked at him stonily. "Is that all you can say, Neel? Just those bald words? No explanation—nothing more?"

"My reasons haven't changed. You know what they are, Piyal."

"Do I really? All you've ever given me are inadequate words which tell me nothing. Are you not going to add something? Don't you think you owe me more, Neel?"

He flung out his hand. "As I've told you before—I can't say more than that."

Suddenly, I was utterly weary. I had hoped and hoped that this time together when we had been as close as a man and woman can ever be, would change everything, and Neel would at last feel he could tell me everything. I sagged against the wall. If I spoke now, I would say a great many wrong things. Even if I'd had the spirit, the energy left—which I didn't—my words would be futile. A bitter quarrel would ensue in which we would both say unforgettable hurtful things, solving nothing. My pride would not permit it.

If my lips did not speak, my expression must have, for a sound like a deep groan left Neel's throat. In a kind of lunge, he was across the room, pinning me against the wall, rough urgency in his movements. He held my head through my hair, turning my face upto his.

Hoarsely, "Piyal—don't—don't hate me. If only you knew—what this is doing to me. As it is, I'm tearing myself away from you. Inside—I'm being torn to pieces."

"Then why won't you tell me the truth—let me understand?" I whispered. "These days—when we've shared so much—don't they mean anything to you? Haven't you learnt to trust me yet?"

"Oh God!" He pulled me tightly into his arms. "This has been the most beautiful time in my whole life, Piyal. And I love you. I love you so much I don't have words to tell all I feel." He looked into my eyes searchingly. "Tell me you believe that. Tell me, Piyal."

"If you mean what you say, why do you want it to end? You say we'll never meet again, is that it? That when you go tomorrow, everything we mean to each other will become past history? Just a sweet memory?" His hand came up to cover my mouth. Over it, we stared at each other.

He said huskily, "Piyal, please let's not spoil these last hours when we've been so happy together. I beg you, Piyal."

I thought, less than twenty-four hours left. How can I survive after he goes? He isn't going to tell me. Always his loyalty to Romola wins out over our love. That was my last coherent thought. Neel's frantic kiss wiped out everything. The elemental passion between us that always smouldered beneath the surface opened the floodgates of our need for each other, made desperately urgent by the separation that lay ahead which would sever our relationship for all time.

"Piyal, I don't want you to come to the airport."

Unable to believe my ears, I turned.

"I don't want you watching the plane depart, and coming back alone. You mustn't go through that."

Neel had his back to me. He was placing his bags by the door. My eyes were on the big frame as he bent to check a name tag. Shattered, I sank to the settee. So, I thought numbly, what little time we have left is being cut just like that.

I thought of a possible reason why he didn't want me to come. "Are your aunt and uncle going to be there?"

"No. I said my farewells yesterday. In any case, he had to go out of town, and she's at work all day."

It was late afternoon, but knowing New York's rush hour traffic, Neel had asked for a cab well before time. Since last night, we had not spoken another word on one forbidden topic. Neel had been right. What use to spoil our last hours together? We could change nothing. All day, I had carried this heavy feeling in my breast like a stone. Now the old bitterness threatened to swamp me, but I held it at bay.

My eyes leaped to the clock. Five minutes.When I looked up, Neel was watching me. He crossed the room swiftly, and knelt down, wrapping me in his arms. We had no words we could utter without breaking down. My eyes burned with unshed tears, my breast with feelings I could not find release for. Neel leaned back, cupping my face in one hand, the long sculptor's fingers of the other moving tenderly over each feature.

"Piyal. My most beloved Princess. You're the most beautiful thing that ever happened to me," he said huskily, speaking with difficulty. "Forgive me for hurting you, my darling. You've given me so much happiness—such joy. I remember every single moment we've spent together, every word we've exchanged." He pulled me back into his arms, burying his face in the curve of my neck. The next words burst out as if he could not stem them. "But how can I leave you—never see you again? Oh, God, Piyal, I love you. I love you."

Even if I had wanted to, I could not have spoken. He raised a ravaged face. He said unsteadily, "I have to go, my darling. The cab must be here." He kissed me, putting all his feelings into the embrace. "Bless you, my Piyal." His arms fell away. I stood up with him. He moved quickly now as if forcing his feet to obey him. He opened the front door, and picked up his bags, tucking the light handbag under his arm. I watched silently. He turned to give me one last look. Then he was out of the door. It closed behind him.

Katia was a tower of strength to me in those awful empty days after Neel had gone. That evening when he left, unable to stay on in the apartment where memories crowded in on me, I had called Katia. It had been a cry for help. She had said, "Do you need to ask? Just pack an overnight bag, and come over."

There was no way I could keep the story to myself. Indeed, the need to tell someone, to cry on a sympathetic shoulder became an absolute necessity. And I did. I who had suppressed my tears for so long, now wept. Even so, though my tale shocked the Asschers, I could see they were fascinated. Katia told me later it was like listening to something out of Eastern fiction like *The Arabian Nights*. Dear David, how kind he was, patting my hand comfortingly, placing a box of tissues near me, making enough tea to float the *Queen Mary* in order to soothe my broken heart.

Katia mentioned how her parents had been charmed by Neel. David added he had been spellbound at the Exhibition by Neel's work. "Enormous talent there. He will reach great heights."

From Katia, "Is there absolutely nothing anyone can do, Piyali? Some older person from his family or yours? That nice cousin lady you talk about, or her husband?"

I shook my head. My voice thick with weeping, I told them about Madame Nalin's relationship with her grandson. "He'll never jeopardize her well-being. I've met her twice myself. A truly lovely lady. I wouldn't forgive myself any more than Neel would forgive himself if anything happened to her because of us. And it will surely upset her terribly."

Katia said restlessly, "There must be some way out of this. It isn't in your nature to give up so easily, Piyali."

"Perhaps not. But in this one case, I'm up against a stone wall. No, I just have to learn acceptance—live with the reality."

Daddy sounded different on the phone, and I couldn't fathom why. He actually seemed embarrassed. He cleared his throat several times, and it came out at last. "Piyali, I don't know how to tell you. It's just that—well, Kanan is—well, in the family way." And stopped abruptly. I was flabbergasted. He said my name anxiously. Recovering, I exclaimed, "Daddy, you couldn't have given me happier news!"

"Oh, bless you! I didn't know how to tell you!"

"I'm thrilled! How is Kanan?"

"Very fine—but rather shy over this."

"Tell her not to be. It's splendid news." And it was. In my dark mood, it brought a ray of light. I was glad for them both. I recalled Uday Singh saying, "Tej should have a son." I wasn't belittling my role in Daddy's life, but I hoped it would be a boy.

He was saying, "At my age, I should be a grandfather."

"You're not even fifty, Daddy. Too young to be one. I'm not going to make you one for ages." Unbidden, a picture flashed into my mind of a small curly-haired mischievous child with golden eyes. I thrust it away with determination.

"I don't know how it happened. We hadn't planned—" He broke off.

I teased, "Oh, oh, Daddy, I should have warned you all about the birds and the bees."

That made him chuckle. "Rascal!"

"Is Kanan there? May I speak to her for a minute?"

I made Kanan laugh as well. She overcame her initial embarrassment. "I'm happy," she said simply. "Tej is still stunned."

"And secretly bursting with pride. Take very good care of yourself—and of the expectant father." She chuckled. "Oh, you haven't told the children? They'll be thrilled as I am.

"Piyali, do you realize what a darling you are, I wonder? Another daughter might have felt resentment."

"Then she wouldn't be much of a daughter."

Daddy's voice said, "My daughter is more precious to me than any jewel." His tone changed. "How are things with you, dear child?"

I wanted suddenly to weep, to tell him, "Daddy, I've never been more unhappy in my life. Help me." But I said brightly that things were humming at work, and I had a full social calendar.

"That's good. That's very good."

But after I had hung up, I stood with my head bowed for a long time. If only I could see Daddy, put my head on that broad shoulder, and sob out my woes. . . . No, I must never give him an inkling. He had a right to his happiness, to look forward after long lonely years to the new baby. I squared my own shoulders. This was my battle. I was a Chandravats, and I must fight it on my own.

22

I met Elliott Northrop when he arrived from London after a three-year posting there heading the UK Headquarters of Danae. Elliott had been in and out of New York in the months after I joined, but our paths had not crossed. It was the fact that our Chief, Harrison Roxburgh, was very ill which brought Elliott in to replace him. The grapevine reported that the move annoyed him very much. Before the London assignment, he had been in Paris, and come to love all things European. For the kind of person that he was, an opera buff, balletomane, in fact, lover of all fine arts, such a preference was understandable. Be that as it may, he was reputed to be an excellent administrator, strict but fair, ever open to new ideas. Needless to say, we all were rather nervous. Had Quentin Wirth taken over, we would have been quite relaxed. Quent, however, was now on his way to London as Northrop's replacement.

In the process of taking over the reins with a million things to see to, almost three weeks passed before we designers were summoned to a conference with the new Head. And how well he had briefed himself! He spoke to each one by name, asked questions to bring his knowledge up-to-date. Having the ability to draw out even the nervous ones, a relaxed atmosphere prevailed. When my turn came, he repeated my name carefully to pronounce it just right, then I was asked to tell all about the clientele I had designed for in Bombay. He said he would be interested in the kind of jewellery that had been most popular. I could then sit back and really look at this new boss. Late thirties, tall and lean, a narrow face with angular features, dark-haired, light blue eyes. Superbly tailored clothes, perfectly manicured hands. One imagined as a person, he was hard to know, probably cherishing his privacy.

Later, Northrop met us one by one for more detailed consultations. The first to meet him reported the sessions were exciting. It seemed our new Head was asking for innovative ideas, strikingly different from anything Danae had ever done before. Apparently, he had fired them with such zeal, they were rarin' to go.

When I was summoned, I carried a folder with my Honey Bee designs, plus photographs of fashion shows where my work had been featured. Northrop had specifically asked to see samples. In the imposing Office he had inherited from Harrison, we came down to brass tacks without delay. Soon his big desk was covered with my designs. Incisive questions came at me rapidly. He had an unerring ability to pick out the most striking designs.

At one point, he bent closer to examine a photograph. He said slowly, "This is surely you?" raising his head to look at me. I nodded reluctantly. "Do you model too then?" I explained how my cousin had coerced me into modelling that first time for her. He listened intently. "So it is true. You belong to a royal family. Real live maharajas and all?" I laughed. "Real live ex-maharajas."

By now, I was completely at ease. When he began to outline his ideas for me, I was captivated. No wonder the others had come out of their sessions with him in a state of excitement. I made quick notes, my head already teeming with possibilities. Elliott walked with me to the door. "Good luck," he said gravely.

If I had needed to be jolted out of my misery, this meeting with Mr Northrop had provided it. I hardly slept for the next two weeks. My head spun with ideas, and my hands had a hard time keeping up with them. For a change, even my dreams related to my work. Dark circles under my eyes, a loss of four pounds did not matter. I had much reason to thank my foresight in making sketches and taking pictures of the jewellery Urvashi Devi had displayed for me. They formed the main inspiration for me now, altered, modified, adapted to suit Western tastes, but essentially retaining the grandeur and tradition of the original pieces.

I spent almost a whole day arranging a display of these new designs. Then I asked for an appointment with Mr Northrop. When he arrived, he nodded briefly, and went straight to the display. "Explain everything to me," he commanded. And I did, forgetting my nervousness, my words flowing on smoothly. He often asked a question, always to the point, clearly showing he knew what he was talking about. My throat was parched when I finished. I waited, my eyes fixed on his face. When he spoke, he astonished me.

"Are you free this evening? Good. We'll have a celebration dinner." And smiled when he saw my expression. "This is tremendously good work. Surpasses anything I had visualized. But then I'm not a real live princess." I sagged with relief. "I want to know much more about these designs and the designer. Leave them with me. I'd like to study them more carefully."

I stammered, "Thank you. I'm so glad—you approve. I wasn't sure at all if this was what you wanted."

A gleam appeared in the blue eyes. "We're going to build this into a very big thing. By the way, wear your Indian dress tonight. I'd like to see how it looks."

"I don't wear saris."

"Whatever you have, as long as it's traditional. I have a few other ideas in mind—hence the request."

I went down to the lobby a few minutes before Elliott was due. He looked very suave in formal evening attire. His glance swept over the cloak I was wearing, the hood partially over my head. Katia and David had given it to me for my birthday. She had seen it in a boutique, she told me, and knew it was just meant for me. It was satin, reversible, ivory on one side, and gold on the other. A quizzical expression crossed my escort's face.

"You are very regal tonight," he said quietly, handing me a little box. It held an orchid, pale cream with deeper yellow markings. When I exclaimed it complimented my dress perfectly, he said smiling, "Probably, my ESP working overtime."

Elliott said he hadn't felt like battling traffic tonight, and had a cab waiting. "I hope you like Chinese food?"

"Love it."

We went straight to the heart of Chinatown to The Golden Unicorn. I was glad it wasn't a place Neel and I had gone to. So I could relax now in the elegance of the restaurant with its beautiful marble and brass decor. We were early, but already several tables were occupied by Chinese couples.

There was pure admiration in Elliott's eyes after he had helped me with my cloak.

"I can't help feeling we're in the wrong place for you," he said softly as he seated me. "We should be somewhere like the Taj in the moonlight—sandalwood and jasmine scenting the air, with music to go with it all. A *sitar* maybe." He studied the ivory caftan-like gown I was wearing, its low round neck heavily embroidered in gold and seed pearls, as were the cuffs of the loose flowing sleeves. Very long pearl and gold earrings matched the choker around my neck. A broad gold belt studded with pearls, and gold slippers completed the ensemble.

"That's very fanciful. You wanted me to wear something ethnic, Mr Northrop."

"Elliott. Yes, I did for a very special reason. But," firmly, "not another word till we've dined royally."

The food was superlative. As more and more people arrived, many of them Chinese, one could assume the cuisine was authentic. Nor could my companion be faulted in any way. He was as polished and urbane a person as one could find anywhere. Easy to guess that the wonderful ballet and opera performances he was describing had been attended in the company of some very glamorous sophisticated ladies. Fleetingly, I thought of someone else, also an opera lover, who would have enjoyed and contributed to this exchange, and then sternly banished the thought. Elliott also drew me out, and I found myself telling him more about myself.

"You spoke about the way I am tonight. Actually, this kind of dress isn't worn by ladies in our family. They wear the traditional sari—at least the older ones do. But then, I never have. I suppose this is Indian enough even if it does bear a touch of the Middle East. I have to say these are merely external trappings. I was born in Ithaca, New York, and if not in appearance, in outlook and as a person, I'm as American as apple pie. With a soupcon of Europe and India each," I concluded firmly.

Elliott threw back his head and laughed with true enjoyment. When he sobered, he said, "You have the best of three worlds, and that makes you a rare person indeed." Our dishes were being cleared. "I suppose this is as good a time as any to tell you what I've been dreaming up."

Soon I was so absorbed in his words that I sipped the fragrant tea in my cup without really being aware of it. Elliott's idea was to launch a new collection of jewellery to be called The Maharani Collection. Like other houses of its kind, Danae had had similar themes. The idea had been born when he first met me, had taken firm root during our consultation in his Office, and when he saw my designs this morning, the matter had decided itself. I visualized it all in growing excitement. It was going to be the high point in my career so far, and who knew where it might lead? If I knew Danae, they would give the Collection a spectacular build-up.

Eyes on my face, Elliott went on. Emphasis would be laid on the fact that a princess was the designer, inspired by authentic jewellery from her own royal background. "And," he now brought out his final surprise, "I've been thinking you could model them yourself." My face must have reflected my shock, for he said gently, "Why should that surprise you, Piyali? You have the looks, you've modelled, and are familiar with cameras. Those high cheekbones, those amazing eyes which seem to change colour, that disdainful look, all add up to a fabulous model for the Collection. I'm not going to force you to do anything you don't want to do. In any case, Rothman has the final say. But I know his cameras will love you."

I was silent. It was a little too overwhelming for me. As long as I was an anonymous designer, a small cog in the vast enterprise that was Danae, I was secure and happy. This was like being catapulted into the realm of international fashion where the most beautiful models in the world were featured. Suddenly, I longed for Neel to be there, to support and sustain me in this difficult decision. I could almost feel his strong hand clasping mine, pouring strength and courage into my heart, feel the powerful frame as I leaned on it like a shelter from all storms, and hear his voice saying, "But of course my Piyal can do it." I came back with a thud. I was here at The Golden Unicorn where people were dining, and opposite sat a man who was my Boss. I gave my head a little shake to clear away the sense of desolation.

Elliott said quietly, "I think a walk through Chinatown will be interesting." I gave him a watery smile, and nodded. I could not have spoken if I had wanted to.

Elliott's prescription worked. We strolled along the streets thronged with people, brilliantly lit and colourful. The change of scene, the cool fall air, all helped to restore me. Wisely, Elliott said no more on the subject. I meant every word when later he dropped me off at the apartment complex, I thanked him for a wonderful evening.

One has to observe at firsthand how Americans do things. No time was lost in preparations for launching The Maharani Collection. Whatever went on in the departments involved was kept in the utmost secrecy. No one was busier than I. This was one time when my advice was sought constantly, for the essential royal aura forming a fitting background played a most important part. If it weren't so exhausting, I would have to admit it was unimaginably exhilarating. There were humorous moments too. Amid a welter of tiger and leopard skins, and gorgeous Oriental rugs, one of the advertising people suggested a little black slave boy wearing only a loincloth and turban, wielding a fan over the Maharani, something like the Nubian attendants one saw in Hollywood Roman epics. Possibly, Cleopatra had them. I had to laugh to myself over this because it seemed extremely unlikely that any one of these little people ever reached Divyasthala! One could have a *punkah*-coolie, of course, but somehow the idea didn't appeal.

I had told Elliott that I wasn't prepared to model for the Collection. He was very understanding—which relieved me greatly. I should have realized Elliott could not have reached where he was without possessing the tenacity of a bulldog when he had set his heart on something. He was out of town attending a conference when I received a rather desperate summons from a minion of Leon Rothman. Roberta, known as Bobbie, came personally to call me. The preliminary shots for the campaign were a disaster. The model simply couldn't seem to grasp what was required of her. Rothman was ready to tear his own hair, and scalp everyone else too. Would I please get to the studio pronto, and see if I could help the model to do it right? Amused and intrigued, I went along—to find chaos reigning. Rothman was scowling, the others waiting tensely. My first glimpse of the model brought instant dismay. Oh no, I thought, she doesn't even look the part, and is all wrong for the Collection. Yet Andrea was famous enough, very beautiful, and photogenic, but those Nordic looks would not do at all. They had draped a sari somehow around her, but frankly, for all its grandeur, neither sari nor model did a thing to enhance each other. No wonder, Rothman was feeling so mad over it.

"Piyali, show her," he said tersely.

For the next half hour, that was exactly what I did. Every time Andrea did it wrong, no matter how carefully I instructed, Rothman breathed fire. Finally, Rothman gestured to me. I was to pose for a few shots to show Andrea what was required. I wore my usual makeup. Some trial pieces of jewellery were supplied. Bobbie draped a length of fabric interwoven with gold thread cunningly around me. I followed instructions faithfully under the brilliant lighting. In other circumstances, posing for the great Rothman would have alarmed me. Now I was quite at ease. In any case, I had modelled before, so if the milieu was different, the exercise was perfectly familiar. Rothman nodded to me at last. My part was over. I was glad I had been useful. Bobbie winked at me, her lips shaping a 'thank you'. I smiled and went off, back to my own work, forgetting it all in the flurry of some new designs I was working on.

When Rothman himself showed up the next day, I was quite exasperated. Now what, I asked myself crossly. He walked into our room unceremoniously. Peter looked at me puzzled. At least, Rothman wasn't breathing fire this morning. He stalked to my desk, and emptied a big brown envelope over its surface. Glossy photographs lay strewn about. Peter bent over them. He breathed, "Heavens above, will you look at this one! Or this!" picking up one at a time. I was truly startled myself. The camera work was spectacular, but that was hardly surprising, given the identity of the master who had photographed hundreds of beautiful women.

It was the model who riveted the eye—proud, almost scornful, the eyes picking up colour from the fabric, the long line of throat a perfect backdrop for the glittering stones of the necklace that clasped it. Yes, I thought dazedly, this is the Maharani to the life.

I became conscious of Rothman's unwinking gaze upon me. Uninvited, he had seated himself comfortably, the fingertips of one hand against those of the other. Not knowing what to say, Peter and I waited silently.

"Well, Princess?"

I stammered. "The pictures are unbelievable! Andrea should have no trouble now."

Rothman snorted. "Who's Andrea?" I opened my mouth, and closed it again. "I want you. You're my Maharani."

"But—"

Grandly, "There are no buts. Rothman has chosen you."

I said desperately, "Mr Rothman, I've already told Mr Northrop I can't model for The Maharani Collection."

"And why not when any one of fifty thousand girls would give their eyeteeth for the opportunity to be photographed by Rothman?" The last word was intoned as if it were Michelangelo or Da Vinci.

"I'm aware of that, and it would be a great honour—but I'm a designer, not a model."

"Oh yes, you are. You were born for the camera. That face, that wonderful sultry look in the eyes, that luscious mouth—all so exotic. I could tell you'd done some modelling—too practised to be a novice."

"I—"

He made a sweeping gesture with his hands. "I shall tell Elliott Northrop Rothman cannot do it. No Princess, no Rothman."

I stared at him. This was a veritable Sword of Damocles hanging over my poor head. I thought of the back-breaking labour that had gone into designing the jewellery for the Collection. If I said it myself, it was magnificent, perfect for the theme. I wasn't the only one to be involved now. An entire team was pursuing the finer details of launching the project. This was Danae, not The Honey Bee where that understanding woman, Madhur Monal, ran her own small empire. My personal preference, my emotional state, simply didn't matter in the vast scheme of things. I had to admit the truth of Rothman's point about fifty thousand other girls. I asked myself why I was fussing so much. No one could actually force me to model, yet here was Rothman virtually holding me to ransom. When Elliott came to know of the latest developments, would he be as accommodating as he had been earlier? Rothman was so acclaimed, having him work for Danae was itself enviable. Any fashion house would snap him up in the twinkling of an eye. To say Elliott would be displeased with me would be the understatement of the year.

I have to grant it to Rothman that he did not crow when I finally looked at him helplessly, and spread my hands in surrender. He held out his hand, and when dazedly, I put mine in it, he said succinctly, "Now." I looked at Peter mutely, and he grinned, lifting his thumb in encouragement. So there I was, being led at express speed by the great Rothman to his studio while heads popped out of doorways, and people stopped working and stared at us in suspended animation. I heard a babel of voices break out behind us. Then the studio door opened, and I was ushered in.

Danae's Maharani Collection was launched with much fanfare. It became the rage for that season. From Danae headquarters in Paris came accolades for Elliott Northrop. You can guess the attention I came in for. Wise in the fickle ways of fashion, Katia told me to bask in it while it lasted. I did just that. Being only too human, I enjoyed being interviewed, and written about, being photographed at restaurants and shows I attended. I was featured on the covers of magazines. One saw the Maharani surveying the scene from the heights of giant billboards, jewels flashing from throat, ears and wrists, and on TV screens. Rothman's master hand was seen in every likeness.

I sent sheafs of clippings and copies of magazines to Urvashi Devi, and Lata. The former told me excitedly on the phone that she had never dreamed the jewellery she had displayed for me at the Palace would turn out to be so inspiring. She had loved each piece I had designed, and they were all so proud of me. And I looked more a Maharani than anyone she had ever known! Lata's response was equally heartwarming, if typically humorous.

Two more things resulted from this whole episode. One, that as the model, I was the recipient of fees which swelled my bank balance to a degree undreamed of. Two, that Elliott, having dutifully escorted me as part of the publicity campaign for the Collection, became much closer to me. I wasn't ready for a new emotional relationship. I was still hurting badly. I told Elliott this very honestly, adding just enough details to make him understand. Dear man, he accepted that. We were friends and companions, he said. I knew it was too good to last, but for the time being, we were content to enjoy the companionship we shared.

23

I was surprised at the message on my answering machine. What would Suneet Pal want with me? I'd met him and his wife a few times, but we were hardly friends. Since I had come from India this time, I had avoided meeting anyone who might remind me of the recent past. Bittersweet as my memories were, I had no wish to brood over them. It was with reluctance that I dialled the Pal's number.

Astonished, I listened to Suneet's voice explaining that the leaders of the Indian community in New York had decided to invite Lekh Sebastian and his troupe as part of their annual cultural programme. The proceeds were always used for some worthy cause. Sebastian had been in and out of the country in the last one year collaborating on a new album with British singer Julian Chatwick and American singer Ham Brubaker. When approached, they had received an encouraging response. However, the composer had many commitments in Bombay, and wished to consult his schedule before giving them a date which he had now done. To organize the entire programme which would also feature other performers, a Committee had been set up. My name was suggested. They hoped very much I would accept.

I listened with very mixed feelings. On the one hand, I could not but applaud their choice. Lata and I had attended a concert in Bombay where Lekh and his troupe had held the audience enthralled. Yet meeting Lekh again—and most certainly Tara—for they were inseparable—

would bring me mixed pain and pleasure. I told Suneet I was honoured, but doubted my usefulness. Surely there were people here far more capable and experienced than I. He drowned me in a flood of words. No, no, I had figured at the top of the list. Everyone was very proud of me. Besides, wasn't I related to Sebastian? Not related, I said firmly, just connected to his wife. Not for nothing had Suneet reached the top of his profession. I found myself agreeing at least to attend the first meeting at his house before making up my mind.

So it was that I found myself in the Pal's grand living room chatting to his vivacious wife, Chatura, while all others were engaged in animated talk. When I had arrived, and was introduced, they had been a little awkward, as if not quite sure how to behave. Only one man seemed to greet me like a long-lost friend—I had never even seen him before—and told me he was one of Bhaiyya's favourite people. I had smiled politely, rather doubting his claim. When the door bell chimed, Suneet let in one more person whom he greeted with great cordiality, clapping a hand on his shoulder, and leading him in. The newcomer was hailed boisterously from all sides.

I thought queerly, but what is Daddy doing here? And he's shaved off his beard! Why didn't he tell me he was coming? Then it came to me I was being a complete ass. This man smiling and responding cordially to all greetings, obviously the leader here, wasn't Tej Pratap Singh even if he was like him enough to be his blood brother. If there was truth in the saying that somewhere in the world, everyone has a double, then here was Daddy's.

Chatura was saying, "Good! Now that Rom's here, we can begin." As if the man had heard his name, he looked across the room, saw his hostess, and came straight across. "Chatura," he said warmly, taking her proffered hand, "how good of you to let us meet here! Under your roof, this is going to be a really productive meeting! Yes, Margot's fine. Sends her greetings."

As if feeling my unwinking gaze, he turned his head. The feeling of familiarity was now so strong, I was quite dazed.

"Oh, you haven't met Piyali—Princess Piyali actually. Rom Nalin, Piyali, who's the inspiration behind the whole thing."

Mechanically, I put my hand in the big one held out to me. I must have murmured the right words. In his eyes, there was appreciation, but no recognition whatsoever. How could there be? That was all there was time for. Suneet had come to fetch him. Everyone was finding seats. We were about to begin.

Through stiff lips, I asked Chatura, "What does Rom stand for?"

"Romain. He's married to an American. Margot is a brilliant

lawyer," in a whisper. "They have two lovely kids—a daughter at college, and a son in high school."

For the next half hour, my mind seemed to work on two levels. On one, I was listening to the man who appeared to be the acknowledged chairperson outlining the many points that needed discussion. He spoke quietly but forcefully. Everyone gave him respectful attention. On the second level, I was studying him intently, a whirl of thoughts spinning in my head. In the nature of the gathering, I could stare at him without anyone noticing since they were all looking at him as he spoke.

The final piece of the puzzle has fallen into place, I thought painfully. And Neel has been carrying this secret in his innermost heart. This is his uncle, the one he avoided letting me meet. And with good reason, as I see now. He is unmistakably a Chandravats. Here unknown to any of us is Digvijay's son. Does he know about his paternity? He has the looks which any knowlegeable person will recognize immediately. I thought of Madame Nalin. Had she known when she fled Divyasthala that she was carrying a child? What had she felt when she discovered her condition? This could have been no joyous discovery for her. Now that I thought back, Madame had mentioned her daughter often, to the point of telling us how the entire incident had affected her, so that she avoided marriage for several years. And yes, she had spoken of her son just once at our first meeting—but never again. "My son tells me I ask too many questions," she had said laughing. She had told us so much of the story—and left out this one vital detail. No, she wouldn't want us to know—especially not us. So Madame had avoided all danger, and played it safe by naming her son Romain. It was an apt name for the one believed to be the posthumous son of Kushal Nalin, and his wife Romola. So Rom had been in New York the whole time, and Neel had made sure we never met. He had distrusted me that much. And, finally, the searing truth. If I had entertained the smallest hope that some miracle would take place, and Neel and I would come together again, the living reality of the man sitting a few yards away, answering questions which were being directed at him from all sides, destroyed it totally.

Suggestions came thick and fast, were tossed around for practicality, some adopted, others dropped. Committees were set up to oversee all aspects of the coming event.

Suneet looked in our direction. He said gallantly, "I'd like to suggest that the two beautiful ladies in our midst would add the perfect touch to the Reception Committee. All invited guests will be dazzled."

Beside me, Chatura said dryly, "This is the first time my lord and master has used those adjectives about me." The men chortled at the dig. One man clapped Suneet on the back, and he grinned sheepishly. Chatura turned to me, "Do we consent, Princess?"

"Yes, I think so. What exactly would we be expected to do? I shan't be able to get much leave."

Shortly, the men descended on Chatura's buffet table as if they had not eaten in weeks. I was stationed behind the tea and coffee pots, but had few takers, most having made beeline to where Suneet was dispensing drinks. Only the fellow who had claimed to be Bhaiyya's friend hovered. His name was Sudanshu Kumar Jaswant, he told me, and he was a most successful stockbroker. I was polite enough, but wished he would go away. He was too glib, too over-familiar for someone I had just met. Nor did I like the way his eye wandered all over me. When a now familiar voice asked, "Am I too late to beg a cup of tea, Princess?" Jaswant moved away at last.

"Not at all, Mr Nalin."

"Please call me Rom."

"I will if you drop that pretentious title, and call me Piyali, "handing him his cup."

"Honoured to, Piyali," spearing a slice of lemon.

Somehow we gravitated to chairs close by. I had questions to ask. Apparently, so did he. I watched his face closely when he wanted to know which State I came from, and I told him.

"Really?" he said astonished. "Speak of coincidence! My family belonged to Divyasthala originally! Of course, there are no Nalins there now. Haven't been for—well, a half century or more, I guess." He lifted his cup to his lips. "If I may ask, what is your last name? Chandravats," he repeated when I told him. "A famous name, is it? Found in all the history books with tales of derring-do?" smiling. "No, I've never been to Divyasthala. No occasion to. And we don't know anyone there now. Perhaps sometime, you'll tell me more about it. Tell me, are all Chandravats—am I saying that right?—as beautiful as you are?" He laughed at my reply. "Have you been in New York long? You are? But if you're designing for Danae, you must be enormously talented. You can't be much older than my daughter, and you've achieved so much! I'm most impressed. Wait a minute—yes, that's it! You're the model in the Maharani ads!"

"And you, Mr Nal—Rom? You must have been a New Yorker for a long time?"

He had come when he was twenty-two, he told me, fresh out of college, nearly thirty years ago now. His cousin had come to America first to study. They were very close, almost like twins, having been born within days of each other. Raised practically in the same cradle, he said smiling. Rom had followed soon after. To supplement their scholarships, they had worked part-time for an Indian importer. One thing had led to another until a few years later, the cousins had set up their own establishment, selling carpets at first, then expanding into handicrafts not only from India, but from all over the globe. They now had branches all over the country. His cousin looked after their West Coast concerns while Rom stayed in the New York Headquarters. I thought it was as American a success story as any I had heard. Starting with practically nothing but one's two hands, the will to work unceasingly, an uncanny ability to judge the market—that was what it took. And here I was, actually feeling a strong sense of pride and admiration! A sudden thought came to me. In the strangest circumstances, Rom Nalin was my uncle as he was Neel's.

"It's a wonderful story," I said softly. "Do you ever go to India?"

"Yes, indeed. I make it two or three times a year. Partly business, and buying, of course, but also to see my mother. Now there's one stubborn woman for you! I've given up trying to get her to stay with us here. She tells me at her age, people don't transplant easily. So I found this rather pleasant place with an excellent climate, built a bungalow where she stays very happily. Fully staffed with a companion who is very nice, domestic help, a car and chauffeur. My sister drops in—when she's in the country. I have a nephew whom my mother practically raised. Dotes on him. She has her own circle of friends. Fine neighbours. The main thing is she's content."

"I'm sure she looks forward to your visits very much."

"She does. But then so do I. She's a very lovely and gracious lady. My wife and children adore her. We go together whenever it's possible." I could well believe that. Hadn't Lata, Tara and I succumbed too?

"You say none of your family remains in Divyasthala?"

"Not any more. My uncle Paul moved away when he was quite young. You see, my father died—was actually killed—in very tragic circumstances before I was born. I'd guess my mother had these terribly sad memories, and couldn't bear to stay on. I believe he was only 32 or so. It's been one of the sorrows of my life that I never knew him. I understand he was very fine—a brilliant man who would have gone far."

"I lost my mother when I was very young, and felt the loss so much."

He patted my hand. "I know. And that makes the remaining parent extra precious."

We smiled at each other in perfect harmony. We are drawn to each other so easily, I thought. I wondered if kinfolk always felt this instinctive familial pull.

In the weeks that followed, other sessions were held for various committees. Having accepted the assignment, I was able to get into the spirit of the whole thing, looking forward to the reunion with the Sebastians. One matter plagued me. Sudanshu became something of a nuisance, phoning, trying to invite me to go out with him. I managed to fob him off every time, but he refused to take the hint. He had been put on the Reception Committee—his doing, I was sure—and at meetings, he stuck to my side. Normally, I would have felt amusement, and considered him no worse than a pesky fly, but in my present mood, it was irritating.

But for Rom Nalin, my respect grew steadily. I thought with a pang that here was a born leader. Given other circumstances, he might have had the onerous responsibilities of leadership thrust upon his shoulders. To us, he was always kind and considerate, making sure Chatura and I were given duties within our capabilities, and no more. It seemed, he looked upon me as a daughter—which though very satisfying, made me sad, for our relationship could go so far and no further.

24

When Ruhi called, I couldn't believe my ears! She and Robin were actually going to be in New York! It seemed Robin had meetings in Toronto in connection with some films in the line of documentaries which were being commissioned by a Canadian TV company. Ruhi was calling from Melbourne where they were visiting her mother. They would fly to Canada next, and then to New York before leaving for India. I lost no time in inviting them to stay with me, and was delighted when they accepted. What a remarkable coincidence that they would be here for the concert! More, that the Sebastians and Nevilles should all be in New York at the same time!

Ruhi, lovely as ever, was as excited as I was. We hugged each other with great affection. From Robin came a big bear hug. They more than liked the apartment, were unhappy about displacing me from the bedroom, but laughed when I said I was glad I could provide a bed that would accommodate Robin. We had the happiest reunion. Robin knew New York well, and had umpteen friends who invited them home. Sometimes, we ate out, but at others, Ruhi and I made a simple meal, and we stayed at home to enjoy each other's company. There was so much I wanted to know, all about family, friends and Bombay that often in the wee hours, Ruhi would say, "Oh, Piyali, look at the time, and you have to work tomorrow!"

In their turn, the Nevilles were excited about my successes. Robin studied Rothman's photography with an expert's eye, and asked if he could meet the man himself. So I took them to Danae. It was instant attraction. Rothman took one look at Ruhi, and was instantly appreciative. He was not surprised to hear she was a model. I swept her off to see the rest of Danae. Before we had even left the studio, the two men were already talking away sixteen to the dozen. I took surreptitious note of whatever Ruhi fell in love with, for I needed ideas for gifts to give her. She had brought me some stunning tops from India, very ethnic which, teamed with matching pants, would be perfect for dress-up occasions, and smaller items from Australia and Canada.

One evening, we decided to stay in after the busy day all of us had had. After dinner, we two sprawled on the rug, and Robin had his favourite deep chair. The Sebastians were arriving the next evening, the concert being just five days away. I had attended more Committee meetings, and was one of those detailed to receive the composer and his troupe at the airport. The other performers—a danseuse with her troupe, a comic actor, and a couple of starlets whose recent films had been hits, were on other flights to be met by other Committee members. To my relief, Sudanshu was assigned to one of these. Speaking of Lekh, Robin mentioned Sinhadurg. Inevitably, the next name he uttered was Neel's. It was a moment I had been dreading, having very adroitly avoided all mention of him so far. My expression must have given me away, for Ruhi's eyes didn't leave my face, and Robin stopped in mid-sentence.

Ruhi said warily, "Neel had some sculptures on exhibit here in New York, didn't he?" I murmured an assent. "Piyali, you don't have to tell us anything. But we are your friends—and Neel's. And we hate to see him so unhappy."

I said between clenched teeth, "You surprise me. He must be unhappy for some other reason. After all, he's the one who broke off our relationship for all time. He should be rejoicing that he was able to shake off an embarrassing unwanted liaison."

Robin said gently, "Neel hasn't said a word to us. Even knowing you two were—well, in love, was something we guessed. If he broke off, the reasons must be very valid. And I'm sure he was cutting his heart out when he did it."

I went on stonily, "We came together because we couldn't keep away—yet every time, he retreated, telling me it was an impossible situation. Each time, it tore me to pieces. Finally, I couldn't take it any more, and decided I must leave India."

"Yet you met again in New York. Was it a bitter encounter?"

"No, a glorious one. And then when we were having the happiest time, he announced he was leaving the next evening—and this was to be our very last meeting. No explanation—except the same old one—that we could have no future together because it would hurt someone very dear to him."

"Piyali—"

I wouldn't let Ruhi speak, but went on passionately. Neel couldn't really have loved me as he claimed. When two people loved each other, there had to be trust between them. Neel should have explained the reasons fully. I would have accepted them. But he never would. So now I had made a new beginning in my life, as I was sure he had.

They were both silent when I had finished. Then Ruhi said, "We're very sorry, Piyali. So very sorry. We wish there was something we could do for two people we love so dearly."

"You're very sweet. But Neel is out of my life for all time—by his choice."

"Robin, I think we'd better give—"

He rose to his feet, and went into the bedroom, returning with a large flat wrapped object. He placed it in my hands. I looked into his face, but found no clues. Ruhi nodded encouragingly. I took off the heavy wrapping—and was transfixed.

It was a painting of a sunlit meadow full of waist-high grass, splashes of brilliant colour marking clumps of wild flowers. Against the backdrop of a clear blue sky, a few fluffy white clouds sailed majestically. But what riveted the attention was the figure of a girl running through the grass, hair streaming out behind her, laughing exuberantly in sheer joy. She was wearing a blouse and a long skirt, the pretty flower print of which added more gay colour. The features were not particularly recognizable, but she was unmistakably beautiful. Joie de vivre, youth and laughter created a special ambience around the slender figure. Overall there was this marvellous radiance of light, so much like a Monet I had seen. The whole scene was so realistic, one could feel the very warmth in the air of that golden summer day. I did not need the initials NKG in the corner to identify the artist. All the while as I drank in every detail, there was a lump in my throat. So Neel remembered that last day as much as it was stamped on my memory. It was one of the most beautiful pictures I had ever seen. It was too much for me. I bowed my head, and wept.

Ruhi came to kneel beside me, and put her arms around me in wordless comfort. Robin laid a hand on my head for a moment. So now they knew I wasn't all that indifferent, that whatever I had declaimed moments ago about putting together the broken pieces of my life, of starting anew, were hollow words.

I don't know how long I sat there in Ruhi's comforting presence, but the chink of crockery roused me. Robin was putting a tray down. The hot tea was infinitely welcome.

After we had emptied the teapot, Robin said, "Piyali, we aren't going to let this spoil the rest of our stay with you. We shan't refer to it again. But I want you to know we are your friends—and Neel's. If you need us at any time—if there's anything we can do in any way at all, we are there. Will you remember that, dear girl?"

I could only whisper an affirmative.

Tara gave me a loving squeeze and kissed me. "I'm so glad you're here, Piyali!" Lekh kissed me too, and told me I looked more beautiful than ever. Yes, it was wonderful to see them again. There was hardly time for more than that exchange before they and the troupe were being swept off to their hotel by some male Committee members in their cars, but I promised to call later.

From the next day onwards, Lekh was fully immersed in rehearsals. Ruhi became Tara's companion in exploring New York. Sometimes, Robin went along as guide. One night, we dined with the Sebastians at their hotel, a merry quintet. Another time, Katia and David who knew all about my guests, and wished to meet them, took us out to dine and wine in style. I confess that I was avoiding a private session with Tara and Lekh, for surely, even in casual conversation, some awkward matters would come up. Was I only putting off the inevitable?

As might be expected, the concert was a glittering affair. To our mutual regret, the Asschers had to be away on this night, and couldn't attend. My special guest was Elliott. An imp of mischief made me want to see my suave Boss at an Asian show, as far a cry from the subdued elegance of the opera and ballet as could be imagined. Elliott had never been further east than Egypt. Speak of cultural shock, I thought, smiling to myself.

I shan't deny that Tara, Ruhi and I made a striking threesome. Tara was in leaf green, her eyes vivid in her small exquisite face, enhanced by the emeralds she wore; Ruhi the picture of delicate loveliness in cyclamen and pearls. I had chosen to wear Urvashi Devi's peacock brocade, designed by Lata into an ankle-length gown, cut very simply like a *cheongsam* so that it clung to my body in fluid lines, slit halfway to the knee, but the neck was cut low and had two thin straps over the shoulders. The rich fabric demanded simplicity, and needed no embellishment. I had put up my hair to do justice to the lapis lazuli necklace, long earrings and bracelet of my own design. Our two male escorts could not be faulted either. Robin was grand in evening dress. Needless to say, Elliott was at his impeccable best. Even before I introduced Tara and Ruhi, I read admiration and pleasure in his eyes at the sight of us three. He had to know if all Indian women were as beautiful as we were. If Elliott felt admiration, Robin was not inspired by the same feeling for my Boss. His smooth expression gave nothing away, but I knew behind the courteous manners, Robin was not pleased. What Tara and Ruhi were feeling was not easily apparent, but I was fully aware that from Tara at least, I was in for some serious questioning.

Be that as it may, I was determined to enjoy myself—and I did. It was that kind of occasion. It was amazing to see the vast throngs of Indians who had come to see their favourite composer perform. One could have been in Bombay, and not here in this very American city. The excitement and anticipation were intense.

And then the heavy curtains were going up, and Rom Nalin was at the mike welcoming everyone, speaking briefly about the untiring efforts of the Committee which had piloted the entire project. Roars of approval and thunderous applause greeted his reference to each performer. Beside me, I saw Tara looking at Rom in puzzlement. Of course, I thought, how could she miss the resemblance? When she whispered, "Piyali, who is the man at the mike?" I said quickly he was the Committee Chairman, the chief organizer of the show—which was in fact his brainchild. "He's amazingly like your Dad. Had you noticed?" I said truthfully it was the first thing I had noticed about him. Elliott commented, "An extraordinary and dynamic personality."

Need I say that from the moment Lekh and his ensemble appeared on stage, he held the audience in the hollow of his hand? At first, all went according to plan, but toward the end, he asked for special requests, and was flooded with them. The crowd chanted "*Bhavishya. Bhavishya.*" Tara murmured, "As expected." Elliott asked for a translation of this famous composition which had become Lekh's signature tune. Tara and I being woefully lacking in Hindi, it was Ruhi who obliged. "That's rather beautiful," he commented when she finished. He listened intently to the melody. Elliott had been charmed by the dance numbers, though a bit lost during the comic skits, which, however, delighted the audience.

With the requests raining down upon him, the show went on for a good forty minutes beyond the stipulated time. Tara said sotto voce that it always happened that way. The crowds were loath to let Lekh go. And then as a quiet finale, Lekh played The Princess Sonata. When I explained, Elliott said, "Incredibly haunting." His assessment of Lekh was, "Tremendous showmanship. And what a composer!"

We held back after the performance, waiting for Lekh to emerge. Elliott, to his regret, as he had told me earlier, had to slip away, for he was taking an early flight to Paris for a one-day conference. He took his leave after courteous farewells, and many compliments to Tara on her husband's brilliant performance. I saw him off at the door, and then went back to join the others—and was in for something unpleasant. Sudanshu appeared out of nowhere. I hid my displeasure, and perforce, introduced him to the others. He acted very jovial, very much the host, telling Tara how he was a friend of Bhaiyya. I hated the proprietorial way he looked at me, standing very close. When he asked to see me privately, I wanted to hit him for making me so conspicuous. Seething, I followed him aside. He had to tell me I was looking very beautiful, he said, eyes lingering over my bare arms, and neck, wandering to my decolletage. I gave him cool answers. Who was the American? Oh, my Boss, as if relieved. When could we meet? We had to have serious talks. I said I had to go back to my guests. Wait, he pleaded. He took my hand in one of his, and caressed it with the other. I pulled away sharply, glancing quickly at the group. No one had missed the little byplay. When I managed to get away and join them, the silence was eloquent.

A celebration party hosted by the Indian owners of an exclusive restaurant followed. As Tara and Lekh circulated, meeting many people, I saw Rom with them—and knew that with her sharp intelligence, Tara would reach the right conclusion in no time after hearing his name. Indeed, her eyes searched through the throng till they met mine as if to confirm her discovery.

And then it was over. Goodbyes all around. Tara said she would call me from Colorado for which they were leaving in the morning. The green eyes were eloquent. And that was the end of an exciting evening.

In the cab going home, Ruhi asked in a small voice, "Is Mr. Northrop serious about you, Piyali?"

"We spend a lot of time together," I said evasively. " Some of it is in the line of duty if I'm wearing some jewellery or clothes for Danae, and we attend some do for the publicity."

Robin said, only half-teasing, "It's the non-duty times that are more intriguing."

I refused to be drawn, and only laughed.

From Ruhi, "And the other one, this Jashwant fellow?"

I said demurely, "That one? I'd say he has weddings on his mind."

"Ruhi, Piyali doesn't have to be subjected to interrogation."

"I know," she said shamedly. "I'm sorry, Piyali."

"It's all right. You're concerned about me. At this point, all I can say is that I won't do anything rash."

Before the Nevilles left, the next in the series of Maharani advertisements appeared in magazines that hit the newstands. Robin declared he was coming with me to Danae to see Leon Rothman to coax some copies of the photographs. In any case, he was carrying a stack of magazines with him on my behalf which carried the full-page advertisement to send to various people. Ruhi said, "It's perfect! And I'm so proud! This one is truly fantastic! And I mean both you and the jewellery. Will you be modelling for Danae from now on?"

I said feelingly, "Not I. Once was enough!"

Robin was vastly amused. "I doubt that. Northrop and Rothman will pull another trick some day!"

I was saddened to see my friends go. I did not know when I would see them again. Ruhi was very quiet. She was feeling the loss of parting as well. I had Danae gifts for her—sandals, a whole range of cosmetics, perfumes and a set of jewellery that would suit her delicate beauty. She was overwhelmed. To send with the Nevilles too, I had Danae products for Lata and Madhur, wallets for Bhaiyya and Skeet. Robin professed to be delighted with the belt, wallet and handsome tie pin I gave him. And then I produced my last gift. "Will you please carry this for me?" I requested. Robin unwrapped the tissue-wrapped object. He stared at the jewelled Easter egg in his hands.

"It's not what it seems." I forced the words out. "The stones are only semi-precious, of course, and the gold work far from 24-carat."

"It's as fine as anything Faberge could have created, Piyali." He traced the graceful 'N' with his finger gently. Then he raised his head and looked at me. "N for Neel. It's for him, of course."

"I—he sent me the painting. I have to—send something in return," I said lamely. "The egg—I was challenged at a party to create one—Neel was present. He'll get the connection."

Ruhi had the egg cupped in her hands. "How exquisite!" she breathed. "This oval space with its border of pearls is for a miniature or photograph, isn't it, Piyali? Whose photograph?"

I shrugged. "His grandmother's maybe? His own? Or his wife's when he acquires one—which shouldn't be too far off now."

Ruhi glanced at her husband. Neither said anything.

Robin's refusal to let me go to the airport was a sharp reminder of another such decision. Ruhi and I clung to each other. "Piyali, be happy. And don't—don't take any steps—well, in a hurry." Robin enveloped me in his arms. "I echo my wife's words. And we have to thank you for a most wonderful stay in New York."

"Come back soon," I managed.

"Sure—after you come and see us at Waverley."

A wave of such longing swept over me, I had a hard time preventing my face from crumpling, and myself from falling on that broad chest to weep out my feelings. I managed to control myself. And then they were gone.

25

INTERLUDE

Sheena slobbered all over him, and Manohar gave him a welcoming grin. Yes, Neel Saab was in his studio. He walked along the corridor with Robin, talking volubly, then departed, leaving him to enter alone. With the privilege of an old friend, he pushed open the studio door, and went in.

The first thing he was struck by was the absolute quiet. The music one expected when Neel was working was missing. If that were not unusual enough, Neel himself was nowhere to be seen. Robin stood thoughtfully looking around, then mounted the steps to the gallery. For so big a man, he trod lightly, and no sound of footfall alerted the lone occupant of the study who sat at his desk slumped over, head buried in his arms. Robin waited for a moment, then called softly. And had to hide his shock when Neel raised his head. This wasn't the Neel he had last seen three months ago, this hollow-cheeked man with the hopeless look in his eyes. Where was the Neel who made all his friends laugh with his witticisms, ever to be counted on to lighten their mood?

"Robin." Neel was on his feet, coming around to embrace him. "I thought you weren't expected till tomorrow."

"We weren't. But neither Ruhi nor I wished to linger on in Bombay when we were longing to get back to Waverley—and peace. We've been away too long this time."

"I'm glad. It's been lonely here without you."

They settled on the long sofa. "Successful trip? Good. Ruhi enjoyed it? And I want to hear all about it from her." But the words seemed forced. "You're looking good, Robin."

"Wish I could say the same about you," bluntly. "Lost a lot of weight, haven't you? Not been well?"

"Who I? No, I'm fine really. Too many deadlines. Every time I swear I won't take on another commission, and will work on my own, something comes along which I can't turn down."

"Even so, I don't care for the way you look—the Tom Selleck moustache notwithstanding."

"This?" touching the luxuriant growth. "I thought I looked rather dashing. So tell me about your trip."

"Well, as a starting point, we had the privilege of attending a Lekh Sebastian concert—in New York," Robin said, his keen gaze noting the startled reaction over the last two words.

A pause. "That must have been—great. Tara was there, of course? Quite a coincidence that you two should have been in New York at the time."

"It was. A fantastic experience. The audience—it was the Indian community in New York which invited Lekh and his troupe—went wild. Ruhi and I had front row seats."

"So you had the best view. Where did you stay?"

Shock was reflected in the sunken eyes when Robin told him. "I—see. That—was nice. How—is she?" looking down at his hands as if he had never seen them before.

"In her work, spectacularly successful. For the rest, as well as can be expected."

A spark lit the dull eyes. "What do you mean? Hasn't she been well?" urgently.

"Healthwise, she's doing okay. Emotionally, I guess she's taken a battering." Deliberately, "And that at the hands of a certain sculptor I know."

A long silence. "Did—she tell you that?"

"Yes. And only because Ruhi forced it out of her. Do you know what Piyali said after she'd filled in some of the details? She said the parting had torn her to pieces, and not for the first time. It was why she had left India." A choked sound instantly suppressed. "We gathered you had met again in New York and it had been a joyous reunion?" No movement from the bent head. "And then when you left, you told her it was the last time you two would be meeting. As before, you did not spell out the reasons except the same one that a relationship between the two of you would hurt someone very dear to you. Piyali said, 'He claimed he did, but he really couldn't have ever loved me. Between two people who love each other, there has to be trust. Don't you agree, Robin? I feel the least he could have done was to spell out the reasons fully. I would have accepted them. But from the start, he maintained this silence. I tell you, Ruhi, it pierced me to the core. How could we be as close as only a man and woman can be, and still have secrets that can't be shared? Well, Neel has spoken. So be it. I've put the broken pieces of my life together. Started anew. As I'm sure he has.'"

As if he could no longer sit still, Neel was on his feet, going to the railing which enclosed the gallery, tightly gripping the smooth surface of the top bar, staring down blindly into the vastness of his studio. Poor chap, Robin thought in pity, I don't know what dark secret he's keeping on someone else's behalf, but he's as shattered as our beautiful Princess. Robin went to stand by Neel, and laid a comforting arm about his shoulder.

"I'm sorry, Neel. But I felt you had to know. We care about both of you—hate to see you unhappy. You see, Ruhi and I have been through the worst crises. I behaved with her in the most cruel manner possible for reasons she knew nothing about. I married to avenge a great wrong for which she was in no way to blame. I had waited for long bitter years for it, and since the one who had done the wrong had died, she was my victim." Neel listened, his body motionless. "She was completely bewildered, Neel. Just out of college, launching on a career as a model. I hurt her to the point where she became a shadow of her former self. Still, though I could see it, I didn't let it rest. Then I went away on assignment. I'd had enough. I was to explain as soon as I came back—tell her the dark secret—beg her forgiveness. But she was gone! I went after her, Neel. And found she was not available—out of bounds to me. I was told if I was really as concerned about her welfare as I claimed, I must leave her alone. Emotionally, she was in very bad shape. Worse was to come. I was told she had filed for divorce."

Neel turned a shocked face to him. "No! I had no idea!"

"How could I blame her? That was when I came after you, brought you to Sinhadurg to see this place. I desperately needed your companionship. It was the one thing that kept me sane. Today you said you were lonely without us. We're often away, Neel, and you never said that before. It's Piyali you're missing, aren't you, just as Ruhi's going left a gaping void in my life? For me, I was reaping the whirlwind. That it all came right again is a miracle I thank God for every day on bended knee. That's how I understand your circumstances, Neel. I told Piyali so—that you probably were plunged into a situation over which you have no control."

"What—did she say?"

"That it's all water under the bridge now."

Neel was silent. "Is she—seeing someone?" The anguish in his face went straight to Robin's heart.

"I'd be less than honest if I said she wasn't, Neel. Two men seemed very much in attendance. One is an American—happens to be her boss at Danae—very sophisticated, urbane. In fact, was her guest at the Sebastian concert, so sat with us. Impressive guy. The other one is an Indian—highly successful. A stockbroker, I think. Friend of Tara's brother. Openly smitten. Piyali gave vague answers when Ruhi asked, and just laughed. But how serious this is, I couldn't say."

At the look in Neel's eyes, Robin came to an abrupt halt. They stood for a long time without words. Then Robin said, "By the way, she appreciated the painting very much. Complimented you on your talent." He put a hand in his pocket. "She sent you this. Said you were both at some party—and you'd get the connection."

Robin turned away from the sight of his friend holding the Easter egg as if it were the most precious object in the world. He said quietly, "Neel, I've brought some photographs and magazines which might interest you. I'll just leave them here on your desk. They're for you. I have some copies for us." Neel had not moved. "Lots of unpacking to be done. We'll expect you for dinner tonight." And went away, not certain if Neel had registered those last words or his departure. He walked up the driveway to Waverley lost in somber thought.

"Mama, I'm very worried."

Romola's hands stilled over her knitting. "It's Neel," Jana continued. "Something's very wrong. He's become very quiet. You know how he keeps one laughing—how witty and entertaining he can be. Not on this visit. He seemed to be forcing himself to respond to my talk as if mentally he was far away. At first, I thought it was overwork. Then I observed he was driving himself deliberately—almost as if trying to bury himself in his work—so he won't have time to think."

Romola listened intently. "He hasn't visited me since he came back from America—though he calls regularly. Pressure of work that piled up in his absence, he told me." Anxiously, "He's all right, isn't he, healthwise?"

"Oh yes. He's much thinner, but with the pace he sets himself, anyone would be. No, it's something else, Mama, and I feel so helpless. What can I do for him? God knows, I haven't been the world's best mother. He's always looked to you for mothering."

Romola thought deeply. "Jana, was there no clue—no pointer you can think of which might help with the answer? A word dropped by chance?"

Her daughter said slowly, "Not a word. But there was something—I wonder—could it be? I was looking for an envelope in Neel's desk drawer where he keeps stamps and such stuff. No envelopes on top so I rummaged around. At the very bottom, a folder came into my hands. I wasn't snooping, Mama. I wouldn't, you know. But the contents of the folder spilled out. They were photographs—of a girl. And a colour page from an American magazine, beautifully photographed, of the same girl. I couldn't resist taking a good look."

"A pretty girl, of course?"

"That's too tame a word. Ravishing is more apt. She'd have to be, wouldn't she, in order to model jewellery?" At the last word, her mother's eyes widened. "Now why would Neel save an ad for jewellery from an American journal even though it was of Indian design? Unless he could use it for some sculpture? Or his artistic eyes found the girl of interest? Perhaps she looks like someone he knows. But maybe I'm reading too much into the collection of pictures. Letting my imagination run wild."

The knitting slid off Romola's lap. "Jana, describe the model for me."

Not a little surprised, Jana tried to remember accurately. "Well, as I said, strikingly beautiful." She groped for words. " Rather—well, exotic. Extraordinary eyes. I noticed them particularly. Sort of grey—no, I'd say more blue. Straight nose—shapely. Looking at the camera—how shall I put it—disdainfully. No, that doesn't sound right."

"Perhaps—regal—queenly?"

Jana was surprised. "Yes, that's it. That's it exactly. Have you seen the ad too?" puzzled.

For several minutes, there was no answer. Then her mother said sadly, "I've been so blind. So very blind. And they actually told me in so many words. They said the lives of two young people were involved. But I've been so taken up with myself, I could see nothing else. Poor Neel. Poor children."

Jana came and picked up the knitting which had slid to the floor. "Mama, what is it? What are you talking about?"

"The three princesses." Alarm bells went off in Jana's head. Something was very wrong with her mother.

"Princesses?"

"Yes. One from Sonal Mohur. And two from Divyasthala."

Jana's heart sank. Mama's mind was deteriorating alarmingly—and she hadn't even realized it. Now she was hallucinating—and about a place which hadn't been mentioned in the family for decades because it was strictly taboo. I shouldn't have told her about Neel, she castigated herself. He's probably the dearest one in the world to her. "It's all right, Mama," she said soothingly, putting a hand on the frail shoulder. "Perhaps you should lie down."

Romola shook the hand off. "Stop treating me like the village idiot, Jana! I may be old, but I'm not senile yet! And my mind is perfectly clear, I'll have you know!" And, indeed, her eyes were bright and alert as always. "Now sit there and listen. I should have told you long ago."

As a listener, Jana's reactions were eminently satisfactory to the narrator. Her eyes grew rounder; she choked back exclamations; put her hand to her throat; clasped her hands together tightly; and finally, wiped her tear-wet face on her sleeve. When Romola was done, they both sat silently.

"I find it so terribly hard to believe," she said at last. "My son—and a girl of royal blood—and wonder of wonders, a Chandravats at that." Hesitantly, "She looks so haughty, Mama. Can we be sure of this?"

"Oh, Jana, those looks are so deceptive! She can't help being born with them, you know. She was kindness itself to me when I became upset." And Romola explained.

"What next, Mama?" Jana said at last.

"Obviously, something has to be done, and that quickly. And I'm the one to do it."

"You'll talk to Neel? Yes, I suppose you'll have to."

"If it's to protect me from shock that he's been making this sacrifice, then I can't let it go on. In any case, I want to know. Some of this is conjecture on our parts, but my ESP tells me we're right. Unless I talk to him, we shan't know."

"Mama, about R—?"

Romola sighed. "Another grave error on my part. I'll have to give that some thought."

"You won't let this upset you though, will you?"

"No," was the brisk reply. "My days for being upset are long past. It's my selfishness which is responsible for all this. I've been an ostrich, burying my head in the sand. Thinking only of myself. Trying to conceal what are, after all, facts of history. No, Jana, I've been very wrong. I have to make amends before it's too late."

"Jana said you have some very big commission in hand," Romola said brightly. It's not just weight loss, she thought sorrowfully, surveying the still figure opposite to her. It's as if some awful calamity has left a great void in his existence. As if there's no joy left in life.

Neel stirred. "Commission?" He spoke with effort, as if trying to give a lucid answer. "Yes, it's a larger-than-life size statue commissioned by the Samartha Group of their Founder, the first Jaisingh Samartha. The grandson bears the same name."

"Oh!" Romola was impressed. "You must be working with photographs then since he died quite some time ago?"

"Yes. And a couple of portraits done in his lifetime. They were very useful." He lapsed into a reverie again.

When on the phone, Romola had asked Neel to come and see her, he had been instantly concerned. Wasn't she well, he had demanded. Reassured by her reply, he had said he could manage just one day that weekend. The strain he was under was instantly visible to her, but he had kissed her with affection. Only later had his manner been restrained, as if he felt awkward in her company. It had never happened before, and the fact pierced Romola. My Neel, she thought sadly, who has Kusum and everyone else laughing all the time, hasn't smiled once. If he's leaving in the morning, there's no time to lose. I doubt if he'll come again very soon.

"Did I ever tell you about the adventure I had with two chance visitors?" He looked at her blankly, his mind obviously elsewhere. "Well, I was sitting on the veranda one day. Kusum had gone shopping. And I noticed this car having trouble." She watched his expression as she went on, barely interested at first, then more attentive until when she came to a description of each visitor, a look of disbelief crossed his face. He was sitting up now, fully concentrating on her words. When she mentioned 'shooting assignment' and 'jewellery design', he came to his feet. "And then I made an utter fool of myself," she went on. "They said they were originally from Divyasthala—and I went cold, Neel. And they noticed at once."

"My God!" He crossed the floor in two strides, and sank down in front of her. "My God, Piyal was here? Actually here? And you met her?" He passed a shaky hand over his face. "Did your name come up—and mine?"

"I never mentioned either—though I did speak of my children and grandson—with pride. But they must have asked Kusum—she came back just as they were leaving, and I asked her to see them to my car since theirs was not functioning—because the sweet-spoken Princess sent me a gift as a token of their appreciation."

Neel had put his head in his hands. "They came back, Neel." His hands fell away, and he raised a shocked face. She nodded. "The one I call sweet-spoken telephoned, and asked if she could come and see me. I was alarmed—but how could I refuse when she was courtesy itself? And the tall beautiful one came with her." A deep sound of anguish from his throat. "Also a third princess, so very lovely—Lekh Sebastian's wife." Neel did not seem to be conscious he had seized a fold of her sari, and was crushing it in his hands. Romola went on quietly with her story.

"You told them? Everything? Oh, God! Piyal knew! Piyal knew all the time! And was waiting for me to trust her enough to tell her! And I—I've hurt her time and again. Right from the time I met her, and learnt who she was. Put her through hell." He buried his face in his hands.

Romola was quiet for a few moments. "You were protecting me, Neel. I'm the one who stood between you and happiness. But not any more."

His head lifted. "Why do you say that? You're not to do anything drastic, Grandmama! I shan't let you endanger your health for me."

"My health is fine—but it won't be unless I have peace of mind. Neel," she went on, "there's one vital link in the story which I didn't tell them about." At the question in his eyes, she nodded. "I may have mentioned—yes, I distinctly recall—but nothing more." She put a hand on the broad young shoulder. "Oh, it's been very wrong on my part to keep the facts from the one person who has every right to know."

It's going to be shattering.

"Who can doubt that? But as a grown man, a person of maturity who's seen much of the world, I hope and pray that after the initial shock, he will calm down. Don't you see—I shan't rest in peace till I've told him? I love him. Nowhere in the world could one find a finer person. You agree with that, I see. Then is it right for me to go on concealing the truth? I've waited too long as it is."

"How will you do it? Write? Or call?"

"Neither. He'll be back after a fortnight. And spend a couple of days with me as usual."

Neel put a hand over hers. "It won't be easy for you either. Do you want me to be here then?"

She squeezed his hand, and brushed away the sudden tears in her eyes. "And leave Jaisingh Samartha the First languishing? No, Neel. You're being thoughtful as always. This is something I have to do myself." Romola put a hand on his head. "What are you going to do, Neel?"

He shook his head blindly. "I? Nothing. I've inflicted enough hurt to last a lifetime. There's no way she will forgive me. I can't go crawling back again. It's happened too often." He rose to his feet, and went to the window, staring out into the darkness. "I told her last time—it was in New York—that it was the end. We would not meet again—ever. I have to face the fact that there's someone else in her life now."

"You can't be sure of that, Neel."

He swung around. "Can there be a single doubt? A girl as beautiful as that? She has every reason—and right—to be involved with another man after the way I've treated her. Besides, Robin told me so. He and his wife stayed with her in New York." His voice cracked suddenly. "I've lost her! I've lost her now—and it's killing me!"

The woman in the rocking chair sat motionless, his anguish hers.

26

It was one of those blustery New York nights in November. I was glad enough to stay at home, and work on a fresh set of designs I had begun. The necklace was inspired by the one worn by Nefertiti, and it had presented no problems. The earrings, however, were more challenging—the kind of challenge I loved to take on. I must have been working steadily for well over two hours, well past suppertime, not stopping for even a cup of coffee, when the doorbell rang. It took me a moment to come out of my intense concentration. Who could it be on this windy night when the weather was so nasty? The bell pealed again.

A surprise awaited me when I looked through the peephole. Uttering an exclamation, I unbolted the door. All words died on my lips when I saw Rom Nalin's face. Oh, God, I thought, it can't be bad news about Madame? A second thought pierced me. Oh no, not Neel! Pray God, nothing's happened to Neel!

"I'm disturbing you, Piyali," seeing the dining table strewn with my materials. "I'm sorry. I should have called first, but I had to take a chance you'd be at home. And am so relieved to find you here."

I let out my breath slowly. It wasn't Madame or Neel.

"You aren't disturbing me at all. I was just going to wind up." I hung up his coat in the closet. He appears very disturbed, but not grieved—not in mourning—I think, I told myself. "May I get you something?"

"Thank you, but no," waiting courteously till I sat down before taking his seat. He looked at me, and said helplessly. "I don't know where to begin, Piyali. I had to come to you—to trouble you because you're the only one who can help me—to answer some questions. To enlighten me."

"Not—bad news?"

"I don't know what to call it—bad—shameful—degrading." His eyes met mine—and realization came to me. He knows, I thought in pity, and read confirmation in his face. "I came back from India last night. While there, I visited my mother as usual—and was told something which I still haven't taken in fully. Apparently, I'm the only one in the immediate family who was kept in the dark—though it affected me the most." His mouth twisted. "I was being protected, it seems." He looked at me directly. "And even you knew, Piyali. I find that hard to believe—that my mother would tell you—and keep it from me."

I said steadily, "She didn't tell us about you. Not even a hint. I didn't know you existed till I saw you at the Pals' home. Madame Nalin told us only so much of the story—till the point when she fled Divyasthala. She stopped there."

Incredulously, "Yet when you saw me for the first time, you knew who I was? I find that hard to swallow!"

"Yes, because my first—rather foolish reaction was that Daddy—my father—had suddenly appeared from nowhere." Rom stared at me. "The resemblance is so striking anyone will spot it. Except that Daddy has a beard. That was when I guessed Madame had left the story unfinished."

He was on his feet, walking the length of the rug and back, visibly agitated. My heart went out to him. He came to stand in front of me. "Are you telling me—that the resemblance to—to the Chandravats—is so strong that you spotted it at once, Piyali?" I nodded. " Oh, God!" and he sank down again, face in his hands. The muffled words reached me. "That's why I don't look like anyone in the family—why I've always been so different!" His hands dropped. "I'm not a Nalin at all—not the son of the man I've idolized my whole life. I'm—I'm the son of a wicked evil man—a ravisher of helpless innocent women!"

I couldn't sit still a moment longer. I pulled a padded stool in front of him, and sat there. I said urgently, "You are not to think that for a moment, Rom! It isn't true at all!" For the first time, I uttered the name aloud. "Digvijay Singh was a great and good man. His name is revered to this day for all the good things he did for his people."

He caught my hand. "How can you say that, Piyali, after what he did?"

"Because it's the truth. I don't blame you for thinking the way you do. It's how the three of us—my cousin Lata, and Tara, Lekh Sebastian's wife, who were with me when Madame told us—felt. Can you imagine Lata's feelings and mine—that a Chandravats had done this?" Rom was listening with his whole concentration, his body tense, not realizing how tight was his grip on my hand. "We felt bitterly ashamed—and yes, guilty. Madame told us we were not to feel that way, that we were in no way to blame. These things had happened before we were born." Rom bent his head in agreement. "The very name Divyasthala repelled me. In my heart, I hated the Maharaja. Then weeks before I left India for New York, I decided to go and investigate for myself. Otherwise, I would carry a whole lot of unanswered questions with me when I came away.

And what I found has made me think and think since then."

"Will you—tell me what you discovered?"

"Of course, Rom. Gladly."

Not once as I spoke did Rom's eyes leave my face, but the changing expressions on his were an index to his reactions. My throat ached with unshed tears for him. When I reached the end of my narrative, he leaned back, and closed his eyes. I knew he was trying to absorb all he had heard.

"I'm going to make us some coffee," I said, and went away, leaving him with his thoughts.

When I came back with a tray, he rose and took it from me, courtesy foremost even in his state of mind.

We had drunk two cups of coffee each when I asked, "Rom, would you like to see some photographs? I took a great many when I was in Divyasthala, and there are others of my parents and family members." He agreed almost with eagerness. My first action was to take the photograph of Daddy off the mantelpiece, and hand it to him. "You can see if you look like him," I said cheerfully, and went to collect my albums.

"Uncanny!" he said, speaking for the first time when I came back. "Except for the beard, we could be twins! He's younger than I am, I think? Is that so?"

We settled on the rug. I did not rush him, knowing how important, how necessary it was for him to see and know at last. They were all there, the Palace, the Durbar Hall, the surroundings, Uday Singh and Urvashi Devi, Rika, uncles, aunts, cousins, Lata and Bhaiyya, Daddy's wedding photographs—and finally, I laid the likenesses of Digvijay Singh before him. He was utterly still, taking in detail after detail.

He muttered at last, "This man is my father. And it took me fifty-two years to know the fact—and look upon his face." He held his head for a moment. "Why—why? How could he deliberately set a trap for my fa—for Kushal Nalin to die—and in the most cruel way possible?"

I said quietly, "Can we know for sure that this is true? In a court of law, wouldn't this be called circumstantial evidence? Bhairav Singh could very well have sat down and negotiated with the delegation—they could have arrived at a compromise. I told you I've been thinking so much since my visit to Divyasthala. I went fully convinced as you are now, then I began to wonder if it was right to put a man on trial, and condemn him when he wasn't there to defend himself? I'm not denying that most family members believe he did it. And certainly, Madame Nalin believes it. Yet when I put the whole composite picture of the Maharaja together, this simply did not ring true."

"But he did set up Kushal's widow as his—oh, how can I say this word about my own mother—mistress! You can't deny that, Piyali! My very existence proves that!"

I said softly, "Did Madame tell you about his feelings for her?" Rom shook his head. "He told her she was the only woman he had ever loved—though he was old enough to be her father. He had seen her in the *tonga* and been unable to believe anyone could be so beautiful. I saw the things he gave her—she left everything behind, as you know—and they were exquisite, obviously chosen by him personally to suit her especially. At the Palace, for professional reasons, I had made a point of examining all kinds of jewellery. Much of it looked almost vulgar and ostentatious in comparison. Whereas the pieces in the other collection were as delicate and beautiful as the one they were intended for."

"If he really had such feelings for her, why did a bastard child come out of the liaison? Is that how he showed his love and concern for her?" Rom asked bitterly. He still held the photographs of Digvijay in his hands.

I was silent. Who could deny the stark reality of his observations? A thought struck me. I said gently, "Don't you think if he'd known about you—known in time—he would have loved you in a very special way—as the son of the woman he loved?" I saw I had startled him. Patently, the possibility had never occurred to him. "I'd guess there's nothing he wouldn't have done for you." Rom's eyes went back to the photographs in his hands as if he was seeing the subject anew from a fresh perspective. "And, Rom, another thing. Ever since we met—and I identified you—watched you in all the doings relating to the Sebastian concert, came to know of your achievements, I've been struck by how much you and Uday Singh have in common. You started with nothing, and look at the heights you've scaled. By the time Uday Singh reached majority, and took over from the Regent, the princely states had been abolished, and shortly after, the privy purses which had been granted to the ex-rulers were withdrawn. Some of them are in wretched straits. Not Uday Singh. He's a financial whiz—especially in the stock market."

I saw the import of my words sinking in. After a moment, he said, "What you told me earlier—about my resemblance to your father, that I have the family looks—do you mean to say if I go to Divyasthala tomorrow, the similarity would be noticed?"

"Absolutely. Interestingly, Uday Singh doesn't have the Chandravats looks. I believe he takes after his mother who was the Junior Maharani. But the two daughters born to the Senior Maharani strongly resemble their father." I touched his hand. "Rom, if you did go to Divyasthala, you'd be given the warmest welcome from Uday Singh, and no doubt, from everyone else."

He threw out his hands. "We don't know that, Piyali! They might revile me—throw me out!"

"I know because of what Uday Singh told me. I asked him a hypothetical question about how he would react if someone from the Nalin family showed up. Do you know what he said? 'I would welcome him or her! I can't make amends for someone else's actions, but I can do my small bit by being cordial.' I found that in Divyasthala, the very name of Digvijay Singh is uttered with the greatest admiraton and respect. He dedicated his whole life to his people." My hand covering his, I went on, "Don't let this blight your life, Rom. You must see this from another perspective. Forgive him for his one awful lapse, and think of the great and good man your father was otherwise."

Rom took a deep breath, turning over my hand so that it was now held in his. "How can you who are so young be so wise?"

"I'm not wise at all. I wish I were, then my life wouldn't be in the mess it is in now."

He said quietly, "You mean about Neel?"

He must have felt the quiver that ran through me, seen the shock on my face. I said through stiff lips, "How—could you know that—unless Neel told you?"

"The last time I met Neel was in New York, not on this trip to India." Our positions had reversed in the twinkling of an eye. Now I was the troubled one, turning to him for succour. "No, it was my mother who told me."

Disbelievingly, "How—could she know? Oh, Rom, Neel couldn't possibly have told her! She was the one he was protecting all the time!"

"Not Neel, Piyali. It was his mother—my sister, Jana." I stared at him in confusion, gripping his hand. "My mother, my beautiful Romola, has seen so much in her life, Piyali. This situation—she was the one who put two and two together—far from shocking her, as Neel has always feared might happen, brought her to the moment of decision to break the silence at last. You have no idea how precious Neel is to her. The past couldn't be allowed to cast its shadow over his young life—or yours. I have to tell you she liked you very much. In all the praise she heaped on the beautiful queenly Chandravats princess—her words, not mine—she said you had been kindness itself to her." Rom said in a different voice, "Piyali, I didn't mean to make you weep! Please," offering me a snowy handkerchief from his pocket, "you've been splendid throughout. I can't tell you how sorry I am that you and Neel parted ways, and all because of my mother—and me. Is there no way of healing the breach?"

I mopped up, and blew my nose on the pristine square. Then I shook my head. "It's over, Rom. That's what he told me. You see, he never trusted me enough to tell me the truth. At first when he met me, he was very rude and cutting, told me I wasn't welcome ever at ROMOLA, practically threw me out. Can you imagine my humiliation, my bewilderment? Later when we fell in love, he said time and again 'This can't be. Not with you—ever.' He never would explain. Only told me someone he loved dearly would be very hurt if our relationship became known. Which meant my hurt in comparison was of no significance to him. When he was in New York, he wouldn't invite me to meet his uncle and aunt. I see why now. But that hurt me too. His last words made it very clear that it was over. And it is. I shan't go through life mourning what cannot be. I've rebuilt my whole life. There are other men with any one of whom my relationship could become permanent."

"Piyali, don't do anything on the rebound, will you?"

"Not I. If there's one lesson I've learnt it's to be wary. But the possibility is very much there."

Rom's eye fell on his watch. "No! That can't be the time! Margot will be calling Missing Persons Bureau if I don't go home right away!"

"Rom, does she know? Have you told her?"

"Yes, and the kids too."

"How did they react?"

"Disgustingly! Will you believe it, they were actually thrilled? Margot, my brilliant lawyer wife who mows down the opposition in court, is terribly elated. Can't wait to meet you—will be inviting you for dinner soon. Our son said, 'Yippee! Imagine being related to a maharaja. You mean I'm actually the grandson of one?' Now what does one do to such a crazy bunch!"

I had been laughing. "I think they're wonderful! They certainly have the right attitude." More seriously, "Rom, won't you take some pictures to show them? Take whatever you like."

"May I? You're sure? Yes, Margot and the kids will love to see them. You're very thoughtful, Piyali." He chose several, and I noticed he picked up the ones of Digvijay Singh first. I found a big envelope for him to put them in. I took his coat out of the closet and held it for him. When he had buttoned it up, he put both hands on my shoulders. "Piyali, how can I find the words to tell you how grateful I am? You've given me a whole new perspective on everything—lifted my spirits enormously."

"Not to thank me. After all," mischievously, "I did it for my Uncle Rom even if he won't let me use the title!"

For the first time that evening, his face lit up with laughter. He held out his arms, and I went into them, hugging him warmly. He kissed the top of my head. "Goodbye, my dear child."

An enormous bouquet of hothouse flowers arrived next evening, brightening up the whole apartment. They must have cost the earth. The accompanying card simply said, "Eternally grateful. Rom."

27

New York was gay with the Christmas spirit. It showed in the brilliant decorations everywhere, enticing shop windows, Santas in stores and on sidewalks, and, of course, the magnificent Christmas tree at Rockefeller Center. The sound of carols filled the air wherever one went. It was very cold but the first snow had yet to fall. At Danae, they said that there might not be a white Christmas after all. I went shopping with Elliott to buy gifts for his family. He was spending his holiday with his parents in Boston. For the last three Christmases, he had been in Europe. Quite a few Northrops gathered at such a time. He had invited me to join him, but I explained I was spending Christmas at my new-found uncle's home. I had told him the bare outlines of the story, completely deleting Neel's part in it. Even so, Elliott was disappointed. I knew he wanted me to meet his family. I wasn't ready for such encounters because the thought of any commitment alarmed me. I had sensed Elliott was becoming rather restive, and that one of these days, he was surely going to become more assertive. Fleetingly, I wondered how they would have reacted if Elliott had shown up with a girl who wasn't remotely a WASP, for the Northrops were very proper Bostonians. Oh well, if such a confrontation ever took place, then I could think about it.

I had not expected to look forward to Christmas, but now that I was going to Rom's home, the prospect was most pleasurable. I had already been there twice, the second time for Thanksgiving. Margot Nalin had wasted no time in inviting me for dinner after Rom's visit, and I had gladly accepted. Their home was surely one of the most beautiful in New York with its magnificent view of Manhattan. It combined luxurious comfort and exquisite taste without a hint of ostentation. It went without saying that rugs and smaller carpets, the wall hangings and objets d'art gave evidence of that.

The welcome I received from Margot and the children was heartwarming. Tall, svelte, auburn-haired and hazel-eyed, reputedly a brilliant lawyer, she had hugged me and exclaimed, "I can't tell you how impatient we all have been to meet you, Piyali! Rom has told us so much about you!"

"And I've been dying to meet my long-lost relatives!"

Kimberley had come down especially for the occasion from Bryn Mawr in Pennsylvania where she was a sophomore. I thought she was lovely with the height both parents had passed on, her mother's colouring, and a distinct resemblamce to her grandmother Romola. Laurier, named after Margot's family, about to graduate from high school, topped them all by inches, had dark hair like Rom with his grey eyes, and a strong Chandravats look about him that delighted me. Within minutes, it seemed as if we had always known each other. The evening flew, and all of us were astonished to find it was midnight. They would not hear of my going home that night. Everyone pitched in to make up a bed in the guest room with fresh sheets and blankets, Kim found me a nightie and robe, Laurie a new toothbrush. Eventually, Margot swept everyone off to bed. That night as I lay under the fleecy blankets, I felt warmed and happier than I had been for a long time. What Margot had said was true. This was my family. This was my home.

It was Margot who dropped me off at the apartment next morning. "When Rom came back, I took one look at his face, and knew something was terribly wrong," she told me in the car. "My first guess was that it had to do with his mother. It did, but hardly in the way one might expect. When he told me, I was dumbstruck. What does one say at such times to a man whose very identity is in question, and everything he had accepted about himself, including his name, is taken away from him?" She stopped for a red light. "And when he has come to know what his beloved mother endured at the hands of the man who sired him—My heart bled for Rom. He needed desperately to talk—and we did for hours. But I have to confess that deep down I couldn't suppress a teeny bit of excitement. This was stuff fantasies are built on! I told Rom the children had a right to know. We've always been very open with them. He agreed. Now they made no bones about their elation! Rom was disgusted with us!" She took a right turn. "But the fact was that Rom was still deeply troubled. He said, 'I must see Piyali. I need so much to talk with her.' I told him to go. He didn't come back for so long, I was quite agitated. But when he did, he was a changed man—and at peace with himself. All thanks to you, my dear."

Since then, Margot and I kept in touch by phone. It was a mutual attraction, fascinated as we were by each other's professions. So it was that I learnt Rom's cousin, Jagat Alexander, son of his uncle Paul, and his family, were also expected for Christmas. They too looked forward very much to meeting me, Margot said. I shared the feeling. This was the son of the brother Madame had mentioned in her narrative, and the cousin Rom had spoken of with such affection. He was also Neel's uncle.

Neel. I wouldn't allow myself to think of him. The memory only brought anguish. Months had passed since he left, and momentous events had transpired in my life. He belonged to the past. Then why, I asked myself, did I often wake up, my face wet with tears because I had dreamed so vividly of Neel? Well, someday I would forget, I comforted myself. Probably the coming of the Nevilles and Sebastians had contributed to the prolongation of the agonized feelings. And Rom, of course, large as life, and Neel's own uncle.

In a chat with Margot, I learnt Rom was out of the country on his quarterly buying expedition, and it was lonely for her in his absence. However, he had promised to be back well before Christmas.

A round of parties kept many of my evenings occupied. Elliott escorted me to some thrown by mutual friends; others given by close friends I attended alone. They were not of the kind my suave Boss would have enjoyed anyway. To my great relief, Sudanshu was away in India, and for now at least, I was free of his attentions. I told myself that if I couldn't shake him off myself, Rom would certainly do it for me. I begged off the party I was invited to on December 18th. A respite was badly needed. For one, I had things to do around the apartment; for another, I had to call Daddy. I did the first in record time, made a quick trip to the supermarket to stock up on groceries, then feeling rather pleased with myself, decided to wash my hair and attend to my nails before making my call, which in any case, was last on my agenda due to time differences.

A shampoo and shower did much to restore me after the cleaning I had done. In a warm velour robe in a delicious shade of blue, a matching ribbon in my hair, I sat down to write to Rika.

When the phone rang, I was delighted to hear Rom's voice. He was back, he said, as he had promised his wife. Had arrived the night before. He sounded very different from the man who had come to see me, all shocked and hurt. Now he was in the highest of spirits, actually effusive.

"A wonderful trip! The best ever! Highly successful. I was in India, you know. Mama's absolutely fine, thank you. Piyali, I've brought you a gift. No, I don't want to wait till Christmas. This is a special one from me to you. Are you home now? May I come over?" I glanced at my watch. Barely eight o'clock. Suddenly, I was dying to see him again. Hang letter-writing! I told him to come. "About 45 minutes," he told me.

So there went my quiet evening, and I was glad of it! I went to make fresh coffee. Vanity, thy name is woman, I told myself grinning, as I put on a little make-up. My robe was perfectly respectable, but a pair of embroidered slippers replaced the frivolous mules with pom pons which I wore around the house. I looked around with justifiable pride at the sparkling clean apartment. A small but perfect pointsettia which I hadn't been able to resist buying added a festive touch in keeping with the season. The fragrance of coffee filled the air.

I flew to open the door when the bell rang, and was promptly enveloped in a warm embrace. It did my heart good to see Rom looking so well and happy, laughing at me, answering the flood of questions from me.

"As I told you, the best trip ever! Mama? Looks younger if such a thing is possible. My sister, Jana, was there with her husband. I hadn't met her or Denzil for more than a year." Rom had slipped off his big overcoat, but left it draped over a chair. "And you, dear child, how are you?"

"Swimming in eggnog and punch. Too many parties. Tonight I simply rebelled at going to one more. There's still the big one at Danae I can't avoid."

"I know it," he said sympathetically. "By the way, Margot wants you to come and stay with us as soon as your holiday begins. Can you? That's great. You won't mind sharing Kim's room? Mmmm, it's going to be a wonderful full house. No, my dear, I shan't stay for coffee—though it smells enticing. I just came very briefly to say hello, and give you what I brought. No, I couldn't have kept it till Christmas. It's not that kind of thing. I left it outside. A bit too big to lug in. No, no help needed. I'll just fetch it." He hesitated, then, "I hope you approve. Piyali, do be—" His voice trailed off. He bent to kiss my cheek, and picked up his overcoat. "I'll call you later." He went out, leaving the door open. I was at a loss. What could he have brought that was so large? Within seconds, I had the answer. Neel stood in the doorway.

I was motionless, rooted to the floor, no words coming to my rescue. In the bulky lined jacket he was wearing, he looked big, but also different. I didn't have the time or the wit to analyse that.

Neel broke the silence. "Hello, Piyal. May I come in?"

So formal, I thought, like a stranger who's just met me. The reality of seeing him there in flesh and blood was almost too much for me. I could not speak. He said, "If my presence bothers you—if you don't wish to speak with me, I'll go, Piyal." He half turned to do just that.

My tongue obeyed me at last. "No. No, it's all right. Come in. I'll get some coffee," and fled into the kitchen. Once there, I clung to the counter, breathing deeply, trying to take hold of myself. My head was whirling with thoughts, none of them clear, my legs less than steady.

With a shaky hand, I reached for two mugs, poured the dark steaming liquid into them. Automatically, I added the sugar bowl to the tray, and carried it to the living room.

Neel rose from the settee, and took the tray from me. He had slipped off his jacket, and laid it over a chair just as Rom had. So it seemed he didn't intend to stay long. Just a courtesy call because he happened to be in New York, and that because Rom had requested him to do it. The thought gave me a pang. I handed Neel a mug, and placed the sugar bowl near him.

"So," I said brightly, "what brings you to New York? Another exhibition?" I sank to the rug, and picked up my own mug.

"No."

I took a sip of coffee. It scalded my tongue. Neel had not moved to take the spoonful of sugar he liked in his coffee. I cast about in my mind for another topic.

"How is your work coming along? What have you been doing lately?"

"A few commissions." His eyes were on the painting above the mantelpiece.

"That's a beautiful piece of work, Neel. Very much like a Monet I've seen. You ought to do more painting in between sculpting."

He did not answer. His head was bent, the long curling lashes concealing his expression. He was thinner, I saw, the face showing it most. It wasn't just the moustache which made the difference, though I had to admit it made him look extremely handsome. This wasn't the man who laughed himself, and made everyone else laugh. He looked weary, as if he had been driving himself too hard. He hadn't even smiled. The hollows in his cheeks did not come from the flashing of dimples. Unbidden, I suddenly remembered the evening I had come home from Katia's house, and found Neel stretched out on the same rug I was sitting on. 'How shall I greet thee/after long years?/In silence and in tears.' The memory threatened to fell me. The silence was becoming very awkward. "Rom mentioned meeting your parents after a year. Are they in India now, or about to leave on some dig?"

Neel roused himself. "No. My father has to have a hernia operation. So they're grounded for the time being."

"Too bad. Did you all assemble at Madame Nalin's for a reunion?"

"They did. I wasn't there. But I did join Rom in his travels."

I drank some coffee. "It's nice you had a little holiday. Where did you go?"

"It wasn't a holiday. We first went to the Simla Hills."

"Lovely there, isn't—" I put my mug down carefully. "Why there?"

"Because your father invited us." I stared at him, unable to credit my ears. Neel was looking at me now. "He's a grand man. A prince in more ways than one. And the resemblance between him and Rom is incredible."

I whispered, "I don't believe it!"

"He gave us not only the warmest welcome and hospitality, but left his wife for a couple of days—she can't travel now and couldn't come with us, but let him go very graciously to accompany us to Divyasthala. His presence truly smoothed the path for Rom."

"How—did it all come about?" I asked slowly. A slow anger was building up within me. All these things had happened, and not one—not even my own father—had bothered to tell me. Why, I had spoken to Daddy just a week ago, and he hadn't breathed a word.

"My grandmother." I opened my mouth to speak, and closed it again. This was no more unbelievable than the rest. "She called your cousin, Princess Suvarnalata." Of course. Why hadn't I realized Lata must have had a hand in this? "Initially, she was stunned over Rom's existence. Once she got over it, she lost no time. Called your father—who invited Rom at once. Then it was he who called the Maharaja. Again the same stunned reaction followed by the warmest invitation. He and the Maharani offered us the most gracious hospitality. One seldom meets such fine people."

I exclaimed to myself, But I should have been there! It should have been my privilege to tell Daddy and Uday Singh, to go with Rom! Instead it had all been done behind my back without my knowledge. As for introducing Neel, wasn't it my inalienable right? If any one of them—Rom or Daddy or Lata—had had the decency to keep me abreast of developments, I would have rejoiced over them. I had figured nowhere in the picture. Was I that unimportant? My anger grew by the minute. It made me cruel.

"It sounds like Old Home Week—a jolly gathering of the clan."

"Rom will want to fill in the details himself."

"Tell me, where do you fit into all this, Neel?" An expression I could not read crossed his face. "I suppose you went along as a dutiful nephew to provide moral support to Rom. Otherwise, wild horses couldn't have dragged you to meet the Chandravats you hate."

After a moment, "It appears you resent my going. Do you think it was presumptuous of me, Piyal?"

I shrugged. "It has nothing to do with me. If Rom needed you, who am I to question your going? And you're a grown man. You can go where you please."

I was startled and quite unprepared for his next move. In a single lithe movement, Neel was on his feet. He picked up his jacket. Surely, he wasn't leaving!

"I came to ask your forgiveness. For causing you pain time and time again. Perhaps it no longer disturbs you—or you've forgotten it already—but I had to say it. I want you to know I'm truly glad for you—the way your career is going—the spectacular successes." I listened numbly to the deep low voice. Neel slipped on his jacket, and zipped it up. "I shan't be troubling you again. I—pray for your happiness. God bless." The last words came out almost inaudibly. It all happened so fast, I hadn't the presence of mind to stand up, or to speak. Still on the rug, I saw the tall figure reach the door and go out of it. It closed firmly with a click.

It was the click that galvanized me. Oh God, I thought, Neel's gone! What have I done! I can't let him go! I was on my feet, running to the door, flinging it wide open, and racing down to the elevators. There was no one there. What shall I do now, I asked myself in utter despair. I looked down at myself. In just a robe and slippers, my apartment wide open, where was I to go in search of Neel? In any case, he must surely have vanished. Slowly, dragging my feet, I retraced my footsteps. Once in, I shut the door automatically, and put on the safety chain.

The untouched mug of coffee stood on the table. I felt awful, the deepest sense of loss mingling with shame and guilt. Neel. I had been cruel to Neel of all people. What else could I expect but that he would walk out? I covered my face with my hands. What next, I asked myself despairingly. Should I call Rom? I knew I couldn't do that. What would I say to Rom who had come in such high spirits after the events that had transpired, and which had changed his whole life? To crown it all, wanting our happiness, Neel's and mine, he had brought Neel to me. And what had I done? With a few barbed words, destroyed everything. No, I couldn't call Rom. At this very moment, he and Margot were probably listening to Neel's account of what had taken place. I covered my mouth at the thought. How was I to face them again, spend Christmas in their home? But most of all, I was haunted by Neel, by the way he had looked, by his last words.

I spent most of that night huddled on the settee. The thought of going to bed was abhorrent to me. I wrapped a duvet around myself, only to sit motionless, head on a cushion. If I closed my eyes, scenes unreeled behind my closed lids. I heard murmured words, the scent of crushed thyme and wild flowers strong in my nostrils. I faced the stark truth. What I had felt for Neel, deny it as I would, was all there, vibrant, pulsating. Elliott, all the other men I went out with—no wonder I couldn't advance in relationships beyond friendship.

The night had never seemed so long. I was up early, showered, and dressed. With Christmas so much in the air, no one seemed to be doing much work. Certainly, my concentration was at zero level. Coming by late afternoon to speak to Peter, Elliott took one look at me, and exclaimed, "Piyali, aren't you well?" I shook my head. "What is it? A headache? A cold coming on? You need to lie down. Go home," he commanded. "Take a couple of aspirins. Do you want me to call a cab? Sure? Well, go on then."

I reached for my coat without another word. I had no intention of going home. I had never been to Rom's Head offices, but that is where I found myself steering the car.

28

The Offices on the 35th floor of an imposing building had been decorated with exquisite taste, but I was too distraught to pay much heed. In response to his PA's call, Rom had me shown in at once. He was waiting. I searched his face to see if it showed anger.

"Piyali, what is it?" he asked gravely.

I stammered, "Rom—Rom, it was terribly wrong—to be so rude—to Neel."

He neither denied it, nor defended me. "Yes," still gravely, "why did you do it, Piyali?"

After giving me a chair, he had perched himself on the edge of his desk. "I—don't know—what came over me," I said wretchedly. "I'm bitterly ashamed, Rom. It's just that—so many things have happened—and I've been kept in the dark. It made me see red, I guess. I even spoke with Daddy recently, and he didn't say a word."

"At my request. I wanted to give you a very big surprise. Tell you the whole story in person." He shook his head. "I see I was very wrong to insist on that. I should have called from India to tell you. In truth, everything happened so fast, not one of us had a moment to spare. Momentous events do that, I guess. It started with my mother's call to Lata, and after that, things just snowballed." He looked down at his folded hands. "You seem to think that Neel pushed himself into accompanying me." I opened my mouth to deny it, then closed it again. "Nothing could be farther than the truth, Piyali. Lata and I, my mother, Jana, all of us had a time of it trying to get him to agree. Yes, Lata was there. Left Bombay at once to come and meet me. Said she couldn't wait.

What a grand little lady she is! It seems Lata had already talked to Tej about Neel. I believe he knew there was someone special in your life, and that it was an unhappy situation. Just that much. When it became clear who Neel was, Tej didn't hesitate in telling me he was invited too. Neel simply wouldn't agree. Only when Tej spoke to him personally, did he accept finally."

I was silent, visualizing the entire scene.

"No need to tell you how everyone liked Neel both in Simla, and later at Divyasthala. Yes, they were so impressed by his achievements, but it was the person, Neel himself, who made an impact. I don't think they've ever met anyone quite like him. Urvashi Devi simply adopted him. Uday Singh carried him off more than once to his Library just to enjoy his company. And little Rika just stared at him wide-eyed, quite speechless, which I believe is a most unusual state for her. The one happiest over it all was Lata. It seems soon after the New York concert, she and her husband had taken Lekh and Tara to Divyasthala for a break. A young cousin of Lekh's went along too. Quite a party. Though the one place they didn't go near was—Sonal something—where Tara and her brother come from. I believe you're the one who introduced Uday Singh to Lekh's compositions? Mmmm, I thought so. That was when he asked if they knew anything about the man in Piyali's life. Couldn't have asked better people. Neel received such a big build-up that when the actual meeting took place, it was almost a reunion of old friends. I guess Neel was astonished by the welcome not just to me—and that story I'll save for another time—but also to him."

It was a tale full of wonder for me, yet I could imagine it in every detail.

Rom went on when I did not speak. "Tej told me privately after meeting Neel that he had never been more relieved in his life. His daughter is that precious to him. When the idea came to me to bring Neel back with me, it was met with unqualifed unanimous approval. Uday Singh gave me a very special message for you. Which is quite redundant now. Neel was the one who held back."

"Why?" I whispered.

Rom's glance held mine. "Because apparently, he had grave doubts about how you would react. I assume he's heard about Northrop—and Jaswant. That shouldn't surprise you, Piyali. Northrop was your guest at the concert, wasn't he, where both the Sebastians and Nevilles met him? To say nothing of Jaswant indicating his state of feelings for you right there after the concert. Has spoken to Devendra Singh of his hopes. In any case, I was wrong, and Neel was right. He's a proud man, Piyali. Not many people have seen that side of him." Rom shook his head sadly.

"Coaxing him to come was the worst blunder on my part. Last night, he tried to comfort me. Said I'd meant well, and it wasn't my fault it all blew up in his face. He'd half expected something of the sort. Well, maybe. But not in that harsh way."

My throat was aching with unshed tears. "I've disappointed you, Rom."

"I wouldn't put it that way, my dear. The error in judgment was mine. It's your life, after all, and you must choose whom you wish. What the clan feels—Lata, Tej, Uday Singh, even I, is not important. It's just that I can't bear to think of what Neel is going through. The boy sacrificed his own happiness for an old lady—and for me." Yes, I thought numbly, that is what Neel did. Ever since we fell in love, he's been pulled in two directions. And all I've been thinking about selfishly is myself—my hurt, my anguish, my loss—which Neel was feeling equally, if not more. Rom was saying sadly, shaking his head, "And this is how I repaid him."

"Rom," I managed, "do you think Neel would be willing to speak with me?"

Surprise showed in his eyes. He said slowly, "He's been hurt very badly, Piyali. Why rub salt in the wounds? What can you want to say to him?"

"I want to tell him—" my voice broke, but I managed to go on "—that I love him."

Rom had become motionless. He said slowly, "Do you mean that, Piyali?" I nodded because I could not speak. "Then why—" He pressed his fingers to his brow.

"Can you call home—and ask him? Please, Rom?" He stared at me. "But my dear child, Neel's gone!" I came to my feet, and he off his perch. "His flight leaves in—" glancing at his watch, "just a little over an hour." Perhaps the stricken look on my face did it. "Come on!" grabbing my wrist. He snatched up his big coat, as I did mine, and we struggled into them on the run to the elevators. As we shot past his astonished PA, Rom called, "On our way to JFK." The cold December air hit us in the face. Someone must have been watching over us, for in a moment a cab came by, and we were on the way. I sat staring out at the darkening sky. On this short winter's day, the street lights had come on, and the headlights of cars. Rom was as tense as I was. Traffic was very heavy.

"How could he—get a return flight booking at such short notice, and in this rush season?"

Rom turned his head to me. "Neel booked his ticket that way. He wasn't sure at all, you see. And if he'd needed to postpone his return, the agent said there was a waiting list as long as his arm. People would fight for his seat."

Had Neel been that unsure of me, I thought bleakly.

At the airport, Rom thrust some notes at the cabbie, and then hand-in-hand, we were racing into the terminal, glancing at the list of flight timings as we sped past, noting that in less than half an hour, they would be calling passengers to start boarding. My heart pounding in my chest, I thought, thank God, the plane hasn't left yet.

Rom and I scanned the crowd. Adults, children, babies, and that indefinable atmosphere which marks the period just before departure, passengers poised for the summons. Our eyes leaped from person to person.

"Rom," I said desperately, "he isn't here!"

"He has to be. If we don't spot him, I'll have him paged."

And then I saw the lone figure sitting apart, slumped, head in hands. I touched Rom's shoulder, and pointed.

"Go on," he told me urgently, "I'll be here if you need me." He gave me a push.

I needed no urging. Heart in my mouth, I flew across the intervening space to crouch down in front of the still figure. I whispered, "Neel?" His head came up slowly. At the sight of the ravaged face, I wanted to weep. As if he was sure he was hallucinating, he stared at me. I spoke his name again, and covered both his hands with mine. The touch must have convinced him finally, for he said my name wonderingly.

"Piyal. Piyal, what's wrong? Why are you here?"

I clutched his hands more tightly. "I came—to see you, Neel." And at the question in his eyes, I burst out, "For many things, but first, to say I'm sorry—so sorry about last night. That I was so mean to you."

He lifted me to my feet so that we were both standing.

"It doesn't matter, Piyal. It's all right. I understand."

My voice wobbling, I exclaimed, "You don't understand anything! It isn't right at all! I didn't mean it!"

"And you came all the way to tell me this? You needn't have, you know."

I pulled myself closer to him. "Yes, I needed to come. And there's something else I have to tell you." He looked at me with tired eyes as if expecting to hear the worst news. I couldn't bear it a moment longer. I flung my arms around his neck, and buried my face against his throat. Words burst from me. "Neel, don't go! Don't go! Don't leave me!"

His hands had come up instinctively to hold me. "Why do you say that, Piyal?"

I raised my head. "Because I love you."

A pause. Then slowly, "Can that be true, Piyal? It didn't seem so last night."

"It's true! It's true!" Agitated, I pressed my mouth to his. "I've never stopped loving you, Neel. I've tried. God knows, I've tried. Nothing worked." I kissed him again, the warm mouth so dearly familiar. He did not kiss me back. "Tell me you won't go, Neel."

"Piyal, why are you doing this to us when—when you're marrying someone else?"

"I'm not marrying anyone! How can I when I love one man even though he's as stubborn as a mule?"

He said carefully, "You're not marrying someone else—some friend of Devendra Singh's, or this man from Danae?"

"Nor the Man on the Moon."

"Piyal,—are you sure of this?"

Over the loudspeaker, passengers were being asked to start boarding. There was a flurry all around. People stood up and began gathering up their belongings.

I was afraid now. I couldn't help the tears that rolled down my cheeks. I had gambled—and lost. Neel was going, and I couldn't stop him.

"Piyal, I must boa—" And when he saw my face, "You—you're crying. Don't. Don't, Piyal." He took a deep breath. "Do you really want me to stay? Are you quite quite sure?" I couldn't have uttered a word to save my life. I was shaking, my lips tremulous, but I managed a nod through my tears, reaching a hand out to touch his chest in mute appeal. He turned his head to look around as if wondering how we came to be here. The orderly queue of passengers was moving rapidly past the barrier. Neel said unsteadily, "I'll have to report to the counter I'm not going."

I found my voice. "Your baggage, Neel!"

"It's just one small bag with a few changes of clothing. They can send it back from London."

"Rom's waiting. He came with me."

Their eyes met across the width of space. We went swiftly to him, he meeting us half-way. I ran the last few feet, and threw my arms around him, hugging him tightly, then I stepped back. For a moment, they stood silently just looking. Rom had tears in his eyes. Neel's tired ones held the sheen of moisture. Then they embraced, Rom patting his nephew's back. "I'm so glad, son," reaching for his handkerchief to blow his nose.

I sat quietly while they reported to the counter, and took care of other formalities. I was far from being overjoyed. I had managed to stop Neel from going, but something of grave magnitude was making Neel hold back. Instead of my heart singing for joy, I was deathly afraid. And then they were back, and Rom was saying, "All done. Take him home, Piyali."

In the cab going to the apartment, we were silent. Neel stared out of the window. I glanced at him several times. Has he changed so much in this short span of time, I wondered. Where is my laughing Neel? I turned my head back to the never-ending stream of New York traffic.

29

At this time, approaching the shortest day of the year, night had fallen when we reached the apartment. Once there, Neel stood silently as if remembering the circumstances under which he had been here just yesterday. Only then did he recall the airbag in his hand, and set it down. I switched on the Indian lamps by the settee, and went to turn on the kitchen light.

"Will you have something to drink, Neel?"

As if I had startled him, he raised his head. "No. No, thanks."

"Then won't you sit down?"

"Thank you," and chose a seldom used padded chair.

Oh, where do we go from here, I asked myself despairingly. Neel is tired and jet-lagged. More, I can't make out what he's thinking. And he hasn't said he loves me. What next?

Unexpectedly, he said, "Thank you for the Easter egg. It is exquisite."

"Oh," relieved, "did you like it? I'm glad. I wasn't at all sure how it would turn out." At least we were conversing. "How are the Nevilles?"

"Very well. Ruhi just discovered she's going to have a baby."

The news was delightful. "But that's lovely! I'm so happy for them. Are they pleased?"

"Exceedingly. Robin is so protective Ruhi had to explain she wasn't in that delicate a condition."

I laughed, feeling much more cheered, and not just over the good news. Neel seemed to be relaxing slowly. He hadn't smiled once though. Nor did he look at me except fleetingly. But at least we had made a beginning. Should I dare to touch upon more delicate matters now? Better to take the plunge, I told myself.

"Did you like Daddy's estate—and the Simla Hills?"

"Extremely picturesque. I'd never been to that part of India before. Neither had Rom."

"And Divyasthala?"

"Another new experience—to stay in a Palace."

I wanted to know so much more—personal matters. And was shocked when Neel beat me to it. "I had the impression you resented my going to either place."

I flung back my head. "Oh, Neel, how can you say that?"

"It was an unmistakable impression I received yesterday."

"That was just pique. I was upset because—well, as I told Rom, no one said a word to me when it was happening—nor afterwards. I—resented being kept out by everyone, Daddy included. I know now that was because Rom had requested secrecy."

"I think you were happy Rom could go—that it all cleared up—but that you felt rightfully I had no business going with him."

I jumped to my feet in agitation. "Neel, stop it!"

"I have to clarify that if your father hadn't spoken to me personally, and invited me, I had absolutely no intention of going. All through the time when the Chandravats were extending the most gracious welcome and hospitality, I kept feeling like a fraud." He answered my unspoken question. "I knew they were being kindness itself because they assumed you and I—had a relationship."

I stepped closer. "And we don't have one?" in a low voice. "Is that what you're trying to tell me, Neel?"

He threw me an unfathomable look, then stood up only to walk about restlessly. He picked up a boomerang-shaped candy dish Ruhi had brought from Australia, half-turning away so I could not see his expression. "Robin had these pictures of you modelling the Maharani Collection. One was a magazine advertisement. The others were blow-ups. He said he'd managed to coax them out of the photographer—some famous fellow. I believe they've already appeared in ads."

"Did you—like them?"

"What words can I use? The jewellery—I hardly need to tell you it's fabulous. And you—" He laid the dish down gently. "There was one that caught my eye particularly. You're in some kind of shimmering iridescent fabric all shot full of colour, holding a tiny leopard cub in both your hands close to your face as if it were a kitten, and laughing. His yellowish eyes and yours—very blue here—set each other off in the most arresting way. The array of colours in the jewellery is amazing—multi-coloured gems in the necklace, earrings, rings, and the bracelet around your bare upper arm. You look like—a dream princess." His eyes met mine directly. "That's what I've been telling myself, that you're a dream princess—so far from my ken, as far as the Moon from which the Chandravats derive their name."

When I could speak, I said unsteadily, "I'm not a dream, Neel. You more than anyone know that. I'm only too human."

"And then when Robin warned me—he was only trying to be kind—about these other men—"

"Neel, they mean nothing to me."

"Yet Jaswant told Devendra Singh he was about to approach your father formally. Indicated it was almost settled between the two of you. Your cousin Lata said—" He halted.

"Please go on."

"—that the New York air must have addled your brains if this oily fellow was your choice, and she wouldn't have it. Otherwise she was coming in person to see you. She's met him—and Tara was introduced to him, she said."

Even in my state of mind, I wanted to laugh at Lata's words. I wouldn't have been surprised if she had turned up on my doorstep.

"Lata is right. he is oily—and more, obnoxious. I dislike him cordially." Neel made a surprised sound. I shrugged. "I can't help it if people jump to conclusions. I'd have to be mad to accept that one!" I changed the subject. "What did you think of the family?"

After a moment, "The one thing I realized was that we had all built them up in our minds as some wicked medieval all-powerful debauchees. Nothing could be further from the truth. Your father works as hard as anyone I know. His efforts made his orchards what they are today. In a different sense, the Maharaja works equally hard. Both are devoted family men. Two events stand out in the midst of several memorable ones." I gestured to him so that he resumed his seat. "In spite of assurances from your father, Rom wasn't at all sure of his reception from the Maharaja. And who can blame him for that? Yet they were at the Palace doors, a royal couple actually waiting for our arrival. And the Maharaja came forward with both hands outstretched, 'How glad I am to meet my brother Romain at last!' Rom had no words to give him. Then they simply embraced. We all had tears in our eyes."

I dashed away my own. "That was a wonderful gesture on Uday Singh's part. But then that's the kind of man he is. How did they explain who Rom was to everyone?"

"Oh, a convoluted tale about a Chandravats who had migrated to the US a generation ago. Rom is supposedly his son. It was accepted without question."

I smiled through my tears. "That was very imaginative! And the second event?"

"Your father insisted on flying back to Bombay with us—he said he was sort of a representative of the Chandravats, but was also coming on his own behalf—to meet my grandmother."

Sheer shock held me speechless.

"It was the most extraordinary encounter. Your father was wonderful—all gentleness and courtesy."

"How did—Madame take it?" I whispered.

"How else but by falling for him within moments? Rom and I had been extremely concerned. We need not have been. She cried a little, but not for long. I think the Chandravats reception of her son—and grandson—had warmed her so much—Rom had called her from Simla and Divyasthala, knowing how dreadfully anxious she was, to keep her informed. Your father had brought messages from the Maharaja which astounded her as much as they moved her. He couldn't stay more than a few hours, but they more than achieved what he had set out to do. His visit wiped out much of the pain she had kept in her heart all these years.

How well I could picture the whole scene. I felt choked up at the thought of Madame Nalin at last finding peace because the son whose existence she had concealed so well for most of her life had found acceptance and affection from his father's other son, as well as from the family.

Neel had fallen silent. He looked drained and exhausted. A feeling of guilt assailed me. Telling me so much had only added to his fatigue. What he needed was food and rest.

I said, "It's way past supper time. We'll eat now."

He roused himself. "Don't go into any trouble for me."

This from Neel who always enjoyed his food? It was a measure of the change in him. I said, "No. I made a quiche yesterday." And vanished kitchenwards. I worked at top speed, putting the quiche in the microwave, getting some coleslaw together, and heating wholemeal rolls. I was carrying the plates and cutlery to the dining alcove when Neel took them from my hand. He had moved so silently, I hadn't known he was there. I thought with a pang of how the kitchen used to be filled with laughter when we were putting a meal together, Neel bursting into song, or an appropriate snatch from an aria, catching hold of me in the midst of my chopping and slicing only to kiss me soundly.

The meal wasn't noted for its scintillating conversation. We spoke of this and that desultorily. Neel ate mechanically as if not really aware of what he was eating, refused second helpings, but accepted a pear from the bowl in front of him. We cleared the table, I rinsed and stacked the dishes, then placed them in the dishwasher. All the while, a nameless dread was growing in my heart. I had sent Neel to the living room while I made coffee. We had talked, and Neel had filled me in with so many more details of Rom's visit, but of our future we had not spoken one word. What would I do if after coffee, he said he was going back to Rom's house? Once I could have coaxed him into staying, but with this stranger, what could I do?

I carried the tray in—only to find Neel in the big chair which matched the settee, head tilted against the backrest, eyes closed. He's asleep, I thought, and who can blame him? He's jet-lagged anyway, and last night, could not have slept any more than I did.

I set the tray down noiselessly, and went to him. I knelt down, and bending, put my cheek to the big hand that lay on his knee. This man is the most beloved person to me in the world—then have I lost him because of my own stupidity? False pride, childish anger on my part have done it. He came halfway across the world to meet me, and I hardly let him stay five minutes, speak no more than a few sentences. Doubts assailed me. Neel had asked for my forgiveness. He hadn't said he still loved me then or at the airport. In growing panic, the conviction grew that he had outgrown his feelings for me. He had come because Rom—and everyone else—had made it impossible to do otherwise. Was there someone else in his life now? Was that what I was about to find out?

"Piyal." Startled, I lifted my head. "You mustn't kneel down in front of me. It isn't right."

"Let me. It's what I want."

"You . . ." and fell silent when I put my face in his hand. Still, he made no move to touch me or lift me up. I raised my face at last, only to see unutterable weariness on his. "You're exhausted! You need to sleep." I rose swiftly to my feet. "Come, Neel." He rose slowly as if only dimly aware of what he was doing. Then, "Piyal—" hesitantly, "I—don't want to deprive you—of your bed. I'll—use the settee, if I may."

"Of course," I said with whatever composure I could summon in my shocked state. "If you want to use the bathroom, I'll get some sheets and blankets."

Without another word, he turned away to fetch his bag, and went into the bedroom, all his movements made with effort. I worried about him falling asleep under the shower, but no, he was back in five minutes, hair tousled from rubbing. "Thank you," he murmured when he saw his bed was all ready. I did not linger. "Sleep well," and saw as I turned away that he fallen on the settee before I could quit the room.

If I hadn't slept at all the night before, tonight, my rest was erratic. I couldn't believe Neel was actually here. Several times, I tiptoed into the living room to make sure. The first time, I pulled the covers up to his shoulders, for obviously, he had just gone off to sleep after sliding under them. He slept so deeply without moving, position unchanged practically the whole night. Two questions warred in my mind as I leaned over the still form. One, should I be happy Neel had consented not to go—or was this to be a hollow victory? Two, was his choice of the settee a portent of the future? Perhaps Neel had stayed on simply because he was too weary to go to Rom's home, and when he woke up, he would move there. What next, I asked myself, wracked by uncertainty.

I was up at first light, making no sound as I showered, and made myself a cup of coffee. Knowing how early Rom was up, I slipped out of the apartment, and went to a pay phone to call him. He listened quietly, then told me, "Give him time, Piyali. He's so weary in body, mind and spirit that he needs space to rest and recover. Put yourself in his position—how much he's had to give up, how much to conceal from you because he dared not utter a word—he's taken a beating in so many ways. So you'll have to be very patient with him. Not force any issues, and let him set the pace himself. It's not going to be easy, my dear child. We are here, Margot and I, at all times. Will you keep us in touch? And call any time of night or day if you need to."

My voice was choked with tears as I promised. I went to the corner bakery for fresh croissants. Before I went up, I made one more call. My voice must have been nasal enough to convince Elliott of my heavy cold. Of course, I didn't need to report on duty, he assured me. No one was doing any work anyway. Was I taking something for the cold? Did I have fever? No? That was good. What I needed was to rest and keep warm. Should he drop in? My heart sank. Hastily, though I hated to, I had to tell him a falsehood. My uncle had insisted on carrying me off home, I said, I was being looked after and cossetted. It was very sweet of Elliott to think of it. Yes, I was definitely planning on coming to the Danae Christmas party. Oh, I would be fine by tomorrow night! When I hung up, I leaned against the wall of the booth. Dear Elliott, I hated to deceive him, but I couldn't imagine what disaster would follow if he showed up at the apartment.

It was the strangest day. Neel slept on. I sat down quietly to work on finishing a design. My hands moved mechanically, but my thoughts scurried around like mice, without any logical sequence. Just before noon, I went to make myself a cup of coffee, and prepare a tuna salad for lunch. Neel must have woken up, for the next I heard was the sound of water running in the bathroom. When I peeped into the living room, the settee had been cleared of all bedding. I thought with a pang how once I would have walked into the bathroom while Neel was shaving only to be anointed with shaving cream. How wonderful it had been listening to his glorious singing in the shower. Now Neel was silent.

When he appeared in the kitchen doorway, I saw he was much more rested. "I'm sorry," he apologized. "I seem to have slept for half the day. You should have woken me up."

"You needed the rest. And you look better. Do you still feel tired?"

"Not at all. Did you stay at home from work because I'm here? You haven't started Christmas holidays yet, have you? I thought not. You mustn't skip work for me."

"A cup of coffee?" I changed the subject. "And lunch is ready."

How formal we are, I thought later when after lunch, we sat talking. Neel brought me up to date on what was happening in India. I asked questions, and he answered them. It was all very proper and polite.

In the afternoon, we went for a long walk. The sidewalks were crowded, for everyone seemed to be out, busy with matters relating to the festive season. When we came back, the security guard on duty handed over a bag which he said had been delivered by my uncle. Dear Rom, he had brought some clothes for Neel which the latter always left in his house. Included were two new shirts still in their wrappings. That evening after supper, we watched a Christmas Special on TV, talked a bit, and then Neel said apologetically that he was sleepy again. Would I mind very much if he went to bed now? Not at all, I told him politely. It was all to the good that he should rest as much as possible. Getting used to the time change always took a while. Neel insisted on fetching the bedding himself, and making up the settee. Fifteen minutes later, he was asleep. And so ended another day.

I couldn't take it alone. I needed desperately to talk to someone. I slipped out of the apartment quietly, and called Rom. This time, Margot was on the extension. They listened without interruption.

Margot said quietly, "I think Neel is tired in a way you and I can't imagine, dear. It isn't just travel fatigue. This is the culmination of long months of a very painful time in his life. All these years, keeping the secrets to himself presented no problems—till he met you. The secrets now turned into a monstrous yoke around his neck, strangling his relationship with you. I don't need to tell you of all people how it's been. Then there's been the guilt element—what he's had to put you through, to say nothing of meetings which always ended in separations."

I said in a choked voice, "Margot, I'm scared this meeting is going to end the same way. All the signs point that way. I can't seem to get through to Neel. He's a distant stranger whom I don't know. I haven't seen him even smile much less laugh. I'm thinking I shouldn't have stopped him from going because—because . . ." my voice broke, "he has no feelings for me left."

"My dear," she said compassionately.

Rom broke in. "Piyali, that isn't true at all! The Neel who came home after he left you was so terribly shattered at what he thought was your rejection of him that I felt I had made the biggest mistake of my life in bringing him to America. No, Piyali, you're not to lose hope this way. It will all come right, I'm sure."

The exchange had not reassured me, but I felt better for having shared my sorrows. Neel was deeply asleep. This time I did not go near him, but went straight to the bedroom.

I went to work the next day. Neel urged me to, and I didn't see the sense of spending another day exchanging pleasantries. A great weariness of the spirit had overcome me. I had no thoughts on what I should do. A change of scene was an absolute necessity.

This was the last working day before Christmas. Only the Danae stores would remain open during the Christmas season. They had been mobbed by eager shoppers for days, and from the way it looked, a last-minute frenzy of buying was in progress.

I had no idea what Neel would do all day, nor did I ask. I came home after the offices closed early to dress for the party. Elliott had offered to pick me up, but I told him all that had been arranged. I didn't know if Neel would be at the apartment, and I was too dejected and hopeless to care. But he was very much there. I asked if he would like to come to the party. He refused politely. Margot had invited him for supper, he said. I said no more, but vanished to get ready.

I don't know what prompted me to choose the dark red dress I had last worn at Tara's wedding. It was hardly new, but its classic style did not date. If it did not fit in with my mood, at least it did with the Season. I left my hair loose in a shining curtain, only sweeping one heavy swathe across and fastening it with the pin that matched the ruby-gold set. I could not read Neel's expression when I walked into the living room to call a cab. With a calm I did not feel, I took out my dress coat, and slipped it on. I asked if I should call a cab for him. No, he would pick up one downstairs. We rode down together in the elevator. The cab pulled up, and Neel opened the door for me. He wished me a pleasant evening. I responded in kind, and that was that. He set off along the sidewalk, and I lost sight of him.

At the party, I laughed and chatted, kept firm hold of a single glass of champagne in my hand from which I took a sip or two. I danced mostly with Elliott, but also with Leon Rothman and Peter. Elliott told me I looked absolutely stunning. He said wistfully that I ought to be going with him to Boston for Christmas. Was I feeling all right? I didn't seem my usual self. I was fine, I told him quickly. Probably just the after-effects of my cold. I seized the opening this bit of exchange gave me. In fact, it was wise for me to have an early night, I told him, so I would slip away shortly. He seemed about to protest, but thought better of it. He said frustratedly that he couldn't even take me home. He was duty-bound to stay on at the party for quite some more time. Even so, Elliott managed to steer me to a secluded place and kiss me. It was to wish me a merry Christmas, he said with a gleam in his eye. He held my face in his hands, "Piyali, when we get back, we have to talk," he said huskily.

It was nearing midnight when the Harters dropped me off. They had a babysitter to relieve, and had been glad to bring me home. The apartment was silent. Such a wave of desolation swept over me that I flung off my coat, threw my purse on a table, and sank down on a chair, my face in my hands and sobbed my heart out. I did not know how long I sat there, lost in my dark misery.

I was startled when the key sounded in the lock. It was too late for me to reach the bathroom and cover up the signs of my weeping. I sat there, intending to get away as soon as I could manage it.

Neel's voice sounded from somewhere near the closet.

"You're back! I thought these parties went on till dawn."

"They do. I—had a headache." The classic excuse.

His footsteps must have been muffled by the thick pile of the rug, for his next words came from very close. "Have you taken anything for it? Can I get you something—some aspirin?"

I was annoyed at the way my voice came out, still thick from my weeping. "No, thanks. I—I'm all right."

For a moment he stood very still, then he was on his knees in front of me, hands on my head, turning my face to his. He drew in his breath sharply. "Oh God, Piyal, you've been crying! And it's because of me, isn't it?" I could not deny it, but stared mutely. "I've done it again—made you unhappy all over again when the last thing I want to do is to hurt you."

"It's the first time—you've touched me," I whispered. "Or looked at me. Is there someone else in your life now? Is that why?"

An incredulous look from him. "*You* ask me that? Oh God, Piyal, how can you even think that?" His arms came around me, and he buried his face in my breast. My hands came out instinctively to cradle the beloved head against me. I bent to hear the muffled words. "Piyal . . . when I saw the photographs . . . the magazine picture . . . and the jewellery that was so spectacular. . . . The ad said 'Jewellery by Piyali for Danae' . . . I knew your career was reaching a peak in every sense of the term . . . I felt I had no right re-entering your life as everyone was urging me to do. . . . You told me at the airport those two men meant nothing to you. . . . Perhaps that is so. But there'll be others . . . men of great stature, millionaires, perhaps titled . . . whom you'll meet with these Danae connections. . . . I couldn't tell them all this . . . not even Rom. . . . They were all so good about it, so happy for us. . . . Somehow the thought of us together seemed to wipe out so much of the past . . . the pain and the bitterness. . . . We symbolized a process of cleansing . . . of healing, apart from the romantic aspects . . . for all of them . . . my grandmother . . . the Chandravats . . . and for Rom. Only I . . . was filled with uncertainties . . . they wracked me. . . . That was why I took the safeguard of booking my return ticket . . . for the next day. . . . And it seemed I was justified . . . you showed your resentment so clearly . . . suddenly I didn't know what I was doing here . . . why I had come against all my better judgment. . . . I damned myself for being the world's biggest fool. . . . Probably you had accepted this man from Danae . . . were about to marry him . . ."

"I'll call Elliott now, and tell him I'm resigning from Danae."

Neel lifted his head to stare at me. He said slowly in wonder, "You'd do that for me, Piyal—give up everything for which you've worked so hard?"

"Nothing has any meaning for me if I lose you. I tried so hard to forget you . . . tried even to hate you for not trusting me. . . . I was just fooling myself."

"Piyal . . . Piyal. . . ." He lifted me up and sat down holding me on his lap. "I didn't try to forget you. . . . I knew that was impossible. . . . I've been driving myself . . . working night and day trying to assuage my pain. It didn't help. . . . I kept imagining you with those other men. . . . I've been torn. . . . The worst of it was I never could help the situation. . . . It's ever been like that . . . bringing us separation and anguish. . . . These last two days . . . I haven't been able to shake myself out of this dark mood . . . haven't been able to believe the past is really behind us at last. . . . And I've truly felt you could find someone very grand. . . . It is only what you deserve. . . . Tonight, Margot and Rom told me I had to snap out of it. . . . I was hurting you . . . and if I loved you . . . I must not cause you more pain. . . . When I saw you in this dress . . . I remembered how I fell in love with you at Lekh's wedding. . . . you were wearing it . . . I had never seen anyone so beautiful in my life. . . ." His mouth twisted with pain, eyes mirroring it.

I couldn't bear to see them. Neel who was meant to laugh. I put out my hand to touch the luxuriant moustache. "This is new. It makes you look—different."

"It will come off first thing tomorrow morning," gravely, "if you don't like it."

"Don't you dare! I love it! It makes you look very handsome."

Still gravely, "Then, by all means, it shall remain."

I whispered, "Neel, you haven't kissed me once."

For the first time in all these days, his eyes took on that merry look, and the dimples creased his cheeks. He said thoughtfully, "Well now, I think that can be rectified, Princess."

He kissed me, not with that wild passion which had marked our lovemaking in the past, but tenderly, putting all his love into it, sealing for all time the covenant between us.

It was at Christmas dinner that the final word was spoken. It had been a heartwarming experience to be in the centre of our family—my family as much as Neel's, and his other uncle, Jagat Alexander, also there, and his wife and children completing the circle. Seeing the quiet happiness on our faces, Rom had simply put his arms around both of us, and held us close. We raised our glasses for toast after toast. Jagat had proposed we drink to the memory of Kushal Nalin which we did, greatly moved. It was Neel who proposed his grandmother Romola's name, and this was received with great enthusiasm. Rom stood up now, and said quietly, "I would like us to acknowledge the contribution of a great and revered ruler, one who worked tirelessly for his people—my father, Digvijay Singh." Margot had tears in her eyes, and mine were wet. What a long way Rom had traversed through shocked discovery, outright condemnation, bewilderment and bitterness to acceptance, the warmest welcome from the clan of which he was rightfully a part, and as was now evident, not only forgiveness, but actually pride in the man who had been his father. Jagat whom Rom had said was as close to him as a twin brother smiled at Rom, and nodded gently. We raised our glasses, thanksgiving in all our hearts.

Rom said genially after we had drunk one last toast to Neel's future and mine, "And now I can pass on Uday Singh's message to you, Piyali." I glanced around the table, and realized everyone, Neel included, knew what he was about to say. Quite at a loss, I waited. "The message is," Rom said with relish, "that your wedding is not to be a repeat of Nayantara's, or an American-style one here in New York. It is to be in Divyasthala with all the fanfare befitting a Chandravats princess—and he as Head of the clan is personally going to oversee the whole thing." They all watched my stunned reaction. When I clutched my head, the room filled with the lovely sound of spontaneous joyful laughter. I turned to Neel, and he was smiling in the way I loved best.